the
takedown

CORRIE WANG

FREEFORM BOOKS
LOS ANGELES   NEW YORK

First Edition, April 2017
10 9 8 7 6 5 4 3 2 1
FAC-020093-17055

Printed in the United States of America
This book is set in Century Gothic/Monotype and Janson MT/Monotype
Designed by Marci Senders

Library of Congress Cataloging-in-Publication Data
Names: Wang, Corrie, author.
Title: The takedown / Corrie Wang.
Description: Los Angeles ; New York : Freeform, 2017. |
Summary: "In this near-future mystery, Kyla Cheng, the smartest, hottest,
most popular student at her Brooklyn high school, gets taken down a
peg by a faked sex tape that goes viral"—Provided by publisher.
Identifiers: LCCN 2016028339 | ISBN 9781484757420
(hardback) | ISBN 1484757424 (hardcover)
Subjects: | CYAC: Cyberbullying—Fiction. | Social media—Fiction. |
Popularity—Fiction. | High schools—Fiction. | Schools—Fiction. |
Brooklyn (New York, N.Y.)—Fiction. | BISAC: JUVENILE FICTION / Social
Issues / Dating & Sex. | JUVENILE FICTION / Science & Technology.
Classification: LCC PZ7.1.W3647 Tak 2017 | DDC [Fic]—dc23
LC record available at https://lccn.loc.gov/2016028339

Reinforced binding

Visit freeform.com/books

SUSTAINABLE FORESTRY INITIATIVE — Certified Sourcing
www.sfiprogram.org
SFI-00993

THIS LABEL APPLIES TO TEXT STOCK

To my mama,
for always answering

NOW

'll warn you in advance.

You're probably not gonna like me.

No matter what I write, you'll think I got what I deserved. So I won't bother sugarcoating my story or trying to pretend I'm someone I'm not. I mean, you don't get over five hundred million views and care what people think anymore. Fine. Maybe you care a little. Contrary to what it might seem, I'm *not* some soulless vampire. But I did always say there were only two ways to emerge from high school.

Scarred or Worshipped.

And ever since freshman year it wasn't hard to guess which track I was on.

Before I begin, I should mention that I'm not like other girls you read about. Never once have I adorably collided with a large stationary object. I mean, come on; I have eyes. And since being debate-team captain kind of obligated me to come up with the exact words I needed exactly when I needed them, I don't bumble my sentences around cute boys. Or anyone else, for that matter. And thanks to French-meets-Chinese genetic dumb luck—merci and xièxie, Mom and Dad!—I ended up prettier than almost everyone else at school. And I was never the girl who says, "Oh, I'm *okay*," when she knows she's gorgeous. Who are you kidding, poser? Remember. I forewarned you that empathy would not be issuing forth.

So never mind that on top of all these things I also tried to be a good daughter, a protective sister, and a loyal friend. Never mind that I was on friendly terms with almost all my classmates. When the video dropped, all anyone saw, all you'll see, was that I was one of a group of four in that nefarious high school species known as *Popular*.

(Why we equate "popular" with being liked, I still don't know. Maybe "popular" always meant most-viewed. In which case, I was undeniably the most popular teenager in the entire world last year.)

But I parenthesize.

I guess what I'm trying to say is, I get it. I get the backlash. After all, the girls and I took the lucky gifts we'd been given and we flaunted them. We flaunted our bodies and hair and friendship and fashion sense, and let's not leave out intellect. Because I think we all knew that if we didn't embrace our good fortune, we would spend our high school years hiding in our houses every weekend, eating junk food, and waiting for something important to happen.

Still, I maintain that I didn't deserve it. Because did I ever cyberbully anyone? No. Did girls go home in tears because of me or dread the classes we were in together? No. Did I ever deliberately make anyone's life hell? No.

Why would I need to? I was on the worshipped track.

Notice the past tense. Turns out, there's only one way to emerge from high school.

THEN

WEDNESDAY, DECEMBER 22

ooking back, the video's launch day was evil from the start. It had snowed two feet by six a.m. Then I overslept and missed my time slot in the bathroom. Then my brother proceeded to take forever getting his mussed look just right. And then, making matters the worst, my rushing meant I hadn't contributed at all to the morning massive group txt-athon with the girls. Thereby, at only eight a.m., Audra was probably already pissed at me.

So as I hurried out of the house, I barely glanced at the first txt I received from the creepy no-name sender.

[   ] T minus ten, nine...

I figured it was a countdown app from one of the twenty universities I was applying to. My top ten schools all had January 1 deadlines, and I hadn't hit submit on any of them. But fifteen minutes later, wading up the snowdrift that equaled the steps of school, I had bigger issues than my unfinished college essays. I was flustered, hot, and seven minutes late for the Walk.

Oh, the innocent worries of an unruined life.

5

School, by the way, was Parkside Preparatory, a three-story white stone sprawl of turrets and stained-glass windows on the border of Prospect Park. If you've never been to Brooklyn, think Central Park but quainter with a few more sketchy parts. And if you've never been to New York City . . . txt me; we need to get you out more.

Inside, frayed oriental rugs coated the floors. Instead of trophy cases in the hallways, there were wall hangings from the 1800s. Was it off-putting going to school in a mansion? Sí. Some days I felt like I'd get expelled if I so much as burped. But most days I loved it. Park Prep exuded an almost British air of higher learning, as if Austen or Dickens or Rowling could have studied there.

Slipping in through the two-hundred-year-old solid-oak doors, I clutched my Doc to my stomach like a security blanket. Cálmate, I told myself. I was only seven minutes late. Audra wouldn't lose her SHT over seven minutes. I quickly tossed my coat in my cubby (because what two-hundred-year-old mansion has lockers?), smoothed back my hair, inhaled, and began.

Fawn was immediately at my side. Poor Fawnie had gotten stuck with a cub on the third floor near the art room, so every day she had to try to look busy until the Walk without a first-floor cubby to use as a prop. Lucky for her, there was usually a boy more than willing to help her stall. She left one now, midsentence, to fall in next to me. Her arm linked around my waist. Our hips swayed side to side in perfect time. Heads turned.

"You're late. Ooh, cute red bow tie." Fawn's fingers danced at my throat. A moment later, her hands were lightly patting my braids. Nothing existed for Fawn unless she touched it. "And I all-caps LOVE your hair."

If any parent set deserved an A-plus for naming their child, it was Fawn Salita's. Half–Irish-Filipino, and half-Iranian, the result was Bambi mixed with old-skool Disney princess: perfect oval face; eyes that were huge and doe-y; cascading spiral curls—that was Fawn. Currently in a hippie phase, she wore a tight cropped tee

6

under a red minivest with a flowing skirt that sat low on her hips so you could just see tummy pudge and her jeweled belly-button ring. One of Fawn's life goals was to eat at every restaurant along Flushing Boulevard in Queens. *"Seventy different countries all repped within, like, two blocks. It's a chubby's dream."* If Fawn had her way, she'd be working on a farm in Peru come summer. If Fawn's mom had her way, she'd be enrolled at the French Culinary Institute in Manhattan.

"Love the vest," I said to Fawn. "It's so..."

"Eye-searingly red?" She laughed.

Red. That was Sharma's theme of the day, because Sharma always cut right to the chase. Just as she did as she broke away from Sir Joan—what we called the coat of arms that was next to her cubby—and fell in line with us.

"Late," Sharma said. "Also, president signed new jobs act and creep congressman stepped down re chat sex scandal. Special elections ASAP."

While Fawn killed time before the Walk flirting, Sharma swiped. She was our morning roundup of videos to watch, celebrity gossip, and news.

"Tell your parents to vote for the female candidate," I chimed in. "She's the most progressive. And she's got realistic ideas for environmental safeties."

Postgraduation, Sharma would be joining the military's Code to Work program. They'd been recruiting her since she was a freshman and won that Young Minds Programmed coding challenge. So we never teased Sharma too much that her outfit themes were mundane and usually color-related, not when she'd be protecting our cyberborders some day soon. Besides, not everyone was Audra, who did the best, most cerebral themes. Rainy Parisian Afternoon was still my all-time fave.

I slipped my arm around Sharma's nonexistent waist. Sharma was all nerd in a model's body. If I didn't see her eat, I'd assume she got her calories from the same place she got everything else that nourished her life—the Internet. Her pin-straight black hair fell to her waist. As always, her light-brown eyes were rimmed with gold—iris *and* liner—and today were protected by a pair of red glasses.

"Sweet bow tie," Sharma said, studying me in the holomirror on her Doc because it was easier than turning her head.

"Thanks, it's my dad's."

As I lifted my Doc to send him a pic, I saw that a new no-name creeper message had popped up.

[ ] T minus ten, nine, eight...

"Late *and* distracted?" Audra. She broke away from the antique hall mirror where every morning she fixed her lipstick or txted (us) until it was her turn to join in. Our quartet was complete. "Always a pleasure being fit into your schedule, Ms. Cheng."

"Geez, it was only seven minutes." I slid my Doc into my bag as Audra wedged herself between me and Sharma. "And the weirdest thing just happened—"

"Gasp, President Malin actually responded to one of your Quips?" Fawn teased.

"You got an A but no plus on your gov exam?" Sharma asked.

"No, no, no, I've got it," Audra chimed in. "Your mom made you pancakes *without* chocolate chips this morning?"

Audra's arm slipped around my waist, mine around hers. Even with the red stilettos she wore, I had to stoop to get it there. Audra was pint-size. When she was all done up—like today—I felt like I had a porcelain doll as my best friend. Two weeks before, in honor of her eighteenth birthday, Audra had hacked off her long tresses and dyed her hair platinum. Her new pixie cut was gelled and held back by a red heart-shaped clip. Everything else she wore was black, except the lacy red bra that peeked out beneath her tight blouse. No one did cleavage quite like Audra, because, as tiny as she was, her package was slamming. What Audra was doing after graduation equaled anyone's guess. All soph and junsies she'd been set on applying to FIT. But when we started Prep this fall, she suddenly began talking about taking a gap year . . . to "grow herself."

I sighed inwardly. I loved my girls, but they definitely required a certain level of on-ness. It was like I constantly had ten screens up and if I didn't interact simultaneously and wholeheartedly with each one my entire system would crash.

"Why, gee, gals, funny enough it's none of those things, but thank you for the touching insights into my apparently frivolous existence. What is actually weird is that my Doc is acting uber-glitchy and—"

All the girls groaned, the potential that I might have juicy gossip clearly obliterated.

"So have Sharmie take a look at it in class," Audra said, tsking. "Which we now need to speed to as some lanky betch was seven *and a half* minutes late and I still have to finish my E-N-G essay. Kisses?"

We'd come to the sweeping staircase in the back that led to all the humanities classes on the upper floors and was the endpoint of the Walk. Since the stairs were right next to Coffee Check, the tiny snack-and-coffee bar that resided in a former coat closet, this particular foyer was the gathering spot for almost every upperclassman in the building. With all eyes on us, we brought our Docs together and commenced our much-Quipped-about morning tradition.

Like it's not obnoxious enough that they air-kiss with their Docs, one of our classmates had posted, *they European air-kiss and do each cheek.*

When I pulled mine out, yet another creeper message was on it.

[   ] T minus ten, nine, eight, seven . . .

This wasn't an admissions app reminder or a glitch. Someone was intentionally stretching out the suspense before . . . what?

I felt it then: hate eyes on me.

It wasn't hard to spot the source. Over by the potted ficus, Jessie Rosenthal and Ellie Cyr were staring at us. The Walk warranting laser death eyes wasn't unusual, but this combination was. Ellie Cyr was Park Prep's basketball star. Junior year, college recruiters had taken up their own section at our home games. She'd get a full ride anywhere she wanted—luckily, since her wicked three-point shot wasn't much helping her C-minus average.

Meanwhile, Jessie was the sole student in Park Prep on an art track. She exclusively cloaked her painfully thin body in vintage couture, and her permanent vibe was world-weary disdain. (Life with her collection of Puccini bags and shoes must be *so* hard.) A loner by definition, her Quip stream was all about how soul-destroying daily life was with "the locals"—i.e., us, her classmates.

I won't say that the only reason Jessie was my competition for valedictorian was because all her classes consisted solely of spreading color on paper. I'll just think it.

I flashed the girls a bright smile. Ellie smiled back. Jessie did not. I held up a fist and then four fingers. Point four. The exact number of points Jessie's GPA was below mine.

I could hear Mom disapprovingly gasp, *Kyle!* But Jessie's family was loaded. She'd be the kind of artist who had Chelsea galleries representing her straight out of art school and would be in MoMA by the time she was thirty. This would be the one time in her life she didn't get exactly what she wanted. A little healthy razzing was good for her. She needed to build character somehow.

Jessie held up only one finger back.

It wasn't the nice one.

"You're bad," Fawn laughed.

Grinning, I refocused on the girls only to find Audra casting a half-genuine, half-benedictory smile over my shoulder. Behind me, curls and an eager-to-please look of puppy devotion were pushing their way through the crowded foyer. Speaking of weird pairings . . . not this again.

"Konichiwa, Ailey-chan," Audra cooed.

"Konichiwa, Senpai." Ailey beamed.

Ailey.

Ailey was my BFF K thru eight, but we drifted freshman year when we came to Park Prep. Or, skip the sugarcoating? *I* drifted. Ever since, Ailey and I had swum in entirely different circles. Her, quite literally, as swim-team captain and all-around likable jock. Since she still cropped up in my feeds, I knew she went to perfectly adequate parties, was now the aforementioned Ellie Cyr's bestie, and did plenty of the enviable cultural stuff that is the hallmark of any NYC teen's life.

And that was all great until, in a weird turn of events, Audra deemed Ailey "cute" this, our senior, year. They'd only been in the same classes for three years prior, but then they found themselves the lone two seniors in the Japanese Life, Art, and Love elective, and suddenly my new best friend was talking my old best friend up to me as if she were Brooklyn real estate at the turn of the century and I'd passed on the chance to buy her.

Whenever they saw each other, to the exclusion of everyone else—namely me—they embraced in, I kid you not, a full-minute-long hug. I pretended absorption in Sharma's zombie-dedicated screen until it was over and Ailey was back on her way.

And then my Doc chirped a familiar tone and I didn't give a swipe about any of it. Not the creepy txts or my lateness or the fact that I lived in a constant state of stress over my bestie's mood while she merged new, apparently more fulfilling, friendships in maddeningly adorable Japanese. My heart skipped in my chest.

Mac.

mac Boys' room. Now, betch.

I snorted.

"Toodles, lovelies," I said as my battery light went from yellow to red. "Ran *so* seven and a half minutes late this morning, didn't have time for a proper pee."

"I-C-K." Sharma crinkled her nose.

"Sharma," Fawn said, and tsked. "Pee is natural."

"Boo!" Audra called after me. "We aren't going up together?"

"Audy, I'll see you in *two* minutes."

"But how am I supposed to survive in the meantime?"

Just like that, all was right with the world again. Tossing me a coquettish wink, Audra linked arms with Fawn and Sharma. I blew them a kiss. And even though my favorite part of the morning was almost there—Mac time—I paused to watch my vivacious girls climb the stairs. We only had six more months together, and then it would be separate schools, states, social calendars, lives. This time was precious. Precious and finite, because more than ever, right at that moment, I had the worst feeling it was all about to go away.

And what do you know? Like always, I was right.

barged into the bathroom, very Audra at a sample sale: *What I want is in this room and I will have it.* A freshman was picking at his face in one of the mirrors.

"Out," I said.

"Oh gawd, I'm sorry."

The boy bumped into the sink, dropped his Doc, fumbled to pick it up, then fled. I laughed, not so much at his freshie antics, but because there at the end of the row of sinks, also laughing at them, was the latest, yet most indispensable, addition to my life.

Mac.

"Did you just kick a boy out of the boys' bathroom?" Mac arched the eyebrow of ruin. "That's a pretty boss move even for you, Ms. Cheng."

Utilizing my best impersonation of Mac's strut and light Chicano accent, I said, "You're, like, not the boss unless you make people work for you, you know?"

As much as I would miss the girls in the fall, I couldn't even grapple with not being around Mac. But he'd accepted early admission into NYU, and my top five schools were out of state.

"All right, my little Szechuan baguette." Mac snorted. "Let's promise you'll never do that impression again. I just heard my primos cringe all the way from Sunset Park."

"Wouldn't want you to lose further cousin cred. Maybe I should stop meeting you in the little boys' room altogether."

His eyes widened in mock horror. "No, don't do it."

Grinning again, Mac wrapped me in a one-armed hug. As the full length of half our bodies pressed together, my brain made analogies. Hugging Mac was like crawling into a lifeboat after a day lost at sea. It was more invigorating than a pot of Dad's Chemex. It was like setting foot on Mars after decades spent traveling through space. His soft, wild curls brushed my cheek. For the nine thousandth time, I was floored by how beautiful he was.

Bachata beats sounded tinnily from his EarRing. As averse as Mac was to tech dependency, he proceeded through life accompanied by an endless playlist. During school that meant caving and trading in his enormous old-skool headphones for the nearly invisible slim ear cuff that everyone else permanently wore.

He started to dance me side to side in a bachata two-step, singing under his breath. My EarRing's Translate whispered the lyrics in English: "Time passes and passes, and I keep wanting you in my arms. . . ."

I gently disentangled myself.

Before letting me go, Mac placed his lips lightly against my cheek. Just as I was about to utter my regular, discouraging "Mac," he blew air so it made a loud farting sound. Then he cranked the volume on his Doc, did a fancy little bachata spin, and elbowed the wall-mounted paper towel holder. It popped open, revealing a jar of hair product. As he felt for his comb, hidden on the high ledge by the bathroom windows, I hopped up onto the garbage can. He said he didn't slick his hair back until school because he was barely on time as it was, forget grooming. But he knew I liked seeing his curls crazy.

14

In the mirror his eyes flicked to me because whenever we were in the same space that was what our eyes tended to do. I could still feel the press of his lips on my cheek.

"Bow tie, huh?" he said. "Am I gonna get squirted with water if I get too close?"

"Um, it's called fashion? What's that look? Flannel shirt layered under a tee? It's so retro it's already been out twice."

"Nah, I'm all the rage. *Bra&Panties* told me so."

"Ew." My fingers paused over my Doc, mid-Quip. "What were you doing on the *B&P* slut's feed?"

"Audra sent me a link."

"She did?"

"Yeah, they did a year-end music wrap-up that she thought I'd like."

"Oh. That was nice of her."

This past summer, a Brooklyn teen got e-famous for streaming half-naked pics with the username *Bra&Panties*. When she launched her site in the spring she wasn't any different from all the other slutty girls who posted trying-to-look-alluring, boobs-pushed-together pics online. Then the *B&P* chick did a post about those girls and all the reasons they were degrading themselves. She harped on them for showing their faces. She never showed hers.

Let's celebrate and adore ourselves but not confuse our bodies with our identities. Screw boys. Let's be sexy for ourselves.

"A teenager wrote that?" Mom asked when I showed her the feed. "Sounds like a marketing firm."

In June the *B&P* slut (my name for her) got mentioned on bigger media channels and even *NYMag*. Next click, she had a full-on designed website, her pics looked *Vogue*-worthy, and she was giving fashion and dining-out advice. Nowadays her skimpy outfits were regularly "brought to us by" the next-big-deal fashion designers, and she ran a column on new products she called Die-For-Worthy.

Girl was making bank.

Since day one, my girls were obsessed with her.

Me?

Progressive or not, she got rich off of boob pics. I'd rather follow girls who were advancing in life solely thanks to their brains.

Mac grinned. "Aww, amorcita, are you jealous? Why would I need to see faceless pics of half-naked girls when I'm friends with the most beautiful girl who refuses to let me get her half-naked? Hold on, it's like the perfect combination."

"Har, har."

My Doc dinged. Mac groaned. Since our class schedules never overlapped, every five minutes we could get together was sacred.

[   ] T minus seven, six . . .

He loudly cleared his throat. I held out my Doc.

"I plead extenuating circumstances. I think someone's messing with me."

Scrolling through the creeper messages, he frowned. "What happens when it gets to zero?"

"Does something have to happen?"

"Why else have a countdown?" Noticing my insta–panic expression, he set down his comb—only half his head gelled back—and adjusted my bow tie. "Tranquila. It's probably spam. Sharma can fix it. Or maybe it's only clocking the seconds till you jump from the high dive into a barrel of water."

"Still with the clown jokes." I rolled my eyes, hopped down off the garbage can. "You're the funniest one, Rodriguez. Come on, time to go learn stuff."

"Be right there."

Completely unconcerned that the bell was about to ring, Mac hummed as he tweaked his curls, a residual smile gracing his lips. Mac was the primest cut of meat at Prep *and* he was rumored to be better at crunching numbers than all our math teachers combined.

Don't think he wasn't entirely aware of both these facts. I'd almost made it to the door when he called out.

"I heart you, Ronald."

Here we were again. Audra would have played it coy and said *I know*. Fawn would have told him the truth, that she hearted him too—like, a lot—because her philosophy was to spread love every chance she got. And Sharma...actually, I have no idea what she'd have said. She wouldn't have been in that bathroom to begin with. Boys were so beneath her.

So what did young, confused Kyle Cheng say to the boy she adored more than anything yet refused to date? Why, she played it off like it was a joke, pretending to hear only the least meaningful word in his sentence.

"Ronald? As in McDonald? Ugh. Let it go, Rodriguez."

In the mirror Mac's easy grin faltered.

"Skip out of calc to see me in lunch?" I asked.

"Sure," he said, resurrecting his smile. "Always."

4

[   ] T minus five, four...

M ad dash to English. I slid into my seat next to Audra, late for the second time that day. Luckily, Mr. E. was tardy, too. As usual, our chairs were arranged in a circle so we'd be forced to talk *to* one another about the literature we were reading.

"Sharmie duck out for an emergency zombie strat session?" I asked, noting her empty seat. "Twenty bucks plus her crack code that downloads *Teenzine* on your school tablet says that Mr. E.'s skiing in Vail and we have a sub."

Audra's red heels were kicked off beneath her desk. She'd barely glanced up as I sat down, and I couldn't tell if it was because she was miffed that I'd been gone longer than promised or because she was just that absorbed in who-knew-what on her Doc. As had been the case more and more frequently these past few months, she had it set to privacy mode. Since the screen only decoded for her retinas, all I saw was black.

"Deal," she said, still without looking up. "Now credit my account and zip that crack over because Brittany Mulligan posted that she saw Mr. E. go into Dr. Graff's office before first bell. My guess is meeting ran long?"

"Damn."

"How's your friend without benefits doing this morning, Ms. I Didn't Have Time to Pee?"

"Hmm?" I grabbed a Sani-Wipe and swabbed down my school tablet. "I was in the restroom."

Audra cleared her throat, then read from her Doc in a slightly falsetto voice.

"'Kyle Cheng just kicked me out of the boys' bathroom. Awesome.' That was Josh Tolbern's status six minutes ago. You could have just said you were going to meet Mac. Though I still say not screwing around with Mackenzie Rodriguez is like not speeding in a Porsche. You didn't have to lie. Or hide, for that matter. Or are you just into vertical urination now?"

Sharma had set up our Docs so we were pinged anytime our name was mentioned anywhere. Only Audra's system was set to receive all our pings. I hated when she actually checked them.

As I hid my Doc in my lap, my cheeks burned. Audra prided herself on saying exactly what she thought, exactly the way she thought it. "Boys do it all the time," she'd say. "Why do girls get shackled with having to be *nice*?" It used to be one of my favorite things about her. But these types of Porsche comments were exactly why I hadn't told her I'd gone to meet Mac. They were why Mac and I were meeting in a bathroom to begin with. He used to wait for me at the end of the Walk by Coffee Check. Until Audra's judge-y looks and in turn catty, then fawning, Mac-focused snipes forced us into hiding.

"Whoa, there, cowgirl," she said, finally glancing at me. "No need for the between-the-eyebrows crease. I was teasing."

Sometimes it was hard to tell. When I didn't respond, she

switched to a nicer Audra tone. "Must not have gone so well today, huh?"

"No," I said, letting down my guard. "It always goes well. That's kind of the problem."

Going back to her Doc, Audra sang under her breath, "Only you would think that's a problem."

Before I could reply, a familiar voice said, "Mr. E., rewriting essay equals waste."

In one synchronized movement the entire class looked up from their laps and smirked as Sharma followed Mr. E. into the room. Their constant butting heads about Sharma's lack of proper usage regarding, well, anything in the English language was a running joke in class. I wished I had something that tied me to Mr. E. like that. Leave it to Sharma to track down our missing profess. Guess it wasn't an undead-related emergency.

"It's a waste of what, Ms. Clarke? Complete your sentence. Is it a waste of time? Energy? File space?"

"Tap all three," Sharma said.

"Don't let someone else fill in your blanks."

Whether it was that Sharma was on his heels or that he was late from his meeting with Dr. Graff, I had to say, teach looked flustered. He didn't take his normal perch on the corner of his desk. Instead he stood behind it and knuckled his chin as his eyes cast around the classroom, barely seeing it. Glamour Stubble—that was Mac's nickname for Mr. E.

The man could get mani-pedis for all I cared. Hot was hot.

As if he could read my thoughts, Mr. E. looked directly at me. It wasn't a casual glance. It was like he was looking for me, purposefully. My face flushed. Audra snickered. There wasn't anything more stereotypical than having a crush on your hot, young teacher, but, well, there it was. Audra and I were obsessed. Sharma had stopped sitting with us in class because she said our raging hormones interfered with her Wi-Fi reception.

"The essay reads like code, Ms. Clarke." Mr. E. finally looked away from me to rifle through the drawers of his desk. "And if I know anything at all anymore—which I don't think I do—it's that I'd rather read your unique thoughts on a novel over some regurgitation of online opinions."

"'Unique thoughts'?" Sharma laughed. "Don't exist. And not regurgitation. Essay equals the best selections from lifetimes of collected knowledge of people way smarter than me."

moi Point 123,083,505 to Sharma.

audy Mr. E.: 0.

"I hope I never see a day when 'collected knowledge' trumps an individual's visceral emotions." Mr. E. slammed a drawer shut. "And dare I ask, if enough people wrote that the sky was green, would you believe that? Knowledge needs a source. Or else there's no way of differentiating guerilla propaganda from true learnedness. Don't believe everything you see online, Ms. Clarke."

There was a gentle knock on the classroom door. It was Mr. Parish, the art teacher. Forgetting about his perfect pompadour, Mr. E. ran a hand through his hair and nodded. Audra txted me question marks and a disconcerted face. Another creeper message bumped hers away. But it wasn't just one. It was a wave of them.

[ ] T minus...
      Three.
      Two.
      One.
      Ready?
      Smile ☺ ☺ ☺

"Oh God," I said.

Audra craned her neck to see what I was looking at. I held my

Doc like something might burst out of it. But nothing happened. I looked up. Mr. E. was staring at me again. This time, when our eyes met, he blushed and mumbled something about having to take a personal day. "Mr. Parish will be sitting in for me until a sub gets here."

We all shifted nervously in our seats as Mr. E. shrugged into his blazer.

"Everything okay, Mr. E.?" Audra asked.

"Of course, of course. Before I go, I just want to say..."

Mr. E. took the bust of Mark Twain's head off his desk, then simply stood there, cradling it. Someone in his family must have died. There was no other explanation for his stunned expression.

"T MINUS TEN, NINE, EIGHT..." the numbers shouted from my Doc.

The entire classroom jumped. Mr. E. almost dropped Mark Twain. My Doc was furiously vibrating, speaking in its no-name sender voice, volume on high.

"Where is that coming from?" Mr. E.'s eyes landed on me. "Ms. Cheng?"

"I'm sorry. I thought it was on mute." I fumbled to shut it off.

None of the other hundred txts I'd received in the last few minutes had come through in audio mode. This one was preset that way, like it was meant to get me in trouble.

"SEVEN, SIX..."

"Gosh, I'm sorry." My classmates snickered, like I was doing it intentionally. "It has a virus or something."

"FIVE, FOUR..."

"Geez, Kyle," Audra said under her breath. "Swipe it off already."

Why hadn't I asked Sharma to look at this before class? *Because you were too busy clandestinely meeting with your unboyfriend,* said Audra's voice in my head.

"THREE, TWO..."

Pinpricks of sweat formed on my forehead. No one was snickering now.

"Ms. Cheng, please shut that off this instant!"

"I'm trying!"

Before I could swipe it off, the next-best thing happened. My charge died. My Doc powered off. I tossed it on my desk. Shaking his head, Mr. E. left without another word. For the first time in my life, it felt good to put my Doc down. Little did I know, right at that moment, my life as I'd known it?

So. Totally. Crashed.

5

The whispering started immediately. Stupid, shallow girl, I imagined that people were talking about my bow tie. I actually
smiled at a group of freshies who pointed at me, like I was doing
them a social favor. Sharma and Audra had second period together
and always took off right after English, which meant Fawn found
me first. A cartoonist couldn't have drawn her eyes any bigger.

"Kyle, what the fudge?" she squeaked, dragging me into the
nearest girls' bathroom.

It was empty. She braced herself against the closed door, intent
on keeping it that way.

"Audra already reamed me out," I said. "Sorry. I won't lie about
our meet-ups again."

Fawn also thought I was wasting Mac's valuable resources, but
her exasperation made sense. She was tagged kissing so many
random boys that she used a sort filter. Anytime a pic surfaced
where her face or lips were pressed against a boy's (or the occa-
sional girl's), the image was immediately sent into a G-File album
labeled oops. Fawn was completely boy-crazy.

"Meet-ups? I had no idea you two were...I mean you...and

24

everyone's saying he was sent home. How are you in one piece right now?"

Sure enough, there were her hands, skittering over me to make sure her words were true.

"Wait. Mac was sent home?"

"Oh gawd. Mac. Has he seen it? What did he say?"

This was becoming less humorous by the second. I put my hands on Fawn's shoulders, forcing her to meet my gaze.

"Fawnie, what's going on?"

"You don't know?" Her eyes filled up. "You haven't seen it?"

"My Doc died." I didn't mean to shake her, but I did. "Seen what?"

Fawn was the most dramatic crier ever. The first time I saw her cry—over a documentary about the NYC public school system—I thought she was kidding and laughed. But now, watching her pouty lip quiver like she'd downed ten grande lattes, I didn't find it the least bit funny.

"Oh, worried face." Tears gushed down her cheeks as she gave me her Doc. "It's getting worse. Thirty-five people shared this link."

I jabbed play. The screen whirled and connected to a YurTube video titled HOW DOES IT FEEL?

"Oh, gross," I said, because the video was of Mr. E. He was with a girl in his classroom and they were, well, doing it. I handed it back to Fawn. "Swipe it off, Fawnie."

"No, watch."

Since the girl's face was completely obscured by her long black hair, I watched Mr. E.'s face, trying not to think how his whole career was over. Lots of us probably imagined doing stuff like this with him, but when we imagined it, it was in a foggy, fairy-tale way. Seeing it in real life was gruesome. I couldn't look. Instead I watched the video's time run down. Twenty more seconds.

"How could he be so stupid as to make a sex vid of himself *in school*?"

There was no doubt it was the real deal. It wasn't grainy or blurred the way fake videos were. It looked like it had been recorded from the exact hub that always bombed out in class. And here I'd felt flattered by his extended looks this morning. When he came to class he must have already known about this. Everyone knew I was one of Mr. E.'s favorite students. Those looks he'd given me were looks of mortification. I shivered.

"Almost there," Fawn said, her eyes glued to the screen.

Throughout the video the girl kept her head down. Now she lifted it up and shook her hair out of her face. It was like I could almost hear it. Like when you step on ice and it makes that satisfying crunch under your heel.

Except now it was my life cracking and splintering.

If you hadn't already guessed, I was staring at myself.

The next two minutes weren't flattering. I'll spare you the details. The sudden drenching underarm sweat. The insane-person pacing. My insisting it had to be some kind of joke.

All you need to know is that it didn't look like a joke. Or like a face-swapping filter. It looked like me in the video. And not just "like" me. It *was* me. For one click, I worried I'd experienced a massive brain reset and had actually slept with Mr. E. All my classmates knew I was completely obsessed with him thanks to the swooning Quips I posted daily. The last one from barely fifty minutes ago, sent while Audra was grilling me:

Almost time for Huck Finn in English. Me. Raft. Mr. E. Now that's a story I want to get lost in.

Whose parents hadn't warned them about the content they posted online? But I thought they meant, like, don't post pics of your butt. Everyone superfanned over some guy, girl, or other. Right?

Or this was what I told myself as I tried to remain calm and watched Fawn cry. Good lord. It was like someone had told her she'd never eat butter again. I pulled her in for a hug, then wiped giant tears from her cheeks.

"Fawnie, you goof. Stop crying already, betch," I said in my best Audra impersonation. "I'm sure this isn't that big a deal. Ms. Sandoval in New World Borders just said that at one point or another every living person in modernized society will fall prey to some kind of online scam or identity takeover. So this is mine."

Fawn nodded, not meeting my eyes. There was an urgent knock on the door; then Audra and Sharma slipped into the bathroom. Considering Audra must have been getting pinged like crazy, why hadn't she immediately shown me this after English? Her Doc must have been off.

"Sharma got us off-grounds passes." Audra handed me my coat.

"Been saving for an emergency." Sharma shrugged as Fawn's jaw dropped.

"Wait. We're leaving?" And this was an emergency? My brain was having trouble keeping up. "You can't tell me this is any worse than Boobgate. I mean, you guys, that's not even me. You know that, right?"

Three pretty heads looked from one to another, then too readily bobbled up and down.

"Okay," Audra said, albeit a little stiffly. Mentioning Boobgate still did that to her. "It's not you."

"Wait," Fawn sniffed. "Come here."

Only later, when I dissected every second of the previous and future twenty-four hours, would I appreciate what Fawn did next. She grabbed my bag, took out my compact, and dabbed at my face. Then she applied a light pink gloss to my lips. In the next eight minutes, 104 different pics would be snapped of me. Yev Baker would PhotoMix half of them into a video titled "Walk of Shame." At least I didn't look stunned *and* shiny in them.

"There. Now you look lovely."

Audra linked her tiny arm protectively through mine. "Two hallways, two flights of stairs, and we're there."

"What is this?" I laughed. "Witness protection?"

"Yeah, kind of, Kylie," Audra said, and tsked.

The girls all took a deep breath. Then Fawn opened the bathroom door. It was still between periods, and the halls were packed. Fawn took my other hand. Sharma trailed behind, her fingers a blur above her Doc, hopefully unleashing a world of doom on whoever had made the video. It was like the morning Walk all over again, except faster with no banter, and now there was a whole different reason we weren't meeting anyone's eyes.

Someone took my pic. Audra's Doc dinged when I was tagged in it. Yulia Yap muttered something about "got him fired." Her best friend, Heather Ru-Weinberg, shot me some serious eye daggers. I blew them both kisses.

"I don't think that's helping," Audra said.

I needed to find Mac. He would make this better, either with a totally inappropriate comment or a really long hug.

We went down two flights of stairs in utter silence. At the new attendance and security sensor, our clunky tablets beeped. The sensor lit up green as it registered our passes. Mr. Watkins, the jovial guard the sensor had replaced, never would have let us leave this easy. For once, I didn't miss him.

Outside, Park Slope had that hush that only a snowstorm could instill in the city. An interborough taxi navigated the unplowed street at half its normal speed. White Christmas lights twinkled mutely beneath the snow-encased potted pine trees that guarded the school. I took my first real breath since Fawn showed me the video. And then there he was, my Mac. I wondered if one of the girls had txted to tell him we were leaving. His tablet was flashing red. No off-grounds pass for this boy. Unless he went back inside quick, detention would ensue. For once, I couldn't care less about Mac's truancy record.

"Macky."

He hadn't heard me. Barely off school grounds, he'd already swapped out his EarRing for his headphones. They were supposed to keep sound in, yet I could hear his music twenty feet away. He was completely absorbed in his Doc, the way he only got when he was searching for exactly the right song. I broke into a trot. The girls called out, trying to stop me. Didn't they know everything would be okay as soon as those arms were around me?

When Mac finally noticed me, he quick swiped at his eyes, then nonchalantly turned away and continued to tap at his Doc. Now that I was closer, I saw that he wasn't searching for a song; he was scrolling through pics of us, deleting them.

I'd expected his hands cupping my face and a stream of affectionate Spanish. Not to be ignored and erased. I almost laughed from the shock and hurt. Like that time Mom yelled at me, "Stop it already, Kyle," in the middle of GoodMart because I wouldn't stop citing reasons why microalgae should immediately be incorporated into all our meals.

"Rodriguez."

He looked awful. Like he'd come down with a sudden scorching fever. His face was flushed. His eyes were red and puffy. I could tell he debated ignoring me again, but seeing as I was only inches away, that wasn't really feasible.

I put a hand on his arm. He immediately shook it off.

"Don't touch me." Maybe it was because his music was up so high, but he was kind of shouting. "I have nothing to say to you."

"Mac." I was like some useless bot only programmed to say his name. "Hold on. Can you please lower that so we can talk about this?"

He pulled a headphone forward off one of his ears.

"No, you don't get to talk to me anymore. You don't get to send me cute pics before you go to bed or make plans with me of what we'll eat for after-school snack. You don't get to call me crying every time you fight with your mom. You don't get to be my 'just friend' anymore."

Behind us, the girls moved in, their shoes crunching on the

snow. I couldn't believe it. Mac thought the video was real. Me. The girl who covered her eyes during sex scenes in movies. The girl who refused every single one of his advances, even though it would have been much easier and more enjoyable not to. She had suddenly up and done this? With her teacher?

There was little doubt it was me, except for the important fact that it wasn't. I thought that'd be clear to anyone who knew me even a little. Panic and rage coursed through my body in equal measure.

"Kylie, honey," Fawn said. "Let's go."

At their approach, Mac's eyes took on that faraway, heavy-lidded *it's all the same to me* gaze that his primos were so good at. It was the expression he wore on constant at Prep. The one that covered up how funny, sweet, and silly he was when he wasn't surrounded by kids who had their own assistants and drove beamers.

As calmly as possible I said, "Macky, you know that isn't me in the video."

Still not meeting my eyes, he gave me a slow, lazy smile. I'd seen this before too. It was the same smile he gave Avery Gibson the time Mac pulled Avery's soda can out of the trash—Mac hated when people didn't recycle—and Avery saw and said, "Hey, Rodriguez, if you're that desperate for the deposit money, I'll just txt you some credits next time."

And Mac replied, "Hey, Avery, eat SHT," and then whipped the can at his head.

"No preocupes, princesa," Mac now said, calmly, like he was over it. "I should have seen it coming, right? Only, you know the part that gets me? All these months, you've acted like *I* was the slut."

I felt the sting of his words as sharply as if he'd smacked me.

"Hey," Sharma said.

"No," Fawn snapped. "You don't talk to her like that."

She began to push past me, but Audra grabbed her back. Mac held his hands out, like *You want me? Come get me.* Luckily, a cab pulled up. Mac's cousin Rupey was hanging out the passenger-side window. Two of his other cousins were in the back. Rupey and Mac slapped hands.

"Have a nice life, Kyla."

Mac was the only person who ever called me by my real name. His voice cracked a little when he said it. He hopped into the backseat of the cab, exchanged a series of handshakes with all the primos. Then, because whenever we were in the same space that's what they tended to do, his eyes flicked to mine. *How could you?*

Before the cab pulled away, Rupey spat on the sidewalk at our feet. Now the tears came. If Mac believed this, who wouldn't?

Fawn immediately absorbed me into a hug.

"I'm fine," I said, angrily wiping my eyes.

Audra stared after the boys, then shook herself a little and said, "Let's take you home."

Home. All I wanted was to put my head in my mom's lap and have her stroke my hair, like she did when I was little and had woken up terrified from a bad dream. Sharma handed me a half-used tissue from her pocket. I gratefully blotted my eyes with it.

"No, not yet," I said. "We have to go to Sharma's and figure out what the H-double-L just happened."

7

Since I'm sure everything will be different by the time you read this, allow me a mini ancient-history lesson for the young'uns in the audience. Once upon a time there was something called the Internet.

I'm kidding! I won't go that far back.

As you *do* know, the first site to do Worldwide Facial Recognition was ConnectBook. Anytime someone took a picture, everyone in it—even twenty rows back—was tagged. So a day shopping in the city meant a hundred different tourists' vacation photos now attached to your profile. You had to un-star them or, like, click diss-connect in order for them not to show up in your feed. I can't remember. There was a lot of starring and clicking back then.

Worldwide Facial Recognition (shortened to WWFR, pronounced "Woofer") was controversial from the start. A cheating husband was the first to sue. He and his mistress were captured in the background when some kid took a pic with his first car. As soon as the kid posted the pic online, BAM! The wife saw the husband tagged—along with the wife's best friend.

Oops.

Wife divorced husband. Got millions in settlement.

Double oops.

The cheater claimed Woofer ruined his life. The court of public opinion said he did it to himself by cheating in the first place. ConnectBook said he could have selected to opt out of Woofer under his account's personal settings. The lawsuit worked its way up through the court of appeals to the door of the Supreme Court. In a five-to-four decision, the court ruled that Woofer didn't infringe on an individual's privacy rights. After all, anyone at any time could opt out.

Nobody opted out.

Instead the world got smaller, or so says my mom. She says Woofer changed everything. In a few months, those star-stalker e-mags became obsolete, because you could now go to your favorite star's CB fan page and watch him move real-time through the world. It was lose-lose for undercover cops. And it became near impossible to lie to your parents about, say, "sleeping over at Sharma's," when you were out at a salsa club with Mac. (Lesson learned on that one.)

ConnectBook patented their 3-D-based, surface-texture-analysis tech so when Goog started attaching Woofer photos to G-Files, ConnectBook sued and won. Now to access Woofer, and all the star and fellow-man stalkery it allowed, you had to be a CB member. ConnectBook's user numbers exploded. It's estimated that 94 percent of the people in the world have a CB account.

Mom said it was the nail in the coffin. Thanks to Woofer and the new personal holographic devices, i.e., PHDs, i.e., Docs (get it? Because they're PhDs?), no one would ever look up from their tech again. Randomly pull up any Woofer tag from the first year it came out, and nine out of ten times that person was staring at their device. After that, audio txt took off. I mean, who liked looking at pics of people looking down?

Now, as we silently filed into Sharma's brownstone and down into the garden apartment that was her lair, I figured someone must have pulled a Woofer video to make the one of me and Mr. E. And all I knew was that whoever did this had it backwards. I'd be over this video in a matter of minutes. They'd be the one who'd live to regret it.

8

That is, assuming I could get any of my friends to actually believe that the video was fake. Because an hour later, despite their Park Prep nods of solidarity, it had become all too clear that the girls weren't concerned with who had virtually violated their best friend, but why their best friend still wouldn't admit that she'd slept with her teacher.

"I guess what I'm getting at, Kylie," Fawn was saying, "is I hope you know that it's okay if Mr. E. *was* your first—hypothetically speaking, of course."

"'Reading Prez Malin's old debate transcripts,'" Sharma said out of nowhere. "Ha. Knew that excuse equaled suspicious."

"You guys—" I started to say, only to have Fawn talk over me.

"I mean, mine was the counter kid from the bodega on Thirteenth Street. What a waste that was. Did we expect that Mac would win the goods? Of course. But aside from the age difference, which honestly, whatever, it's like six to ten years tops, and Mr. E.'s chubby lips—is he a wet kisser? I always wondered...."

I laughed. I couldn't help it. This was getting more and more absurd.

"I mean, aside from that stuff, sleeping with Mr. E., you know, theoretically, is nothing to be ashamed of. The part that would bother me, assuming it were true, was that we didn't even celebrate. There should have been pink bubblies. You should have told us."

"Agreed," Sharma said as Fawn wiped at her cheeks.

This was the third time she'd cried. As calmly as possible, for the hundredth time, I said, "First of all, I wasn't keeping secrets. Second, Fawnie, there's nothing to celebrate."

"Got that right." Sharma nodded at her mammoth wall screen, where the video's YurTube page idled.

Since Sharma's mom was a heart surgeon and her dad was an emergency room nurse, their differing schedules meant they were rarely home at the same time, or ever. This meant if Sharma was at her Fort Greene brownstone, she was usually alone. Also, that her parents' guilt in turn bought her every high-end gadget on the market. Sitting in front of Sharma's wall screen was equivalent to being first row at a movie theater. Needless to say, despite it equaling a marathon walk from Park Prep and all our houses, we were at Sharma's *a lot*.

"Three thousand three hundred and thirty-four views," Fawn intoned. "That's . . . Sharma, math."

"One eighteen."

"One hundred and eighteen new views in three minutes."

On the ride to Sharma's—Audra pinged an Elite, *What, like anyone wants to* walk *to Fort Greene right now?*—Fawn flagged the video. I didn't expect YurTube to remove it. If anything, they'd slap an NC-17 rating on it, which was almost worse. Now Sharma swiped the video from YurTube into PostProduction. On the wall screen my right eye was magnified by 300 percent.

"Eye see you, too, Sharma," Fawn giggled.

Sharma leveled a look at her, then said, "No obvious mask or filters. No color discrepancy. No motion disjointedness." Now the video went into an HTML program. It was like the JFK Terminal Five of HTML. Code flew in; code flew out. "No breaks in code."

"I'm telling you." I crossed my arms. "It's fake."

Sharma took off her glasses and rubbed her eyes. "Kylie, this isn't like someone FaceSwitched you. Remember the HG trilogy from the two thousand teens? That actor died during production of the third film and they superimposed him into scenes and it was all-caps *and* italics *OBV*? Current vid-editing tech hasn't progressed much beyond that."

Sharma was breathless with so many words. Whenever she spoke more than one sentence at a time, a little of her mom's Indian inflection infused her words. When she was angry, it was her dad's Jamaican accent that crept in. It was adorable.

Fawn inched away from me on the couch and snuggled in next to Audra instead.

"Meaning this video, which isn't of me, has to be of me."

"Essentially, Y-E-S."

"Audy," I said. "*You* know that's not me, right?"

Audra had been suspiciously silent since she'd helped kidnap me from school. Splayed out on the chaise section of Sharma's huge wraparound couch, she was all-caps ABSORBED in her Doc, like she refused to even acknowledge the video. Now she gazed at me. And, completely un-Audra-style, she took a moment to consider her words.

Finally, carefully, she said, "I know you're not a liar. So if you say it's not you, I guess I have to believe you. Which means, for the record, this isn't like Boobgate, because I never denied that was me in those pics. But it doesn't matter what I think. By now it's been downloaded onto so many Docs and hubs, pads, pods, and personals it can live as long as it wants to. So I think what needs to happen, whether it's you or not, is that you have to accept, embrace, and move on."

Embrace? How was I supposed to embrace something like this? And she *guessed* she had to believe me? Audra was my best friend. No matter what the evidence said, believing me ought to be a prereq.

"And now," she said, "can we please take that thing off the screen? I mean, why are we even still watching it when we have an unscheduled day off and *Unicorn Wars* has new episodes?"

"No. Look," Sharma said. "Audra, you're wrong. You can't download it. There's only one true posting. Everything else is a link. It's an unbreakable DRM."

We all watched as Sharma tried to copy the video to her Doc. An error message immediately popped up.

"A DRM?" I asked. "Translate."

"Digital rights management," Sharma replied.

"Translate again," Fawn said.

"An anticopying system." Sharma pulled up an Encyclo page on DRMs. "Lets you watch, stream, or link to a vid, but not copy it. So only the person who posted it benefits. Notice the ads."

A continuous barrage of ads kept popping up along the top of the video, blocking out Mr. E.'s pompadour, making him look oddly bald. Most were for different sexy apps, things like *Get Girls Meeting Girls* and *Play* Undress Her *Now!!!!* One popped up for an expensive shampoo, and I couldn't decide if that meant my hair looked great or needed help. Annoyingly, one even flashed for the *Bra&Panties* chick. Something about a New Year's Eve app.

"So I only need to shut down this one video, right? That's a good thing."

"No." Audra sprawled across Fawn's lap so Fawn would scratch her back. "A DRM means you need to physically delete the source material from the Doc of whoever 'made' this. Otherwise, if YurTube shuts it down, the same person who posted it will retitle it, and it will be back up a click later."

It was so quiet you could hear a page load.

"What?" Audra's lips were still a perfect bright red. On the second-worst day of my life, Audra kept reapplying her lipstick. "Sharma's not the only one who knows this stuff. Can we please stop talking about this now? It's done."

I massaged my temples. So I had to delete the video from the

Doc of the person who made it. Then all these other links and tags would connect to nothing.

Across the room, in the charging bay, my Doc spoke. It was my brother, Kyle. Yes, he was also called Kyle. It was my fault. His real name was Étienne. But when we were little, I was convinced he was part of me, just born ten months later. Kyla and Kyle. By the time we were four and five, we both went by Kyle. Everyone still called us the Kyles, even Mom and Dad.

I'd txted him as soon as we got to Sharma's. We went to different schools, but our online worlds synced up faster than a Doc to its home hub.

moi Don't worry. It's FAKE.

He promised he'd skip basketball practice so we could face Mom and Dad together. Every five minutes since, he'd been audio txting to make sure I was okay.

"Aww, your bro is loaded nachos," Fawn said, blowing my Doc a kiss.

Unlike Mac, who hadn't txted or FaceAlerted even once. I could still see the rage and heartbreak on his face. I bet now he saw the merit in the "just friends" stance I'd been taking for the last three and a half months. Imagine how much worse it would have been if we'd been *together* together when this thing dropped.

"I can't believe this is my life."

"No offense, Kylie," Audra said, tossing her Doc aside, "but only because you've never had to deal with a problem before. This *is* life. On the bright side, at least now you won't have to keep fending Mac off. What? I'm just saying what we're all thinking. Or is everyone else *also* thinking about lunch? Pizza delivery? Or no, let's go out. Mussels and frites, on me."

Fawn made apology face at me but proceeded to scratch Audra's temples. Audra closed her eyes in contented bliss. And it was only then I realized that her Doc was lying next to me and that for once, shockingly, it wasn't on private. The screen was still aglow with her latest search. I spun it toward me.

Her eyes sprang open.

"Wait." She scrambled to sit up.

Although she'd made it clear that my video drama bored her, a little part of me still hoped that she was tracking my online life as heavily as usual. Maybe scrolling message boards or chat forums looking for someone bragging about making the video. But no.

"Really, Audy?"

I pushed her Doc back over to her.

Audra was stalking the *Bra&Panties* slut.

For a moment she looked guilty, like she knew she'd been caught, but then she did her little *so what?* Audra head toggle and sniffed, "I can't help it. She just announced she's revealing it all—*all*, her face, girl parts, everything—on New Year's Eve, and she's made this countdown app—"

"So my life might be over but at least we'll all know who the *B&P* slut is. And here I was upset that you were doing something trivial over there. Wait, a countdown app? As in 'T minus ten, nine...'"

"Nooo. As in every morning you get a code to look at a close-up pic of one of her features. It's groundbreaking marketing, actually. You have to see it."

She sat up and swiped into her Doc. Maybe she was instantly ready to move past my video, but I wasn't.

"Audra, for the last time, I don't care about the stupid *B&P* slut."

Audra's tiny doll hands balled into fists. "And I don't particularly care that you lost your V online and are afraid to admit it, but I sat here and listened to you, didn't I?"

The room went silent. Sharma chewed on her lip. Fawn's eyes filled for a good fourth cry. Audra inspected her nails.

"At Prep you said you believed me."

41

"I *believed* you'd launch into rebuttal mode if I didn't one hundred percent support your resolution. How else were we supposed to get your stubborn little butt out of there?"

There it was, then. They didn't believe me and there was no convincing them. It felt even worse than Mac calling me a slut.

"I'm outta here." I stood up. "Enjoy your lunch."

"Kylie," Fawn protested.

I didn't need their help. I already had a pretty good idea who did this. With any luck, Kyle and I wouldn't even need to talk to Mom and Dad. I could have the video offline before dinner. And then Mac, the girls, and all my classmates could kiss my ampersand, because I was never speaking to any of them ever again.

Happy senior year.

I n debate we called it a takeout. It meant you decimated an opponent so thoroughly they couldn't recover. Once when I'd recapped a win for Mac, enthusiastically detailing how absolute my takeout was, he'd raised that eyebrow of his and said, "Takeout? Aces. I'm starved. Tell me you ordered sweet and sour chicken."

Ever since, I'd thought the wrestling term was more fitting—a takedown. It essentially means the same thing without bringing to mind white cartons of lo mein. One minute you're standing. Next you're completely floored.

Couldn't the girls see? This was a takedown. Pure and simple.

And I could only think of one person who might care enough to decimate me completely. The same person whose dad was some big-deal head honcho of development at Eden and had access to all the latest software. The same person who had been cozying up to my best friend for weeks now. As I sat in a café in Bed-Stuy, ordering one pastry at a time and waiting for Prep to let out, my profile told me she'd watched the video twenty-seven times. A few times for laughs, I could understand, but twenty-seven? That spelled guilt (only with entirely different letters).

So two hours, one really long walk, and five baked goods later, I pressed a doorbell I hadn't rung in over three years. No matter who answered, they wouldn't be happy to see me, but I prayed it wasn't her mom. The last time I'd seen Mrs. Amundsen was at the school talent show. Her withering gaze burned worse than that home hair-removal machine Audra had once inflicted on my toes.

The door opened.

Did I have no good karma chips left?

"Kyle." Ailey's mom took a graceful step back inside. Not to let me in. More like she might slam the door in my face. "What a surprise."

Ailey's mom ran a Bronx-based modern dance company. A former ballerina, her posture was pin straight, her skin coal black, and her manner elegant. For as long as I could remember, she'd worn her salt-and-pepper hair cropped to her head.

My voice cracked as I said, "Hi, Mrs. Amundsen. Is Ailey home?"

I still thought about the exact day we stopped hanging out. It was the first week of freshman year, lunch. Audra came up to us and set a fresh-squeezed green juice in front of me. It perfectly matched the one she was holding.

"There are four seats at my table," Audra said without preamble. "Which means one's empty."

I looked over at Fawn (who waved) and Sharma (who was glued to her Doc) and their two other identical juices, and I'd never wanted to be anywhere so badly in my life. I'd noticed the girls during freshie orientation. The ease between them was palpable, like only in each other's company were they all whole. I guess that's what being friends from birth got you. Their mothers were in the same Lamaze class, then after the babies were born it was weekly playdates, then shared babysitters and summer camps, and eventually aligned middle schools.

"Can Ailey sit with us too?" I asked.

Audra looked into the distance, twisting the swoop of her

black flapper's bob. She took a sip of her juice. "Like I said, there are four seats."

I shrugged at Ailey, like Audra's answer was the most logical argument in the world, trying not to look as giddy as I felt. Ailey and I had been friends since kindergarten. But even though she knew everything about me, from the mole I'd had removed when I was six to my speech impediment with the letter *R* until I was eight, I would never have called her my missing piece. Maybe because when eighth grade hit and I got prettier and people were nicer to me, she began acting . . . what's a word that means fake sugary, worried, and proprietary all in one? Anyway, she started acting *that*. When Audra walked up to me a year later because, as she later told me, I "wore cute shoes *and* a powerful aura," all I felt was relief.

Ignoring Ailey's panicked expression, I went to sit with the girls. After all, they'd gotten me a juice and there were four seats. Never mind that it left Ailey at a table with three empty ones. At least I'd asked if she could join us.

In a way, I'd been waiting for Ailey to take revenge for years. Part of me (a very minuscule part) even kind of thought, *Good for her.* But now it was time to make it stop.

"I just came home myself," Mrs. Amundsen said. "Let me see. . . . Ailey might still be at the pool."

Before she went to check, Mrs. Amundsen closed the door. Mrs. A. used to call me her other kid. This same door that she had just shut against me would have been thrown open. She'd have chatted about this or that as she walked away, letting me lock up. I used to spend the first ten minutes at Ailey's talking to her mom. Now she didn't invite me into the vestibule.

Five minutes passed. I clicked on Ailey's CB profile. It said she'd shared the Mr. E. video with her entire peer contact group—over a thousand people. I was about to jab my thumb down on the doorbell when the door opened and there was Ailey. Study Glasses were pushed up on her head, partially holding back her curly bangs. Ailey had her mom's willowy body and oval face, her dad's Norwegian nose and cheekbones.

She glanced around outside hopefully, like maybe the other girls were there too.

"I'm alone."

"I see that," she said.

"Can I come in?"

She hesitated, part in awe that I was on her steps, part fearful as to why. I figured that had to be a good sign.

"Ailey, you can't not let me into your house."

Sighing, she held the door open.

Walking inside felt like how I imagined it would if I stepped into my house after it had been sold and strangers moved in. It was 100 percent familiar and foreign at exactly the same time. The dance prints on the walls, the African blankets piled in multiple baskets around the living room. Ailey's father in the back doorway, glaring at me like the flu virus had just invaded his home.

"Hey, Mr. A.," I said mildly, waiting for it.

He wanted to have a go at me? Let him. It would give me a better opening for what I had come to say. Ailey was already at the top of the stairs, probably secretly praying her father would say everything she'd never been able to. But debate was all about preparation. And though he'd had over three years to build his arguments, Mr. Amundsen now only had two minutes to put them together.

"It's been a long time," he said.

"It has," I said, matching his cool inflection.

For as long as I'd known the Amundsens, Mr. A. had hated his job at Eden, but it paid him buckets of money and it meant Ailey always had the latest tech. In turn, Ailey was as addicted to her Doc as Sharma. Could Mr. A. get his hands on unreleased video-editing software? No doubt.

I waited, but that was it. That was the best he could do? A disdainful sniff and "It's been a long time"?

"Later, Mr. A."

"Leaving in twenty for that thing in the city," Mrs. Amundsen called, as I jogged up the stairs after Ailey.

This was Ailey's out, in case things went badly. The nostalgic comfort I'd felt walking into Ailey's house dissolved. When we got to her room, Ailey left her bedroom door open a crack as if she might need to call for help.

If I had anything to say about it, she would.

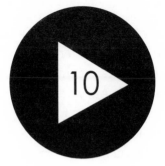

Only Ailey didn't give me the chance to say anything.

"So holy gosh, how are you even breathing right now?"

No sooner did I step into Ailey's room than she was a blur of activity. Picking clothes up off her floor, her chair, her bed. She must have had one of those mornings where nothing looked right, because there were clothes all-caps EVERYWHERE. And as she flitted from one disaster area to another, her mouth ran just as quickly.

"That video is mega terrible. I watched it, like, a thousand times. Sorry, I swear I tap replay right before you see your face. It's just Mr. E., you know? Having S-E-X. With you."

The thought brought her to a standstill. With all the cleaning and the mile-a-minute talking, she was a little out of breath. A curl fell into her eyes. She blew it away and then laughed, as if she'd just caught sight of herself standing there with that enormous armload of clothes.

"Sorry, I wasn't expecting company." She nodded at me to sit on her desk chair, then dropped her clothes back on the floor and sat next to them. "And I'm just so surprised face you're here. But I'm equaling totally rude. Are you okay? More important, do you have any idea of who posted it?"

"Posted it?" I stayed standing. "I'm here to figure out who made it."

I expected her to stutter and apologize or to at least be caught off guard. Instead she shook her head like she had water in her ears.

"You mean it's fake?" she said with incredulousness that was too doe-eyed to be anything but genuine. "Oh holy gosh, I didn't even think about that possibility. It's just so clearly you. Wow. H-A. H-A. Give me a minute here."

As she processed, Ailey separated and then rebraided her hair. I'd forgotten how perfect Ailey and her hair were for each other. Bouncy, crazy, fun. Her nervous energy evaporated.

"Right. Sign me up. How can I help?"

And it's weird, because in the face of the first nonfamilial support I'd had all day, even though I remembered a thousand things I liked about Ailey, I suddenly remembered the things I disliked more. How she reeked of insecurity and clinginess. How every decision was wracked with anxiety—*Ummm, I can't decide. Which burrito are* you *getting?* And the worst, how fawning she was around the in crowd.

My mom still held my breakup with Ailey against me, but at the time, detaching from Ailey had felt like shrugging off a bad mood. I had refused to feel sorry about it.

Until now. Within two minutes Ailey had been more supportive than the girls had been since we left Prep. Other than being looped into our ongoing group thread—which continued to make my Doc hum with pics of food we needed to eat and funny animal vids—no one had individual txted me even once since I left Sharma's. I sank down onto Ailey's desk chair. Someone *believed* me. Suddenly having a friend who liked me too much didn't seem like such a terrible thing.

But alongside my realization, Ailey had one of her own.

"Oh," she said softly. "I just clicked replay. You said you came here to figure out who made it. You didn't come for my help, did you? You came to blame me."

"I think you should go."

Ailey made a sad face. Not like the pantomime of an emote, but a genuinely sad expression, and I knew right then that she couldn't be anything but innocent.

"Ailey..."

"No. That's okay. I understand why you'd think it'd be me, I guess. But I still think you'd better go."

I didn't move.

"I'm sorry, Ailes." The nickname erased her frown lines and brought her shoulders down an inch. "But logically speaking, if it's not you, I couldn't think of anyone else who might have it in for me. I mean, other than *maybe* Jessie Rosenthal..."

Ailey made a face. "Yuck. Jessie. Ellie, for some reason, adores her. I think she's all-caps SO pretentious. And, just, so weird. I tell Ellie all the time that Jessie's not right, but she won't listen to me."

"Not right?" I asked as I scrolled my contacts for Jessie's info. "How do you mean?"

"Ellie told me Jessie keeps these 'human projects' on her Doc. They're, like, collections and videos of these people that Jessie stalks around the city. Ellie said there was one of this man who always eats alone at the same diner every night. This woman who feeds the birds in the park. Jessie woofers them, so now she knows everything about them. 'Human projects.' It gives me the creeps. You don't think..."

I shivered. Weirder than Jessie's human projects was that in thirty seconds of searching, I'd found zero ways to reach her. No e-mail, profile links, Doc digits, nothing. How was that possible? Thanks to Park Prep's alumni breeding program, my Doc was constantly updating my classmates' contact info. I could txt the entire student body, going back twenty years, if I wanted. Yet for Jessie all that came up was a physical address in Brooklyn Heights. What good was that?

Also, there was her Quip stream. It said she hadn't logged in for two months. Still I sent her a private Quip asking her to txt me, then sighed and tossed my Doc on Ailey's desk.

"I don't know what to think."

"So you came here?"

"I just thought maybe you were still mad at me for—"

"Scraping me off like something nasty on the bottom of your shoe?"

"I wouldn't describe it like that." I laughed. "Okay, maybe I would. But I mean, people grow apart, Ailey."

Ailey was fidgeting with her bra strap, a lacy lime-green number, way fancier than anything she'd owned when we were friends. The Amundsens' household was like a thousand degrees. I took off my hat, scarf, and then, after another second, unsure how long I really wanted to stay, my coat.

"You think we grew apart?"

"I dunno. I mean, I guess we just grew different. I'm sorry, Ailey. Chalk it up to being fourteen?"

Ailey flapped a hand, waving away my transgressions.

"Of course. Forget it. That's all nothing now, for real."

It was then, as we sat there, not meeting each other's eyes but uncomfortably smiling in each other's direction, that I realized something strange. Ailey wasn't on her Doc. And Ailey was always on her Doc. I'd checked mine at least twenty times since I'd been there, and I wasn't nearly as Doc-dependent as Ailey. In fact, I didn't see her Doc anywhere. She must have stashed it somewhere when I came in. But why would she do that?

I popped out of my chair and opened her walk-in closet just like I used to, pretending I wanted to admire her boring shoes and sweaters. Ailey got stuck with the smallest bedroom in the brownstone, but glass half-full, it had the largest closet. When I was out of sight, I checked the floor and along her shelves. No Doc.

"Oh holy gosh," Ailey squealed. "I know who it is. Who's the one person who could get their hands on video-editing tech like this?"

You? I wanted to say, but instead guessed, "Reed Winters? He's doing that internship with Magnus Pictures."

"No." I could hear Ailey shake her curls with exasperation. "Don't get frowny face, but it's Sharma. It has to be."

"Sharma?" My head rocked back in surprise. "Why would she do something like this?"

"Because she equals the fourth friend. Like Abel in *Twilight Girls*. Nobody cares about Abel. Who needs more motive than that? I mean, how much do you trust *any* of the girls, for that matter?"

Ailey said it innocently enough, but it was still trash talk. And nobody trash-talked my girls but me. Before I could stop myself, I snapped, "Sharma isn't the fourth anything. We're all integral." Then I lied, "Plus the girls are outraged about this. They have my back, always."

"Of course they do," Ailey said quickly. "Sorry. I was just thinking out loud."

This was pointless. Ailey's closet was identical to Ailey: long, slim, and hiding nothing. I went back into her room and began to gather my stuff.

Above her desk she still had her Wish Board. A rinky-dink corkboard that always held dozens of cutout images of cars she liked, houses she wanted to live in, and boys she had crushes on. It had dwindled over the years as printed materials became harder to come by. Now the board was filled with photos of her and Ellie Cyr. Actual printed photos. Apparently, they did everything together. Ball games, Coney Island, the ballet, sleepovers.

"I can't believe you still do this."

Something constricted a little in my chest. Maybe it was that I could so easily envision myself in those photos replacing Ellie. If I hadn't ditched Ailey, it would have been me. But I guessed things had all worked out the way they were supposed to. Seeing the girls' pretty, happy smiles, I knew that Ailey had clearly found her people. People who, unlike me, wouldn't dump her because better ones had come along. And then I noticed something else: almost in equal number to the shots of Ailey and Ellie were pics of Ailey with a boy.

I lightly touched one of those photos as if it were an ancient artifact. In it, Ailey and the boy were wearing enormous sunglasses, hugging. The photos made me notice the dried roses pinned next to the board. The lone teddy bear on her bed where a pile of childhood ones used to be. It stopped me in my tracks.

I gasped. "Ailey, do you have a boyfriend?"

"Triple smiley face," she said as an actual smile lit up her features. "I hoped you'd notice. We met at the Y. He's a lifeguard and goes to that new charter Learn in Excellence. That's part of why Mom takes my Doc away when I come home. He's on it, like, equal sign, always. 'Homework first, Ailey.'"

And that was why Ailey didn't have her Doc.

I had an urge to rip up the pic of Ailey's boy. I don't know if it was jealousy for the normalcy of it all, or that the boy looked wholesome—obv no checkered past there—or that Ailey was so clearly happy. She stayed good, didn't abandon anybody, and she still got the friends, the boy, and the smooth complexion. For the first time I had a tiny sense of how she must have felt when I dumped her. It was a thick, gooey kind of awful—like existential tapioca.

"Congrats, that's awesome," I said, trying for the enthusiasm I didn't feel. "B-T-W what did your mom have to say about the video? Did you show her yet?"

"Gawd no." Ailey laughed. "She gets worked up enough when we talk about you. I didn't want my next two days equaling a dissection of every lurid detail of your downfall. Is it weird? Knowing so many people are watching you? I mean, it already has over forty thousand views."

Forty thousand views? At Sharma's it had been in the low single-digit thousands. *Maybe if someone hadn't watched it twenty-seven times and shared it with her thousand friends,* I wanted to say, *it wouldn't be at forty thousand views.* The warmth I'd felt at being back around Ailey burned off.

"Ailey, it's hardly a downfall. I had over a hundred likes on my outfit before I left the house this morning. *Fifty* thousand views is nothing. I'll post one old video of me and the girls at Fire Island this past summer and the Mr. E. video will be buried in no time."

I put on my hat and scarf. I shouldn't have come. I should have just txted. This was why I cold turkey stopped talking to Ailey. Faced with her saccharine good-girl personality I always, all-caps ALWAYS, said something that made me hate myself later.

"Oh, sorry, I know, I just meant with your college apps in and all..."

My knees turned liquid. As discreetly as possible, I steadied myself against Ailey's desk. My applications. Everyone knew admissions boards began at your ConnectBook page before they even glanced at your app. I mean, what was a more truthful depiction of a person than their CB profile?

I could feel Ailey watching me. So although I was finding it hard to breathe, I zipped into my coat and managed a breezy laugh.

"I haven't hit send on those yet. I have lots of time to figure this out. You know me. Tenacious is kind of my thing. I know you have to get going. Sorry I barged in on you, Ailes."

"Oh, I don't mind. It was nice. Kyle, for what it's worth, I swear I didn't make that video." Ailey bit her lip, and for the first time since I arrived, her eyes met mine. *Swear.* There was no lying when you called a swear. Or there didn't use to be. "And hey, seriously, let me know if you need anything."

The best argument was always the most logical. I'd known Ailey since kindergarten. She wasn't a liar, which meant she was telling the truth.

What was I going to do?

I want to warn you, what you're about to see isn't pretty, but it's *not* me."

Ailey said she probably wasn't going to "that thing in the city" anyway and did I want to hang and stay for dinner? But seeing as dining in a group where two out of the three people hated me was the most unappetizing idea ever, I demurred.

Now I was home. Three pairs of Kyle's shoes were strewn across the living room floor. Mom's crocheting sat in a lump next to the couch. Dad's basswood replica of the Brooklyn Bridge was spread out on the coffee table. Half-burned-out strings of colored Christmas lights blinked haphazardly from the mantel and windows. Our house was a mess. I'd never been so happy to be anywhere in my whole life. Finally, my people.

"Honey, what's going on?"

Kyle and I had waited an excruciating hour for Dad to get home before we called both our parents into the living room. Mom had on the same expression she wore that time Ruichen Li shoved Kyle into the street when we were kids. I hadn't even shown her the video and she looked ready to end the world.

"Please don't tell me this is about shoes," Dad said. "If we're not having dinner because you ordered another pair of expensive no-refund, no-return vintage shoes that pinch your pinky toe, I'm going to be one big unhappy face."

"Frowny face," Kyle and I corrected together as Dad grinned.

When my dad was younger, he was in a Chinese gang in Flushing. Now he was a librarian who had *R E A W* tattooed in Old English on his knuckles. It stood for "Read 'Em and Weep." He was better at gaming than Kyle and, in all honesty, he was probably hipper than me. His misspoken slang was solely meant to annoy us.

"Sung, this isn't a joke," Mom said. "Less levity for once, please. Kylie, you're scaring me. Enough with the preamble."

I used my Doc to bring up the link on our hub.

"Kyle, tap play." I couldn't stay for it. Maybe it had to be stuck in their memory banks, but their watching it didn't have to be stuck in mine. "Call me when it's over."

I motored into the kitchen.

"What the—?" Dad immediately sputtered.

"Kyle, what is this?" Mom called.

"A fake video, remember?"

I rested my forehead against the refrigerator door. I already felt exhausted by the effort it would take to convince my mom the video wasn't real. When Dad bellowed, it was my cue that the video was over. I pried open the fridge and grabbed a beer. Dad would need liquid strength to help me deal with Mom's ensuing atomic freak-out.

I slunk back to the living room. Kyle gave me a weak smile. Mom was still staring at the screen, stunned. I handed Dad his beer. He waved it off, pointed at the stairs.

"Go to your room."

"Daddy...?" My voice did this weird quaver. "Seriously?"

"It's not her," my brother said.

"Sung..." Mom interceded.

"I said go to your room." For a normal person it wasn't shouting, but for my dad it was. Softer, he said, "I need a minute. Okay? I need a minute to process this and speak with your mother. Kyle, go to your room. You too, Kyle. Both Kyles. Rooms. Now."

It would have been funny if it just wasn't.

13

spent the next half hour wheeling around my room in my desk chair waiting for my parents to knock and say they had somehow fixed this. How, exactly, was beyond me. I'd been tagged in 4,749 posts. I had 536 new Connect requests and 133 private messages, and 2,652 people had commented on a link I was tagged in. I was trending.

I chewed on a cuticle, very much wanting to cry. I txted my brother instead.

moi Thanks for not asking if it was me in the vid, Kyle.

boi-k Duh, Kyle. You're my sister
       I know you wouldn't
       OBV
       I mean, duh.

Yes, my brother resembled an enormous bipedal puppy—I was always tripping over a techie toy he'd dragged out then forgot about, and if I left food in the open it was eaten—but I was still convinced he was the best part of me. I sent him a pic of two babies hugging. To which he replied:

> boi-k You don't think they forgot about dinner, do you? I'm STARVING.

At least some things hadn't changed. On my Doc I typed, *What would Malin do?* and then Quipped it.

The girls could tease me all they wanted, but President Malin was my hero. In her first term she'd pushed through more legislation than any other president in history. She'd declared a fight to end date rape in her lifetime. She'd launched the Global Water Resuscitation Program by going on record as not having used a disposable feminine product in over twenty-five years. I mean, with *one speech* she'd changed the entire feminine product industry. (I preferred the Regal Cup®: For the New Woman's Body.)

(Sorry. The Regal Cup thing was too much. I'll be done now.)

President Malin wouldn't be helplessly chewing on her cuticles. She'd put on her thinking sweats (or the closest facsimile thereof), swipe her Doc to share mode, put her room screen to 3-D touch, and *find her hater*. So that's what I decided to do.

Park Prep was known for its small class sizes. How hard could it be?

Correct answer: extremely hard.

It would have been easier to find the people at Park Prep who *hadn't* commented on the video or linked it. Now when you looked up my G-File, you could see that Kyla Cheng's friend Charity Knowles thought: *Ha! What a TRAMP.*

Charity had shared my hand sanitizer in Civics all last year. Just yesterday she'd cooed how much she liked my blazer. Now I was a tramp? My mouth was briny with anger. No matter how far down I scrolled, not a single person questioned the video's authenticity. And not a single person defended me.

"Won't you look ridiculous, Charity," I told her profile pic, "when I prove it's not me?"

In debate Coach Ota told us to find the facts first, then craft our narratives. So what did I know about the video?

First—surprise, surprise—it had been posted as Anonymous. Mine was the only video this user had ever posted. And the time stamp on the account's creation was yesterday. When I swiped into the user's profile, I knew more, especially since it was set to "open" (amateur). In fact, in two swipes I knew Anonymous's name.

Now who the H-double-L was Ennie Li Sunmaid?

On my room screen, a preset girl avatar popped up next to my personalized avatars. Underneath her it read: *Contact: Ailey.*

Asked my dad, preset girl said. *He knows of no software that could make vid. If you need to talk, I'm here.*

Great. Thanks. Block.

What kind of a name was Ennie, other than completely gender-neutral? I knew an Annie in elementary school, but she was the sweetest thing ever, plus she moved to Buffalo in the third grade. I swiped to another screen and searched for Ennie's G-File.

No matches found.

He/she didn't have a G-File? That meant there was no proof of his/her existence anywhere online. What, did a senior citizen have it out for me?

I swiped back into Ennie's YurTube profile and found the e-mail address that had been used to create the account. My stomach got all squishy. Whoever had made the video had a bigger grudge against me than I'd imagined. Ennie Li Sunmaid wasn't a real person's name. It was just nonsense to fill in the name fields—phonetic, creepy nonsense.

The alias they chose was @AnyLiesUnmade.

My eyes filled with stress tears. I angrily wiped them away and swiped into my messaging program. Who needed facts when I had a direct line to this AnyLies? I pulled up the no-name-sender thread from the morning countdown, and before I could think better of it, I added a line.

moi Why are you doing this to me?

Then I waited.

Mom called upstairs to tell us she'd put soup on the stove. Across the hall, Kyle's bedroom door smacked against the wall. Next second he was thundering downstairs. I shouted back that I wasn't hungry.

Then I waited some more.

Suddenly, into the silence of my bedroom, my FaceAlert notification rang. Without thinking, I hit accept. To FaceAlert you needed my Doc digits, and *those* I kept private. Only about four hundred people knew them. As I waited for the FaceAlert window to connect, I stared at the AnyLies txt thread. I almost felt AnyLies staring at her screen too.

"You'll fix this, Kyle," I murmured. "You'll fix this."

As if in reply, my room screen emitted a high-pitched laugh. The FaceAlert window was still black. I glanced at the contact. The number was blocked.

"Hello?" I enlarged the window. "Your FaceAlert's not working. I can no puedo see you."

There was a digital beep. It sounded like the recording video sound that most Docs made.

"Oh my gosh..."

Someone was filming me.

I tried to push back, out of sight of my screen's camera. The wheel on my desk chair caught on my rug, and the whole thing tipped backwards. My arms pinwheeled. I righted myself, but just barely. As I tapped frantically at the disconnect button, whoever was watching me said in a joyously evil singsong, "Kisses."

I couldn't push air in or out fast enough. I closed out of

FaceAlert. I shut down my room screen, then powered off my Doc entirely. I closed my blinds and checked the locks on my windows. I couldn't have felt more exposed than if you'd shoved me into the middle of Union Square naked. And no matter how secure I made my room, I couldn't stop hearing that voice. They must have used a voice changer, because no human vocal cords could reach that high a pitch.

Kisses.

14

It took three lathers and rinses to wash away the creepy ick. In future debates I'd argue that a hot shower could solve most non-life-threatening problems. As I shampooed my hair into a soapy tower for the fourth time, I tried to mute the high-pitched evil doll voice I kept hearing in my head. *Kisses. Kisses. Kisses.* I'd tried to call the blocked number back, but it was one of those single-use, untraceable, offshore e-mails that the US government was trying to shut down for exactly these reasons. I also tried to think about all the recent lies I'd told.

I mean, "any lies unmade," right?

Here's the problem. I could see people calling me BTCHY (partially true, especially when uncaffeinated), arrogant (lightly true), or entitled (definitely *not* true), but a liar?

A requirement of best-friending Audra meant I was on a first-name basis with brutal honesty.

After my shower, I popped the door and stayed in the steamy bathroom, unable to shake the chill I felt. I was twisting my hair into pin curls when a sudden knock made me jump.

Kisses.

Mom leaned against the door frame. If my dad crushed the coolest dad category, my mom hands down won coolest human. In her late twenties, she'd started StitchBtch, an online Brooklyn arts-and-crafts collective that now had brick-and-mortar stores in almost all fifty states. She still made most of her own clothes and was cofounder of the Sustainability Now local business movement. When I was growing up, even though she was in her forties, strangers regularly thought she was my babysitter.

Now I couldn't help mentally airbrushing her: dyeing the white streak out of her copper-brown hair, erasing the wrinkles from around her gray eyes. It was only recently that I'd started this airbrushing thing. It was only recently that Mom had started looking old. Like everything else about us nowadays, I hated it.

"I'm going to school tomorrow, aren't I?" I asked.

"Your dad and I think you'll only look guiltier if you don't. Not to mention, you can't ruin your perfect attendance."

Tranquila, I told myself. She meant it as a joke, even if it sounded like a criticism.

"Does Daddy hate me?"

"Kyle." Mom gave me a look. "You know Daddy: he just needs to absorb this at his own speed. Let him dredge parenting forums for a while. He'll find someone who's encountered something like this and be ordering apology Mexican food before the night is over. Your brother ate all the soup, by the way. Four bowls. I swear he has a tapeworm."

"Do you believe me?"

If anyone wasn't going to, it would be my mom.

"Did you sleep with Mr. E.?" she asked carefully.

I stopped twisting my hair. "Ew, no. No way."

"Okay, then I believe you."

I was so stunned I almost asked her to repeat herself. Instead I kept pinning up my hair.

"I messaged Dr. Graff," she said. "The earliest she can see us tomorrow is second period. If it's terrible before that, you can

66

always leave and come home with me. And then it's only the half day on Friday and everyone will be too excited for Christmas on Saturday to talk about that video anyway. By Monday it'll be completely forgotten."

Not likely.

If this were a normal year, I wouldn't even have to go to school on the twenty-fourth as one of Park Prep's Senior Perks. Then with a full week off between Christmas and New Year's, yes, maybe everyone would have forgotten all about this. But because of all the days we'd missed thanks to Hurricane Riley in September, and then the October blizzard, this year our winter break was literally nonexistent. And I actually *mean* literally. Christmas and New Year's fell on Saturdays. We were back in classes on the following Mondays.

Prior to the video, I'd been fine with this schedule. It would be only the second Christmas we'd be spending without my näinai, my grandma. None of the Chengs were much thrilled by the prospect. The last thing I needed was one more day sitting at home missing her.

Plus, all the way back in October, Audra had declared a moratorium on Christmas, saying there was no possible way she'd be able to deal this year. Seasons past, the days leading up to and after the holiday had resulted in more Audra meltdowns than any of us knew what to do with. Christmas might be all about the gifts, but it's also still *a little* about family. And Audra's was awful. Since I'd known her, Audra had shown up at one or another of our houses at some point on Christmas Day, usually drunk, her face a wreck, asking if she could borrow our family and yuletide cheer.

This year, when Audra declared she was ignoring the holiday entirely, we other three girls all immediately said it was fine by us. If it weren't for the Community Club's holiday party—*the* best day of my entire year three years running—I'd also prefer to ignore Christmas entirely.

"Want me to do the back?" Mom asked.

"Sure."

I handed her the comb and sat on the tub. For a minute we were quiet as she divided my hair into sections. Minus lots of laughter, this almost felt like old times.

"So why would someone do this to you?"

And *this* felt like new times. Now we were on our regular footing. Maybe Mom believed I hadn't slept with Mr. E., but she sure as H-double-L believed I'd done something to deserve the attack.

I often wondered who was more upset by the fact that Mom didn't like me anymore. Me or Mom? I'd go with me.

The thing is, back when Mom was in high school, she was essentially the same as me—driven, top of her class, and geeky about her extracurrics. The only difference was that Mom had glasses the size of hubcaps and she crocheted most of her clothes. Today, she'd have been (and was) an e-fashionista. But back then, she had no friends, spent lunch in the art room, and was ruthlessly picked on by the popular girls.

Never mind that Mom turned out a thousand times more successful; I still caught her browsing her old nemeses' profiles every so often, wine in hand. If we saw a group of attractive in-crowd kids on the train, her go-to reaction was an eye roll. She wouldn't watch any shows with me if the lead teen character wasn't a social moron. In a thousand little ways, my mom was prejudiced against popular.

So imagine her horror when her own daughter escaped bad vision and turned out hot. (What? It's okay for girls to say they think they're ugly.) Imagine her double horror when her daughter shed her lifetime best friend and gained three gorgeous crazies instead. Never mind that the girls and I were *nothing like* those nasty losers who had abused Mom.

My whole life we'd been close. Now we were this.

I groaned. "Mom."

"Kyle, there must be some reason someone would do this to you."

"Clearly, because I'm an evil, awful person."

She wrapped a strand of my hair a little tighter than it needed to be.

"What did Mac say about the video? I'm surprised he's not glued to your hip tonight."

I forced myself to take a deep breath. Audra would be thrilled if her parents showed this much interest in her life.

"He thinks it's true."

Working to keep her expression blank, she reached around me and took another bobby pin off the sink ledge. Mom had been so grateful for her high school boyfriend that she'd dated him into her late twenties. I was barely out of the womb a decade later when she began telling me what a mistake that was.

"Before I met Daddy I dated a lot of jerks," Mom said.

"We weren't dating," I clarified, again. "And Mac's not a jerk."

"All I'm saying is there will be other boys."

Like Mac? I doubted it.

But I didn't say that; instead I went with "Duh, Mom. I'm seventeen. I know how upgrades work. Why settle for a Series Twenty-One when you can get a Series Twenty-Two Invisible?"

It was Audra's line, not mine. And it couldn't be further from how I felt. I figured Mom would whap me in mock disgust and then we'd both laugh. Dad would have laughed. Mom would have too, a few years back. Now she scraped the last bobby pin along my scalp.

"Ow."

"Oops. Sorry. Well, I'm glad you have it all figured out."

She thought I was serious. As if she couldn't stand one more second of my presence, she sloppily made one last huge pin curl, then left with a "Don't stay up too late."

Frowning into the mirror—because I refused to cry over this again—I separated the last giant curl into four normal ones.

"Kisses."

I'd never felt so lonely in my life.

I was in bed by nine. For maybe the first time in my life, I didn't call out *good night* to my parents. I just shut my door and turned off my light. Then with the covers over my head and Teddy wedged beneath my chin, I hesitated only a click before whispering, "Call Mac."

Fine. Somewhere in the world a feminist was gagging on her coconut water because I was calling the boy who'd just about cursed me out on the street, but would it have been better if I'd waited for him to call me? Eighteenth-century was more like it. Sometimes need ruled out circumstance. And Mac danced with me anywhere, *anywhere*—subway, street, cafeteria—if he knew it'd make me smile. He took me for mystery bike rides that ended in tacos and chocolate–peanut butter ices. Mac thought I was a good person, just the way I was.

Or at least he used to.

Our origin story went like this: I'd crushed on Mackenzie Rodriguez since the first day I laid eyes on him our freshman year. Forget his perfect bone structure, that soccer body, and those curls; he was mysterious, aloof, and rumored to be some kind of mathematics savant. The *entire school* crushed on Mac our fresh-man year. Nobody launched a Bet on who he'd pair off with, but considering the interest, someone should have.

And I'd have put every last credit on myself.

There was little doubt Mac liked me back. Whenever we passed in the hall or bumped into each other outside my freshie math class, our eyes locked. Beats blaring from his headphones (this was before Dr. Graff threatened suspension if she had to tell him one more time . . .), he'd dance that eyebrow up and give me this adorable, sexy lopsided smile. Afterwards I'd have to lean against a cubby to catch my breath, Mac peeking back at me over his shoul-der as he ambled away.

Taylor Louise threw the first party that fall. Her parents went to Tulum for the weekend, leaving her in charge of their Prospect Heights brownstone. A mistake they only made once.

In my honor, Audra picked our clothing theme even though it wasn't her turn—Love 'Em and Keep 'Em. The girls had decided a full week beforehand that Taylor's party would be the night Mac and I got together.

It was my first high school party. We made our entrance, appropriately late. I still wonder if things would have worked out differently if we'd arrived on time. Fawn and Sharma went to scope out the kitchen, and Audra and I went in search of a bathroom. We found a line snaking through the second-floor hallway. Audy cut right to the front.

"Tiny girl bladders out here." She pounded on the door. "Hurry it up."

Silence. She pushed against the door. It popped open. And there was Mac. With his face plastered to Keisha Hutchinson's.

"Ew." To her credit, Audra did not whiplash her head to catch my reaction; instead she reached for my hand and said, "At least have the courtesy to lock the door."

"Está roto," Mac sang out, barely coming up for air. "Why do you think everyone else is waiting?"

I never knew if he realized I was standing there or not. Regardless, ice cream, tears, and a sleepover at Sharma's followed. I felt worse than when I saw the McClellans' dog get hit by that cab. I quickly got used to the feeling.

Just that fall alone, I witnessed Mac making out with Empire Quinn, Sukie Moon, and Trinity Henry. Over the next three years, almost every time I saw him outside school, and half the time in school, he was welded to a different female's face. Girls who didn't even go to Park Prep waited on the steps to walk him home after class. And don't even txt me about the rumors. As if the RL version of Mac weren't bad enough, tales of his conquests, spoken in hushed awe, circulated the grades.

Did I know Rodriguez was dating *two* seniors at Bloomberg?

Did I hear Rodriguez "did it" on the great lawn of Prospect Park—during the day?

You can't help who you're attracted to? Baloney. Try harder. Luckily, our different focus tracks kept us on different floors of Park Prep. Yet for three years straight, Mac seemed to cross my path at least once a day up on three. And every time, he would tilt an imaginary hat or execute a tiny dance step for my amusement. And every time, I ignored him entirely.

By that point, I'd gotten a rep of my own—one for not dating.

Why would I? Never mind that growing up sharing the same search engine with a boy made the entire species lose much of its charm, but I mean, was Izel Kemp worth missing Model UN or not organizing the Walk for Paws benefit? President Malin didn't have her first serious boyfriend until she was twenty-nine and had already won a congressional seat. President Malin didn't get married until she was *forty-two*. I had loads of time to date.

That's not to say I didn't kiss a few other guys, or, like, flirt chat, but the only person I had any interest inserting an ounce of free time into was rumored to have inserted himself into just about everybody else.

Sorry. That was gross. I couldn't help myself.

There was no way I was dating Mackenzie Rodriguez.

Plus, he never asked.

Until senior year.

Calling Mac, my Doc screen read, because txting was too imprecise and FaceAlerting wasn't my friend between ten p.m. and ten a.m. *Calling Mac,* because ever since September, we'd talked every night right before we went to bed. Even if only for a minute. Without exception. *Calling Mac,* because tonight I didn't want to hear Mac's avatar's voice via audio txt; I wanted to hear his *voice* voice and the adorable way he rolled his *r*'s. I quickly got my wish.

Éste es Mackenzie Rodriguez. Háblame.

He'd sent me to voice mail. My pic had shown up on his Doc and he'd swiped it away. I hung up. Why bother leaving a message?

Mac's silence pretty much said it all.

16

A little after one in the morning, my Doc buzzed. Instantly awake (barely asleep to begin with), I snatched it off my bureau. It had to be Audra. It wasn't entirely rare for us to get annoyed at each other—actually of late it was all too common—but the great thing about us was that we didn't hold grudges and our mini disputes never lasted more than five minutes at a time.

However, it had now been over thirteen hours since I'd heard from her. And every time I went to txt her, her avatar was red. For once her sleeplessness was working in my favor. Girlfriend insomniaced hard. If she wasn't sleeping over and prodding me awake, she was doing it via txt. Rare was the night when I didn't hear from her at all.

But when I glanced at my screen, my skin reprickled with chills that hadn't fully left. It was definitely not Audra.

moi Why are you doing this to me?

[   ] Isn't it obvious? To hurt you.

THURSDAY, DECEMBER 23

'll let you in on a little secret.

The in kids know you're watching.

And just the way you could search Brittany Mulligan's Woofer all day and not find a single double-chinned pic of her, even though she swore she didn't pay to have her face Pulled—what you see is a crafted image.

Around you, the in kids smile brighter. Laugh louder. And it's no accident that their every conversation sounds like an inside joke.

It's not that it's fake. They *are* enjoying themselves, only more so when you're around.

This could work for you, too, you know. Nothing annoyed Audra more than Jacqueline Menendez and the uppity chem geeks. Liked. Hated. Popular. Unpopular. It's all how you spin it.

And it's definitely all a ruse.

So the next morning as I walked through Park Prep's double doors and the first-floor hallway grew deadly quiet, I met that silence with a tiny smile. I knew it would be awful. Everyone else didn't have to know that too.

The video was at 250,000 views. I tossed my hair. I hadn't heard from any of the girls since I left Sharma's yesterday. Even our group thread had taken on a morose hush. I smirked and waved at Charity Knowles. What would I do when I got to Coffee Check and it was obvious I had no other Docs to clink against mine? No clue. I put extra sway in my walk.

I was used to the head-angled-down, eyes-angled-up way that my age group viewed the world, but I'd never had an entire silent hallway give it to me. AnyLies could be any of them. I mean, when Oscar Hawley had asked me out last year, I'd laughed.

Him?

Or what about Mr. Huge Ego Ulee Ostrander, who I'd crushed in debate practice for two years running?

Him?

It was like a hallway of Justice League villains. Just beyond Ulee, Jessie Rosenthal and Ellie Cyr were again wedged together like two badly mismatched shirts on the same sales rack. As I passed, the girls stopped chatting and watched me with the grim silence of seeing a funeral pass.

Them?

I swiped at my Doc, pretended to laugh at something I saw there.

And then a mountain of curls was beside me and a hand slapped my butt, giving it a reassuring squeeze. Fawn. My Fawn had come through, adorable in a black pantsuit. Then Sharma, in a long black sheath dress and arm bangles, was on my other side. And seconds after, Audra completed our line.

"I didn't know if you guys would be here."

I tried to sound casual, but my voice shook.

"It's *the Walk*," Audra said under her breath. "We didn't even miss the Walk when Fawnie took us to that seafood buffet in K-Town and we all got food poisoning."

"In my defense," Fawn said, "it had good reviews."

Audra looked like a British dominatrix in her fitted black

blazer, teeny skirt, and knee-high boots. Black. That was Sharma's theme of the day for her color-themed week. It felt appropriate.

"For the record," Audra continued, "I apologize if I didn't seem supportive yesterday. After you left, Fawnie and Sharm explained why this is such a big deal to someone like you. So I guess I can see why you kept it a secret and why you still don't want to admit to it. Only I don't want to be fed any more lies. So maybe until you're comfortable talking about it, let's just pretend it didn't happen and move past it." Her lips puckered to the side. "I know that didn't seem like an apology. But, well, I love you, Kylie-cat. I really am sorry for not being there for you. I know there's no worse feeling."

Actually, there was. The feeling when your bestie essentially calls you a liar to your face. My breakfast cereal curdled in my stomach. Wow. Thanks, friend. I could have continued to deny that it was me in the video or told them about AnyLies, but it'd sound like I was grasping at excuses. Besides, if I didn't accept this lackluster support, I wouldn't have any at all.

"Thanks, Auds. I know that wasn't easy for you to say."

She beamed at me. "Super-mature for me, right? I panic-attacked about it all morning."

"This is actually kinda neat," Fawn breathed.

The Walk normally garnered looks, but today *all* eyes were on us. So Audra chatted away brightly about nonsense. An always-unflappable Sharma swiped at her Doc. Fawn wore her sexy daydreamy look, which meant she was probably thinking about biscuit sammies. Unsmiling, I went for BTCH confidence. And we rocked the Walk that morning. To this day, it still stands as one of the most horrifying experiences of my life.

See? It's all how you spin it.

In front of Coffee Check, I fumbled out my Doc. "That's it?"

"That was nothing," Fawn giggled, pulling out her own Doc.

Cue the moaning.

It was quiet at first, but it quickly filled the foyer like a choir crescendo. It was like everyone had tapped play on the Mr. E. sex video at the same time with their volume on high. I mean, it wasn't *like* that. It was that.

Everyone in the vestibule had their tech out. It was impossible to know who was participating and who was innocently txting or doing last-minute homework. The sound came from at least fifty Docs. There was no way this many people had this big a grudge against me.

Channing Gregory grabbed Bryan Alders and started imitating the video. Stupid Channing thought he could get away with anything because his father was VP of the most popular online network. Yvonne Rose Harper paraded past, her Doc in the air, Mr. E. going at it on-screen. At least four people were filming us, laughing. Fawn still had her Doc raised half in the air, waiting for a kiss that wasn't coming. There wasn't anything to be done. Reacting would only make for a popular related link.

"Come here, betch." Audra smiled brightly, shoving her Doc in her bag.

Placing her tiny hands on my shoulders, she pulled me to her and kissed me, like *kissed* me, full on the lips. Fawn swooped in and planted a kiss on my cheek. After only a brief hesitation, Sharma lightly pressed her lips against my other cheek. The moaning was now covered up by catcalls and a murmur of whispers. The girls kissed me until after the video ended. When they pulled away, we were all flushed and smiling.

"This builds character. You are bigger than this." Audra tweaked my nose, then over my shoulder said, "That's how you protect the people you love, güey."

When I turned, Mac was at the edge of the crowd. He was wearing a baseball cap pulled so low it was impossible to see his eyes. His hands were shoved into the pockets of his hoodie.

"Macky," I called.

Shaking his head, he backed away, dissolved into the crowd, and was gone. The funny thing was, I knew just how he felt. He looked exactly as heartbroken as I'd been every time I'd seen him making out with someone who wasn't me. But there was one huge difference. He'd gotten with those girls. I'd never touched Mr. E. And if he'd tried to talk to me about something terrible that had happened to him, regardless of his guilt in it, I would have been there to listen.

Audra watched me watch Mac, then grabbed Fawn's arm and sashayed away to first period, never mind that Fawn would immediately have to come back this way for physics. Guess today it wasn't important that we all walked together.

A bony hip bumped mine.

"Why I prefer living online," Sharma said. "Let's go see how Mr. E.'s holding up."

18

First period. Mr. E. wasn't in class. My classmates stared at me, waiting for my reaction. Despite her apology for not having been there for me and her miraculous save during the flash prank, Audra stayed thoroughly absorbed in her privacy-mode Doc when I sat next to her, barely registering my appearance. Two people recorded me.

Cue the substitute teacher: "I know it's only two days before Christmas, but I won't stand for any nonsense or improper behavior. I expect you all to read or work quietly." Cue my Doc dinging loudly a dozen times. Cue classmates' laughter as everyone hid their Docs on their laps and flicked on some kind of EarRing device.

Cue me checking my profiles for the first time that day and trying really hard to keep it together. My whole life, my G-File had come up as the second Kyla Cheng. The first Kyla was a film editor out in LA. Now when you searched my name, I came out above her. I had figured I'd be in my twenties before that happened, when I'd won an election as a junior senator.

Ha!

What's worse, there were now dozens of tribute videos attached to my G-File. (Didn't anyone have a life?) A few were simple vlog posts. Only one was in my defense: Ailey's. She said that if I were a boy I'd be getting high fives right now instead of being ruthlessly talked about and ostracized by everyone I knew for being a slut.

Um, thanks.

The rest, the majority, were remake videos. Derek Boger's had the most views. He dressed up like "me," and the whole time another boy moved around behind him like Mr. E., Derek said idiotic things like

"O-M-G, can you believe I have hair?"

"I like clothes."

"O-M-G, look at my boobs."

At the end, when the dude behind him moved in for a kiss, Derek held up his Doc and said, "Kisses."

Cue Audra's Valley Girl avatar voice whispering in my ear, "Look at this instead." When I glanced at her, she winked.

The link she sent was to the *Bra&Panties* slut's most recent post.

BRA&PANTIES

Hey there, mavens and empresses. I picked up on something that happened in my locale today. Apparently there's a high school minx in Brooklyn who slept with her teacher. Let me be the first to say—good job, honey! Now can we all get back to our commercialized holidays and please stop assassinating this woman's character because she knows how to use her vagina?

In honor of Li'l Miss Straight-A and all the other persecuted vixens out there, I hope you enjoy today's special photo series. And don't forget to tune in to my big New Year's Eve reveal, only eight days away.

The post was followed by a half a dozen shots taken in a room similar to our English class with two girls in different barely there outfits reenacting the Mr. E. video. As always, both girls' faces were obscured by their hair, blurred out, or lopped off entirely.

I like sex was written above each picture.

The last photo in the series was of the girls, heads cropped off, cleavage exploding, as they gave the camera the finger.

I like sex, it read. *That doesn't make me a slut.*

Great. The one person supporting me had disrobed her way to stardom. I could tell Audra was impressed and expected me to look equally so. But this wasn't the kind of support I was looking for. Not to mention, the *B&P* slut had over a million followers. How soon would that reflect in views on my video?

I gave Audra a thumbs-up. Cue her wiggling happily in her seat and humming as she flicked through her celebrity pages. Classic Audra—annoying and adorable all at the same time.

I'd only been in school for thirty minutes.

Instead of focusing on my present life of SHT, I decided to think about my future and finish my college admissions essays. But in five hundred words or less, when I swiped over to Scholar: *The* Place to Track and Submit Your College Applications, I saw twelve new unread messages. This was why my Doc had dinged at the start of class. I clicked on the one from Yale.

Thank you for submitting your recent application to Yale University. This e-mail verifies that the admissions committee has received your electronic submission and will be considering it shortly.

What? *No.* I hadn't submitted anything.

I swiped into my pending submissions. Harvard. Brown. Columbia. Every application was marked "completed." Half the essays weren't even finished.

Cue me abruptly standing up. Cue my chair falling backwards. Cue Audra—hand to chest—staring at me like I was insane. Cue the substitute shouting, "Ms. Cheng, sit down now," as if I were a notorious troublemaker. Cue me grabbing the lav pass off the wall, then sequestering myself in the tiny third-floor faculty bathroom so the girls wouldn't find me.

Question: Why haven't hiding rooms been built into high schools?

I mean, when things go wrong, we flee to *bathrooms*. I didn't know where to sit. On the toilet? On the grody, pee-splashed floor tiles? Finally I sank to the floor by the sink. At least the door locked, so no one would see me.

Clenching my head in my hands, I told myself maybe this wasn't so bad. I could finish the essays, then call the schools one by one and beg to resubmit, explaining that Scholar had screwed me over. *Yeah, right.*

As if reflecting my state of mind, my Doc let out a horror movie–style scream. Last night, I'd updated my contacts. So, before looking, I knew that AnyLies had just txted.

😈 Aw, having a bad day? Don't worry. I think community college has rolling admissions.

Wait. What?

moi You cracked my college apps?

😈 ☺ ☺ ☺

As hard as I could in the small space, I threw my Doc at the bathroom wall. It bounced, unmarred, to the floor. That's what crack-proof coating got you.

Too bad they didn't make it for people.

19

Twenty minutes later, my face now composed, I sat in Dr. Graff's outer office, in one of the mansion's two turrets, completely numb. My surroundings felt like a reminder of everything I'd been robbed of. When I imagined myself in Congress, I secretly imagined that space, with its Tiffany lamps, worn brown leather chairs, and floor-to-ceiling old-skool bookshelves.

I'd plotted my future out perfectly. Excellent service record and grades would lead to an excellent college and excellent internships. Except now they wouldn't. A mean-spirited video prank was one thing. But submitting my college apps? That wasn't just making my life miserable. AnyLies had just successfully derailed my entire future. Girls with sex scandals attached to their name need not apply.

"Excuse me one moment," I said to Dr. Graff's secretary; then I hurried into the hall and went to the closest water fountain, afraid I might vomit. Only pretending to drink, I let the lukewarm water run over my lips as I waited for that throw-up feeling to go away.

"Pull it together, Kyle," I murmured. "You will not puke in a water fountain on top of everything else." Please tell me I wasn't going to puke in a water fountain on top of everything else.

The sheer pitifulness of the thought made me straighten up. I purposefully scrolled through my Doc until I found it: President Malin's quote about the South Korean blackout.

Evil might have won today, but we are cleverer, more resourceful, and have the most powerful friends in the world. We are not to be beaten by them. *We are the ones who will conquer Evil.*

Audra said something like that, too, on a near daily basis:

"FCK them small betches."

Calmer, I went back into the office. No sooner had I sat down than the outer door opened. Forgoing a hello, Mom tossed her bag next to me and said, "You didn't respond to any of my txts. How's it going?"

I flipped my hand back and forth, saw that it was shaking, and sat on it instead. "No one dumped a bucket of blood on my head or stabbed me in the belly with a sharpened spear, but it's still early."

Although they *did* submit my admissions applications.

I should have told her right then what AnyLies had done, but I couldn't stand corroborating Mom's suspicions that this was an act of revenge. What I needed to figure out was how they'd cracked my Scholar password. Even though it was too late, I flicked into Shield, scrolled down until I came to the Scholar icon, then tapped *Change Password.* Sharma had insisted I set Shield to change and record all my passwords on a weekly basis, but well, a lot of good that did me. Before closing out, I selected *Apply Change to All,* thereby updating all 112 of my profile logins.

I swiped my Doc off and set it a little ways away on the bench, unable to shake the feeling that AnyLies was actually right there in my Doc, watching me.

Dr. Graff blew in a few minutes later and swiftly ushered us into her office. In her most approachable moments, Dr. Graff could best be described as efficient, no-nonsense, and chilly. But she'd always been friendly to me. After all, in her top-performing high school I was her top performer. Once we were all seated, she swiped right to the chase.

"I'm sorry to see that the video has only gained traction since last night. Luckily, the news outlets haven't picked it up yet. But first things first. Mr. Ehrenreich insists this video is a forgery. I hope you don't mind, Mrs. Cheng"—Dr. Graff took a breath—"but I do need to confirm this with Kyle. As I'm sure you're aware, video-editing technology such as this is not easy to come by, if it exists at all."

My mom turned to me with a furrowed brow. Oops, had I forgotten to mention that part?

My lips pressed into a straight line. If Graff believed that the student who organized a self-esteem seminar for freshman girls would sleep with her twentysomething teacher, then there wasn't much I could say to dissuade her.

"Maybe just answer the question, Kylie," Mom said.

In monotone I said, "Of course the video is a fake."

Dr. Graff was infamous for her unblinking stare, which she now leveled on me. Like eye contact would make me change my story, like I was lying.

"Of course it is," she finally said.

In the tense silence that followed, my mom launched into her talking points about my college applications rapidly approaching their due dates (check that one off the list, Mama), my White House Internship Program application already being submitted, my wrecked G-File, and this video's detrimental effects on all three. I peeked at my Doc. I had a txt from Sharma.

> sharm After school—city. Know hacker at Eden. Agreed to meet you.

I forwarded the txt to the other girls, with the new intro:

> moi Operation Video Takedown in effect?! Sí?

Apparently no.

fawnal Can't today 😣 Picking up our CSA farm share.

audy Have plans.

sharm Capturing Silver Tower (zombie stuff).

Ouch, ladies. Not to play the diva, but this was my life. I couldn't imagine telling one of them that I couldn't be there because I had to pick up vegetables or had vague plans or had to kill M-F-ing zombies.

"We understand your worry," Dr. Graff was saying when I looked up. "And while we take cyberbullying very seriously at Parkside Prep, I must be frank. We are a small staff, tasked with expanding students' minds, not policing their Internet tendencies. If it were our responsibility to ferret out the source of every slanderous e-attack on a student, we would do little else."

"Please tell me there's *something* you can do about this, Dr. Graff," Mom said in her calm-before-the-storm voice.

"Certainly there is, Mrs. Cheng. Just this morning at my DOE breakfast, I raised the topic of creating an exploratory panel focused on online defamation. And of course, we've already taken steps where our staffing is concerned."

I was stunned.

"Does that mean you fired Mr. E.? Dr. Graff, he didn't do anything wrong. He's a victim too. Maybe Park Prep could issue a statement on his behalf and—"

Dr. Graff shook her head. "I don't believe that's wise at the moment, Kyle. Truthfully, it's best to draw as little attention to this as possible. Mrs. Cheng, believe me when I say that no one cares about the reputation of Parkside Preparatory or its students more than I do. But sadly, as most schools are learning through one painful example after another, when it comes to online vileness like this, our hands are frustratingly tied."

Final bell.

I'd made it. School was finito. Maybe the girls had been conspicuously absent from all our between-classes gossip spots. And maybe Mac hadn't used the lav pass in AP Calc to come visit me in lunch. But now it was time for the good stuff, namely Park Prep's Community Club's pre–holiday party gift-wrapping session.

Say that one time fast.

Tomorrow afternoon, Christmas Eve, we were throwing a party for families from a women-and-children's shelter in South Slope. Today was the gift-wrapping bonanza. We'd been fund-raising since September. The kids were going to leave with more presents than they could carry. The moms would go home with new clothes and coats and, most important—thank you, Swiped Tech on Fifth—a solar Doc-lite. Meaning their kids' current situation wouldn't force them to fall behind on the latest tech, and hopefully ensuring they'd still be in the running for a quality future.

Every year, Mr. Hugh, the AP Government teacher, dressed up as Santa Claus. And for the past three years, I'd dressed up as

Mrs. Claus. I'd been looking forward to this since the previous year's party ended.

I breezed into the library, my arms filled with shopping bags I'd wrestled out of my cubby. Last week I'd convinced a card store on Seventh Ave. to donate fifty rolls of wrapping paper and nearly a bushel of ribbons and bows. I couldn't wait to see the kids' faces when they got a load of their fancy swag bags.

"Hey, everyone."

I set down the bags. The library was empty.

Ms. Tompkins, the librarian, came over with a garbled cry of distress.

Thanks to Dad, I had an affinity for librarians in general, but I loved Ms. Tompkins in particular. She sat alone in a tiny room that looked across the hall at where the old library used to be before it was turned into a student café. She also geeked out over the Suicide Games series and gave all-caps GREAT e-book recommendations that my suggested-likes lists had never even heard of. And she always bought cookies for our Community Club meetings.

"Brittany asked me to tell you that they're wrapping presents in Mr. Hugh's classroom."

Brittany was the vice to my presidency. She was a know-it-all junior who I might have admired for her overabundance of well-meaning if she weren't so utterly lacking in imagination. We got along fine as long as we worked on entirely separate projects. Suffice to say, we had not run on the same ticket.

"Okay." I started to collect bags. "Thanks."

"Wait." Ms. Tompkins held me back. "Kyle, she also wanted me to tell you . . . they're impeaching you."

I laughed. "What?"

"They have Dr. Graff's approval. Brittany's going to be interim president."

There were a thousand things I wanted to say, like how this fall when I told the group I wanted to tackle a major community-wide project before I graduated, Vice President Brittany Mulligan's best idea was sticking dog-waste bags onto every garbage can in Park Slope—i.e., Brittany Mulligan thought dog poop was our community's biggest issue. Not to mention she nearly failed algebra freshman year and her voice had more whine in it than Uncorked on Fourth Ave. How was she going to stretch the budget? How was she going to convince local businesses to donate nearly all our supplies? Have I mentioned she thought dog poop was Brooklyn's biggest problem?

The rest of what I wanted to say was curse words.

I managed a shrug.

"Good prep for politics, huh? I'll just do the behind-the-scenes stuff."

Ms. Tompkins was staring at me like I'd just told her I'd never read the Narnia books. Sympathy mixed with remorse mixed with awkward.

"Oh." Even I could hear the awful hurt surprise in my voice. "I'm, like, totally out. But I started the Community Club. I'm not even allowed to go to the party?"

She gave the barest shake of her head, *no*.

"But who will be Mrs. Claus?"

I knew from Ms. Tompkins's expression exactly who was going to be Mrs. Claus. I set the bags back down, redid my ponytail, and tried to tell myself that the important thing was that the party was still happening.

"Kyle, I'm so sorry." Ms. Tompkins squeezed my arm. "For the record, I told them I disagreed with their decision. Especially considering how much time you put into the club. If it makes you feel better, I didn't let them take the cookies."

Her gaze flicked to the door. I turned in time to see Brittany backing out of the room, her eyes wide with horror, trying to make a silent escape.

"Oh, hi, Kyle." Brittany bumped into the door frame, then

rubbed her elbow. "Sorry to interrupt. Just came to see if you'd brought, well, those yet."

She reached toward the shopping bags that were still sitting at my feet. The shopping bags full of lovely free goodies that I'd scored for the kids. I stepped in front of them. Brittany stepped back.

"You know," I said, "the Community Club bylaws state that you can't just decide to impeach a person. You have to have a two-thirds vote, otherwise it isn't legal even if Dr. Graff gives her approval. I should know, seeing as I wrote them. The whole point of Community Club is that we're student-run, Brittany."

"I know what the point of Community Club is, Kyle. You remind me of it every week. And for some of us, excessive dog waste *is* important, okay? Have you tried running in the park lately?"

"Girls," Ms. Tompkins warned.

But Brittany was on a roll.

"And for the record," she continued, "you can contest it if you want, but I have a two-thirds vote. Or I will. Because maybe you get things done, but you're pushy and impatient and there are *nice* ways to say your opinion, you know. I'd rather get nothing done but know that people like me than solve every problem in Brooklyn and have people think I'm a BTCH."

As soon as she finished speaking, her lower lip began to wobble. She inched toward Ms. Tompkins for safety. As if I might physically hurt her. Why use violence when I had words? Ms. Tompkins was too stunned to say anything. I wasn't.

"Congratulations, Brittany. With one speech you set the women's movement back a hundred and fifty years."

I picked up the bags of wrapping paper and held them out to her. After a very hesitant moment, she took them from me.

"Don't be stingy with the bows," I said. "And don't worry; I won't contest the impeachment. I wouldn't want to be a part of any club that would even consider having you as president. I'll start my own community club, again, after the holidays. So get ready to lose enrollment, because don't kid yourself, Brittany. Nice or not, nobody likes you. Later, Ms. T."

I was out in the hall before Brittany figured out her comeback.

"You'd better watch your back, Kyle. That vid isn't even the start of what's coming your way."

I wanted nothing more than to wedge myself into a cubby and hide beneath my coat until everyone else went home. But a cluster of boys started cracking up when they saw me. Chief among them was Derek Boger of the nine-hundred-times-viewed Mr. E.–and–Kyla Cheng remake video. Park Prep's faculty loved to tell us that in ten years most of us would be leaders in our chosen fields. I'd always felt proud of that thought. Now it terrified me. This was the best and brightest?

"I like clothes," Marcus Graham mimicked.

"Excuse me, milk brains," I said as I pushed through them. "Victim of a spurious and fake defamation campaign trying to walk here."

Only once I was a good ten feet away did Derek call out, "Slut."

I stopped. Inhaled deeply. In debate there was nothing worse than an opponent who refused to get riled up. So, with a cheery smile, I turned. It's all about the ruse, right?

"That's it?" I asked pleasantly. "Come on, Derek. You attend one of the most prestigious high schools in the country. Put your parents' tuition dollars to use. If you can't be clever, at least be intelligent."

Farther down the hall, an overly thin, black-clad form came out of a classroom, saw us, and then hurried away in the opposite direction.

Jessie.

"For example," I said as I backed away, toward Jessie, "your video might have a few hundred views, making you popular for an afternoon, but mine has a few hundred thousand, so you errone-ously call me a 'slut,' but I can truthfully call you a 'nobody' or a 'waste of space' or, if we're sticking to single words, 'forgettable.' I could get personal and say 'acne.' Or, if you want to talk sex lives, 'virgin.' Or I could play it infantile and simply say, 'F you, Derek *Boner*. I never should have let you copy my Civics homework all last year.' See? The possibilities are endless."

Derek blinked a few times, stunned. Crickets from his crew, until in unison they burst out laughing—at him. Alex Stu jogged over and high-fived me. Farther down the hall, Jessie turned the corner by the framed photo of Park Prep's first graduating class. It had been taken over seventy-five years ago, when suspenders seemed to be a thing.

"Ta-ta, boys," I said, then called out, "Jessie, wait."

I trilled my fingers, then hurried down the hall. Jessie didn't wait. When I turned the corner, she glanced back, then cut a hard right and sprinted down the spiral staircase nicknamed Ankle Breaker thanks to more than a few incidents involving Doc-focused students. I leaned over the railing.

"Jessie, hold up."

Now she took the stairs two at a time. And normally I would have laughed to see her tottering like that on her vintage Manolos, but I was too annoyed, plus lightly vertigo-stricken.

"Please don't make me chase you."

Holding on to the rail, I ran down Ankle Breaker, cursing under my breath. On one, I bumped into Ellie Cyr.

"Oh," she said, surprised.

We did a side-to-side shuffle, trying to get around each other. I couldn't tell if it equaled purposeful or not. Either way, by the time I'd followed Jessie outside, she'd already hopped into a black sedan. It wasn't an interborough taxi or an Elite. It was her personal car, with her personal driver. I ran up to the window as the car pulled into traffic. She gave me a weird grimace, mouthed what looked like "Smile," and then sped away.

Discreetly as possible—plugging one nostril, inhaling; plugging the other, exhaling—I did Audra's insomniac breathing exercises all the way to the train. Audra swore it soothed her enough to occasionally sleep. And while I didn't feel the least bit calmer, I figured the added oxygen couldn't hurt my psyche, unlike remembering how placid Jessie's face was as she was driven away.

It wasn't until the B train emerged aboveground to cross the Manhattan Bridge that I began to feel like a semiadequately capable person again. Attempting to leave my drama in Brooklyn, I focused on the girl across from me, who was in *the* cutest parka. I Sourced her to see where she got it, then used the Woofer-based Hey, Neighbor! facial-scanning app to see if she was in fashion. But she must have Hey, Neighbor!-ed me first. Her CB profile showed that she was watching my video. Ten clicks later, my Doc dinged as I was tagged in a pic—sitting as I was still sitting—above the caption: *That sex vid girl sitting across from me on the B train.*

Instantly I uploaded a pic of her to CB with the caption: *Thanks for making your burrito my problem #fartsinsmallspaces.*

Woofer took care of the rest. Her Doc whistled. She glanced at it, then quickly looked at me, huffed, and moved down the train. I was too busy Hey, Neighbor!-ing other people to care. It wasn't just her. The next person and the next and the next—in fact, the entire car of nearly sixty people—were watching my video. Chains like this were common. But I'd never been the subject of one.

I got off at West 4th and decided not to transfer to the A train, even though it was two stops too soon and meant a fifty-minute walk. Outside on Sixth Avenue, it felt even warmer than it had in Brooklyn and to prove it, the sidewalks were coated with an inch of gray slush. Still I put up my coat hood. If that was what public transportation was going to be like, I guessed I'd better get used to hoofing it.

22

Almost an hour later, I stepped inside the enormous open-air atrium of Eden's entrance. It was like entering a hybrid of a space-agey future utopia and the coolest parts of Brooklyn. There was a hotel, gourmet food shops, restaurants, cocktail bars, and an entire floor that was a play zone for kids. The level I was meeting the hacker on was an open-air market, with food trucks, sidewalks, and trees that wove throughout. As hologram snowflakes fell, requisite holiday music was piped into the air. Around every bend were Expert desks and displays of Docs to buy.

As a backdrop, the largest screen in the world—no, literally; it was in *Guinness*—showed the most popular G-File users who were doing their last-minute Eden holiday shopping right at that moment. Presently, it was the two-time YurTube Planet Award–winning actress Lucy Helen Banks. The screen showed the most-viewed clip from her latest film.

How cool was NYC?

For the umpteenth time I wished the girls were there. Cool or not, I was dead nervous. I'd never met a hacker before. I mean, other than Sharma. And Sharma showered with her Doc because she was afraid she'd miss something.

We were supposed to meet at 4:30. It was currently 4:16. Sharma txted, *Don't laugh,* but that she'd met this hacker through an apartment-decorating game. I wandered around the market. At 4:18 I bought a lemon bar for Kyle. A minute later I ate half of it. I still had ten minutes to kill. So I did something stupid: I txted AnyLies.

> moi They won't let me be Mrs. Claus.

I know this doesn't read like the smartest move, but if you had a direct line to your hater how would you not txt them?

No response.

I didn't stop, or more like I couldn't stop.

> moi Or even go to the party.
> I look forward to it all year.
> Brittany Mulligan is the new Mrs. Claus. She has the charisma of plastic packaging.

I didn't explain that I was talking about Community Club, figuring my hater went to Park Prep and would simply know. If not, then, well, that was one big clue, no? Also, I *really* hoped my hater was Brittany Mulligan and that she'd read that last line. But still no response. Maybe AnyLies was busy, but I didn't think so. I gave it one last try.

> moi Why do you hate me so much?

Now the reply was instantaneous.

 So many reasons.

moi Like?

😈 You are everything that is wrong with everything.

moi So we know each other?

😈 You can say I despise you from afar.

No, *that* wasn't creepy. I thought about all the people I interacted with but didn't really know, at debates, Model UN, volunteering, my clothing swap.

moi Contrary to whatever it apparently seems like, I'm not a bad person.

😈 Keep telling yourself that.

Annoyed, I swiped the thread away. It was 4:30. I positioned myself in a very visible spot at the entrance to the market. I assumed the hacker had viewed the video and my profile. Spotting me wouldn't be hard. A minute passed. Another.

At 4:40 I walked toward an expensive izakaya and stood next to a bench outside. Pretending everything was normal between us, I snapped a pic of the menu and sent it to Fawn. She was hard-core about boycotting overfished fish.

moi Sashimi of the day is yellowfin tuna.

She'd combust.

"That's lab tuna," a soft female voice behind me said. "Not natural-caught. Twice the taste. Triple the price. None of the murdering-endangered-species guilt. You even think about turning around, I virus your Doc."

23

"You're the hacker guy?" I asked.

"Gender bias much?"

I risked a glimpse. Dyed-pink hair and what looked like an Eden tie and name clip, which she detached and shoved in her pocket. So she was an employee. Hiding in plain sight. Nice.

"I said *don't* turn around."

"I'm not allowed to see you, but you can hack my Doc?"

"Didn't hack your Doc. You use holoscreen to txt. Anyone within five feet can see your message. Not smart. Name's Ivy. Watched your vid. It just tipped six hundred thou views. Speak."

"Uh, okay, for starters, can you tell me anything about the person who made it?"

"Who made it?" I could hear her smirk. "That's how you're swinging this? All right, already asking the wrong question. This is out there. Done. Question is: How to recover? Next question. Go."

I needed to sit down. But in order to sit on the izakaya's bench, I'd have to turn around. And since I didn't want to disobey Ivy's rule a second time, I put a steadying hand against the wall and knelt on the bench instead, like I was worshipping the menu.

"I said, next question. Go."

"Geez, okay. Gimme a sec to think." Mac teased me that I spoke and processed things so fast he was always three thoughts behind me. (Or he used to tease me about that.) Now I knew how he felt. "Pretend I'm not asking the wrong question and where the video came from does matter. I mean, it's a DRM. I go to a small school. There might be a chance I can delete the source file—"

Ivy cut me off. "Gold Goes with Everything told me the orig IP was fragmented. Said defragging's in progress, but that takes a few days, min. Is there a time stamp on the vid? Could use your GPS history to prove you"—I could sense her forming air quotes—"'weren't there.'"

"No. There's not a time stamp."

"Hmm. Too bad. Gold Goes with Everything also said the YurTube account was fresh?"

"Wait. Who the H-double-L is Gold Goes with Everything?"

"Our shared contact."

"Sharma?" She'd been working on cracking this without telling me? "That's her screen name? Gold Goes with Everything?"

The girl tsked. "Your privacy-protection etiquette needs serious CPR. You never tell a hacker another hacker's name. It's, like, the first rule of hacking. And I see you looking at me in the mirror on your Doc. Keep it up and I will ruin you."

"Worse?" I snorted. "How? Fine. Sorry. Yes. The YurTube account was freshly made. They used an alias. AnyLiesUnmade."

"Creepy." I imagined Ivy's frown deepening. "There is one possibility. Heard whispers about software from Asia—Korea or Japan, maybe—that lets you do face forgery. None of my contacts has it in hand. Or if they do, they're not saying. Thought it was a myth. Said to be gove'ment grade so it means this AnyLies has mega coin *and* mega connects."

Holding my Doc up, I holoscreened my messages.

"Any way to attach this contact to a person? AnyLies and I have been txting."

"That sounds unsafe." Ivy tsked, but then, too intrigued not to look, she added, "It's not a contact. If they were txting via a Doc, and they blocked it, that field would read 'Contact Unavailable.' You're dealing with an old-skool cell phone. If it were a smartphone—thanks to GPS—it would still show a phone number. I bet those messages are coming from an old-old-old-skool burner cell. They're so low-tech, Docs don't even recognize their existence. That's completely untraceable. Mama's smart."

Oh, terrific.

"Mama?" I said. "So you think it's a girl?"

"I think the vid is perfect. It's not a prank or gag. The hacker wants to x you out. You have any spurned boyfriends?" I shook my head *no*.

Boyfriend. Unboyfriend. Friend. Unfriend. Whatever his title, Mac would never do this.

"Then it's def a chick. Pay attention to enemies that have come into considerable sums of money. And stay tuned for a second attack. She needs to keep views up or bye-bye revenue stream. You could try following the dollar signs, but if she finds you poking around her bank accounts? With her hands on tech like this? She'll end you. Way I see it, you have two choices. Capitalize on your new popularity and embrace your notoriety—"

"Or?" I asked.

"Erase yourself. There is no way to prove this isn't you."

24

With a curt "Have a nice life," Ivy left. And although I was supposed to count until twenty before I turned, I spun around after "one" and watched as Ivy reattached her Eden tie and name tag, then slumped onto a stool behind a help desk at the front of the market. As I walked past her, a grandmother with her three wailing grandkids approached and asked to "borrow a phone" for help "calling a cab."

Karma, baby.

No sooner had I left the market floor than my Doc lit up with messages from Audra. Not *How was the meeting?* or *What did you learn?* No, the latest read:

audy   Dinner at six, betch.

Dinner was always at six. The timing of the Rhodes meal was as predictable as the intense dreadfulness of it. Normally, among us girls, dinner at Audra's was the standard against which all other instances of torture were measured. Example:

Me: "I can't believe Linkman is making us watch *Transcending*

Transgender again. That's four years running. Doesn't he get it? There's a reason the film's dated. Nobody cares anymore."

Fawn: "Unconscionable. I'd almost rather have dinner at Audra's."

Audra: "Yuk it up, ladies; it's only my abysmal home life you're laughing at."

I'd been planning to go home, take a long bath, and then have a hot fudge sundae on the couch with Kyle. Then I was going to shirk my homework and reread the new installment in the Suicide Games series. Just proving how desperate I was for my friends' companionship, dinner with the Rhodeses actually sounded *nice*.

> moi Still in the city. Might not make that in time. ☹ Can you believe I just ☹'d that?

> audy HA! Like I'd let you off that easy. I already hailed you an Elite. It'll be waiting for you out front by the time you get there.

When Audra pinged an Elite to drive us to Sharma's the day the video dropped, I figured she was splurging because it was dire circumstances. Nobody except the uber-wealthy took them. Not only were they self-driven vehicles—assuring utter privacy and no unnecessary messy human interactions—but their minimum fare was fifty dollars. An Elite to Brooklyn? That was at least a hundred-dollar ride. Apparently girlfriend was as desperate for company as I was.

Suddenly, I felt kinda good. Fine, I wasn't making monumental (or any) progress, but I was in the coolest store in the world, it was slathered in Christmas green and red, hologram snowflakes twinkled in the air like stars, and my best friend wanted to be around me so badly that she'd pinged an *Elite* for me.

Before the video I'd always known I had a good life. Maybe I still did.

As if echoing my joyous thoughts, the atrium filled with laughter. On the hour, Eden did a Christmas show. Tourists from all over the world trekked to NYC to watch it. When I looked up from my Doc, I expected to see hologram Santa and his crazy-realistic hologram reindeer rocketing around the atrium dome. But people weren't looking up at the dome. They were looking at me. Not in the pretty-girl-in-a-short-skirt kind of way, either. In like a naked-guy-in-the-subway kind of way.

A father, there with his small children, shouted, "Turn it off, already."

More people stopped, scanned the room with their Docs, landed on me, and simply stared.

A boy in a glammy fake-fur coat and sparkly blue eyeliner tapped my shoulder and nodded behind me. At any given moment there were thousands of people shopping at Eden. I should have expected it. It was simply a matter of mathematics and technology. Apparently, Lucy Helen Banks had left the building, because now I had the most popular G-File in the place, and the certified largest wall screen in the entire world was showing my most popular clip. It couldn't have been on for more than twenty seconds before whatever safeguards they had against exactly this happening caught it and the feed cut out. But it was long enough.

"Do you have a safe way to get home?" the boy asked.

"My friend called me an Elite."

"Fancy. Well, lock the door when you're in, honey, because I do not like the pervy eyes that man has been aiming at you. He's been watching you since even before they played your debut. Trust me, I notice these things."

The man in question wasn't much older than me. College or shortly out of it. When our eyes met, he opened his mouth like he was about to speak. Maybe it was the unblinking way he was watching me, or that he kept fidgeting with his belt, but I'd Bet a semester of early registration that whatever he wanted to say wasn't G-rated.

"You get out of here now, sister, and for heaven's sake don't share that ride. This world is filled with not-very-nice people." Then, disproving his words entirely, the boy in the fake fur walked up to the creeper and created some interference. "Excuse me, sir, I think you dropped something. No, look, this gum wrapper. I believe it's yours."

I hurried off into the crowd. And maybe this will sound naïve, considering the video had been playing on a football field–sized screen, but right then, I finally got how huge it was. Never mind my college apps or my ruined reputation at school. With this many views, the video would never be pushed down in my profile. My children would see this. *Their* children would see it (even considering my whole not-till-I'm-thirty-eight agenda). If I didn't take down the video, it would forever be the first thing anyone knew about me. If I didn't take down the video, I wouldn't be able to escape it for the rest of my life.

I was finding it hard to breathe. A guy wearing tight pants and white sunglasses nudged me and said, "Yo, girl, you famous. Can I get your autograph?"

"Can I get your digits?" His friend laughed.

I pushed past them. To calm myself down, I thought about what President Malin would do. She'd say, "I will not mince words. This is a nearly insurmountable problem. But we will roll up our sleeves and try to fix it, because we have everything to lose." Just like she did in her October web address about the challenges of reversing our escalating environmental collapse.

Me?

I ran.

25

The Elite Audra had pinged me honked when I went outside. I was wondering if having a fully automated car identify me officially made me the most recognizable girl in the world, when the back window rolled down and a petite platinum blondie waved at me.

"What are you doing here?" I asked, running up to the car.

"I told you." Audra grinned. "I sent you an Elite. I just didn't mention I was in it." She let out her best evil-villain laugh. "Come on, silly; get in."

Brooklyn to the city *and back*? This would be at least a two-hundred-dollar ride. I tried not to think about what a waste of coin that was. After all, I was *in* an *Elite* for only the second time in my life and the last time I'd equaled too upset to notice how prime the experience was. Adjustable tint on the windows, audio controls for temp, music, and speed. A bus passed us and splashed our front windshield. The Elite's wipers immediately flicked on. It even still had that new-car smell. Unthinkable in a normal cab.

As Audra slid next to me on the unmarred leather seat and tucked her arm beneath mine, I txted my mom.

moi On duty for dinner at Audra's.

mama Heard!

"What coordinates did you give it?" I asked as we turned out into traffic. "Brooklyn's that way."

"Kyle, are you seriously trying to backseat-drive a computer? Or are you just that anxious to see the Parents? Chill, please. I'm taking you somewhere special first. Someplace I've never taken anyone else."

"How come I'm so lucky?"

"Must be that charmed existence."

After our light banter, we fell into the inexplicable silence that had been creeping between us for months now whenever the other girls weren't present. Still our arms stayed entwined. Based on our recent history, maybe it was better that we didn't talk.

After a few minutes of quiet, unable to take it anymore, Audra streamed our favorite nightcore song and cranked it through the Elite's speakers. One verse in, we were singing along, trying to keep up with the lyrics. When the Elite cut through the music to tell us we'd reached our destination, we were both breathless with laughter and nightcore and using each other's fists as microphones. We were also parked outside the Met.

"You're taking me to look at art?"

She tweaked my nose. "Better."

We hurried up the steps to the museum. Dinner started in fifty minutes. Even if we encountered only green lights and all the other cars on Fifth Avenue miraculously disappeared by the time we came back outside, we were going to be late. The Parents hated lateness.

Once inside the Met, we walked straight to the members' line. Audra's Doc blinked green. *Welcome, Ms. Rhodes* flashed on the turnstile screen. She selected a *with guest* option. And then we were through.

"Are the Parents members?"

"The Parents wouldn't know good art if it OD'd in front of them. I'm a member because the Met is home to my favorite place in the entire wide world."

Audra glanced at her Doc and quickened her pace. I thought for sure we were headed to the sold-out special exhibit by the famous artist who tattooed on lemons, but instead of going up to the second floor, we stayed on the first and made our way through the European Sculpture and Decorative Arts wing. I kept expecting Audra to stop in front of a particular painting or sculpture, but instead she wound through the museum until we were in a deserted section that held ancient African urns and an easy-to-miss door in the farthest corner of the room.

Although there was an exit sign above the door, it for sure seemed like one of those doors that emitted high-pitched alarms if opened.

"Almost there."

I could hear the giddy in her voice.

"Audra..." I warned as she pushed through the door and stepped into the space beyond.

I glanced around, expecting a guard to come and yell at us, then realized that the only other person who would think that happened anymore was my mom. Most museums now implemented static barriers around the artwork. Since this room stayed emptily ancient, I figured we were entering allowed space. Besides, if whatever was on the other side of this door led to my girl's favorite place in the world, minor electrocution would be worth it.

Or so I thought.

As Audra turned to me with wide, happy eyes, I couldn't help asking, "Did we take a wrong turn?"

For on the other side of the door was a plain, gray, institutional stairwell. And we weren't climbing it to get someplace cool. Audra planted herself on the steps, halfway up.

"We are exactly where we're supposed to be."

We were risking the Parents' ire for this? I didn't get it. I checked my Doc, but there was no signal.

"That won't work in here," Audra said, then patted the space next to her. "The first time I came in here was because my Doc told me it was the quickest way to the bathrooms. It only goes up and down. It hits all the most boring exhibits. I've never encountered another soul in here, no matter how long I've sat. I thought you could use a little shh."

Leaning back on her elbows, she closed her eyes.

"Isn't it wonderful?"

"You have a membership to the Met so you can skip the line to sit in an empty stairwell?"

"Mm-hmm," she said without opening her eyes. "Try it."

I dropped my bag and sat next to her.

"Audy, I didn't sleep with Mr. E."

"Shh," she said. "Listen. Isn't it amazing? Nothing. No sound, no ambient noise, no buzzing or dinging. And look around. No cameras or holoscreens. No motion sensors or triggered ads. No one can see us right now, Kyle. No one can hear us. Or find us. These walls are so thick even the best PHD can't access Wi-Fi. This stairwell might be the last place of untraceable freedom in all of New York."

"Audy, is everything okay with you?"

I thought about her excessive mood swings. How her Doc was always on private. How she hadn't slept over at my house in weeks. She leaned her head on my shoulder.

"Don't take this the wrong way, Kyle, but you wouldn't understand. Just know whatever happens, everything I've done—"

"What have you done?"

"Everything I've done," she pushed on, "has been because I'm trying to make life better for us. Now close your eyes and just feel it."

Thoroughly freaked-out, I shut my eyes. And, weird as it was, Audra was right. Even two days ago, when I was invisible, I wasn't. I'd been seen daily in a hundred different ways even when I was alone. I'd just never minded because all the images of me were good and praiseworthy.

Except I wasn't invisible in here, either. When I opened my eyes Audra was studying me.

"Nice, isn't it?"

I nodded, and she clapped her hands, pleased.

"I can get you your own membership. Skipping the line equals the best."

"I'll be okay," I said.

She patted my knee. "I know you will, sweetie. Now, let's hurry the FCK up. The Parents will kill us if we're any later."

26

Bridge traffic, an hour later, and thirty minutes late, Audra and I were sitting at her teak dining room table. Everyone had their Doc out. The Father and I were both browsing the news on ours. The Mother had hers on holoscreen and was flicking through a patient's case history. Audra had her larger Home Doc up on a stand, so none of us could see what she was looking at. Our late arrival made the oppressive silence of the meal even more punishing than usual. It was the eve of Christmas Eve, but in the Rhodes brownstone, not a single holiday bauble was in sight.

I wasn't surprised. The Parents' religion wasn't faith-based. It was purely clinical. Audra's parents were both psychiatrists. Even the most banal comment was so ruthlessly dissected that I hesitated to thank them for dinner lest they diagnose me with a flattery complex. They were parents in name only—the Mother, the Father—who must have had their daughter completely by accident, because not an ounce of affection or interest went into raising her. Yet, strangely, they insisted on these nightly dinners. Most likely so they could hold them up to their patients as parenting done right.

If I'd grown up in Audra's house, I'd hide in empty stairwells, too.

On the wall behind Audra, life-sized American soldiers shot at some desert culture's rebels. These wallpaper screens had come out a year ago. I'd always thought it was strange that the Rhodeses had installed theirs in here instead of in the family room.

"Why would they put it in the family room?" Audra said. "It's the least-used room of the house."

I looked down at my plate as the position of the screen made it look like the soldier was taking aim at Audra's head. I'd had more than enough screens for one day.

As if she weren't breaking into utter silence, the Mother asked, "And school, girls?"

The Mother was a carbon copy of Audra—tiny, with delicate features, slim wrists, and impeccably coiffed hair. For the most part she was a cold, aloof woman, but on the occasions she had a bad day or drank too heavily, she could put Audra's nasty streak to shame. At one of the worst dinners I'd attended, she'd derided Audra to the point that my friend was whimpering. Audra had stayed at my house for a whole week after that evening.

Still studying her holoscreen, the Mother nibbled on a small green bean, chewed it thoroughly, and washed it down with an equally tiny sip of pinot blanc. If people in Audra's family took normal-sized bites, dinners could be finished forty minutes earlier.

"Unstimulating as usual," Audra said. "Oh, and yesterday someone posted a sex vid of Kyle—"

"A *fake* sex vid of Kyle," I corrected.

"And she thinks her life is . . ." Audra paused, sent a txt, then said, "All-caps OVER. But on the bright side, *everyone* now wants into her pants and thinks she has amazing tatas."

I wrapped my cardigan tighter around me.

"Audra, I appreciate your effort to shock us with the content and quality of your language. Don't you, honey?" The Mother directed her words to the Father. "It shows quite the need for attention and acceptance, wouldn't you say?"

"Yes, dear." The Father reached across the table without looking and patted empty air as if searching for his wife's hand, but then he picked up the home-hub controller instead. "And I am oddly put at ease that our daughter still tries to shock us."

As the *New York Times* banner filled the wallpaper screen behind her, Audra scoffed like it was an art form.

"I'm not trying to shock you. I was trying to converse with you."

I never understood why Audra spoke to her parents, why her method of adapting in this household hadn't evolved into simple one-word answers. I guess I had to admire her pluck.

"Oh, darling." The Mother directed her voice at her husband again. "I had a breakthrough with the coked-out model today. Did I mention it?"

After what felt like a full minute's pause, the Father replied, "You did."

My Doc buzzed.

audy I hate them. I hate them. I hate them.

moi I know.

This family did the impossible and left me at a loss for words. Audra's tiny nostrils flared as she snorted. I hurriedly added,

moi I don't have the best relationship with my mom either, y'know. My life is officially far from perfect nowadays. At least when you and your mom fight, she sends you shopping to make up for it.

Audra glared at me. "You think I care about shopping? Your life *is* perfect—*still*. You're just too naïve to see it."

"Then enlighten me."

"For starters, *your* mother is an amazing woman."

"Insult noted, Audra," the Mother intoned.

"You two are going through a tough time," Audra continued. "That is all. Meanwhile, a video drops of you and you're instantly famous. People would kill for this much attention, and do a lot more to get it. Yet you can't even see all the possibilities it presents."

"Possibilities?"

"Yes, Kyle. You would be the perfect person to prove that being an intelligent female *and* a normal sexual being aren't exclusive concepts. You can cast it as 'For so long I struggled trying to fit into society's good-girl stereotype. And then, bam! My secret was out. And look, I'm still the same intelligent, ambitious woman who rocks nice clothes.' This could be hugely feminist. Yale would be tripping over itself to enroll you. I think you should be thanking whoever posted that video."

Ever since I met her, Audra had been trying to get me to come out of my proverbial prude shell. But why couldn't she see that as much as some of us—her, Fawn, that *B&P* chick—were huge, flaunting sexual beings, some of us weren't. Why wasn't that okay too?

"And don't even get me started on Mac."

"No, go ahead," I said. "You're clearly on a roll."

Audra was practically standing now. "The primest papa at Prep trips over himself to see you smile, yet you hold him at arm's length, Buddha only knows why—the best I can figure is because he's acquired previous skills. Girls would kill to date Mac. Poor frickin' you. Kylie, I would give anything—anything—to have your life even for one day."

In a normal household, the parents would have interceded by now. I could swear the Father was taking notes. Meanwhile, the Mother took a tiny sip of wine, then raised the volume on her EarRing.

"For the last time, Audra Rhodes," I said slowly and clearly, "I did not sleep with Mr. E."

"Stop lying to me!"

Audra slammed down her silverware. She stared at her plate, her lower lip quivering. Then, composing her features, she said, "Looks like the grocery avatar forgot again that I'm pescatarian."

The Mother sighed. "You have been looking wan. I thought you needed iron. Thank you, Mother. You're welcome, Audra."

The Mother didn't cook, but she definitely knew how to add to cart from the local foo-foo prepared-foods market. Audra could easily change the settings. It was a matter of a few swipes. But this had been her complaint five weeks running, almost as if she liked that her mother kept proving her neglect.

"I can't eat this."

The Mother scrolled through files. The Father flicked through news stories. Audra looked between them, then violently shoved back from the table. Like she was on the catwalk, she whisked her plate into the kitchen. The drama of the garbage can lid slamming against the wall rang through the house.

"I hope you put that in the compost bin," the Mother called as I stared at Audra's deserted Doc. "Teenage tantrums shouldn't add unnecessary waste to landfills. Gregory, make sure your daughter put that in the compost."

"Hmm?" the Father asked.

Before I knew what I was doing, I reached across the table and swiveled Audra's screen toward me.

"My Doc's not getting a signal," I explained.

Neither Parent so much as blinked. Maybe it was that Audra thought I should be "grateful" for the video or that she would give anything to have my life, but as I swiped at her screen, I told myself that it wasn't that I suspected Audra had made the video; it was that I didn't want to suspect her. Those were two different things, right? But when I swiped at her Doc, the password prompt

115

came up. She had it on fifteen-second mode? I drew Audra's password. It was the shape of a broken heart.

Incorrect password.

No it wasn't. I'd watched Audra make this password just two days ago.

"Whatcha doing?"

Audra stood in the kitchen doorway holding a premade macrobiotic veggie wrap.

"I was gonna watch this link Fawn sent on a bigger screen. You changed your password."

"Yup." Audra primly sat back down.

"Aren't you going to tell me what it is?" I asked as I leaned back.

"Maybe if you're a real good girl..." Audra swiped into her Doc. Her mother laughed, though it was unclear if it was because of Audra or something from her EarRing. "Go ahead, what's the link?"

"I'll txt it over."

Sometimes Audra and I hung after dinner, but not that night. I couldn't stand being in that house one more click. I was outside moments after I put my fork down. Our good-bye was said via audio txt.

She never did tell me her password.

27

The year I was born, Mom's company was still in the red. Dad had a solid job at the NYU libraries, but only a tiny paycheck to go with it. Every month, more money went out than came in. At the time, we were all crammed into the tiny garden apartment of our house on Carroll. Mom had moved there right after graduating from Brown. A few times a month, she and her landlady, Marie, met in the yard to drink wine and talk men and books. When Marie moved to Florida the year Kyle was born, she sold the house to my parents at half its value.

"You have been a gift to me for two decades. This is my gift to you."

Even renting out the upper floors, my parents barely made the mortgage those first few years. There was no way they could afford day care as well. So every day until I was six, Mom took me and Kyle on the G train to meet my Grandma Cheng at the Court Square stop. Then we three would take the 7 train back to Queens, where we'd spend the entire day in the closet-sized Chinese-medicine store that my nǎinai owned.

"This will all be worth it when we get to vacation in San Sebastián every summer," I remember Mom saying when she zipped me into my coat in the mornings. "Or get a day off, period."

Sometimes the girls and I talked about how lucky we were. Because when you're beautiful, your parents earn good incomes, and you live in the best city on the planet, that fact doesn't escape you. But I didn't want my good fortune to rest solely on luck. Volunteering at homeless shelters, I saw what bad luck did. And I knew it sounded trite coming from a girl who presently owned a two-thousand-dollar Doc, but I could remember teetering on the cusp of Not Okay like it was yesterday. My family had made it, but we easily could have failed.

Audra was incessantly on me about this perfect-life nonsense. Didn't she see? We all had stuff.

On my walk home, Mrs. Gallagher audio txted. I babysat for the Gallagher boys at least once a week. Her message was brusque. There'd been a change of plans, and she wouldn't need me on Monday. I hoped Milton and Ernie were both okay.

I swiped into one of my prematurely sent college essays to see how terrible it was. Describe Yourself in Five Hundred Words or Less was the topic. I had a few different responses saved in Write on my Doc, but on the actual application screen I'd written: *At 8 a.m.? Sleep deprived.*

Oh. Great.

I txted Mom.

moi Just left Shrink Castle.

Any night I ate at Audra's, this was our ritual. Knowing the Rhodes environment was too intense to eat in, Mom always had a plate waiting for me at home after I left Audra's. She'd sit with me while I devoured it. It was our one or two moments of truce during the week. Naturally it involved laughing about how awful my friend and her family were, but when it came to bonding with Mom, I'd take what I could get. She immediately txted a reply.

> mama Ohh, sorry, honey. Didn't have time to cook or
> order yet.
>> Fend for yourself tonight?
>> Kyle's at a friend's. Daddy's working late.
>> I'm on deadline for Paris store.

When I didn't reply, she added,

> mama Can't wait to hear about the rest of your day. Still
> steamed over our meeting with Graff.

Dad never worked late. Clearly he was avoiding me. And fend for myself? More? I'd never felt more unloved and alone in my life. Awash with self-pity, I stopped on the crowded corner of Fifth Avenue and Third Street. Blocking hordes of last-minute Christmas shoppers carrying their expensive hand-stamped brown-paper shopping bags, I finally let myself cry.

It wasn't that there were now over seven hundred thousand views of the video. Or that taking it down was impossible. It was that ever since the video had come out, I'd felt filthy in my own skin. It was an awful mix of shame, embarrassment, and guilt, and it wouldn't go away. Worse still, I didn't have anyone to talk to about it.

My Doc buzzed. Kyle! My sweet little bro's sibling sixth sense must have picked up on my misery.

> boi-k Hey, sis, not to make you go more girl over this but
> it's getting worse.

> mama That's not an appropriate descriptor, Kyle.

I hadn't realized we were on group txt.

boi-k Sorry, but the Times Online wrote about the video.
       It's one swipe into the local section. Titled: Sex Scandal
       Rocks Prestigious Parkside Prep. The video's views just
       exploded (more).

Neither my mom nor I replied. Kyle kept going.

boi-k Also, Mom FYI. The video's attaching itself to us.
       On ☺ side: I have 10k new friends. On ☹ side: video
       comes up when you G-Search StitchBtch. It's the
       second link after your website.

My mom had been talking with her lawyers about going public.
A new string of stores were set to open in France. She'd given this
company her all since her twenties. And now I'd ruined everything
because someone at school had it out for me. It was like I'd proved
her right.

There was a long pause where no one wrote anything. Then:

mama This is what lawyers are for.

Then her avatar went red. *Do not disturb.*

When I got home, I didn't bother going inside. The mini blizzard of two nights ago had shifted right into a warm front. The
temp had steadily risen all day. At eight o'clock it was sixty degrees
out. Sorry, Fawn, I guess no white Christmas after all. Fine by me.
I needed fresh air and exercise stat. As I sloshed down the steps
from the sidewalk to haul my bike out from under the stoop, a
shadow separated from the tree next door.

"Excuse me, miss?" It was a soft voice that belonged inside a
white van with tinted windows. "Do you live here?"

His Doc gave off a silver glimmer. I couldn't tell if he was pointing it at me or simply holding it. I quick tried to think of how I'd describe the man to police. Tallish. Dark clothes. Light skin. Twenties? Thirties? Tell him you're only the babysitter! Tell him it's your friend's house! my brain shouted. Don't tell him you live here!

"Yeah, this is my house," I said.

Why do we feel obligated to tell perfect strangers the truth? If I ever have kids, I'm encouraging them to be good liars.

"Cute." He paused, like I was supposed to fill in the uncomfortable silence. "I was hoping you could tell me what your Doc digits are. Just kidding. Which way is Seventh Avenue from here?"

"Straight up the hill. Can't miss it. Especially if you use your Doc."

He seemed surprised to find it in his hand.

"I'm suffering through the Series Twenty-Three." He laughed softly. "The map app gives you 3-D directions. It's the most confusing thing. I think it gives me motion sickness."

I'd read that the Series 23 did that to people, but this guy didn't look sick. He took a step forward, as if to show me the maps feature. I took a step back. He stopped.

"Sure, I get it. Don't talk to strangers, right?" Now a longer, weirder pause. "Anyway, happy holidays. Hope you've been a good girl and Santa brings you everything you asked for."

Two houses away, he looked back, stared at me, then waved. Part of me wanted to run inside. Part of me didn't want to be anywhere near my house right now. That part won.

There was only one place I could conceive of going. And even if he wasn't home, or wouldn't let me in, or I had to knock down Rupey to see him, being in the vicinity of Mac would be better than being anywhere else. I made it to his house in twenty minutes flat. A new record.

I always teased Mac that he couldn't do anything unless he had enough guys with him for a pickup soccer game. So I wasn't surprised that he was outside on his stoop with a handful of his cousins when I rode up. Cans of beer and bags of chips took up the empty spaces on the steps between them.

I skidded to a stop in front of his house and dropped my bike.

"Kyla?" Mac made to stand up, but Rupey put a hand on his arm and he stayed seated. "What do you want?"

I pulled a wadded-up tissue from my pocket and threw it at Rupey.

"I came to tell your primo it's rude to spit in public. That's what tissues are for."

And then because I couldn't take one more mean comment from me or anyone else, I put my face in my hands and sobbed. Again.

I'd cried more in the last hour than I had in a decade. With a quick, annoyed glance at Rupey, Mac untangled himself from the stoop.

"What happened?" He walked me a few paces away from his cousins. Pulling my hands from my face, he brushed my bangs back from my forehead. This was the reaction I'd been expecting yesterday, when the video dropped. We hadn't spoken in nearly a day and a half. I'd been afraid I'd never see this side of him again. "You're shaking."

"I pedaled standing up the whole way here."

"How come? Qué pasa, chiquita? Tell me."

"There was a guy. Outside my house. I don't know if he was one of the guys who have been messaging my CB with pics of their wieners or if he was AnyLies or if he was a total nobody and just lost, but he had a Doc so how could he be lost? And I didn't know him, but he knew me. And, Macky, it was *muy* scary and I don't know what to do. About any of this."

Mac pulled me into a hug. He smelled like beer, clean T-shirts, and cheesy tortilla chips. Just like that, all the bullshite of the previous thirty-six hours fell away.

"Okay," he said stroking my hair. "I got you. It'll be okay."

"I don't see how."

"Come sit down. What have I told you about not wearing your helmet? Muévense, pinches primos. We have a girl in distress here."

Normally he would have said *"my* girl's in distress here." Still, the primos begrudgingly cleared a space for me.

Without exception, Mac scorned the boys at school. He called them kickback, cutback lobbyists in training. It was his primos who were his true clan. So it was kind of a big deal that none of them liked me. Granted, I'd only officially hung out with them once, for like, a half hour. Mac had brought me to his house and introduced me the second week of our not dating. His cousin Victor had appraised me in Spanish. My EarRing's Translate had whispered that it meant something like "This must be the little [unrecognized word] who thinks she's too good for you. She's got small breasts, no?" (For the sake of accuracy, I'm pretty sure Victor had not said "breasts.")

Both Mac and I knew it hadn't gone well. I was supposed to stay through dinner, but instead we grabbed banh mis and rode our bikes to the park to eat them. And, I mean, Mac called in sick anytime there was a new batch of tamales in the house. It was no small thing for him to opt out of his mom's cooking.

I hadn't been around his cousins other than in passing since then.

Mac quickly reintroduced everyone. And for the first time since AnyLies set their sights on me, with these people who I knew despised me, I felt safe. Which is maybe why my tongue unspooled and then, like we'd all been BFFs for years, I told them everything.

All of it. AnyLies's txts. Our meeting with Graff that morning. Brittany and Community Club that afternoon. The girl on the train. The Eden hacker. The video on the big screen. The creep who kept clutching his belt. My guardian angel in the fake fur who'd played interference. How the video had attached itself to StitchBtch, and last but not least how there was a guy outside my house and he sure seemed like he was waiting for me.

Strung together in one long run-on sentence, it sounded crazy paranoid. As the primos traded raised eyebrows (brow dexterity clearly ran in the family), it wasn't hard to tell what they were thinking.

Mac's girl is small-chested and *psychotic.*

I almost apologized, but stopped myself, hearing Audra say, "Why are girls always apologizing for *talking*? Is there some kind of word limit we have to abide by that boys don't?" Instead I stayed quiet and waited for their verdict.

"I'm calling the police," Mac said.

"And telling them what?" Victor asked. "A dude asked for directions outside her house thirty minutes ago?"

"Right," I said. "It had to be a weird coincidence. He couldn't know I live there, right?"

"Your parents own your property?" Alfie asked. When I nodded, he poked me in the arm. "Ding—there you go. You said your vid is linked to your mom now. Search your moms. Bam. Find the real-estate listing from when they bought your house. Boom. Address."

"Nah." Caleb waved a hand at all of this. "It's even easier than that. Anyone in her contacts can just WhereYouAt her. You guys ain't heard? You don't need your contact's permission or anything. You just need their Doc digits and BAM! Current frickin' GPS location. I mean, it's expensive, like twenty-nine ninety-nine, but still."

"That is nonsense." Rupey ran a hand over his face.

"Is there anything to block it?" Mac asked.

"Not this week," Caleb said. "Yo, Alfie, hermano. Cerveza me."

Now that I had stopped crying and the immediate drama was over, Mac took his arm away. The stoop fell silent. I sniffled.

"Need a tissue?" Alfie dug around in a takeout bag.

"I got it." Rupey waved the wadded-up one I'd thrown at him, like it was a white flag. "Sorry, just, you know, I can get kind of protective."

"It runs in the family," Alfie said. "It's our one admirable quality. Along with Mac's useless addition skills. Hola, hermano, ever hear of a Doc?"

There was a simultaneous low burble of laughter.

"Need a cerveza?" Caleb offered me his.

"Need us to beat some people up?" Victor burped.

I blew my nose. "Yeah, only about five hundred thousand of them."

Again, the low appreciative laughter. Now I got why Mac surrounded himself with these guys. It was the same reason I surrounded myself with Mac. Life felt better in their company.

"Mugrosos, not that we don't enjoy your clever repartee—"

"Ooh, 'repartee,'" Rupey interrupted. "Look at the novio go all French for the girl. Réplicas agudas not good enough for you anymore, cuz?"

"All-caps BUT I need to talk to the lady in private." Mac offered me a hand. "I kinda, like, need to apologize for what a dick I was yesterday."

"A super-huge dick," I said as Mac pulled me to my feet.

No sooner were the words out of my mouth than I groaned. Caleb hid his face in the crook of his elbow. Victor choked on his beer. Mac held up his hands, feigning innocence. Alfie made a quiet extended laugh noise that sounded like "Huh-huh-huh-ahhhh."

"So immature." I rolled my eyes. "You guys are worse than my brother."

"Lo siento, you're the one who said it," Mac laughed, then pounded fists with Rupey. "And all I have to say is, thank you for noticing."

29

"Meet me at the park on Saturday. We'll get tacos."

It was the first week of senior year, lunch. One second I was considering a browning avocado roll, wondering where they sourced the nori from; next Mac was there, spinning his Doc between his fingers, smelling freshly showered, and setting my weekend agenda. I glanced over my shoulder to check that he wasn't speaking to the girl in line behind me.

"What," I said in monotone, "am I the last Park Prep girl you haven't been with?"

He laughed. "There might be a couple freshmen I missed. Come on. Sunshine. Tacos. Saturday. Noon. I know you're free. I checked your G-Calendar. I'll meet you on the library steps. Perfect gentleman, I swear."

My lips turned down but my shoulders lifted up; my head tilted forward. Without my consent, my body had agreed. I immediately regretted its decision.

"Ugh," Audra's avatar said, then made a *tsk* sound later that night. (Thank you, *Teen Sounds* extension pack.) "Why are you stressing? It's one *daytime* date." Then Sharma txted:

"Ooh, it can be like a test." Fawn flapped her hand at me over FaceAlert. "See if he gropes you. If he doesn't, he's changed. If he does, you have to promise to tell us everything that comes after. I heard he does this thing with his thumb that will melt you."

On Saturday, when I got to the library, Mac was already there, holding a daisy. When I tucked it behind my ear, he grinned. And not like a wolfish grin, just a pleased one. Over the next four hours we teased each other, talked nonstop, and eventually held hands. We walked through the park, cut over into Sunset Park for tacos, and circled all the way back to the library. I never expected that this amalgamation of bad-boy stereotypes might also be funny, genuine, and kind. It was a great date. But, I mean, Mac had had a lot of practice.

Once we were back on the library steps, Mac untangled the wilted daisy from my hair and tucked it into his jacket pocket.

"And now I'm going to kiss you."

He did. And, well, whoa. If I had been with anyone else, it would have been the perfect, expected end to the best non-school-related afternoon of my entire life. But as we kept kissing, all I could think about was Fawn's test. We hadn't crossed into Groping, but we weren't exactly in High Five country either. I pushed him away.

"I'm not interested in being one of your mannequins."

That's what I liked to call the girls Mac screwed around with. It made it easier to think of them as interchangeably pretty and empty-headed. Mac took my hand, ran his thumb along my lifeline. Was this what Fawn had meant? Because it didn't make me feel slushy so much as flammable.

"You know, I've liked you since I saw you wearing that green dress at orientation."

The best I could describe what Mac was wearing the first time I saw him was "boy gear"—pants, shirt. And that was only a guess. Trying to shake off its misgivings, my heart did a fluttery jig.

Telling it to chill, I softly replied, "You've had a funny way of showing it."

He flashed his lopsided smile, shrugged.

"Yeah, I kinda, like, went through a slutty phase."

"Three years is a kind of long 'phase,' no?"

"Which must be why I'm so totally over it."

He pressed my hand gently between both of his, staring at our entwined fingers. Then he leaned in for another kiss. And maybe it was because I'd seen him do this countless times before, but my hand slipped out of his. I backed away and said for the first time the same seven words I'd been telling him ever since.

"I think we should be just friends."

Mac looked at his now-empty palm, laughed dryly. "Hermosa, you and I will never be just friends."

I expected him to go away after that. Instead we ended up talking on our Docs every night and meeting up every morning. He'd run to see me between classes, so he could walk me to mine even though it guaranteed he'd be late to his. Every Saturday, no matter how busy we both were for the rest of the day, we'd grab food and chill in the park for a bit. He came to my *debates*. Before I knew it, I'd become the president of the Mackenzie Rodriguez fan club while remaining its only unaffiliated member. I'd thought I'd proved him wrong about us not being able to be friends. Right until he called me a slut outside Park Prep.

Now we were sitting across from each other on his bed. Mac had worried his curls into a puffy 'fro.

"You know that isn't me in the video, right? I tried to tell you. Someone is messing with me."

He nodded. "I probably knew when I saw it, but Channing Gregory showed it to me with this mierda-eating grin, and I just got so pissed. At you and him and me."

"You called me a slut."

"Kyla." His expression crumpled. "What can I say? If I could take it back I would. I mean, lo siento mucho, but, like, I think that was the only reaction I was capable of in my state of massive disintegration. I felt like someone used an expansion ray on my heart and then, like, set it to pulverize."

"Isn't that how you killed the final boss in *KillCrush Seven*?"

"Yeah, remember all the blood? I'm really, really sorry."

He wiped his eyes with the sleeve of his hoodie. I put my feet on top of his. When I got upset, Mac said cálmate, tranquila; then he made me play-wrestle or dance with him. Mac was so even-keeled, I'd never had to repair his mood before. I scooted forward so our knees were touching. Putting a hand on either side of his head, but like over half his face, my thumbs right under his eyes, I forced him to meet my gaze.

"Question," I said. "If I'm not allowed to plan after-school snack with you anymore, what point is there to life?"

Rolling his eyes, he lightly clonked his forehead against mine. Then he gathered my hands and held them in his lap.

"Kyla, can we be serious for a sec? Because there's something I've wanted to ask you for a long time." He gently skimmed his thumb over my cheek, and I couldn't help thinking, *Is this the thing he does?!* Because it caused more of a pleasant static shock than a melty sensation. "And maybe this isn't the right time, considering that whole I-don't-ever-want-to-see-your-face-again bit, but I strongly believe, like more strongly than I believe that Manchester United will win the cup this year, that you should go out with me. Or you know, in question form: Will you be my girl? Por favor. Y gracias."

As Mac traced a line from the curve of my jaw to my neck to my collarbone, a thousand different emotions surged through my body. Excitement, giddiness, nervousness, por supuesto, but the largest percentage of me felt annoyed. For nearly four months, I'd waited for Mac to ask me to be his girlfriend. Anytime we were particularly cuddly or he said my name in that serious way he had or he rubbed his nose against mine, I held my breath, expecting to be kissed. And on any of those occasions, despite his past, and my trepidation, and my hard-line—correct!—stance that we'd last longer as friends, I would have said yes.

But he hadn't asked me in those nice, appropriate times. He asked me now. When I'd spent the last thirty-six hours being eye-groped by everyone who saw me. And maybe it wasn't fair, but having Mac ask me out right at that moment didn't feel much different from the hundreds of times that request had been made to me online over the last two days. I couldn't have felt more physically dirty if I had slept with my teacher all-caps PLUS every stranger who had propositioned me. The very last thing in the world I was thinking about was pairing off with someone.

"Macky, I'm not sure now's the right time."

"Okay, so when is? Six more months? Right when we're about to go away to college? A year? How about just one more month?" He took my Doc and tapped in my password. "By then we'll have figured out this video mess, and your college apps will be in, and you'll realize I don't like you any less; I only like you more."

I watched him set a reminder on my Doc for January 23 that read: *Say yes to Mac asking me out.*

"How did you know my password?"

"It's a simple equation, actually; all you have to do is..." He rolled his eyes. "All you have to do is know you even a little, hermosa, to know your password is Malin's inauguration date. And you wonder how someone hacked into Scholar?"

"But I use Shield."

"Yeah, but Shield doesn't update your Doc password. Plus, what's your Shield password? Let me guess. Malin's inauguration date."

"It is not," I sniffed, but only because I intended on changing it as soon as I left.

Mac's eyes met mine. They burned with resolve. "Be my girl-friend, Kyla."

"I won't be bullied into going out with you, Mac. I feel like you're only trying to claim me because the video made you jealous."

"No, dummy, I'm trying to ask you out because I *like* you."

Hey, fellas, a quick word about trying to convince the girl you like to go out with you. Maybe don't call her stupid as a persuasive tactic.

"And if I thought we'd last more than a week, maybe I'd say yes."

As Mac's shoulders rounded in hurt, I let out a rush of air and tried to laugh. Kyle liked to remind me that not everyone chose to argue as an extracurric: i.e., not everyone enjoyed heated discussions or was able to walk away from them completely grudgeless like I was. We'd only just made up. I didn't want to be fighting with Mac. Not about *this*.

"Come on, Macky. You know you don't do relationships. You pillage and then move on."

"Let me ask you something: You think before we went on that date this fall, I had a reason to be up on three every afternoon freshie through junsies? You know all my classes are on one."

After a click of hesitation, he lightly bit my pointer-finger knuckle. I'd prefer not to describe the tingles that this created. Just please know they existed. He smiled. I didn't.

"That's called infatuation."

"Or maybe it's called just the sight of you made my days bearable. I think *this*"—he motioned to the space between us—"is a little different than pillaging."

"My point exactly: You *think* it's different. And what if it's not? In a few weeks' time *this*"—now I motioned to the space between us—"could be nothing. Macky, do you know what everyone says about the girls you hook up with?"

"That they're awesome?"

"That they're skanks. And right now, confirming everyone's opinion of me is the last thing I need to do."

He quietly studied me, squinting. "Nah, that's not what this is about. You care even less what those Park Prep clones think than I do. This isn't about them. It's about you. So tell me, princesa, how long before you stop thinking *I'm* a skank?"

Step. Back.

"Don't you dare 'princesa' me, Mackenzie Rodriguez. It's not like I'm making this up. How long did you date Monique after you marauded her at the welcome-back junior picnic? How long did you and Lizzie last after you did the vertical grind at junior prom?"

"It's called the reggaeton."

"Is that also the name of what you two did in the parking lot after? I'm trying to keep you in my life. I'm not trying to be that girl who—still—buys you energy water at your soccer matches months after you dumped her. I realize your brain might be kind of fuzzy because you haven't kissed anyone for a record-breaking number of weeks—"

"Weeks? Try, like, almost four months."

"But history doesn't lie, Macky. We're essentially perfect as is. We see each other all the time; we're constantly on txt. You practically equal my favorite. Do you really want to mess with that?"

"For the chance to kiss the girl I like? Yeah, I'm willing to take the risk."

"But I'm not. And for what it's worth, my biggest priority right now isn't hooking up—"

"Neither is mine."

"—and that doesn't make me a high-maintenance princess."

Fine. Maybe I'd been suppressing some resentment. And maybe my delivery was harsh. But it didn't make any of what I said less true. He sprawled away from me, frustrated. Grabbing onto his headboard, he stretched backwards so I could just see his perfect stomach.

"I'm not the opposing side, Kyla. You don't need to decimate me." When he sat back up, his features were smooth again. "So indefinitely, then. The answer is you'll hold my past against me indefinitely. Bien, bien. Ya sé. Solo somos amigos, Ms. Cheng."

In an exact mirror of his mom, whenever Mac got flustered or upset, he spoke more Spanish.

"You're mad."

"I'm not mad. Just, no lo sé, disappointed."

I didn't know what was supposed to happen next. We'd never talked about any of this before—it just kind of lived between us—and when I'd imagined doing so, things went smoother and there was more hugging involved. Maybe this was where he rolled his eyes and said, *What am I going to do with you?* Because he realized that the question was more what would he do *without* me. I couldn't deny that he was right. Barring the completely inappropriate timing, I *wanted* to date Mac. So how long would it take to stop worrying that doing so would mean losing him?

"Maybe we can just table the discussion until I can sort out the video mess."

"Sure. Aces." He got to his feet and pulled on a hoodie. When I got to my feet, Mac lightly put a hand on my shoulder. "Can I just ask one favor?"

"Okay..." I stretched the word out with wariness.

"Do you think maybe we can be, I don't know, less affectionate? 'Cause I know we're only friends, but sometimes we act like more, and I think it'll be easier if I, like, touch you less."

This day had officially grown as terrible, humiliating, and heart-wrenching as any day ever lived by anyone in that exact five-foot radius. (President Malin always said it was important to keep a healthy perspective.) He let his hand drop. This felt like my driving test all over again. I could see all the errors I was making; I just didn't know how to correct them in that moment.

So, dumbly, I nodded. *Sure. Yes. Less physical touching would be aces, Mac.*

BTW, I also failed my driving test.

Mac sighed with relief. "Gracias."

"De nada."

Unfortunately, we were standing toe to toe, nearly right on top of each other. This was normally where he'd hop around and pretend to box with me or swipe a finger down my nose or tug my earlobe or flap my hood over my head or fix my bangs or touch me in another hundred little ways that made my tummy constrict.

How were we supposed to say good-bye now that we had "no touching" restrictions in place? How were we supposed to do anything we normally did?

Mac held up his fist. I bumped it with mine.

Oh, terrific.

"Come on, I'll grab Victor's bike and escort you home." Then he scrunched up his nose in a way that meant that whatever was about to come out of his mouth would make for one irritated Kyle. "Unless you're afraid that might make you skanky by association."

30

When I got home, Dad was in the living room, waiting. He clicked pause on the anime he was watching as I collapsed on the couch next to him. Mom and I had a general script to follow at times like these. Huge fight. Tension ebbed. Tension built. Huge fight. Repeat. But this was new ground for me and Dad.

"A new anime, huh?" I said.

"Boy-Kyle turned me on to this one. It's stupidly good."

"I'll believe half of that last sentence."

Dad snorted. "Audra was here before."

"She was? That's weird. I just saw her at dinner. She didn't tell me she'd be dropping by. Was she okay?"

Dad shrugged. "She seemed great. Spent about a half hour talking with Mom in the kitchen."

"About what?"

"I don't know. Nothing, really. They were just chatting."

"Did she leave me a message?"

"Uh-uh."

Great. Rub it in, universe. My mom got along famously with

everyone except me. As if he could tell this conversation was taking us into choppy waters, Dad cleared his throat and said, "So I found a person."

"Are you going to get a medal?"

Like Kyle, Dad always laughed at my jokes.

"A lawyer. He deals with cases like ours." Ours. "He's rated five stars on LawLink. I told him it was urgent, so he squeezed us in at twelve thirty tomorrow. We're his last appointment before he takes off for the holidays."

"Cool."

What I wanted to say was: *Hey, Dad, ever win an argument and still feel like you lost?*

Dad patted my knee. "Not a great reaction on my part. Sorry, kiddo."

I shrugged. "It was mild in comparison to school."

"Ahh," he said, like that made him feel worse. "When I was growing up, if I ever complained about anything, your năinai would say—well, first she would whap me across the back of my head, but then she'd say, 'Jade doesn't become a gem without some chiseling first.' We'll get through this. And we'll be stronger and richer for it."

Năinai.

Năinai would have told me I did the right thing with Mac. "Lots of time for boys," she'd always said, then tapped her head—brains first. As if my năinai were sending me a message from the afterlife, my Doc emitted its horror movie–style shriek.

Dad let out a mock mini wail. "Worst ring ever."

😈 Are you having a good night, pookie?

I chucked my Doc onto a chair across the room. Mac was the best person I knew. And I refused to go out with him. Audra came over *to talk to my mom*, apparently proving that my mother and

137

my best friend had a better relationship than I had with either one. Before the video, I'd have said I had a few problems with a few people. Now all signs pointed to the fact that I was the problem.

"You gonna be okay, Kylie?"

"No worse off than I was before." My voice caught. "I know I didn't turn out like you guys were expecting. I'm sorry if I've been a disappointment."

Dad didn't pretend not to know what I was talking about.

"You're not a disappointment; you're a teenager. Mom knows that too. You two will find your level ground eventually. That's the cool thing about family. We might have our ups and downs, but we're kinda stuck together. There's no question we love you, right?"

He nudged me.

"Sure," I said.

I put my head on his shoulder. He put his arm around me. Not knowing what else to do, he clicked play on the hub. On-screen, a flying squirrel decapitated a blobby demon. Blood splattered everywhere. We laughed.

31

moi My dad just told me my mom loves me because she's
stuck with me.

Normally, I'd have sent the txt to Audra. I'd have whined about
the latest turn in the Kyle-Mac saga. I'd have apologized for
how weirdly we left dinner. But I just couldn't get my fingers to
cooperate with my brain.

When AnyLies instantly responded, I found myself feeling
happy. Which was admittedly weird. But lately every time I txted
Audra, her avatar was red. Instant txt replies felt so refreshing.

😈 Why are you telling me this?

Because after our conversation tonight, I thought it best that I
give Mac a little Doc space for the evening. And because what Dad
had said had got me thinking. When you were stuck with someone,
you had to come to terms with them, no?

moi I dunno where or when, but I think we got off on the wrong foot. So, hi! My name's Kyla Cheng. My friends call me Kyle.

😈 What are you doing???

If there was no way to technically take down the video—a fact I still didn't accept—then this was my only play. Still, I hesitated. Fostering a relationship with my hater was clearly a bad idea. Yet worse things kept piling up. In the time between my bike ride to Mac's house and my return home, two more families had canceled upcoming babysitting dates. And in the time it took to say good night to Dad and go to my room, I assumed that the file sweep programs caught on that the video had attached itself to all my volunteer organizations, because my G-File no longer said I volunteered for We Shelter, We Care, or the half dozen other organizations I belonged to, including Senator Cooper's office. Additionally, all the photos I'd been tagged in at those places had been Pulled.

Even if colleges looked past my unfinished apps, now my profile contained nothing except the Mr. E. video and a collection of assorted family and friend tags.

I literally had nothing else to lose.

moi I'm doing the impossible. I'm going to convince you not to hate me.

32

FRIDAY, DECEMBER 24

The next morning, I groaned when my alarm went off. Nothing about my life made me want to get out of bed. It was Christmas Eve. In normal, non–devastated-city years, I would be sound asleep right now thanks to Park Prep Senior Perks. Instead I had a half day of school to get through and only eight more days until my college applications were due. Or, at least, were supposed to be due. I was pulling my pillow back over my head when there was a kick on my door.

"Wallowing under a blanket of woe is me," I called out.

Three pink-clad bodies tumbled into my bedroom.

"Well, throw it off." Audra frowned. "We brought enormous coffees."

Telling by the circles under her eyes and the tiny cowlick of white-blond hair that was poking up at the back of her head, she clearly hadn't had enough of hers. But it was early. This was the time we all normally woke up. Instead she was at my bedside in full makeup.

"And egg sammy bagels," Fawn said as Sharma tossed me a greasy brown bag. "Organic ones from the new place on Bergen."

"And an apology," Sharma said.

"AnyLiesUnmade?" Fawn cried. "And a stalker outside your house?"

"I still can't believe you were on the huge Eden screen." Audra laughed. "Why didn't you tell me yesterday in the Elite, you stinker? Or at dinner? I mean, there were a few seconds when I wasn't being a self-righteous betch."

"Wait. How do you guys know about all this?"

Answer: Mac. Apparently, he'd txted Audra last night, reamed her out, and updated her on everything. So what they had to say was that they now (finally) believed it wasn't me in the video. If for no other reason than I would never prematurely send off my college applications.

"And we're so super-sorry we didn't believe you from the start," Fawn added.

"Though, for the record, it is an excellent editing job," Audra finished.

Cue Audra falling onto my bed and tickling me in the ribs. Fawn pulling out her gross hanky to mop up her tears. Sharma looking like God creating Earth as she flicked between the seven holoscreens orbiting her Doc to show me all the videos I'd missed. And yes, part of me wanted to tell them they were too late. That I'd been handling things perfectly fine by myself, and that I'd continue handling them by myself. But then my Doc dinged with a message from a Will at Rise High Entertainment, congratulating me on my notoriety and asking if I was repped by anyone yet.

Who was I kidding? I'd take just about any support the girls offered. So, silencing my Doc, I said, "Seriously? Pink?"

"I know," Fawn pouted. "I lobbied hard for red and green. I mean, it's Christmas Eve."

Sharma made a *gag me* face. "Still my week. So yes, pink. Innocent yet in-your-face."

These weren't accents of pink with hair clips and shoes. These equaled the-most-ridiculous-outfits-in-your-closet's-arsenal pink.

Sharma was wearing a pink sari that her mom must have lent her. Fawn was in tight hot-pink jeans and a flouncy pink blouse. Audra was in a full-on tutu, wearing pink ankle booties that were on all the fashion sites' holiday wish lists. When InStitches had first suggested them to me, the comment I left was: *For five hundred bucks you should at least get the whole boot.*

"I guess half a boot is good enough." I nodded at her shoes.

"Ever heard of a splurge, betch? You're just mad they're a size six."

"Truth," I laughed. "You guys look like regurgitated Pepto-Bismol."

"It gets better." Audra brightened as she undid the top two buttons on her blouse.

Across her chest, in bright pink lipstick, was the word *BRAT*.

Fawn undid her blouse the same way. Across her chest it said *SLUT*.

Sharma's said *NERD*.

Audra took a lipstick out of her purse, straddled me, and wrote *INNOCENT* boldly across my neckline.

"I love my friends." The words burbled out of me. "Group pic."

With Audra on top of me, I couldn't reach my Doc, so I dug into my shoulder bag, grasping for my school tablet instead. When I pulled it out, a bunch of papers came with it.

Fawn's face paled. "Where did those come from?"

At first I thought she simply meant because it was *paper*, and other than, like, Fawn's mom and similar crunchy granola eaters, no one used paper anymore. But then I saw what made Fawn's curls droop. There was something written on the papers. My name. Over and over and over again.

Kyle. Kyle. Kyle. Kyle.

Front and back. Written thousands of times in all different styles of handwriting.

"I have no idea," I said.

Someone must have shoved them into my bag when I wasn't

looking. But when? When was the last time I looked in my bag? Last night after I got back from Mac's? Yesterday afternoon when I left Ms. Tompkins in the library? I carried it everywhere but barely used it. At school it sat in my cubby all day. My wide-open, unlockable cubby.

Fawn and Audra exchanged a look I couldn't read; then Audra grabbed the papers out of my hand, crumpled them up, and tossed them in my trash can. I knew it was as creepy as it felt because Fawn set down her egg sandwich.

"Someone's just trying to scare you..." Audra said.

"More," Sharma added.

"But who?" Fawn asked.

That was the problem. I didn't know.

txted my hater as the girls and I climbed the steps to school.

moi Congratulations, the video just hit a million views.
We're famous.

I refused to ask about the papers. As if I were dealing with a child, I didn't think bad behavior should be rewarded with attention.

😈 Just in time for Christmas. And no. Only you're famous. And maybe it's time you stopped tracking the count.

moi Can't help it. Obsessive-compulsive like that.

😈 Or just self-obsessed.

moi Touché.

Though, look who was talking? I wasn't the only one who was Kyle Cheng–obsessed. Who else would have made those sheets other than my hater? AnyLies sent me an emote of a devil face blowing a kiss. The last thing I wanted was to piss my hater off.

"Earth to Kyle," Audra said as we fell in line to commence the Walk. "So to make up for the whole we-think-you're-a-big-fat—"

Fawn loudly cleared her throat.

"Sorry, Fawnie," Audra said. "To make up for the whole we-think-you're-a-big-*plus-sized*-liar thing, we've belatedly done a little work."

"First," Fawn said, "you can thank Jessie Rosenthal for that flash mob in the hall yesterday morning. Ashe Yung told me @JessieRosenthal invited the entire school—minus the four best ones—to participate via Regrets Only. Then she filmed it and posted the whole thing on YurTube. The title is 'How the mighty shall Fall.' Capital *F*."

"Leave it to an art major to capitalize a season," I said. Only Sharma snickered at my grammar joke. "Does that move Jessie to the top spot of AnyLies possibilities?"

"Her fam def has the neces dollar signs for a techie hater campaign this big," Sharma said in a display of staccato abbreviation that was impressive even for her.

"And girl equals twisted," Fawn said. "Did you see her junior spring show?"

I did. They were paintings of beautiful girls in idyllic environments. Only problem was all the girls were dead. Some had been strangled. Others had track marks up their arms. Some had split wrists. Graff had made Jessie put up a parental-advisory notice at the entrance to the student gallery.

"I liked it," Audra said. "What? I did. It was dark. And kind of sad. But why would Jessie go through all this effort? I mean, she def has reason to despise you, Kyle, but you can't tell me this is about valedic."

"'Despise' is a slightly strong word choice, don't you think, Audy?" I asked.

But she was right: with my razzing, I *had* given Jessie reason to dislike me. But was it enough motivation to turn me into one of her little projects Ailey told me about? AnyLies had thoroughly infiltrated my life. And yet ten seconds talking to Jessie and I wanted to punch myself in the face. Mom would love her, the girl absolutely *spewed* angst, and deepness, and significance. But as weird as it was to say, my hater didn't seem annoying. My hater seemed like me. Granted, the most I'd heard Jessie actually speak was in the monotone voice-over she'd done for her video about the final extinction of the polar bears.

Cleo Bradley coughed "slut" as we walked past, amid her friends' laughter. Audra coughed back "ugly." No laughter now.

"Has anyone noticed Jessie's been hanging out with Ellie Cyr lately?" Fawn asked. "Doesn't that seem weird? What do those two have in common? Answer: nothing."

Sharma swiped at her Doc. "Either way, added subtle mustache to Jessie's Quip pic. Also, a thought. Came to me yest when you were talking to Eden hacker. Kylie, you equal natural-caught tuna. You're the real deal. It's your face but not your chest in the vid. Might be a slim chance the vid doesn't have anti-Woofer filter on it."

"How'd you know Ivy and I'd talked about lab tuna?" I asked.

"Tech reply," Sharma said. "Plus, didn't think it was right, you meeting that hacker alone. So, well, you didn't. My avat was signed in on your Doc."

"How is it everyone keeps hacking into my Doc?" I asked, feeling warmly violated and loved all at the same time.

"You never change your password" came the same reply in three different voices.

"And sorry," Fawn said. "What's an anti-Woofer filter?"

Audra gave her a three-second-long sigh. "How do you think

the *B&P* chick conceals her identity? Anti-Woofer filter, Curly Locks. Otherwise anyone could download a pic and run it through Woofer. Already had that thought, Sharmie. Unhappily, there *is* an anti-Woofer filter on the video."

"So the conclusion you've all come to is that everything continues to suck."

"All-caps B-U-T . . ." Sharma said.

"Huge butts?" Fawn teased. "Sharmie, I like it."

Sharma's eye roll said, *Remind me why I form RL bonds.* "B-U-T got the IP address the vid posted from. Traded the Sword of Light and Dark for one huge favor to speed things up."

Fawn flat-out stopped walking. Sharma had been talking about the Sword of Light and Dark since freshman year. She'd finally acquired it this summer after spending an all-nighter battling the same damn zombie in *ESSO,* the world's longest-running MMO, which, as Sharma always liked to point out, had a larger economy than most countries.

"Sharmie, that's about the biggest sacrifice anyone has ever made for me," I said. "I don't know how to thank you."

"Excuse me, do you not recall how I'm the only one in this group that will still watch you eat chicken wings?" Audra said. "Talk about a huge sacrifice."

"It's not my fault you guys are afraid of cartilage. I take after my grandma." I gave Audra a light shove away from me. Laughing, she skipped back to rejoin us. "Speaking of my family, Audy, did you come over and hang out with my mom last night?"

"Yeah," she said. "I stopped over to apologize. Thought maybe I'd crash with you. But *you* weren't home. So we had a chat. Anyway, Sharmie, hope the trade was worth it."

"Consternation face," Sharma said.

It wasn't. In Sharma-to-English translation, the video had been sent via a timed rerouter through a public computer at the main branch of the New York Public Library on Forty-Second Street. Sharma said the hater went through an IP borrowing program called GoFetch, which meant AnyLies had used a public library computer to log in to her GoFetch account, selected the video, and then set the clock. The video had been sent, whenever she'd designated, from the IP addy of the public computer. So it wasn't as simple as seeing who'd logged on to that terminal. She could have posted the video a week or even a month ago.

"Can we search all the GoFetch accounts that were logged in to from the Forty-Second Street library?" I asked.

"If so, I don't know how."

Sharma instantly equaled bad mood. She hated when tech failed her.

I kept waiting for my Doc to buzz. It was two minutes past Mac time. A minute ago, unable to wait any longer, I'd txted:

moi   Our spot? Sí or no?

Fine. We'd had a slightly intense conversation and we weren't allowed to touch anymore, but that didn't mean we weren't still meeting in the mornings, right? I mean, we'd already missed yesterday. I told myself to relax. He'd probably overslept.

"So never mind the library," Fawn said. "Isn't there a program to hack GoFetch?"

"If you're CIA, maybe. Whole point of GoFetch is it makes poster impossible to trace."

We'd reached the end of the hall. The girls held their Docs up to do halfhearted kisses. As I lifted mine, my stomach somersaulted. Mac hadn't overslept. He was walking toward me, curls already nicely slicked back, smiling. And he wasn't smiling because he was coming to get me. He was smiling because there was a girl walking next to him, practically glued to his arm.

"Mac-*ken*-zieee. Explain it again, only this time in beginner mode so I'll understand it."

Oh. My. Yuck.

The girl was Ailey. Ailey would need to be in Cali not to feel my eyes on her just then. She waved goofily, then put her *other* hand on Mac's arm—double the touching—so he'd notice me as well. Right, because even though Ailey was making big, round, innocent eyes at Mac, Ailey had a boyfriend. She wasn't interested in mine.

Oh, wait, that's right. Mac wasn't my boyfriend.

Thank you, self-sabotaging Kyle.

Anytime, trust-your-instincts Kyle.

When Mac saw me, he gave me his sexy lopsided playah grin, flashed me a peace sign, then hiked his jeans and walked *in the other direction.* Ailey shot me a *What the . . . ?* look, then hurried to keep up with him. I could hear her voice chattering all the way down the hall. Wanting very much to scream, I instead wrapped Sharma in a tight hug.

"I'm sorry you traded your sword and lost the ability to be invisible *and* kill your enemies with one stroke. Sounds like a perfect weapon right about now."

Sharma adjusted her glasses. "Don't forget regenerate lost limbs."

"Smile, Kylie-cat," Audra sang through her teeth while holding her Doc up to mine, her eyes narrowed after Mac. "Everyone's watching."

I lowered my Doc before it tapped hers.

"Honestly, Audra, I could care less. F them *and* F my life."

Audra's brow furrowed. "Firstly, I would think that you had learned by now that you should always care who's watching. And second, I don't want to be *that gal*, except we all know I am, so I'm just going to say I warned you, didn't I? If you wanted him, you should have lassoed that stallion while you had the chance."

"Ailey has a boyfriend," Fawn said.

"I'm not saying it's Ailey she has to worry about. Just be ready for some competition. Now that people think you were with Mr. E., they'll see a big old For Rent sign on Mac." Then with seemingly complete indifference, Audra casually asked, "Is Mac for rent, B-T-W?"

"Why, Audy, you in the market?"

Her eyes narrowed with displeasure, but taking her own advice, she pouted her lips and fixed my necklace so it was lying flat against my sternum.

"Maybe. I mean, if you don't want to experience his thumb magic, I don't see why I shouldn't partake."

Her whole body shivered in anticipation.

"Auds, sometimes you can be such a..."

"Brat?"

She gestured to the word on her chest like she was an old-skool game-show girl. Then she cackled and sauntered off to class.

Actually, I would have said *BTCH*.

I really needed to get into her Doc.

34

"The shift to the digital rules we live by all started with SeaWorld."

The law office was on the thirtysomethingth floor of a Gothic building on Lexington Avenue. Looking at it from the street, I imagined tiny, dark offices with low ceilings. Once inside, I saw I wasn't far off. It was a little before one, but three floor lamps were turned on, along with the overheads, and it still felt dimly lit.

Rick Brenner was the lawyer. A few of the people on the parenting forum Dad found had raved about him. He specialized in social-media and entertainment-media law. As soon as we entered his office, I knew he'd be no help. His walls were hung with actual black-and-white photographs framed inside pristine white mats. We were getting media advice from someone who still shot with film.

"SeaWorld," I said. "Terrific."

Mom tensed next to me. She'd surprisingly said nothing about the word on my chest, though she had given me a tissue and some serious directional eyebrows in the elevator ride up. Dad let out a weak laugh. The lawyer gave them a reassuring smile.

"I also have a teenage daughter. And yes, SeaWorld. It was a live-animal theme park."

I laughed. "I'm not that young. I know what SeaWorld was."

I also knew it went under when I was, like, seven, after a tech company opened up a bunch of 3-D ocean holoparks. The holoparks were expensive to build, but a lot cheaper to maintain. The boycotts over animal cruelty and the massive sea-life deaths made it harder and harder for the live-animal parks to keep stock and draw tourists, despite the fact that they'd stopped breeding orcas. And who'd want to just look at animals swimming in water when you could be "in" the water with them?

My Doc buzzed with a txt from Mom.

mama Manners. NOW.

"Good. But did you know that back in 2007," Rick Brenner continued, unfazed, "SeaWorld began making its patrons use their fingerprints to enter the park? Initially you could present a paper ID and avoid the process, but after a few years they took that option away because hardly anyone used it except for privacy spooks. Turned out, most customers didn't care about their data. People thought using a thumbprint for entry was easy, and even cool. The other major theme parks weren't far behind. Other companies and venues quickly followed suit, until agreeing to give up your biometrics became a standard part of going anywhere.

"Take your local grocery store. There was a time when people clipped coupons out of the newspaper to access deals and the store had no lasting connection to you. Thus the invention of rewards cards so the store could track your purchases, fine-tune their ordering, and increase their profits. However, rewards cards were optional, and a large percentage of people chose not to sign up for them.

"Nowadays, as you know, grocery stores are automated to the

degree that you cannot purchase anything in them without submitting some form of your biometrics. In trade for your personal information—including everything from what you buy to the data your Doc sends unencrypted via their Wi-Fi—the store lets you purchase food. If you don't agree, you don't buy food."

I sighed loudly. I might as well have been in my New World Borders class.

Over me, Mom said, "So when my daughter signed up to be a member of YurTube, she signed away all her rights as a member."

"Exactly. And right now, because of the unusually high quality of the forgery, the services that are hosting and profiting from the views can plausibly take the position that it is actually Kyla in the video. Because she's a user, she's agreed to let them use anything they can reasonably confirm as being her, even if it's explicit in content. It's disturbing, but per the agreement that everyone clicks through—and doesn't read—when signing into new accounts, it's perfectly legal. Especially since the cutoff age is only thirteen."

"Isn't there a way for Kyle to permanently untag herself from these videos?" Dad asked.

"Possibly," the lawyer said, "but there was the case of *Barton versus Watchyou.com*. CGI is quickly becoming indistinguishable from reality. In a situation where someone wishes to untag themselves, a service might reserve the right to keep the tag, if they think that the user is untagging themselves from a tag that is accurate. Remember: these services make money from content, and if someone wants to untag themselves, it's probably because the content is something that someone else will want to watch . . . which is why the services will fight any attempt at takedowns."

"I can't believe this is legal," I said.

"For that, you can thank the social-media lobby. Anytime the government tries to crack down on misuse of information, the media outlets compare the situation to the censoring that China still has in place and the overturned 'right to be forgotten' law that the EU passed earlier in the century, and every user gets up in arms about free speech and a free web. Don't get me wrong. A free web is primarily a good thing."

"Except when it isn't," I said.

"Right," Rick said. "You said the IP address was rerouted through GoFetch, but even if we could find the source, an injunction against the hacker would be difficult. Not only would we have to one hundred percent prove it's him, but if the servers are out of the country, the hacker will keep putting up new copies on new servers, and by the time we stop him, well . . ."

"My reputation is beyond reparable. Right. Gotcha."

Why was no one listening? I already *knew* this. Dad put a *please cease your fire* hand on my head; then his expression lit up.

"As is exceedingly evident today, our daughter's still a minor. Can't we go after them on child-pornography charges?"

Rick shook his head. "Since it isn't her in the video, what this scumbag has in essence done is created virtual child pornography. While there are strict laws against child pornography, there is First Amendment protection for virtual pornography. In order for us to go after Kyla's 'hater' on child-pornography charges, she'd have to say it *is* her in the video."

"Ew. No way."

"Right," Rick said. "We could go after the hosting website to remove that content or release the user information that posted it with an implied threat to paint them as peddlers of virtual pornography based on real children. First Amendment or not, most organizations won't want to go quite that far to defend their use of the content."

"But it could get reposted the next day, and I already know that the user information doesn't lead anywhere," I finished for him.

Rick tapped a finger against his lips. "I can bring this to the feds at the courthouse in Brooklyn. They *might* take it on, and they have the resources to slow this down while tracking down the video's creator. Their offices are probably closed for the next few days, but I'll still reach out to them if that's how you want to proceed, though I wouldn't expect to hear back until after the New Year."

"But by then all the admissions deadlines will have passed," Mom said.

I bit my tongue. It was already too late for that.

"Might as well," my dad sighed.

"And the source material didn't get you anywhere?"

"How do you mean?" I asked.

"Your hater took the footage of you from somewhere—Woofer, most likely. Finding out who posted the original clip might give you a lead on who the forger was."

And now you'll have to excuse me, because right at that moment, my brain went into all-caps mode.

OMG. I'M AN IDIOT.

WHY DIDN'T I THINK OF THIS?

SO BASIC = TOTALLY OVERLOOKED.

I KNEW IT WAS A WOOFER VIDEO THEY USED AS THE SOURCE MATERIAL! WHY DIDN'T I THINK OF SEARCHING FOR IT?

A lead. I had a lead. I jumped out of my chair, stuck out my hand. When Rick reached for it, I pulled him into a hug instead.

"Thank you so much, Mr. Brenner. That was the most enlightening lecture ever."

Rick laughed, uncomfortably. My mom shook her head. I couldn't get out of there fast enough. Rick had just told me I might figure this out by doing all the things I did best. I needed to do research. I needed to build an argument. Plus, I had something to work with that I hadn't had in the last three days:

Hope.

35

txted AnyLies.

moi Ever tried to watch 1,298 videos of yourself? I don't recommend it.

😈 Sounds like something you'd be good at.

moi I think you have the wrong impression of me. I'm not conceited.

😈 ...

moi I'm not *that* conceited.

😈 ...

moi Well, it's not my fault. I mean, have you seen me recently? ☺

😈 UGH. I thought you were trying to convince me not to hate you.

Smiling, then realizing it was weird that I was smiling, I set my Doc aside and got back to work. After a quick train ride to Brooklyn, with my parents only too happy to be out of my company and back at work, I sequestered myself at a secluded table in a coffee shop at the top of Prospect Park, as was my way when I dove into work mode. I was getting close and I felt something like confident. I was going to logical think the SHT out of this.

I could do this all day, which was lucky, considering I might have to. I'd swiped sixty-four videos in before I even found a video that was non–Mr. E.–related.

It was footage that Audra had taken of me and the girls in the Rockaways, prancing around in our bikinis. The sight of so much skin and boobs and, in Fawn's case, butt crack was horrifying. When Fawn had first posted the video, I'd thought it was adorable. Now, looking at my beautiful friends, I felt ashamed. Like we should have known better, but about what? Enjoying ourselves? Swimming? Having bodies? Kyle was in plenty of similar videos, naked except for his board shorts. But that would never be used against him. It wasn't fair.

I untagged myself from the video, then multitasked and txted Sharma to see if she'd do a little digging on Jessie Rosenthal. Like, for instance, did her Brooklyn Public Library account also have borrowing privileges for the New York Public Library?

sharm Good thinking. Never cracked the library before, will try. Gonna be off Doc for next 30.

Sharma? Off Doc? Bizarre.

moi Mkays. Thanks, pookie.

158

Me using my hater's slang? Bizarre times thirty. I took out a Sani-Wipe and swabbed my Doc clean as if that could erase my txt slipup. I needed to relax. My stomach was the size of a pixel. But the more videos I watched of myself, the worse I felt. Did we need to record and keep *everything*? I txted Audra:

> moi Freaking out about amount of info that's online about me re vids.

> audy Think you've txted the wrong friend. You know my thoughts. Can never be too much info online. All this exposure is good for you.

Did Audra not remember all those tear-soaked Boobgate-related sleepovers sophomore year? Talk about too much info.

At the time, Audra was dating Cobi Watkins. He was quiet, a little preppy for Audra's usual tastes, and a first-year prelaw student at Columbia. When she told us Cobi had asked her to send him naked pics of herself, my stomach did a serpentine twist with unease. I began to wonder aloud if that was the smartest decision, which, might I note, was also what I wondered aloud when Audra said she was dating a college guy to begin with. I mean, he could ask for nude pics all day as far as I was concerned; that didn't mean she needed to send them, especially not after only a few weeks of dating.

But Audra did her head toggle and this pitying puckered-lip pout, and it was clear they'd already landed on his Doc. Fawn cheered and said, "Welcome to the club," and they both generally acted like it was no big deal to send your boyfriend nudies. Until, not even a day later, Cobi forwarded the pics to all his friends. He didn't do it to be vindictive. It wasn't like he and Audra had argued or broken up. Titillating and bragging to his friends about his hot girl just rated higher than respecting her.

"If you didn't want me to share your whorey pics, then you shouldn't have sent them."

One of Cobi's friends knew a senior at Park Prep. It wasn't long before half the boys at Prep had seen her topless. Audra eschewed her tech for a week. She also spray-painted *CHILD MOLESTER LIVES HERE* across Cobi's dorm-room door and sent a letter detailing Cobi's indiscretion to the dean of Columbia, as well as all his professors, and his mother.

That was Boobgate. I.e., Audra hadn't been at all laissez-faire back when it was *her* body being fully exposed. And the pics hadn't even claimed the top spot on her profile for longer than a few weeks. But I stayed my fingers.

Audy was right. I should have txted Fawn. I immediately rectified my mistake and forwarded Fawnie the original message. She'd be more sympathetic.

> audy   BESIDES, nobody looks at every single vid in a
>   person's cache. It'd take days.

As I waited for Fawn to txt back, I replied:

> moi   I guess that makes me feel better? Xmas Eve movie
>   date night?

> audy   Can't. Gonna meet Sharma in a couple then got
>   other Xmas Eve plans. Xoxoxo

Wait. What plans? I thought we weren't celebrating Christmas this year. So what were she and Sharma doing that I wasn't invited to? Plus, I thought Sharma was off Doc. And why the H-double-L wasn't Fawnie txting back? Whoa there, Kyle, I told myself. No need to go all paranoid. And yet, if this was my friends being supportive, this blank-faced emote was me being underwhelmed.

I swiped back to my ConnectBook, to the first ten Woofer

videos that had nothing to do with the Mr. E. sex vid. The second Woofer was of three Park Prep girls. They were in the cafeteria, talking about a mustard/mayo preference. The person recording them must have gotten bored, because she panned from her friends and zoomed in on my lunch table. Or rather, she zoomed in on me. I reached over the back of my chair to pick up a dropped sandwich eco-baggie. My hair fell forward, curtaining my face. As I sat back up, I flipped my hair.

"Oh my gosh."

It was like the person who took the video, focusing in on me like that, knew exactly what she would use it for. She didn't even use a fake moniker. It couldn't be any clearer: the poster was @EllieCyr.

Stay calm.

Everyone had access to these videos. It could be a total coincidence that my stalker had pulled footage from one that Ellie made, *if* that was even the clip. The angle seemed mostly right, but it would be nearly impossible to blend my hair into the Mr. E. video like that, and, let's be honest, I wasn't unknown for flipping my hair. But ten seconds before the clip ended, I smiled exactly as I did at the end of the Mr. E. video.

My chair screeched on the white tile as I pushed it backwards. Without a doubt, it was the source video and it was filmed by Ellie. Who was suddenly friends with Jessie. I hurried to the entrance. Sharma was powered down for thirty minutes, so I txted Audra instead because she was the last person in my txt thread.

> moi   Finished watching vids. When you see Sharma tell her the Woofer vid is from Ellie's account. Gonna try and get to bottom of this Ellie & Jessie friendship. Regardless, finally have proof it's not me!!!!!

I waited for a reply, but none came. Her txt line spooled for a moment. Then her avatar went red.

36

In retrospect, my next move wasn't the brightest. I should have called my mom or tried to get ahold of the lawyer or at least waited until Sharma and I could do more digging, but I wanted it to be over. So I took a shortcut. Still, I'll blame Brittany Mulligan for what happened next. If she hadn't ousted me from Community Club, I would have been dressed as Mrs. Claus right then, inadvisably leading off-key Christmas carols.

Instead I thought I'd won.

Ellie was changing out of her school clothes and into her gym clothes when I found her in the YMCA locker room on Ninth Street thirty minutes later. (Though why bother? Both outfits involved sweatpants.) Even if I hadn't downloaded the WhereYouAt app that Caleb had told us about and cyberstalked her, I'd have known where to look for Ellie. If she wasn't at basketball practice, Ellie was always at the Y working out. I'm sure it partially had to do with her court game, but every Park Prepper knew her parents were going through a nasty divorce, trying to gain custody of their brownstone while still both residing in said brownstone. The divorce was Ellie's mom's second. Rumor had it, Ellie's stepdad was the parent she liked better.

For the hundredth time, I thanked the universe for my parents' happy marriage.

Whatever mix of nationalities Ellie was, not to be mean, but one of them had to be oak tree. Sturdy and thick with muscle, she wore her brown hair in a short bob, which she always tied back for games using one elastic and a hundred thousand bobby pins. She jumped when she caught my reflection in the mirror at the end of the locker row, surprise dribbling across her round features. But then she laughed.

"Oh boy, let me guess." She faced the mirror and reworked her ponytail so it shot directly out the back of her head. "You're here to blame me for your hair not coming out right today?"

Wait, seriously, what was wrong with my hair?

"No, actually, Ellie, I found the clip of me that was used to make the sex video. It came from footage you took."

I don't know what I was expecting—that she would fess up? Or be floored by my detective work? Or at the very least be creeped out like I was that someone had stolen her innocuous vid to frame me? And, fine, if I'm being 100 percent honest, even though there's nothing lamer than women fighting women over men, a tiny part of me hoped she'd be as nice as she always was, so I could press her for a little insider info on why Ailey and Mac suddenly looked so chummy.

But instead Ellie laughed again.

"Yeah, Ailey told me you tried to blame her, too. That you're saying it's fake."

"What do you mean, I'm *saying* it's fake? It *is* fake. I just told you. I found the original clip my hater used to doctor the video. A clip that you originally recorded."

"The only fake thing around here is you."

"Excuse me?"

This was not the Ellie Cyr I was used to. Ellie Cyr was nice.

Ellie Cyr and I took a boot-camp class in the park our sophomore year and immediately got milk shakes afterwards. *This* version of Ellie was the girl who pushed through two defensive guards to dunk the game winner and smashed the backboard in the process. (Yes, that actually happened. It was amazing.) This Ellie was a girl I didn't at all want to share frosty beverages with. Or be on the opposing side of.

"You heard me, Cheng."

One long leg following the other, Ellie stepped over the changing bench to hover over me, like she was trying to engage in one of those chest-bumping competitions. My knees gave. I sat down hard on the bench behind me. She smirked.

"Ailey also told me about how you abandoned her freshman year all because Audra brought you a juice."

My face was level with Ellie's belly button.

I frowned, mumbled, "She also said there was only one seat."

"So you pull up another one. Ailey was your best friend."

"We were fourteen. Friends break up all the time." I stood back up. Ellie didn't move to give me more space, so the top of my head was right beneath her nose. I stepped out from under her. "Look. I didn't come to talk about Ailey. I came to talk about the video you took."

"The sex video?" Ellie turned back toward her locker, folding her school clothes and shoving them in her bag.

"No. The video that was used to put me into the sex video."

"I honestly don't know what you're talking about." She looked genuinely puzzled, but then gave me that smirk again. "'Put you into' the sex video? How would I do that, with magic? I didn't make that video, Kyle. Because no one did. You can't make reality."

This was getting me nowhere. It was time for a different tactic.

"Look, Ellie, I have no static with you, but I know you're friends with Jessie and I thought—"

"So you didn't come to blame me, you just came to blame my best friend."

"Wait, I thought Ailey was your best friend." And she was scolding me for being disloyal? "And actually, I did come to blame you, but now that we're talking, I'm pretty sure you had nothing to do with it."

"I meant she's *one* of my best friends," Ellie huffed. "I'm not like you. I stand by my people. Besides, Jessie wouldn't do this either; she's not—"

"Creative enough," I filled in, until I realized that wasn't the descriptor Ellie was searching for. "Grimacing face. Sorry."

"I was going to say she's not that mean. Something else you wouldn't know anything about. If you'll excuse me, I'm gonna hit the machines or I might hit something else."

Spinning around faster than I'd expected, Ellie stormed past me and rammed me so hard in the shoulder that I stumbled backwards.

"Geez, Ellie," I said. "Watch it."

And then I did something stupid. I pushed her. Only a little, but that was all it took.

Now, at five eight I wasn't short, but have I mentioned Ellie Cyr was six foot two? Her nickname was Empire State. As in the building. Next thing I knew, a tourist attraction–sized girl slapped me across the face. The force of the slap knocked me back two steps. My head smacked into the lockers behind me.

"Whoa," Ellie said, as I felt my cheek with a shaky hand.

And maybe if she'd apologized, things would have been different, but she didn't. Her surprise was immediately replaced by that smirk, and something inside me snapped. I charged. We flew over the bench that divided the row of lockers and tumbled to the floor. Ellie had a fistful of my hair in one hand and was punching my ribs with the other. I tried to shield the blows while also landing a few of my own. I was not successful.

"Hey!" someone shouted. But not at us, because then they said, "No PHDs allowed in the locker room. What are you recording?"

When I looked up, whoever was filming us was gone. A click later, in that person's place huffed a Y staff member.

"Girls," she said, "what are you doing lying on the floor like that? Come on now. Y's closing early today. I suggest you hurry up, get on with your exercise, and then go have yourselves a happy holiday. Some of us would like to do the same."

Ellie was breathing heavily. Pushing away from me, she sat against the lockers with her head in her hands. Her shoulders shook like she was sobbing. When she looked up, she was laughing so hard she was barely able to breathe. The employee tsked, muttered something about missing Christmas Eve drinks for this nonsense, and plodded off.

"Oh my God," Ellie wheezed, wiping tears from her eyes. "I've never gotten in a fight before. Wait till the girls hear. Your cheek is all red."

"Because you slapped me," I said, which made Ellie laugh harder.

Ellie got to her feet, inspected her arms and legs for damage, then adjusted her ponytail. Stray bobby pins littered the floor around her like fallen leaves.

"You deserve a lot more than that, Kyle. Though it looks like you're getting it. Give my best to Mr. E. Hope you two have a happy holiday."

37

awn lived in the biggest brownstone of any of us. It had been willed to her mom by her grandparents, and ever since her parents' divorce when Fawn was a toddler, to make ends meet her associate-professor-of-women's-studies mom rented out every room in the building to an ever-changing flow of foreign graduate students and professionals. It was a lively, liberal household that was full of heady conversations but low on toilet paper. It was also the closest in proximity to the Y, and since I'd just gotten beaten up, I needed closest proximity. The last thing I wanted was to get caught in someone's Woofer sporting a puffy eye.

A tacky animatronic Santa took up half the stoop and ho-ho-hoed when I rang the doorbell. A few seconds later, an equally jolly Fawn answered the door.

"Kyle." Her laughter stopped midtwinkle. "What're you doing here? You can't be here."

"I just had this awful confrontation with Ellie at the Y...." The curtains in the front window separated and then fell back into place. "Wait, Fawnie, why can't I be here? Are the other girls inside?"

"No, uh...it's, um..." She nervously chewed on the inside of her cheek like it was free-range jerky; then her face lit up. "It's a boy!"

A few weeks back, Audra had plugged us all into her period-predicting app. Blue dots were what you marked on your calendar to mean "had sex." And Fawn had tons of blue dots. When I'd teased her about it, she'd said, "It's no big deal, Kyle. My body needs to poop. My body needs to sleep. And lately my body feels like it needs to have sex." And that had cured me of ever wanting to mention her dots again.

So it was entirely possible she was telling the truth, but the Fawn I knew would have dragged the boy outside and, like, made him do a pirouette so I could admire how cute his butt was. Instead she stepped out onto the stoop and pulled the door shut after her.

"Who is it?" I asked.

"Oh, nobody you know. I didn't want to tell any of you about him because, uh, it didn't seem appropriate if I was all daydreamy, especially with what's going on with you and Audra."

"Wait, what's going on with me and Audra?"

"Oh my gawd, Fawn," she squealed, and slapped a hand across her mouth and then giggled. "Nothing. I meant with you and your video and Audra just being crabby all the time."

That wasn't what she meant. Fawn wouldn't meet my eyes, and normally Fawn all-caps DUG my eye contact. The curtains flickered again. Fawn squealed and rocked on her heels.

"What are you on?"

"Endorphins?"

I tilted her head back and stared into her eyes. They weren't bloodshot.

"Breathe," I said.

She puffed into my face. Her breath smelled like tater tots and ketchup. She giggled again, looked back nervously over her shoulder.

"Kyle, I gotta pee. Too much kombucha. Oh, gosh, and Merry

Christmas Eeeve. My dad's coming by to pick me up in, like, an hour, but txt me laters."

The door shut in my face. I tried not to feel upset. Fawn was Fawn. This was not a friend conspiracy against me. It wasn't. I swiped on my Doc. My finger hovered over the WhereYouAt app. There was one way to know for sure where all the girls were.

Sighing, I swiped off my Doc. Animatronic Santa beamed his approval, like I was a prime candidate for the Nice list.

"Oh, stick a pipe in it, old man."

The truth was, if the girls were all on the other side of Fawn's door?

I didn't want to know.

38

Mac txted as I walked home.

mac   Saw the fight.

The warm front continued. As dusk came on, Christmas lights blinked on with it. It all felt a little surreal. Like Christmas in July. I didn't bother asking how he already knew about the fight. I'd been getting pinged like crazy. @JessieRosenthal had posted it on ConnectBook. It had been her in the locker room. She'd titled it *"Valedictorian?"* Guess she suddenly wasn't too good for the Internet anymore.

Viewed alongside the sex vid—as it now forever would be, considering they were already grouped together in an *If you liked this, then watch . . .* —it looked like my life was in a tailspin. (Looked like? Ha!) More than being creepy, knowing she'd been there listening to us the whole time, it was supremely frustrating. There I was, wasting my time wrassling with Ellie, when Jessie was only steps away. I finally could have confronted her.

mac   What happened?

moi   I honestly don't know. I told Ellie I knew she shot
      the original footage of me that was used in the Mr. E
      vid...

mac   Nice!

moi   Next second we're tumbling over benches.

mac   Kind of an aggressive reaction.

I touched my cheek. Winced.

moi   Yeah, tell me about it. What do you think it
      means?

mac   I guess that Ellie needs to be added to the list of
      possible haters.

Didn't it seem strange that all my possible haters were in the
same friend group? Ailey. Ellie. Jessie. I sighed. I felt like I was
too narrowly focused, like I was missing something. For starters,
Ailey and Ellie had both adamantly denied making the video, and
as aggravating as it was, I believed them. So that left Jessie, who
couldn't even be bothered to post things under a fake name. Like
she wanted me to know she was enacting my takedown. But why
would she so blatantly post the fight and the flash-mob video in
the foyer, but not the Mr. E. vid?
How many haters did I have?

mac   Want some company? We haven't had after-school
      time all week.

He sent me some quick pics of the world exploding, a mad scientist pulling at his hair, and Godzilla ravaging NYC.

Or maybe the fight video was totally innocent. Maybe Jessie had simply gone to pick up Ellie and stumbled on us fighting. Who wouldn't record a fight?

> mac I can come over early. Hang before we all go for ramen.

Earlier in the week I'd invited Mac to come to Christmas Eve dinner with us.

> moi You sure you're not busy?

> mac ???

> moi Hanging with Ailey, maybe?

My Doc fell silent as Mac figured out how to word his response. I'd finally made it home. I let myself in and went straight to the freezer and got a bag of peas to put on my eye.

> mac Are you talking about me walking with her this morning? She had a math question.

> moi So you weren't trying to make me jealous?

> mac What am I, ten? She had a math question.

> moi Was she trying to multiply you times her?

I grinned, perfectly envisioning his exasperated expression. Faintly, I heard the front door open.
"Mom?"

I waited for my mom to come into the kitchen. How in the world was I going to explain my puffy face to her? I thought about just going straight to my room, but I'd have to dash right past her. Mac's txt thread spooled as he wrote and deleted the perfect comeback.

But then all he sent was:

mac She had a math question.

moi I hope you gave her a satisfying answer.

Ever so softly I heard the front door close. It wasn't my mom or she would have said something. I crept to the kitchen door, listening. I could have sworn I locked the front door. To get to the front hall, I'd have to walk through the dining room. It felt like someone was standing just on the other side of the dining room doorway, listening right back.

"Dad?" I waited, and when there was no answer: "Kyle? Is that you?"

Silence. But not an empty silence.

"I hope it's all right," I called out. "Mac and his cousins are coming over. They'll be here any second."

The floorboards in the front hall creaked. I wasn't imagining things. Someone was in my house.

"Oh my gosh."

I was so upset over the fight, I must not have locked the door. What if it was the "don't talk to strangers" guy? I'd been so focused on my Doc, he could have been sitting on the stoop next door and I'd have missed him completely. Or what if it was just about anyone else who now knew me, even though I didn't know them?

There was nowhere for me to go. The kitchen led into the basement—no way, uh-uh—or the backyard. The yard was minuscule, with a ten-foot-high fence around it, but at least out there, people could hear me scream. I grabbed a chopstick from the jar on the counter in case I needed to stab my assailant in the eye. Then as quickly and quietly as possible I went to the back door. The lock was old, rusted, and usually required an iron grip and a lot of willpower to turn. Dad was always talking about needing to replace it.

Struggling with the lock, I looked over my shoulder only to see a big guy in a black hoodie coming at me. I flung my chopstick at him. It struck him harmlessly in the stomach, then clattered on the kitchen tiles. I tugged at the lock. A hand gripped my shoulder. I screamed and sank to the floor.

39

"Geez Louise, you are not having a good day, are you?"

It was Kyle. Dumb, stupid, wonderful, non-rapey Kyle.

"Where did you come in from?"

"Nowhere. I was upstairs."

"But I heard the front door open and close."

"Must be a ghost," Kyle said, his upper body already halfway buried in the fridge. "I've been upstairs for the last two hours. Didn't see any murderers on my way down, either. I did see the fight, though."

He waved his Doc at me.

"How awesome will it be if you have a shiner for the Christmas pic?" he said. "I can't believe I once had a crush on Ellie. I'm totally unconnecting her on everything."

"Thanks, Kylie." I was still trying to catch my breath.

I couldn't stop staring at the useless chopstick lying in the middle of the floor. Audra always said every woman needed to arm herself with confidence and a bottle of pepper spray.

My Doc dinged with a txt tone I hadn't heard in forever. Ailey.

ailey Hey Kyle, Ellie told me what happened between you two. I made the mistake of telling my mom.
She told me to tell you, if you come to our house or approach me anywhere outside of school, she's going to file a restraining order against you.

"Oh my God. That little brat never could fight her own fights."
"What is it?" Kyle asked, but I was too angry to respond.

moi Ailey, this wasn't even about you. And ELLIE slapped ME!

ailey Sorry. I'm actually a little mortified, but she = serious. I just thought you should know.

"Ailey's mom wants to take out a restraining order against you?"

I held my Doc to my chest, but it was too late. Damn holoscreen txting. When would I learn? Kyle's jaw dropped open. His Doc was immediately in his hands. I grabbed his wrist.

"Don't you dare txt Mom."

"What, ow. Why not?"

"Because it's all bluster and I don't want it to be one more exhibit that her daughter's turned into a terrible person. She'd disown me for sure."

"No, she'd call up Mrs. Amundsen and rip her a new one. When will you stop acting like Mom hates you?"

"When she actually stops hating me."

It was different for Kyle. This past summer he'd finally cut the shag of black hair that had hung around his face since he was ten. Now that you could see his cheeks, neck, eyes, it was obvious that very soon he'd be devastatingly handsome. (I'd throw my Doc in the e-recycling bin before I told him that.) Kyle had to get extra storage on his Doc to hold all his contacts. His inner circle called

176

themselves the LMs, for Lordly Misfits. Yet when Mom gave Kyle SHT it was lovingly. It was abundantly clear she wasn't worried he'd turn into a giant a-hole.

Kyle's face had gone all red. I'd been living under the supposition that we all knew Mom didn't like me. I decided to change the subject.

"Okay, Kylie. Sure. Whatever you say, buddy." I felt like Audra trying to convince me that she believed me about the video. "Up for playing *Wooded Escape*?"

He was about to agree when my Doc emitted a familiar jingle. Audra was FaceAlerting me.

Kyle groaned. "Say hello to Aryan Audra for me. See you in three hours."

He'd stolen the name from Mac. Audra had once bragged in front of Mac that of all us girls *she* was the most exotic because both her parents were white—a rarity in NYC nowadays. Mac had tacked Aryan onto the front of her name ever since. It hadn't taken long for Kyle to follow suit. When Audra had asked if Mac was "for rent," she'd just been trying to get at me, right? I mean, there was no way he'd ever go for her, *right*?

"Don't call her that. And I'll only be two seconds." After Kyle left, I swiped my screen to accept. "Gaudy Audy, I need hugs."

Only I was staring at a closet door. Audra's Doc was docked. I hated when she did this. Why FaceAlert and then make me stare at her steering wheel or, like, her feet while she got a pedicure? From somewhere on the other side of the screen she called, "Saw the fight. What you need are boxing lessons. Check your mail. I gifted them to you for Christmas. Your right hook needs serious help. It was like watching a kitten fight a lamppost."

"I'm only good at verbal jousting," I said, patting my eye.

Sharma piped in. "I'll tell Jessie if she doesn't remove vid, I'll sign her up for the KKK e-letter. Goes right to the top of your G-File, flags your whole page red. And B-T-W Jessie, Ellie Cyr, *and* Brittany Mulligan all have Brooklyn library cards plus NYPL access."

It was perfectly normal that Sharma and Audra were hanging out together, but a nasty little voice in my head wondered why I wasn't there too.

"How'd you find that out so fast?"

"Simple. I messaged them."

"Thanks, Sharms, you charge my Doc like nobody else. But how did you get Jessie's contact? Up until this fight an hour ago, I couldn't find her anywhere. And I still can't connect to her."

With the exception of the fight video, Jessie's CB account had to be hard-core private, which I guess explained why I couldn't find her at Ailey's no matter how many of her friends-of-friends' connects I quickly searched. Her G-File was still almost nonexistent. It was almost like she had her face Pulled and her G-File swept on a daily basis. Because other than her uber-elitist Quip stream, the video of the flash mob at school, and now the fight video, she still equaled almost zero online presence. Which in essence meant that two-thirds of what was online about her was actually about me.

"We overlap on a few games. Her call is @DarkEnchantress. You can message her through that."

"Awesome. Gracias."

It was then I realized it wasn't Audra's closet door I was staring at. Hers was painted white and always open and bursting with clothes. This door was varnished maple. Had Fawn been lying? Were they all at her house? But why would she lie?

"Are you guys over at Fawn's?"

"Nope," Audra said, and left it at that.

"Sharmie," I said. "What did you think of the Ellie video?"

"What Ellie video?"

In the background, Audra gasped and said, "Oh SHT, I totes forgot to tell her."

Now I was glad for the docked Doc. Was Audra *trying* to stop me from figuring this out? As calmly as possible, I explained about the source video coming from Ellie's account. No sooner had I finished than Sharma said, "Kyle, tell me you downloaded it."

"Not yet, why?"

Please, no. My stomach was already in revolt. No matter how angry Ellie was, no matter that we just got into a knock-down fight, Ellie had to know that that video was my one way—so far my only way—of proving my innocence. She wouldn't be so cruel as to delete the video. Ellie Cyr was nice.

"Yep," Sharma said tightly. "It's gone."

40

"F'd up, didn't I?" Audra said after a moment of dead silence.

It wasn't Audra's fault. It was mine for not immediately down-loading the Woofer video. I'd been so caught up in getting to Ellie that I hadn't wanted to waste the three seconds it would have taken me. It isn't Audra's fault, I repeated to myself. It's mine.

But come on. If Audra had told me she'd found a way to prove she wasn't in the sex video that was stalking her, I'd have relayed that info to Sharma the moment she walked through my door.

When no one responded, Audra cleared her throat, then trilled, "In happier news, the *B&P* goddess did another piece about you."

"Audra," I exploded, "I don't want to hear it. Not right now. Hello, college admissions boards. My name's Kyla Cheng. This is my sex video, and here are all the related links on this teenager's porn page."

"It's not like that." The Doc violently swung around as Audra grabbed it. "She's trying to get two million views on the post so it knocks the Mr. E. video from the first spot on your G-File. The post is about how if this happened to a boy, no one would care. How he'd benefit socially from it. How Parkside Prep would be working harder to take it down. It ties it together with how our culture only slut-shames girls. It's saying all the things *you* should be saying and is all-caps FE-MI-NIST. There's fifty thousand likes already."

"And let me guess, this deep piece of writing is accompanied by the *Bra&Panties* slut in her barely theres? Auds, if it's on *B&P*, it's not fe-mi-anything. What I'd like is for the BTCH to leave me alone and stop using my misfortune to get herself more views."

When Audra txted me a link to the *B&P* slut's new and improved site over the summer, it was all-caps DISLIKE at first click. Since I made a point of not hating on other girls—the world did that enough for us—I kept my comments about the content of the pics to myself, but under all the posts I pasted links to volunteering organizations, articles about self-esteem, and links to the sites of famous women authors, scientists, and politicians.

Audra had instantly FaceAlerted me, her face bright pink with anger.

"Why would you do that? You're trolling her!"

"Oh no," I said, mortified. "I thought you sent the link because it was ridiculous. I mean, *Die-For-Worthy*? They're rain boots."

"Made out of recycled rubber. I sent the link because I thought you'd think this was cool. *I* think it's cool."

"We don't have to like the same thing all the time, Auds."

Now Audra held the Doc a little farther away from her face. Her hair was pressed against her head as if she'd taken off a tight cap.

"What do you mean if it's on *B&P* it isn't fe-mi-anything? Don't you listen to me at all? My whole point in trying to get you to follow her is to prove that just because a girl is sexual it doesn't mean she's antiwoman or a slut. Fifty percent of her followers are women."

"Agree to disagree, ladies," Sharma called out.

The captain of the debate team? Not likely.

"Half the slut's viewers are girls, not women. Girls, Audra. What example is that setting?"

"What example are *you* setting? Maybe stop calling her a

slut so much. That 'slut' was approached to do a running post for Vogue.com. I think the lesson there is that enough gumption gets you what you want. Maybe she's not your perfect President Malin with her immigrant parents and public-school education, but *I* find her hugely inspiring and *you're* making an argument that you know nothing about. You'd never let yourself be this uninformed in debate. Never mind that you're unfairly persecuting her for the exact reasons you're being unfairly persecuted. But fine, agree to totally all-caps DISAGREE. Kissy face."

The FaceAlert screen went end over end.

"Hey," I said as my screen showed a close-up of carpet. "Don't toss me."

"Sorry, pookie," Audra called out. "It slipped."

"Wait. What did you call me?"

From the other side of my Doc, a door slammed. Sharma came on-screen.

"She stormed out, didn't she?" I let out a shaky breath. "Sharmie, have you noticed that Audra's a little more Audra lately? Do you ever think she'd take anything out on us?"

"Stop. Are you equal-signing Audra to AnyLies?"

Hearing it out loud sounded as bad as thinking it. This was Audra, *my* snarky best friend, not some webisode's cliché mean-girl villain. And so, fine, maybe I'd double-checked—correction, *tried* to double-check—that it wasn't her at her parents' house, but I knew deep down that AnyLies was not Audra.

Sharma and I stared at each other. Or, rather, I stared at Sharma, her eyes flickering over Audra's Doc. Sharma was holding Audra's Doc. And it was unlocked.

"Kyle," Sharma said. "No doubt Audra equals unhappy person. But she's one of us. Would you think I did this to you? Audra wants to be loved more than anything. By you, especially."

"Me? Why me?"

"Simple. Kyle equals perfection."

"Even so, you won't check Audra's Doc for the source video? Just to be sure?"

Sharma frowned, like *Weren't you listening?* But then a sly grin tugged at her lips; she pushed her glasses up on her nose.

"Already did. It's not there."

As it officially became the Eve of Christmas, I slaughtered Kyle in *Wooded Escape*.

"Thanks for shooting me through the heart *and* lighting me on fire," he cried, as I proceeded to trap him in a hedge maze. "We're supposed to be on the same team. Argghhh, vines everywhere."

I couldn't help it. I was all full up with anger. Twenty minutes earlier, right before Dad got home from work and my mom came back from a meeting in Tribeca, Mac backed out of coming to dinner.

mac Gonna stay home tonight, hermosa. Stuff feels kinda weird with us, and you don't seem too keen on my company right now.

moi Is this because I was teasing you about Ailey? Are you mad at me?!

mac No, just maybe need to lick some wounds for a day and don't want to ruin your time with your parents.

I didn't write back.

So it was only the four Chengs who walked to our favorite ramen spot on Vanderbilt. There, at our usual window table, between big bowls of eggy noodles and plates of pork buns and dumplings, I actually managed to find my pre-video self. We laughed and teased each other and, for a little while, life was about family: Mom getting tipsy; Kyle, Dad, and me re-upping our noodles and slurping enormous mouthfuls without biting because in Chinese culture that's considered bad luck. And I didn't need more of that, thank you very much.

Later that night, after a pre-Christmas present—faux-leather gloves!—and cocoa by the hologram fire that Kyle downloaded and then projected into our fireplace, and Dad's traditional readings of *'Twas the Night Before Christmas* and *The Polar Express*, I txted good night to the girls and, after much consideration (too much), also Mac.

moi Merry almost Gift-Giving Day, Señor Rodriguez.

mac And a Happy Standing In Return Lines to you, Ms. Cheng.

I miss you, I typed but quickly deleted, vaguely wondering if AnyLies *was* keyed into my Doc and if it made her hate me less to see how terrible I was at having a simple relationship with a boy. Then I hunkered into bed and pulled up the *Bra&Panties* site on my Doc. Audra knew my weaknesses. How *could* I make a good argument if I didn't know what I was taking about?

On the left of the page was the countdown clock. *Until Legalization and Exposure* was written in a curling script above the clock. The end date was December 31. Beneath the decreasing numbers was a huge close-up shot of the *B&P*'s cleavage, pushed practically to her chin in a lacy nude bra. Beneath the pic it read: *See me bare all (my face and other assets) on the thirty-first.*

The clock had 242,000 likes.

My hand hovered over the teeny *x* that would close out the page. Instead, with a sigh I couldn't suppress, I swiped over to the latest post and started reading. After placing Audra on the suspects list, I kind of owed it to her.

BRA&PANTIES

Hey, party people,

Let's talk objectification. I get this question a lot: Is it objectification if it's to my own benefit and I'm choosing to put myself out there? To which I ask: Do you like what you're doing? Is it fun? Or is it beneficial to you—say, is it providing a much-needed income? If the answer is yes to any of these questions, then no, it's NOT objectification.

Yeah, sure it's not. I was about to skim ahead when something caught my eye—my name.

BRA&PANTIES

Take this Kyla Cheng chick for instance. How great would it be if she had the courage to stand up and say, "So what?" Why can't this chick be Li'l Miss Straight-A, intelligent, a real go-getter, and still—gasp—have sex? Our sexual icons faded out nearly a century ago. Can we all agree that we are desperately in need of an update?

In theory, I agreed with what she said. But come on. It wasn't like her followers—Mr. @BigJack2005 or @DirtyDaddy—were admiring her for her brains or lucid women's-rights arguments. I mean, no one watched *Unicorn Wars* for the wars. They watched it for the unicorns. Maybe the post would have meant more to me if she didn't end it by plugging her big nudie reveal. Or if it weren't me she was calling out for not being feminist enough.

No better than the average teenage boy, I swiped ahead to the pictures.

It was a series of six photos. The sluts wore different lingerie in each pic (keeping the advertisers happy). There was a girl in bed, sheets tucked in just so around her naked body. Then a girl in a skimpy bra-and-panty set, stretching. Then that same girl straddling a pillow. Even alone in my room, I blushed.

I scrolled down to the comments. Some of them were *go get 'em girl!*–type posts, a few were near memoirs about the reader's own struggle with objectification, and a few followers were having an intense exchange about feminism. The rest were completely asinine. *Slut* was written so many times, I stopped seeing it. And it wasn't men writing these comments. All the men's posts were like *girl u hot*. The nasty comments were all written by other girls.

Now I scrolled back up to the third photo. The girl was posed on her bed, face blurred, hair tousled like she just woke up (but who woke up on all fours?). It wasn't the ridiculous pose that kept drawing my attention; it was her bra. I recognized it. It was the same one that Ailey was wearing the day the video came out of me and Mr. E. The one I'd thought seemed exceptionally fancy for no-glitter Ailey.

I swiped off my Doc. The whole point of *B&P* was to get people to buy things. The fact that Ailey had that bra didn't make her one of the *B&P*'s sluts, it only made her impressionable, like the hundreds of other Brooklyn teens who lived and died by *B&P*. Besides, though she and the model did have similar skin tones, there was no way Ailey's boobs were that big.

I sent one more message.

moi Hey Jessie, Kyle Cheng here. Can we talk?

I wasn't expecting much. Maybe just a flat-out no. But my Doc sat unresponsive in my hand, like I hadn't even txted a real address. The thing of it was, if Jessie was AnyLies, why wasn't she using that moniker all the time? I mean, it equaled far creepier and untraceable. Why was she posting anything under her own name? Unless it was precisely to throw me off her trail. As I tried to fall asleep, I wished hard that it was Jessie who made the video. Because if it wasn't her, then I had to admit I still had no idea who had.

42

Two a.m. My Doc screamed.

 You up?

moi Yes. Barely. Insomniac much?

 Insomniac always. How's the cheek?

moi Bruised, like my ego. How'd you know?

 How could I not? You can't stop making popular vids.

moi Unfortunately, this WAS of me. Never been in a fight before.

 Doubt that.

moi   Not a PHYSICAL one. Is it weird to say that it felt kind of nice?

   Yes, it's weird.

moi   I mean, all these other verbal arguments I get into, there just doesn't seem to be an end. One good pop in the eye, and the issue's pretty much over and done with.

   Who do you fight with so much?

moi   My mom. My friends, or at least one of them. I don't know. I guess it's just our thing.

   My thing with my friends is having fun.

You have friends? I wanted to write. But I guess, of course she did. Only why would someone who was happy and had friends be doing this to me?

   You know, for what it's worth, some friendships are worth fostering and holding on to. Some aren't. Good indicator is, are they there for you, is it easy to laugh with them, and do they love you no matter what.

moi   Wow. Good advice.

Hater, I thought but didn't write.

moi   Going back to sleep now.

   Quitter. BTW Merry Christmas.

moi You too.

Then before I knew what I was doing I added

moi xoxoxo

and hit send.

43

SATURDAY, DECEMBER 25

Christmas.

Since I want to go into politics, I'm obligated to say that I am definitely a spiritual person. But religious? Năinai was vaguely Buddhist. Dad and Mom were not so vaguely agnostic. For us, Christmas was about presents. Paid for with money I should have been saving for college. (And since I'd like to go into politics, I shall now redact the previous four sentences.)

Christmas on the second anniversary of your grandma's death, the day after you didn't see Mac in any satisfying way and had a huge fight with Audra, and AnyLies is the first person to txt you Merry Christmas? A hundred times more depressing.

Thank goodness for boy-Kyle.

At six a.m., as he'd done since he could walk, he woke me up by bouncing on all fours on my bed.

"What are you?" I asked, pulling my pillow over my head. "Five years old?"

"Kyyyylieee, it's Christmas."

Two minutes later he dragged me across the hall and we both bounced on Mom and Dad's bed. Five minutes later we were all

192

downstairs. Dad made coffee as Mom took our stockings down from the mantel. The whole present affair only took about ten minutes. I mean, it doesn't take long to open envelopes of store credits and logins. After that it was breakfast, and naps, and me trying on the clothes my parents bought. Since Mom now pulled items directly from my InStitches cart, everything was literally exactly what I wanted. Still my crankiness persisted.

Maybe it was everyone else's good cheer. Maybe it was that we should have been getting ready to go to my grandma's. And when we got to her Queens apartment we'd be greeted by a mountain of food she'd spent the last two days cooking. Hugging me around my waist, she'd scold me in Mandarin for being too skinny. Then she'd give me and Kyle our own plates heaped with food—soy-braised pork belly, those thinly sliced potatoes that brought good luck, homemade dumplings, and pieces of a steamed whole fish—and she'd shoo us from the room so she wouldn't have to hear Dad complain about favoritism and how come he had to wait until dinner?

But on the worst day of my life, exactly two Christmases ago, Näinai had passed away at New York Presbyterian in Queens. Since my mom's parents had retired to the Languedoc shortly after Mom turned thirty, this effectively robbed us Chengs of all the family we didn't have to FaceAlert to see and me of the one person in the world who I knew loved me unconditionally. Now, if we were creating new traditions, in a little while Dad would order Chinese takeout and we'd get six orders of shrimp toast instead of four.

Ba. Hum. Bug.

At noon, the doorbell rang. My first thought, unreasonably, was that it was my hater. But there on my stoop, squinting because the sun was right in his eyes, was Mac. He was holding a tiny box wrapped in the same kind of brown paper bag that a bodega sandwich came in.

Just like that, my Christmas felt merry.

Declining my offer to come inside, he said he didn't want to take up my time, but you know, he knew we'd said no gifts, but it was Christmas *and* Saturday and he kinda, like, got me something. We sat on the stoop instead. With at least two feet of space between us, Mac inspected the cheek Ellie slapped. Beneath the cover-up I'd used to deflect Mom's questions, it was slightly blue-greenish and sore.

"Ouch," he said. "*I* haven't even gotten slapped before."

"Yeah, well, next time you see Ailey, tell her to thank Ellie for me. Yet another thing I can add to my résumé."

Mac rolled his eyes. "I don't *see* Ailey. She had a math question."

"Macky."

One side of his mouth rose up. "And I, kinda like, knew it would make you muy jealous if I answered it right then."

"Thank you! See? I'm not crazy."

Mac laughed. "I don't know about that. I mean, says la chica with a black eye."

I normally would have playfully pushed him, but now I kept my hands in my lap. I imagined an alternate universe where Mac had an arm around me and we were laughing, kissing. I imagined how easy it would be to cross into that universe. And how much I would prefer living in that world compared to this one. At least until Mac got bored.

He cleared his throat. "So I've been thinking about the Virus."

I snorted. "That's seasonal."

The Virus was the world's new terror alert. And it had already happened to South Korea. One day, the Internet simply went away. Like someone ran a demagnetizing strip over the entire country. It took the South Koreans a month to get a bare-bones Internet back up and running after the blackout. During that time, chaos reigned. That was five years ago. Since then, most countries had channeled a lot of their military spending toward tech military branches. That's where Sharma was headed after high school. She would have gone already, except the US military wasn't like CB or Goog. It didn't accept high school dropouts.

"Why have you been thinking about the Virus?"

"First, because that's what it feels like not being normal with you." Mac blinked a lot and looked away. "Second, I keep thinking if the Virus strikes, what will I be left with? Like will I have good people around me to be stuck in the dark with? I screwed up the other day when I asked you to be my girl. I'd been waiting for the right moment for a long time, waiting until after I proved myself. That was definitely not the right moment. I'm sorry."

"And I'm sorry if I hurt your feelings. Just ... if you've really liked me for the past three years, why didn't you act sooner? I mean, September was the first time we even spoke."

Even if he'd asked me out last year, that would have ruled out half a dozen other girls. We would have been dating for over a year. Which actually? Just didn't seem possible.

The twitch of his lips said, *Isn't it obvious?*

"Have you seen yourself walk Park Prep? With that high ponytail and that frowny pout. Intimidating doesn't describe it. Every time I saw you, you acted like I was plague. I figured you were way out of my league. Plus, I was busy kissing, like, *a lot* of other girls."

Now I did shove his shoulder.

"And then I cut class and saw you in that lunch line this fall and kinda, like, saw how you looked when you weren't pretending to be scary and I had to go for it. I figured if I could get you to smile, I'd be aces. And you did smile." The very act of remembering made his eyes light up. Then that glimmer went away. "But I think you're right. If the Virus strikes, the best way to assure you're in my top five lost contacts is probably by doing your friend thing. I won't ask you out again. Está bien?"

I swallowed hard. "Está bien."

"Friends?"

"Siempre."

Mac turned my present over and over in his hands. When Mac was twelve, he gave himself a homemade tattoo on the soft flesh between his thumb and pointer finger on his left hand. He'd done it for a girl he liked, named Marrakesh. "Lucky we had the same first initial," he laughed when he told me the story. Staring at that spot always made me proud we had the relationship we did. I mean, where was Marra now? But today, I suddenly got why Mac had asked me out right after he saw the Mr. E. vid. It was terrible imagining him attached to anyone else. *I* wanted to indelibly leave a mark on him. And not because we had a great *friend*ship.

"Nothing says gift time like awkward silence," I said in my Mac accent.

He groaned. I scooted closer, holding my hands out. He pulled my hat down over my eyes. When I fixed it, his gift was in my lap. I opened it quickly, fearing that at any second I was either going to cry or tackle him. We were back to being friends. I'd never felt more miserable.

Inside the paper bag was a tiny jewelry box. Inside the tiny jewelry box was a pair of delicate woodlike earrings.

"Are these 3-D printed?" I asked, holding one up.

They were stunning.

"Nope." He smiled shyly. "They're made *by hand* of *natural* materials. I bought them in person at the holiday market in the city."

"Macky." I swallowed heavily. "I love them."

He looked down at his feet. "Yeah, well, I knew you would."

Patting me once on the arm, he stood up. I shielded my eyes against the sun so I could better see his expression when I said, "And all I got you was a preordered copy of *KillCrush Eight*. You can download it at midnight."

His eyes widened. He whooped loudly. Holding on to the porch rails, he swooped in to kiss me on the cheek. More out of surprise than anything else, I leaned away. Mac and I roughhoused so much, retreat was my go-to defense. Still, it stopped Mac cold. He pushed off the railing, his lips a flat unhappy line.

"Good job, Rodriguez. I can't even keep my word for one minute before I go pillaging again. Sorry, Kyla. Tell your family I said Happy Twenty-Five Percent Bump in the Economy Day."

"Tell yours I said Merry..."

My mouth felt like it was filled with glue. There I was, the queen of debate, and I couldn't think of a single example of anything Merry right at that moment. So I just shook my head and got up to go inside. When I got to the top of the steps, Mac was already gone.

moi   All I want for Christmas is for you to take down the video.

t was close to midnight. My family was sprawled on the sofa. Mom was sleeping. Dad was on his Doc. Kyle was now on the sixth episode in a row of *Cloaked Games*. I'd just messaged Jessie for the nine thousandth time, asking her to talk, when moments later AnyLies responded.

😈 Can't have it all. I'm sure you got everything else you wanted.

moi   Yeah, tho I kinda miss the years when I didn't.

😈 Meaning?

moi   Meaning I guess I kinda miss the years when my mom got it wrong.

Hmm. Because when your mom got it wrong, it at least meant she still knew you enough to guess what you might like?

Yeah. That was it exactly. After days of feeling misunderstood by everyone who knew me best, somehow my hater kept getting it right.

moi You're pretty all right. If only you'd stop ruining my life.

AnyLies and I aren't friends, I quickly reminded myself. AnyLies understood what I was going through because she—I mean, let's be honest, it had to be a girl—because she'd put me there. Maybe I was txting my hater in the hopes that she would take down my video, but why was my hater txting me back? I reminded myself of the sheets of paper with my name written on them a hundred different ways and I almost called it quits on the whole enterprise.

But then AnyLies txted this:

 You know, you aren't the only one.

moi The only one what?

 The only one who's been through this.

moi This what?

I waited. But that was it. The only one . . . who had grown apart from her mom? The only one . . . who was questioning every single relationship in her life? The only one . . . who hated the holidays? Missed her grandma? The only one who . . .

I quickly sat up, crunching Kyle's feet in the process.

199

"No, that's fine, girl-Kyle, I didn't need to walk ever again anyway."

"Not like you do now," I said as I did a quick search.

I wasn't sure how to word my question, but the Internet helped with that. There were enough results to make your mind spin, but none that seemed to match. I swiped further and further into the search. Then, as Kyle clicked next on the seventh episode in a row of *Cloaked Games*, twenty pages into my search, I found her—a Christmas miracle.

Her name was Trina Davis. And, thanks to my hater, she was about to help me figure out who my hater was.

45

SUNDAY, DECEMBER 26

The next day, when I woke, warm sunshine was filtering through my curtains. The house smelled of Sunday—organic bacon, chocolate chip pancakes, and coffee. I cheered when I swiped on my Doc. Christmas was finally over. Plus, I'd slept until eleven, which meant I was nearly late for my own party. After quickly responding to a string of CB messages that Trina had sent me after I went to sleep, I leapt out of bed.

Twenty-five minutes later, the groggy versions of Fawn, Sharma, and Mac were in my living room, all decked out in their lazy weekend attire. Late last night, I'd invited them all over for an All Brains on Deck meeting. Now Mom brought in a huge pile of pancakes. Boy-Kyle passed out plates and in an effort to save room for dim sum brunch in a few hours, incredibly didn't keep one for himself. My dad yawned. There was only one empty seat.

Audra was a no-show.

I'd expected it would take her a few days to cool down after our Christmas Eve fight over the *B&P* slut, but I hadn't heard from her even once yesterday. And that was huge considering she'd come to my grandmother's funeral two years ago. She knew Christmas wasn't only tough on her nowadays.

> moi Urgent. You okay? Please confirm not dead in
> gutter.

Since there was no worse feeling than not being able to reach someone, our code was that if we added *Urgent* to any message and you still had fingers on your hand, you *MUST*, caps *and* italics, respond. I could feel her gauging just how grudgey she felt like being. It took her a full two minutes to write back.

> audy Sorry can't make your big show and tell. Busy. There
> in spirit.

> moi Busy with what?

> audy Schoolwork.

> moi Schoolwork?

On the room screen, my Doc on share mode so it would sync with the hub, I pulled up the G-File account I'd discovered last night while searching student-teacher sex scandals. Unlike mine, which came up first, the one on-screen was 336 entries in. But that didn't make it any less relevant.

"Meet Trina Davis," I said.

No response. This was one sleepy audience. Kyle's eyes flickered to Fawn. Poor guy. He was crushing hard on my Fawnie and she was years more experienced. Meanwhile, Fawn's eyes were focused on the pancakes. Sharma was absorbed in her Doc. Mom sat on the arm of Dad's chair and absently rubbed his neck. Across from them

Mac put up the hood on his sweatshirt and yawned, "Who's Trina Davis, amiga?"

Ignoring the amiga descriptor, I said, "A girl who had an identical fake sex video made about her."

There. That woke everyone up.

46

"Trina lives in Chicago. She's a solid A-minus student. And two months ago, someone posted a video on their school's faculty page of her and her young calc teacher having sex. Should I play it?"

"No," my dad said.

"Yes," everyone else said.

Sharma was one step ahead. The file was already on our living room screen.

The video had been filmed inside a car. The teacher propped his Doc up on the dash. Except in the beginning, when he hit record, you mostly could only see his back. Occasionally, Trina's face surfaced over his shoulder. It was pretty clear that the teacher hadn't said he was filming this. He'd acted as if he was just putting his Doc somewhere safe.

"I called this All Brains on Deck meeting because I thought you guys could help spot the other similarities between me and Trina. Why were we targeted for these videos?"

I'd asked AnyLies the exact same question right before I went to bed last night but hadn't heard back.

"How do you know they're related at all?" Fawn asked. "This video looks real. I know coitus face when I see it."

As Kyle erupted in violent coughing, croaked that he needed water, and disappeared toward the kitchen, I shrugged. No way was I telling everyone that it was AnyLies who had led me to see the connection. Then I'd have to admit I was txting AnyLies, and I didn't want to get chastised so early in the day.

"That is exactly what everyone thought about my video. Trina and I CB messaged all last night. She adamantly denies it's her. Even now, two months after her video dropped. She said the footage was taken from some video of her that her friends shot at the gym."

Sharma flicked more elements from her Doc at our home hub. On-screen, the gym video of Trina loaded next to the sex video. Trina was on one of those leg weight machines, pumping a SHT-ton of weight. The videos played simultaneously. Other than some high-quality masking, the footage was nearly identical.

"See, Fawnie? Workout face. Not sex face."

"Oh yeah." She squinted at the screen. "My bad."

"So why us?" I asked.

Trina was suburban. Me, urban. She was a sports nut. I was a volunteer junkie. Trina's guilty pleasure was the Colossus Sundae from someplace called Dirty Ice Cream. Mine was reading pop stars' autobiographies.

Please never repeat that.

"You thinking Jessie again?" Sharma asked.

I nodded, and quickly filled my parents in on the "human projects" Ellie had seen on Jessie's Doc. This was quite a project all right. What was it she'd titled that one vid? "How the mighty shall Fall"? Was I only one level of a much more complex game?

"Is it just me or does Trina kind of look like you?" Fawn asked.

"You're right," Kyle rushed to say. "I think so too."

He was back, leaning in the doorway, crossing and then uncrossing his arms so his mini boy/man muscles bulged. Fawn glanced at him and hid her smile with a forkful of pancakes.

"Aren't the Rosenthals in Turkey?" Kyle asked. With Herculean effort he pulled his eyes away from Fawn and swiped at his Doc. "I go to school with Joseph. Yeah, look."

He flicked an image at our home hub and now we were all looking at three smiling Rosenthals (and one very unhappy one). They were out to dinner, sitting in a maroon leather corner booth with enough small plates in front of them to feed Fawn through the entirety of a *My Friend, Ghost* binge-watch. Joseph and his parents were leaning in for the photo, basking in the candlelit glow of their elegant dinner and clothes. Jessie sat on the outside, almost at the very edge, frowning at her Doc. Kyle put up another one. Three smiling Rosenthals were bundled up and posing in front of a mosque. Again Jessie was off to the side, arms wrapped around herself, cold, miserable, impatient.

"So what? They're on vacation. Turkey has the Internet."

"Yeah, but who stalks someone when they're on vacation?"

"Clearly miserable her." I flung a hand at Jessie.

I could practically see my profile on her screen.

"Nah," Mac said. "This isn't Jessie. Jessie's messed up, but I mean, she's not a bad girl."

He said it like he held some deep understanding about the inner workings of the beast. I thought back. Wasn't there a rumor that Mac and Jessie hooked up, when was it, sophomore year? At the Halloween dance? Oh, yuck. As if Mac could see me working through my memories, he quickly pushed on. All eyes flicked to him.

"Isn't it obvious what the connection is?" As if he were on a job interview, he sat up straight and folded his hands in his lap. He cleared his throat. "I mean, running the odds alone . . . the similarity is the guys. Both are teachers, both are young, both were caught with students, and both are in situations where they *had* to be aware the videos were being filmed."

"What are you getting at?" I said.

"Bonita, you're too innocent for your own good."

"I happen to like her that way," my dad said, straight-faced.

"Me too." Mac wiped his hands on his pants. I could see the sweat beading on his forehead from across the room. "All I meant was, Kyla, you keep assuming that because it's not you in the video, it's also not Mr. E. It isn't like someone captured vid of Mr. E. shooting hoops and overlaid it on some porn star doing it. That's him in the classroom with a girl. You're spending all this time looking for who made the video, but you haven't once considered that it could have been the person who participated in it."

"Whoa," Kyle said.

"I always did think Mr. E. had a crush on you." Fawn nodded.

Mac continued, "Is there a way to find out if the other profess taught any extracurrics? I bet you anything he did video effects like Mr. E. Maybe they're old college buddies that send each other vids of themselves with their hot students."

"Mr. E. teaches video effects?" I asked. "How didn't I know this?"

"B-slash-C the only electives you take lead to you in the Oval Office," Sharma said, looking at me over the bridge of her glasses.

"But then who's AnyLies?" Mom asked. "Mr. Ehrenreich couldn't have wanted this out there. Whoever made the video has an issue with you."

It was a good point. And almost exactly what I had been thinking, but when Mom said it, it was attached to her same refrain of *what has my daughter done to deserve this*.

"Mama," I said. "Let's pretend not everyone hates me and look at this objectively."

Mom's eyes narrowed. She collected a few plates, then left the room. Dad pinched the bridge of his nose. Yup, I was going to get it later.

Into the ensuing tension, Mac shrugged. "Who knows what Glamour Stubble does outside Park Prep? He used to date Ms. Valtri, but I guess recently he'd been going out for happy hour with Ms. Tompkins." *That* I didn't know. "I mean, double-dipping in such a small pond? That's just estúpido. Anyone could have found this video and run with it. Take your pick of girls at school who are jealous of you, Kyla."

"Or maybe Mr. E. got hacked," Dad said.

From the kitchen came sounds of plates being slammed into the dishwasher.

"Right." Mac cleared his throat. "All I know is these videos aren't a hundred percent fake. Never mind Ellie Cyr's footage. You gotta find the original source videos of the men. I'm telling you. Mr. E.'s no innocent victim."

I looked at Sharma. She didn't crush on him like I did, but Mr. E. was her favorite teacher too. She sighed and pushed up her glasses.

"I'd say not enough data. But regardless of what the connection is—teachers or students—maybe there's more of these videos out there."

Once everyone left to get back to their post-Christmas afternoons with their families, we four Chengs went to a strained Sunday dim sum brunch out in Flushing. Thanks to my earlier snap, Mom was full-on silent-treatmenting me. I thought a noisy, crowded banquet hall–style restaurant would be the perfect relief, but even in that delectable chaos of steamed buns, squeaking carts, and multigenerational families, I could feel the tension crackling between us. Though we ordered equivalent amounts of food, in comparison to all the other families ours seemed small and unhappy. So I waited until we got home, having spent an appropriate amount of awkward time silently window-shopping in Queens, before I tried to escape. I found her in her office.

"S'okay if I go to Audra's to work on my college essays?" I lied.

"Do whatever you like, Kyle," she said, keeping her back to me.

"Sorry I snapped at you," I said, still from the doorway. "I've been stressed."

"I never use that as an excuse to snap at you. And it's not only today. Sometimes I feel like I don't even know my own daughter anymore." Whose fault was that? She shook her head sadly. "What will happen when you go away to school?"

Remember how I wrote that I didn't bumble my words around cute boys? Well, unfortunately, I didn't bumble them around my parents, either.

"What are you afraid will happen, Mom? I know you think I can't possibly get worse."

"Kyle . . ."

"It's true," I said, suddenly shaking. "I know you think I'm like Violet Mitchell and all those other girls you despised. I'm sorry I'm not some nerd, that we never got to bond over how awful high school is. But now you can be happy. I'll officially be haunted by it for the rest of my life just like you."

This didn't come out as cleanly as it's written. My eyes started to tear up and my voice turned shrieky the first sentence in. Beneath her now-fashionable hubcap-sized glasses, Mom's eyes went wide with shock. As much as I'd been thinking Mom looked older of late, she suddenly looked very young and innocent and wounded.

"And you wonder why I worry about you?"

"Now that you mention it, I do. I don't feel like I've changed all that much."

Mom laughed once: "Ha."

"*I* think I'm a good person who tries to make good decisions. In fact, I'd have thought I was doing pretty okay, until you started making me think I wasn't. So what is it, Mom? What is it about me that you don't like?"

Mom reached for a tissue, shook her head no, like she wasn't going to humor this line of questioning.

"Oh, great," I goaded. "That's helpful."

"It's how you treat people," she burst out. "As soon as you met the girls it was like everything about your old life just wasn't good enough anymore."

"You mean Ailey? I know you liked her, but she drove *me* crazy, Mom. I'm your daughter." A huge sob escaped me. It was only through force that I continued speaking. "You're supposed to go along for the ride with me, no matter what. You're not supposed to pick some other kid over your own."

This was a conversation we should have had over a nice calm mother-daughter lunch. I'd been imagining how it would play out for years. It wasn't supposed to be like this. It wasn't supposed to be nasty.

"I've never preferred Ailey." Mom kept wiping at her eyes. "I just don't like—"

"Me," I finished for her.

She didn't correct me, but instead said, "I worry everything comes too easy for you."

"Too easy?" I hiccupped a laugh. "I've watched you like me a little less every day for three years. I've tried to excel at everything to make you proud and make you change your mind. Instead you hate me. Tell me how that's easy?"

Tears streamed down my mom's face; her shoulders shook with her effort not to break down and sob. Add this to the list of things that made me a terrible person: on the day after Christmas, I made my mom cry. I bolted down the stairs, and ran right into Dad.

"Kylie..."

Wiping my eyes, I grabbed my EarRing from the hall table, dodged him, and hurried out the door.

I understand if you don't want to keep reading. When I get to this point in the story, I hate me too.

48

Question, oh silent, unseen reader. How am I supposed to act? Because I don't know anymore. If I'm only sweet and endearing, you'll never respect me. If I take charge and am in control, you'll think me aggressive. If I embrace my sexy, I'm a skank. If I embrace my inner dork, I'm ostracized. If I'm wildly popular, it's the same.

Minus a couple of hiccups, I thought I'd been acing this teen-age stuff by me being me, but then I got *this* for it—see previous 209 pages—and everyone rejoiced.

So you tell me. How will me being me offend you the least?

A tap of my Doc and I was through the turnstile and on the train. And today I didn't care who Hey, Neighbor!-ed me. I was all-caps PISSED. So I ignored the golden rule about sending angry txts and didn't wait a twelve-hour period before letting my thoughts fly AnyLies's way. And the whole time I txted, all I could think of were those pics of Jessie in Istanbul. AnyLies or not, she got to traipse around Europe/Asia, probably filling suitcases with wonderful trinkets and fashions, spending time with her whole family. Meanwhile, my family's busy schedules meant half our conversations were over txt and most meals—even when we spent them speaking—were eaten at separate times and in separate rooms. Thanks to her private driver and elitist lack of presence online, Jessie could escape RL and her online worlds whenever she wanted. There was no escape for someone like me. Jessie had it made. And what was she doing? Moping.

I don't want to write what I said to AnyLies. Or admit that I sent a similarly nasty stream of txts to Jessie. It's too shameful. I will say that the first txt in the AnyLies series was:

moi   Hey, hater, FCK you.

I continued that I bet she was the kind of person who commented on her own posts with fake profiles so it looked like she had friends. I accused her of all the issues that might prompt someone to make a video like that in the first place—mommy issues, daddy issues, self-image issues, social issues. It went on and on, only becoming more juvenile and mean. I could feel her reading it. So I was as hurtful as possible.

Yeah. I know.

But wasn't this what everyone expected of me? Why keep trying to exceed my mom's expectations, when I could just live down to meet them? And no, I didn't feel *bad* about it. AnyLies took *me* on, remember? She'd *asked* for this.

Seventeen stops went by on the Q train as I txted her. When I looked up I was in Coney Island, two stops past where I was supposed to get off.

It was dark out when I left the Slope, but as I stood alone on a nearly empty Coney Island train platform, it felt like an entirely different kind of night. Like the it's-too-quiet scene in a zombie flick right before all the undead came pouring out. And it was freezing. The two previous warm days must have been a citywide hallucination. Because tonight there was no doubt it was winter. It was so cold my anger couldn't burn it off.

In my dramatic departure from home, I hadn't grabbed a coat. All I was wearing was a light wrap. As I made my way down to the street, I was shivering so badly, my EarRing kept popping off. Still, when I got to Brighton Beach Avenue, the sidewalks were littered with groups of loitering men. At first I felt relieved to see bodies, but five minutes into my walk, I quickened my pace and turned off automatic Translate, wishing it also shut off all the multilanguage catcalls I was receiving.

"Distance to destination?" I asked, as my EarRing told me to turn right.

"Twelve blocks," the GPS calmly responded as three guys in heavy parkas broke away from their street corner and started following me.

"Excuse me, miss," Camo Parka called. "You cold? You look cold."

I swiped into the 911 app on my Doc. My aching, frozen thumb hovered over the dial button. I was surrounded by stores, but at seven o'clock on a Sunday most of them were already shuttered. A train rumbled past on the elevated tracks overhead. GPS told me I had eight more blocks. This was karma. Mugged was what I got for being terrible. I walked faster. The parkas kept up. I remembered Mom saying that before EarRings, people used to look at their Docs to follow GPS. How before that, people didn't have GPS at all.

"What would they use?" Kyle had asked, taking the bait.

Winking at me, Mom had replied, "Actual. Paper. Maps."

"That's just stupid," Kyle had said, floored.

Let's talk about men for a minute. Normally, I didn't subscribe to the all-men-are-pigs theory because I had three men in my life who proved it very wrong. But men could act like cave dwellers with no repercussions, while I had a hater after me because, best I could piece together, I was conceited.

"Hi, gorgeous."

"Hey, beautiful."

These guys weren't like the stalker outside my house. They

didn't know me from the video. They were just jerks. How would they feel if they walked down the street and women aggressively solicited them? Didn't they go home to girlfriends, wives, mothers, daughters? Didn't they know those women in turn dealt with this shitey male attention?

"Five hundred feet until you have reached your destination," my Doc calmly said.

"Excuse me, miss, you lost? You need some help?"

"You need a boyfriend?"

"Turn right at 245 Ocean View Avenue. Turn right, now. Welcome. You are here."

What difference did the video make? As a female, I'd always be dealing with this sort of aggravation. For some reason, that thought calmed me down. But it didn't make me feel any safer as I faced the RingScreen of Mr. E.'s building. The parkas stopped a few paces away and lighted smokes. It was a Sunday, the day after Christmas. Mr. E. was Jewish, but he could still be gone for the holiday at a friend's or a girlfriend's. I could also picture him, staring at his screen in horror, quietly tapping deny.

"Come on, Mr. E.," I murmured, teeth chattering, as I pressed the button again.

"Don't worry. We'll keep you company."

"I'm okay, thanks," I said, pressing the button again, again.

The parkas laughed.

"You more than okay, sweetheart."

"Looks like your boyfriend no home. You want a new boyfriend?"

I'd had enough.

"What is wrong with you?" I whirled on them. "I still shop in the juniors' section at Macy's." (FYI, not really). "You should be looking out for me, not harassing me."

"Baby, I am looking out for you," Camo Parka said. "Or at least I'd like to."

As he came and leaned next to me, I held my finger down on the buzzer. Why hadn't I dragged one of the girls with me? Or Mac?

Or my brother? *Because Mr. E. wouldn't be honest if you weren't by yourself.* Cheap cologne filled my nostrils.

"I'll look out for myself, thanks."

ADMITTED, the RingScreen flashed. Next to it was a smiling photo of Mr. E. As relief swept over me, so did the acute knowledge that this was a horrible idea. As I pushed into the lobby, I heard Mac calling me naïve. Mr. E. actually might have made that video, meaning he wasn't like these parka guys. He kept his creep hidden.

And maybe that was worse.

Either way, I was about to enter his lair.

49

"'m guessing you're not here to give me a fruitcake, Ms. Cheng?" Mr. E. shouted.

He met me at his apartment door. I think he would have kept me out in the hall, only the thudding music coming from the apartment across the hall made conversation, let alone thought, impossible.

"Sorry, what?" I shouted back.

With the same expression of resignation he wore when he packed up his desk the morning the video dropped, Mr. E. reluctantly invited me inside.

We awkwardly negotiated space in the hall as he locked the door behind me. Mr. E. smelled stale, like cigarettes and alcohol and unwashed hair, and like something else that wasn't a scent as much as it was an aura. Mr. E. reeked of misery. I was also pretty sure he was drunk. I followed him into the living room. As a testament to shoddy building practices, the volume on the music across the hall only equaled one or two bars quieter. After scooping a pile of clothes off his ratty sofa, he gestured for me to sit.

The apartment probably listed as a one-bedroom, but the entire space wasn't much bigger than our kitchen. Mr. E.'s living room fit a couch and a coffee table with only an inch between them. A wood-paneled bar separated that space from a kitchenette that was about the same circumference as our living room screen. Dishes were stacked in the sink. Apparently, considering the takeout containers that were piled everywhere—kitchen counter, living room floor, cheapo bar—the appliances either didn't work or were never used.

Using his shoulder, he popped open a door off the hallway and tossed the clothes into an even tinier bedroom, onto an unmade single bed—a single bed! Then he grabbed a beer can off the fake-wood coffee table, rattled it side to side, and took a slug. An entire case of empty cans littered the apartment.

"Sorry to intrude, Mr. E.," I called as he retreated into the kitchen, "but I'd like to know why you told Dr. Graff the video was a fake."

"Because it is fake, Ms. Cheng," he shouted back in order to compete with the bass that was now making the apartment throb. "Or part of it is. I mean, what was I supposed to say?"

When I'd imagined Mr. E. outside of Prep, I'd pictured downloads straight from an e-mag. Hot, intelligent twentysomething females sidling up to him at fancy Manhattan cocktail bars and ubercool, little-known Brooklyn speakeasies. Thick eyeglasses, ratty beard, dingy apartment didn't compute. He was an adult. Get it together already.

Mr. E. picked up a sponge, sniffed it—winced—and lobbed it at the trash. It hit the floor with a wet thunk.

I was a stupid girl. This afternoon, I'd imagined us sitting at his fancy kitchen island—because who would want an apartment this far away from everything unless it was dope?—drinking espressos, syncing our Docs, and solving the SHT out of this mystery.

"Was it—you don't have to tell me who—but was it another student in the video?"

There was no denying that Mr. E. was a flirt. Glancing around his crappy apartment, I couldn't help thinking that the adoration Mr. E. received at school was probably the best thing he had going for him.

"I'd rather not discuss this with you."

Even above the loud beats, the shock in my voice was audible as I said, "Mr. E., with the exception of my face in it, I know the video is real. And since my best theory right now is that you're in some pervert-teachers' AV club, I'd very much like to know who knew it existed other than you. I know you're a victim in this too." *Or so I'm telling myself.* "Please help me."

Maybe we weren't going to Sherlock Holmes this together, but he couldn't refuse to help me. Mr. E. chucked his now-empty beer can at the garbage. It bounced off the wall and then rolled across the floor until it was resting against his foot. He hung his head.

"You know, I used to live in a cute two-bedroom close to the park? I mean, not the fancy side of the park, but *the park*. But my ex was on the lease, so she got to keep it. She was going to get a roommate, she said. Except somehow suddenly they're married."

Mr. E. shouted this last sentence into silence. The music across the hall was suddenly swiped off. He cricked his neck side to side.

"*Finally,*" he said, "Two hours that's been going on. I thought he died."

He shuffled to the sink and began to fill it with water.

"Anyway, yeah," he continued. "It was my first year teaching. She and I had only been together a few months. One night I brought home the wrong stack of tests to grade. We stopped at the school on our way to dinner. Park Prep was empty. She sat in one of those tiny desks and said she wanted to see me teach. . . . This is not appropriate to talk about."

He squeezed soap into the sink, apparently intending to let the dishes soak. I kept quiet. I didn't need to take AP Law to know that when a witness was freely divulging information, you let them talk.

"The whole thing was her idea. I didn't even know she'd hit

219

record on that stupid classroom hub until she showed me the video later that night. I was pissed. She swore she'd erased it from the school hub. I went in at, like, dawn the next day. She was telling the truth."

Mr. E. took a recycling bag from beneath the sink and began tossing takeout containers into it. He twisted the bag, tied it, and then took out another.

"We broke up a year later. It wasn't cordial. Maybe I accidentally smashed her windshield after a night of drinking. Maybe it was some punk from our—her—block. Whatever. Anyway, do you know about that site *My Ex Is an A-hole*?" I shook my head. "It's supposedly a women-only site. Women dump bad photos, stories, and videos of their exes on it. Guess what ended up there? Naturally, she airbrushed out her face."

He pushed his glasses up with the back of his wrist. "She titled the post 'Bad Teacher,' like we broke up because she caught me with a student. One of my friends from college saw it and played it for me. I got in touch with the website. But obviously it was too late."

Now with two filled bags of garbage next to him, he attacked the kitchen counter.

"Fast-forward two-plus years. On Tuesday afternoon when the fake video posted, Dr. Graff called me at home."

"Wait," I said. "Tuesday afternoon?"

Ignoring my confusion, Mr. E. kept talking. "I pretended I didn't know what she was talking about. I mean the video was obviously shot inside Park Prep. That right there goes against everything in the teacher handbook. Maybe if I acted like I didn't know about it, I wouldn't lose my job. Chalk it up to a spiteful ex.

"The next day, first thing, Graff called me into her office. When she said it was you in the video, I laughed, relieved. I thought it had to be a gag one of my students made. For a minute I thought maybe it was even you who'd made it."

"It definitely was not me."

"When I *truthfully*"—he paused in his scrubbing to jab a finger into the air—"told Graff I had no idea what she was talking about, she said she couldn't take the chance. Said I was suspended pending investigation. When I saw the video after it reposted first period, I didn't blame her. I mean, Kyla, I have no idea how they did it."

I thought of the *T minus* countdown txts I'd received all that morning.

"So when it appeared on the Student Activities board, it was a repost? The first time the video went up was actually the day before?"

Mr. E. nodded. "It popped up on the Faculty Activities board on the Park Prep website, right about when school was letting out."

"There's a *Faculty* Activities board?"

"Yeah, where teachers list, like, the readings or lectures they're giving. It gets loads of traffic." Mr. E. shook his head no. "For the record, if I'd known from the start that it was a doctored video, I would have come clean immediately. I swear. I've wanted to ever since, but Graff and Park Prep's legal counsel have 'strongly advised' me against speaking out. I think they're afraid I'll make everything worse."

"Does the original video still exist?"

"NYPD has been searching the *My Ex Is an A-hole* website. Unfortunately, no luck."

"The police are in on this?"

"You're telling me you haven't spoken to them? Maybe your parents ran interference." Mr. E. wrung out the sponge. "I mean, Ms. Cheng, I'm a teacher. You're seventeen. What do you think? Of course the police are involved."

221

I t was time for me to go.

It was *past* time for me to go. Only, there were just a few more things. . . .

"So who posted the first video?" I asked. "The one that cropped up on the Faculty Activities board?"

Mr. E. sighed, like, *What does it matter?*

"Somebody with the number six-six-six. Like 'six-six-six and gone.' I don't remember what Dr. Graff said. But it didn't seem like a name that Mardi—my ex—would come up with."

"So not AnyLiesUnmade?"

"No, though that does sound like a name Mardi would come up with. I called her the moment I got pinged by the reposted video. She didn't answer. But she txted back." He scrolled through his Doc, read: "'Eric. That's awful. Wasn't me.' She signed it with a frowny face. 'Hey, your life is destroyed, frowny face.' The police have been trying to get in touch with her, too."

"When was the last time you spoke before all this?"

"Over a year? Year and a half? Honestly, with Woofer, I've been waiting for this video to come back and haunt me. When I first saw the clip with your face put on hers, it was like my worst nightmare had come true. I'd been worried people would think the woman in the video was one of my students. But I didn't think someone would change it so it actually *was* one of my students. So why *you*, Ms. Cheng?"

"I came here hoping you'd tell me," I said, unable to hide my exasperation. "Mr. E., you teach—taught—effects. Did Jessie Rosenthal ever take that class with you?"

He nodded. "Kicking and screaming she did. She needed to pad out her art track."

"Did she or anyone else ever use your personal Doc? Or do you have access to software that could—"

"Ms. Cheng, as technologically forward-thinking and endowed as Park Prep is, there's no way that video came out of one of our classrooms. And Jessie . . . let's just say Jessie was not one of my more gifted students."

"Why doesn't that surprise me? Does that mean you gave her a bad grade?"

"I gave her a fair grade, though I'm not sure she saw it that way. Still, just based on skill set alone, I can't see her pulling off something like this. What about your friend Ms. Rhodes?"

I wasn't expecting him to say *that*. Flustered, I said, "Audra doesn't have a motive."

"No? A while back, she stopped me after class asking detailed questions about DRMs. She was very . . . intense. Wanted to make sure there was no way a third party could download them; wanted to know how she could maintain all rights."

You should be thanking whoever posted that video.

"It is high school, after all," he continued. "Sometimes there are no motives other than pure, genuine meanness."

"It's not Audra." Only I was allowed to pin it on my best friend, not him. "The file's not on her Doc."

"Could be on an alternate drive or—"

"Mr. E.," I interrupted. "Can I connect with you? If I can compare our CB Connections lists, I might find a link."

He shook his head. "No way. That's all the police need to see after everything that's happened, that we're 'connected.' I'm sorry, but my privacy's been invaded enough. Besides, I'm in the process of erasing myself."

"You mean you're erasing your CB account?"

Only paranoid tech-phobes erased themselves. It equaled insane. First because it meant deleting all your profiles. And everything was attached to your profiles: buying just about anything, bill paying, credit cards, air miles. But it also meant a complete name change and then never being online in any significant social way again. Since CB owned half the social apps out there, it was only a matter of time before old Woofer pics just reattached to you. Erasing yourself also basically labeled you a miscreant. Imagine going on a job interview and having no online history for your prospective employers to look at. Who wouldn't wonder what you were covering up?

But it was true. I swiped to his G-File. Other than the sex-video links there was nothing about him.

"Mr. E., this equals way over-the-top."

He shrugged. "I don't have enough money to indefinitely get my face Pulled and have my G-File swept. So I'm starting fresh. Bartending got me through college. It can get me through this. It pays better anyway."

"But you're such a good teacher."

"Trust me, Ms. Cheng." He laughed, like he had a thousand bitter one-liners he'd like to make. "If there's one thing a teacher's career can't rebound from, it's a sex scandal. And now, if you don't mind, I believe I'll get back to the self-pity you found me wallowing in."

I told Mr. E. about the parkas who'd followed me on my way here. Begrudgingly, he said he'd walk me out. He took the recycling bags with him. Fawn would have insisted he walk her to the train. But frankly, I was as ready to be out of his company as he was to be out of mine. We walked to the trash cans in front of the building. The sidewalk, the entire block, was deserted, proving that the only thing creepier than a block full of sketchy men was a sketchy block completely devoid of anyone.

Across the street, a yellow Hydrogen Coop was parked behind a battered pickup truck. It looked way too new and way too ecologically conscious to be in this neighborhood. (No offense, Mr. E.'s crummy block.)

Watching Mr. E. morosely throw away the recycling, I couldn't imagine what I used to find attractive about him. I'd never give up this easily. The president would never give up this easily. My mom would never give up this easily. Grow some breasts already and woman up. When our eyes met, he flinched at the pity in mine. Shrugging, as if to say, *Add your disappointment to the list,* he held his hand out to me.

"Looks all clear," he said. "Good luck with your investigation, Ms. Cheng."

"You know, there's another video out there like mine. What if this is a thing?"

He shrugged. "The end result is the same for me."

"I'll let you know what I find out anyway."

"To be honest, Kyla, I wish you luck and everything, but I hope I don't hear from you again anytime soon."

51

After a heart-pounding run, I made it to the correct train station in a quarter of the time it took me before and hopped on just as the doors were closing. Half of the train was packed with post-holiday revelers returning home from family visits. The other half was completely empty thanks to a sleeping homeless man who wasn't wearing shoes.

It was so cold outside it hurt the insides of my nose to breathe. Mr. E. had lost his job and was facing criminal prosecution. In comparison to these two men's lives, mine was easy. The only thing truly wrong with it was that I had a wobbly relationship with my mom. But at the end of the day, it was like Dad said: she was stuck with me. And, sure, I had a trending video that I might never be able to come out from under, but I'd still have opportunities and friends and, like, basic shelter.

Overhelmed by gratefulness, I sank into a seat on the empty side of the train and swiped into the message screen on my Doc.

I owed so many people apologies I didn't know where to start.

I txted AnyLies.

moi I'm sorry.

I had a huge fight with my mom and I was angry.

I shouldn't have lashed out at you.

Fine. It was strange that I was apologizing first to the person who'd roadblocked my future, but, well, like *that* was the weirdest part of my week? I'd been mean and when you're mean you're supposed to apologize. And apologizing to AnyLies was a whole lot easier than apologizing to my mom or Audra or Mac. As usual, AnyLies wrote back immediately.

😈 What was the fight about?

moi Oh, that my mom doesn't like me, I'm a brat, the usual stuff.

😈 At least your mom knows you exist.

I'd been txting AnyLies with abandon, hoping it would humanize me and guilt her into taking down the video. But now she was opening up to me. I felt all the pressure of a parent whose misunderstood teen approached them to talk about, like, taking drugs.

Be cool. Don't say the wrong thing.

I wrote a few responses. Deleted them.

Finally I went with:

moi Have you tried to talk to her about it?

I chewed on my hair, waiting for her reply. AnyLies took her time responding, like she, too, was searching for the correct response.

😈 No. It's fine. You wouldn't understand.

Wrong. I got it wrong.

 No sweat for you either way, huh? Bonding time is
over. You should have apologized sooner.

I hurriedly replied.

moi Listen, I just spoke with my teacher—the one in the
video—the police are after him. He's ERASING himself.
This is getting serious. Forget about me. This is hurting
people. It's time to take down the video.

A couple got on the train wearing matching reindeer hats.
When they saw the homeless man, they veered sharply toward
the crowded side. It was then I noticed the exceedingly thin figure cloaked all in black at the opposite end of the train, txting.
She wore a fancy velvet coat with a black mantle of fur around
the hood. Black leather gloves. Heels. A scarf wrapped the lower
half of her face, and while, granted, it was cold outside, the train
was warm. I couldn't see what her device was, but it definitely
wasn't a PHD.
"Jessie?" I called out.
Then, just to be safe, I sent a txt.

moi Jessie? Is that you? Will you at least respond to me?

The figure stiffened. I stood up. My Doc screamed with its
AnyLies txt sound. The homeless man mumbled in his sleep. We
were coming into the station. Keeping her head down, the black-
clad figure stood and hurried off the train. I debated following
her, but another romp in the freezing dark with only a light wrap
on was not on my list of priorities. Besides, this was Brooklyn; it
wasn't like there was a lack of emaciated women who wore black.
And, I reminded myself, Jessie is in Turkey. Sighing, I watched

the figure whisk away, casting a quick glance over her shoulder as she went.

Only once the train pulled out of the station did I glance at my Doc.

😈 I made you something tonight. Call it a belated Christmas gift. I hope you like it.

"Oh, that's just terrific," I said out loud.

Nobody even looked up. I was just another crazy person talking to herself on the train. Now what did I have to look forward to?

moi I'm guessing it's not a tin of cookies.

Before getting off the train, I airdropped ten bucks to the sleeping man's Cred-It Card, which came up on my Doc as *Pleese Help, Gary*. Just as my Doc screamed again.

😈 And for the record, I say when it's time to take the video down.

Not if I find you first, betch, I thought.

52

MONDAY, DECEMBER 27

"Frankly, Kyle. It's incriminating."

"No, it *looks* incriminating," I said.

With only five days until college admissions deadlines (and, no, I hadn't contacted a single admissions office), I didn't make it to the Walk. As if she were our fifth member, Dr. Graff met me at the front entrance. Would I be so kind as to speak with her in her office? Usually Graff messaged your school tablet if she wanted to see you. Her in person? Not good. Fawn had been about to come out and meet me; instead she let the boy next to her keep talking. My Doc dinged.

fawnal Will wait here.

Audra's avat had been red all morning. She hadn't contributed at all to our group thread since Christmas Eve. The only personal txt I'd received from her since yesterday had come only moments before. *Busy* was all it said. I assumed that meant she wasn't coming in. This was the third day in a row I hadn't seen or spoken to her. At least she'd sent around her theme last night: Like a Virgin.

In honor of me, I supposed.

At the moment, I couldn't be more grateful for it, because as Dr. Graff scrolled through the pics of me and Mr. E. standing out in front of his building last night, my one consolation was my knee-length skirt and fitted blazer. It was almost like Audra had known I'd be sitting here.

"Clearly, there's no denying you were at Mr. Ehrenreich's apartment building yesterday."

Nope, no denying it. Especially not with Dr. Graff flicking through the photos that AnyLies had posted on the Student Activities board. There was Mr. E. leading me into his building by my hand. There was Mr. E. gesturing as if we were having a lovers' quarrel. Never mind that I was leaving, not entering, the building. Never mind that we weren't holding hands, we were shaking them, and that he'd only walked me outside to make sure I was safe. Never mind that he was telling me he hoped he never saw me again.

"And I don't even know what to make of this video."

It was the video someone had recorded from the blank FaceAlert window on my room screen the first night after the Mr. E. video posted. Now it was linked to the photos as a related video on YurTube. The whole world could see me with my hair in a topknot, my retainer in, telling myself I could fix this, that it would all be okay. I sounded all-caps GUILTY, like the caller had caught me as I was flicking through the photos in the middle of a huge freak-out. Then my terrified face when I realized they were recording me. And, fine, normally I might have laughed at the almost-fell-over part, if the video had been of anyone else but me.

The video still exists. You can search it. Last time I checked it had 350,000 views. The pics-vid combo was my belated Christmas gift from AnyLies. She'd titled everything "Kisses."

My Doc and profile were blowing up again. The whole school felt as buzzy as on the day the video dropped. At least I knew one thing: AnyLies drove a yellow Hydrogen Coop. And I guess if AnyLies was in the car, that couldn't have been Jessie on the train. Though it couldn't have been Jessie in either place. She was in Istanbul, right?

Dr. Graff took a decorative pen from a holder on her desk and clicked it, unblinkingly waiting for my response.

"Mr. E. and I were brainstorming who might have done this to us," I said.

Or at least I was. Mr. E. was mainly cleaning and acting like a disgruntled child, but I didn't think telling Dr. Graff that would help my case any.

"Kyle." Dr. Graff frowned. "As noble as your reasons were for being there, you must see how much more indelicate this makes an already extremely indelicate situation. I feel that we are working against each other. We need to be on the same side."

"I'm sorry to disagree, Dr. Graff," I said carefully. "But in my view, the most unseemly thing is that I am repeatedly being bullied literally, or well, virtually, on the boards of my school, and my school is doing nothing about it. Why are these pics even still posted?" I cleared my throat. "Doctor...Ma'am."

Dr. Graff flicked the holoscreen away and kept clicking the pen.

"Yes, about that," she said. "I conferred with the head of the board of trustees this morning. He spoke with the other board members and they all think it would be in the best interests of everyone involved if you were to stay home from school for the rest of the week. You can restart fresh in the new year. By then things should have calmed down."

She said it so gently that the words took a click to sink in. When they did, I blurted out, "You're suspending me?"

Never mind my perfect attendance. My whole Park Prep career would be negated. A suspension would go on my record. Every college would see it. Plus, it quite simply *was not warranted*.

Graff cleared her throat. "It's not a suspension, per se, as much as a small leave of absence. Mr. Rosenthal and the rest believe a little time away from school will lessen the disruption this incident is causing—"

232

"Mr. *Rosenthal*? As in Jessie's dad? Dr. Graff, I'm not entirely sure it isn't Jessie who's masterminding this whole thing. And now her father wants me suspended?"

"Jessie's father is the head of a multibillion-dollar company. I'm sure he has more important things to do than involve himself with his daughter's school rivalries or take down one of her classmates."

My eyes grew wide. Only through a strong sense of self-preservation did I stop myself from blurting out, *Can you hear yourself right now?* I mean, when had a multibillion-dollar company ever cheated? Only all-caps ALL THE TIME. Park Prep always claimed it prepared you for the real world. Welcome to it, Kyla.

"Besides, between you and me, he has already spoken to Jessie about the flash-mob gag in the hallway and the video of your tiff with Ms. Cyr."

"He did? What did Jessie say?"

Graff puckered her lips. "She said she had nothing to do with either of those things."

I threw up my hands. "Except they posted from @JessieRosenthal! Dr. Graff, can we conference her right now and clear up this whole situation? I wouldn't have to go anywhere."

"Kyle," Dr. Graff sighed. "The Rosenthals are in Europe through the new year, *on vacation*. He sent these missives through one of his assistants. Now please, let's shift your focus a bit. A lot of parents in the community are very upset. Many are questioning the integrity of the school. Some have threatened to pull their children out and place them in institutions of what one father called 'higher moral standing.' While I don't necessarily agree with the board's decision, I do see how it calms the greatest number of people. And it is a final decision."

"Meaning I have no choice."

Instead of figuring out who did this to me, Parkside Prep was going to remove me and hope this all went away so that they wouldn't lose enrollment.

"My mom is going to be very upset when she hears about this."

It was clear from the set of her features that Graff didn't like this any better than I did. It was also clear that she was going to enforce it.

"I haven't said you're expelled." The *yet* went unsaid, but we both heard it. "What we're mainly discussing here, Kyla, is a few sick days. Might I remind you that when you enrolled at Parkside Preparatory, you signed an honor code?" The holoimage of it now hovered in the air in front of me. "And I quote, 'I, Kyla Cheng, affirm that I will uphold the highest principles of honesty and integrity in my endeavors at Parkside Preparatory.'"

"Which is exactly what I'm trying to do."

"I see," she said. "On a related note, the attendance and security sensor wasn't solely installed to extend class time by eliminating homeroom. It was meant to allow our faculty and funds a higher focus than babysitting the student body. Don't think it makes us naïve. If I catch you or any of your friends using another unapproved pass, the suspension won't be a suggestion, Ms. Cheng."

So if I didn't go quietly, they'd find a way to force me to stay out of school. Dr. Graff, infamous for her stare, now wouldn't meet my eyes.

"I leave it up to you, Ms. Cheng—a week of sickness or one of suspension? You may finish out your day here and then message me this afternoon with your decision. That will be all."

53

Out in the hall, people flowed around me in one big dinging, buzzing, swiping, avat-voice-messaging Monday morning mass. All the Christian-affiliated were harassing the Jewish- and Muslim- and otherwise-affiliated with pics of favorite Christmas gift items, meals they ate, things they had to return. Disruption? Considering the wide swath everyone cut around me, the only life not carrying on as usual was mine.

"What did Graff say?"

Fawn. I dropped my bag and put my head on her shoulder. Her curls tickled my cheek.

"Ooh, loving. Gimme it," Fawn said, wrapping me in a hug. "You okay, mama?"

Before I could answer, Sharma ran up. It looked like she'd pulled an all-nighter. Her hair was in the exact same topknot she'd worn yesterday when she came over for pancakes, but now it was surrounded by a thousand breakaway frizzes.

"Four," she said, grinning like the time her code had worked for unlimited credits in the *Apocalypsa Fashionista* game on her Doc. "Four girls."

235

"Sharma, full sentences," Fawn said.

"Other girls who suffered similar life crashes at the hands of a hater? Answer: Y-E-S. Four. From all over the US: Kansas City girl caught with teach in gym after hours. Cali girl making out with teach in a bar. Florida girl with teach skinny-dipping. Michigan girl and teach, um, cavorting in snowstorm. Plus Trina and you, so six in total. Sent you all the students' and teachers' names. And, wincing face, haven't told you the weirdest part. Kyle, all the girls look just like you."

Stunned was starting to feel like my permanent state of being.

"There's more," Sharma sputtered. "Hope you don't mind, but reached out to the new four last night using your CB account. They responded quick. Swore it wasn't them. Two know the exact Woofer footage the hater used to make their vid. Other two will try finding it today."

"What about all the teachers' CB accounts?"

Sharma shook her head. "All suspended or deleted."

"Can you access deleted accounts?" I asked.

"Not easily." That was the closest Sharma would come to saying no. "Not that it matters—ConnectBook security is so tight, you can't even run a mutual-connections filter on multiple accounts."

"Know anyone that can?" I asked.

Sharma pushed up her glasses. "Other than ConnectBook?"

We grinned at each other.

It wasn't just me and Trina. There were other girls who had suffered through this. And despite what everyone said, there might be a way to crack it. I could glimpse a future in which searching my mom's company didn't bring up her daughter's sex video. A future in which I didn't have to precede job applications with *As I'm sure you've noticed*... Where I could make a difference, and not in spite of what happened to me.

Fawn looked back and forth between us.

"Wait," she said, breathless. "Why are we smiling? You lost me at six total sex videos."

Giddily, I quickly explained. "So far—thanks to Sharma—we know that half of the footage that was used to make these fake sex videos was stolen from Woofer. In order to access Woofer footage, you first have to have a CB account and second have to be 'connected' to the person in the footage. Which means, as we speak, the hater is somewhere in here"—I wiggled my Doc—"as one of my CB connections. If we get CB's help to compare multiple accounts and possibly access the deleted teachers' info..."

"We can weed out your hater," Sharma finished.

"Oh my God, my friends are so brilliant," Fawn squealed, and threw her arms around us.

"Do you know if any of the other girls are txting the hater?"

"Uh, no." Sharma eyes narrowed with displeasure. "They didn't mention it. Why? Are you?"

"No, of course not," I lied.

"So what are you going to message ConnectBook?" Fawn asked as roles reversed and for the first time ever I avoided Sharma's gaze.

"I'm not going to message them. I'm paying them a visit."

"Like in person?" Sharma said, glasses sliding down her nose.

"People do still do things face-to-face, Sharmie. Let them try and not help me."

54

Maybe it was egotistical (I mean, surprise, surprise), but right from the start I'd assumed this was about something I'd done. It had to be, as what stranger would ever hold this big a grudge? But knowing there were five other victims changed everything. What was it AnyLies had originally told me? That she "despised me from afar." Maybe Graff was right. I needed to shift my focus. This whole time I'd been assuming I was dealing with someone I encountered physically on a daily basis—Jessie, Ailey, Ellie, or (sorry, pookie) Audra—because our txts felt personal. Not like some random girl in Duluth hated me, but like someone very near to me in Brooklyn did. But what did distance matter anymore?

Why couldn't it be someone I'd pissed off online? I was a regular commenter on at least half a dozen political sites. And, I mean, what was more divisive than politics? Although, come to think of it, that answer equaled commenting online *at all*. Period. I left reviews on every book I ever read, and let's be honest, it wasn't due to "this generation's lack of attention span" that I rarely got through half of them. I was an avid poster on all things nightcore and possibly one of the only fans of Snap

Cinco, a group of tiny Guatemalan girls who thought they were fly as SHT and everyone loved to hate on. I left honest (negative) reviews for shirts I bought and returned, bad food or service at restaurants I would never set foot in again, and a whole thread of angry missives on the *Unicorn Wars* feed when they tried to swap out a main actress for an entirely different actress without even a minor acknowledgment in the dialogue.

I mean, how hard would a *You don't seem like yourself today, Starborn* have been?

Never mind that Mac had me listed as his Main Squeeze on ConnectBook and Mac had over a thousand connects, half of whom I'm sure would have loved to see me choke on my breakfast. Actually, mental note, that wasn't a bad investigative thread to follow.

As the girls went to class, I went in the opposite direction and rushed up Ankle Breaker straight to three.

The main entrance security sensor had already marked me present, so I wasn't worried about ruining my attendance record. But if Graff caught me sneaking out, there wouldn't be a choice between sick or suspended. Especially after I'd received her don't-mess-with-the-security-sensor lecture less than ten minutes ago. I could think of only one salvation.

"Kyle!" Ms. Tompkins said when I barged into the library. "Did you hear Brittany got puked on at the holiday party?"

"What? No!"

Ms. Tompkins was sitting behind a narrow counter next to a few measly shelves of fiction, one window, and two computers. Park Prep could at least try to keep her relevant. She shoved out a stool next to her.

"Yep," she said. "In like the first ten minutes. Mrs. Claus was forced to make a quick exit. After that only Santa circulated."

"That's so *not* terrible. Did everyone else have a good time?"

"You should have seen all the moms' faces when they unwrapped the Docs. It was the best party yet, minus one of the most important elements. How you holding up?"

"I'm good," I said. "In fact, I'm about to go to the ConnectBook offices to figure out who's hating on me. The only thing is . . ."

Without a click of hesitation, Ms. Tompkins swiped at her Doc. "You'd probably need an off-grounds pass for that, wouldn't you?"

Off-grounds passes were something Dr. Graff created. Considering our location in Brooklyn and our proximity to Manhattan, she thought a Park Prep senior could, on occasion, be better educated outside the mansion's walls than within them—be it at a gallery opening, a ballet performance, a lecture. All we needed was parent and faculty permission.

As Ms. Tompkins swiped to the correct screen, I txted Mac. Regardless of how we defined ourselves, he was the first and only person who came to mind. I didn't want to be around anyone else for this.

moi   Feel like an off-grounds field trip? Hater within reach.

At the end of the day, Mac was still the person I trusted the most. Ironic, considering I'd always thought the biggest reasons I had for not dating him involved lack of trust.

mac   Just off train. Nothing sounds better.

Perfect. Today his lateness worked in my favor.

moi   You'll get detention for skipping.

mac   What's one more?

We agreed to meet at my house because WhereYouAt couldn't find you if you left your Doc at home. My bulky school tablet blipped. On-screen, a bar-coded note said Ms. Tompkins had excused me from all my morning and afternoon classes to do research on

Internet safety and protection at the ConnectBook offices. I txted a copy to my Dad. He immediately responded with his e-signature.

"You have no idea how much this means to me," I said.

"Happy to be of use." She winked.

"Hey, Ms. Tompkins." I turned back at the door. "You and Mr. E. never dated, did you?"

"Nope." She stuck out her tongue, making a *gross* face. "Just friends. I have a girlfriend. And hey, Kyle, when you do figure out who did this to you, let me know. I intend to level some serious overdue fines on them."

55

Without our Docs, Mac and I got turned around getting off the train in the city and walked east instead of west. Mac thought being Doc-free was fun. I felt like I was missing my central nervous system. I had no idea what time it was. I didn't understand a word anyone was saying if it wasn't in English. And there were at least three shirts I saw in window displays that I couldn't add to my Watch List. Not to mention, I hadn't told anyone what I was thinking in at least forty minutes. In lieu of this, I kept audio txting Mac all my observations.

"Txt Mac: It's too quiet."

A bus stopped beside us. Across the street a cabbie laid on his horn. But there was no dinging, buzzing, or alerts. My hand kept reaching into my bag, coming up empty.

"You're like a malfunctioning windup toy." Mac laughed. "Whose messages are you afraid you're missing, anyway? The girls will still be there an hour from now."

"It's not them."

"Found yourself an unskanky novio already?" He tried to keep his voice light.

As if *I* were the one who would immediately date other people.

"Nooo." I linked arms with him. "I got into a txt argument with AnyLies last night and I still haven't heard from her today."

"Wait. Please tell me, por favor, that you haven't been txting your hater."

"I keep thinking if she knows me well enough, she'll take down the video."

I didn't tell Mac it was up to about five hundred txts a day, that I found her constancy comforting. That I'd been kind of crutching on her like she was an Audra replacement. I mean, I'm pretty; I'm not stupid. I knew how crazy it would sound.

"Kyla, that sounds incredibly..."

"Dumb, I know."

"I was going to say dangerous. You have no idea who this person is. You think it's a she? What if it's some fifty-year-old pedophile you're sharing your secrets with? You remember this is all their fault, sí?"

"Of course."

Though what if some of it was mine, too?

"Promise me you won't txt them anymore."

Mac took his arm away from me and turned me so I was looking at him.

"Sure, okay. Promise. Look, Macky. I think we're here."

The ConnectBook headquarters looked like an oasis on the High Line. As opposed to all the red and gray brick buildings around it, the CB offices were entirely fitted with reflective solar-paneled windows that were a rainbow assortment of shiny blues, greens, and pinks. Just visible from the ground were the long grasses that made up the roof garden and the building's huge water-filtration system. When it was first built, the ConnectBook HQ was lauded, and then deplored, by the energy companies for being the first building in Manhattan that functioned entirely off the grid.

Coming in and out of the building were people walking their dogs, toting their bikes and skateboards, and otherwise enjoying this sunny, brisk late-December day. It felt more like a college campus than the headquarters of one of the most influential companies in the world.

"This isn't David versus Goliath," I muttered. "It's David versus all the geek gods inside one giant Cronus."

"Geek gods. Good one." Mac stared up at the building in awe. "Don't forget. David won."

We didn't get past reception.

There were two receptionists—one male and one female—who sat in plush chairs behind an empty glass table. I nudged Mac toward the male receptionist because he gave us a bright smile when we entered while the female receptionist kept staring straight ahead, her eyeballs moving in minute flicks. Every few clicks, she said, "Hello, ConnectBook. How may I connect you? One moment." Even though we heard no ringing.

"Hi there," the male receptionist said when we approached. "Welcome to ConnectBook. How may I help you?"

"Hi there," I said. "Someone's posted malicious content about me. I was hoping I could talk to a tech."

"All right, I see you're having a malicious content problem. If you go to your ConnectBook account and click *Flag Post*, ConnectBook security will investigate the complaint."

If I'd had my Doc, I'd have txted *Creepy* to Mac. Instead I tried to convey the emotion with my eyes and mouth. Mac raised an eyebrow, like, *huh?* Behind us, the front doors slid open. A kid in a slate-colored hoodie, not much taller than Audra, wandered in and waited for an elevator. Did they have day care here, too?

"Oh, it's not one post, it's like hundreds of thousands, but the thing I need help with is—"

"I understand. If you go to your account and click *Flag Links*, ConnectBook security will investigate the complaint. But what I am hearing you say, ma'am, is that there are many links you'd like removed, and I should remind you that as a ConnectBook user, you have signed a terms-of-service agreement that allows all ConnectBook information to be public. You can find this information right online under your *My Account Info*."

My eyes flicked to Mac, and under my breath I said, "Txt Mac: Bot?"

Mac's mouth was slightly agape, his eyes glued to the receptionist. "Not sure."

I glanced longingly at the bank of elevators behind us. I imagined grabbing that kid—who'd put his hood up and was clearly eavesdropping—as a hostage, making a mad dash for any upwards locale and cornering the first tech person we saw.

"But we're here and I don't want to wait for"—I didn't mean to mimic a robot when I said it, but I did—"ConnectBook security to launch an investigation. I don't want you guys to remove any links. I was hoping to speak with someone about accessing closed user accounts so I could remove the links myself."

The smile didn't leave the receptionist's lips, but it tightened. Thank goodness. He *was* human.

"Yeah," Mac said.

"Please," I added, to make up for using the robot voice.

The female receptionist tapped a tiny square piece of metal next to her eye, then spoke directly to me. Mac and I jumped.

"What I am hearing you say is that you would like to access another user's private account information. At ConnectBook we take the privacy of our users very seriously. Account tampering is a serious offense. May I have your username, please?"

"But he just said all ConnectBook information was public—"

"Posts are public and protected by freedom of speech. Identities are private and protected by CB. May I have your username, please?"

The smile now genuinely widened on the male receptionist's boyish features.

"No. Why do you need my username? I'm not trying to account tamper. I'm not even online right now. But I'm pretty sure someone has accessed ConnectBook Woofer footage of me and other girls my age and then turned that footage into fake and highly damaging videos of us doing *stuff* with our teachers. If a user is allowed to do that within CB's guidelines, I should be able to find out who that user is."

The female receptionist tapped the metal square again and resumed staring at her retina screen. "Hello, ConnectBook," she said. "How may I connect you? One moment."

I didn't want to sound like Mom or anything, but cutting-edge tech was getting weird. The kid in the slate hoodie now stood a few feet behind us. He was even leaning in to hear us better.

"This is garbage," Mac said.

"If you have a complaint about the service you received today"—this now from the smiling male receptionist—"you can put it in writing and mail it to our customer service division. You can find the address online under our contact information. Is there anything else I can help you with?"

"But you haven't helped me. You're telling me—ConnectBook is telling me—*to write a letter*?"

"That's correct. Thank you for contacting ConnectBook. Have a connected New Year."

It wasn't supposed to go this way. I wasn't supposed to be stopped at the gates by a tooth-model clone with an unhelpful script. Next to me I could feel Mac tense, like he was ready to coil up and spring on the guy. Grabbing the crook of his arm, I pulled him toward the exit. The doors didn't automatically slide apart.

I jammed my finger against the manual door-open button. When that didn't work, Mac pressed the button again and again.

"I think those are supposed to work on a push-once basis."

The kid in the hoodie was hovering behind us, except he wasn't a kid. He was just short. And extremely pale. He looked like he'd been kept in a closet his whole life.

"Doors used to work that way too," Mac said.

The glass panels parted and let us out. Sunlight. Air. I took a deep breath and glanced back. The building didn't look like an oasis now; it looked like a madhouse. And it didn't help that the shrimpy guy in the sweatshirt was following annoyingly close on our heels.

I whispered. "Txt Mac: We've got company."

"Txt Kyla: I know," Mac said. "Also, I'm right here."

Mac abruptly stopped walking. The little guy plowed into him.

"Dude," Mac said. "What is your deal?"

"I'm Rory, senior ConnectBook programmer."

"And?" I asked.

"*And?* I'm the guy who's gonna help you get your life back." He grinned and pumped a fist in the air. "Man, I've always wanted to say something like that."

57

Five minutes later, the three of us were sitting at a café right around the corner from Headquarters, as Rory called it. Hood up, Rory sat with his back to the café and spoke so softly, Mac and I had to lean halfway across the table to hear him whisper, "I heard your dilemma."

"Shhh," the woman at the table next to us said.

Was there ever a time when coffee shops weren't dens of silence? This café didn't even play music.

Even softer, Rory continued, "What it sounds like is some hater has made a series of nasty DRMs using footage they swiped from CB's Woofer and you're trying to find links between all the subjects hoping they connect back to the maker B-U-T you need someone on the inside's access because half the accounts are closed re nasty DRMs."

"You got all of that from my conversation with the receptionists?"

"I filled in some blanks. So now what I need to kick the SHT out of the person doing this to you are the names of the other victims. Then it's just a simple logarithm that scans multiple accounts and connected lists along with any other related overlaps, i.e., if all those bad teachers were in some dirty CB closed group together."

I reached for my Doc but only patted empty pockets. Mac jokingly mirrored my stressed-out expression back at me.

"I don't have the names with me, but off the top of my head I remember Trina Davis. And another of the girl's names was... Natalie Wong. And, well, Mr. E.—Eric Ehrenreich, though I think he deleted his account, so you might need, like, special access."

"Darlin', *I am* special access."

As Rory spoke, he swiped at his Doc and murmured commands. Pushing his blue-framed glasses up on his forehead, he took out a wired pair from an inside pocket of his hoodie. With all the nodding, swiping, and twitching it was like someone had his head on a puppet string. I missed my Doc even more.

"Txt Mac: It's like he's possessed," I murmured.

I'd only ever seen one person this adept at their gadgetry.

"Txt Kyla: Stop weirdly trying to audio txt me, you addict," Mac whispered back, and then, reading my mind, said, "And, no, it's like he's Sharma."

"I can hear you," Rory said. "People in cafés down the block can hear you. Where are your Docs, B-T-W?"

"We left them in Brooklyn," I said.

"You *left* them in *Brooklyn*?" Rory shuddered.

Being called out on what a terrible idea it was made my stomach feel even queasier. Before I could protest that we were trying to avoid being WhereYouAt-ed, which I already knew Rory would not accept as an excuse, Mac said, "Why don't you just wear those NanoContacts? You wouldn't need all this gear."

"They give me a headache. And call me old-fashioned: I like the gear."

Nobody would ever call Rory old-fashioned. All the gadgetry he was flicking and switching between could buy a family of four a luxury sedan. The woman at the table next to us got up with a loud tsk and moved farther away. I didn't see what it mattered when both her ears were plugged with buds. I mean, if you want to work without distractions, maybe stay in your office.

"How long you been working for the evil empire?" Mac asked.

"Evil empire? I don't have to pay a wired bill ever. Why sit in coach if you can fly first class? I've been with CB ever since I flunked out of college."

"No mames." Mac laughed. "Kid genius flunked out of college?"

"I only enrolled to get scouted. I never intended to graduate."

"Why not just send CB your résumé?" I asked.

"Flunking out sounds cooler." Rory's eyes flicked to Mac.

The boys shared a smile, like they were members of the same rabble-rousers' club.

"Let me ask you," Mac said, after they'd knocked fists. "You get all the perks, how come I bought your coffee?"

"Because I'm the guy who's going to fix your girlfriend's life."

Both Mac's eyebrows went up. *Girlfriend.* I took a huge slug of coffee so Mac wouldn't see me smile. I wasn't about to correct Rory that we were only friends. Let him think what he wanted.

"We're just friends," Mac said.

Rolling my eyes, I said, "If I get you the students' and teachers' names by tonight, how long do you think this will take?"

"What do you mean how long will it take?" Rory sat back and cracked his knuckles. "All I had to do was a quick search of suspended or terminated accounts—which, I mean, are a pretty rare thing—taking into account age and date of account suspensions. Throw a little profession filter on it. Then a quick survey of flagged posts—everyone always flags the posts—bada bing, bada boom, and voilà. We have the teachers.

"Then it gets a little more complicated. I won't bore you with the details—gender filter, school-type filter, recently clenched up on privacy settings, blah blah blah—and voilà! The students. I mean, it's not called waiting with my thumb up my A-S-S. It's called *hacking*. And it's done."

58

"That's what I'm talking about," Mac whooped, reaching across the table to knuckle Rory's head.

The barista held a finger to his lips and loudly shushed us. Rory tried, but failed, to act offended by Mac's affection and barely suppressed a grin when Mac said, "This little dude is killer. So dímelo, Killer, what'd you find?"

"To begin with, there are eighty-two matches between all twelve of your accounts."

He hit a switch on his Doc. The white café table was now illuminated with the eighty-two matching connections he'd found between mine and the other eleven harassed teachers and students' accounts.

"You can rule the famous connections out right off the bat. That takes away thirty. Good-bye, Madam President. Also, these users."

With a swipe of his fingers, the pics on the table diminished by ten.

"Why?" I asked.

"Elderly Asians and Indians? No offense, but your criminal is not going to be Abhay Kapur. Dr. Abhay's got better things to do."

"No, that's not racist at all, Rory."

"Hey, my people died in the Holocaust. I'm allowed to make whatever ethnic jokes I want."

"What if those were fake profiles?" Mac asked.

"Nah, I checked. They were all too detailed and went too far back in time. Same goes for these six—they're all over sixty and their profiles are mainly pics of kids and grandkids; they probably can't sync their home hub to their Doc, let alone scroll Woofer for hacking purposes."

That left just under forty. An assortment of real men and women aged sixteen to forty-two. Thanks to his CB access, out of thousands of people Rory had narrowed down my potential hater to a handful of choices in thirty minutes flat. Sharma would be all-caps PISSED.

"But I don't recognize any of these people," I said.

Some of them used actual photos for their CB profile pic, others used more vague personal images like sunsets or a pic of their dog. About half used an avatar re-creation of themselves. It was one of the ways that people tried to get around being woofered. It also didn't really work. Sooner or later, *someone* snapped a pic and tagged you. Then it equaled total loss of anonymity from there on out.

"Has the person who made the video contacted you?"

"Lots."

"Then chances are just because you don't recognize them doesn't mean you might not know them. Even so, what we're looking for is a dummy account. Nobody would make all these illicit videos using their actual profiles."

Rory swiped away one of the girls.

"Why'd you get rid of her?" Mac asked.

"First, it's a real profile. Second, she lives in South Africa.

Third, I mean, that's some precision work. Your video probably took ten solid hours of edits and airbrushing. Girls are lethal, but I can't see them staring at footage of a couple having sex for as long as it would take for someone to make that vid."

"You must not know a very wide variety of girls, then." If only Audra could hear me. She'd be so proud. "And what if she got her hands on something new? I hear there's this new tech out of Asia—"

Rory snorted. "That's a myth, though your video *is* unbelievably realistic."

"Wait. You've watched my video? Like before I went into Headquarters? You recognized me?"

"Of course I did. You're famous. You have almost five million views, and after that piece they ran this morning on *EToday* about wayward teens, it'll only go up. Oh, don't worry—they didn't use your name—but it'll still spike views. Why did you think I was helping you? I've never met someone who's trending and wants to take their video down. Antifame? I mean, coolest project ever."

Mac ran a hand across his throat in a universal symbol of *Dude, panic attack happening here.* I put my head in my hands. Both boys were quiet. When I looked up again, they tensed.

"Okay, so let's find out which of my friends isn't."

The boys traded a silent look. Rory covered his mouth with his fist. Mac patted my arm in a *there, there* kind of way.

"Apologies my one-liners aren't as freakishly good as Rory's. Can we get on with this already?"

59

Mac and I spent the rest of the day with Rory in the café, going through the names one by one. Around noon, we went to a different coffee shop for lunch, but kept at it because deciding which profiles were fake was way more difficult than it first seemed. But it equaled the longest amount of time Mac and I had spent together in like a week. And is it bad to admit that, sitting next to each other, shoulders nearly touching, joking with Rory, that I had fun? I mean, despite the college kid who came up and asked to take his pic with me, then snapped one anyway when I said no. Despite him, too soon it was over. Once we were back in Brooklyn, we went to my house to pick up our Docs.

"Wanna hang and then stay for dinner?" I asked. "I still don't know what I'm going to tell Graff. And I'm sure your mama is not happy she received a *Not In Attendance* txt from Prep today."

I sat on the stoop. Mac stayed over by our tree, tapping his fingers against his stomach.

"Nah, I can't." Mac cleared his throat. "I have this thing with Victor tonight."

"A soccer thing?"

More than anything I wanted to reach out, grab his jacket, and rest my head against his belly. I wanted to run my fingers from the tip of his fingers, tracing the muscles up his arms until they stopped in the hollows of his collarbone. Before the Mr. E. video, I'd kind of figured Mac and I would eventually hook up. Audra had tried to rush me into it. But there's something to be said for going slow. Letting tension build. Daydreaming about all the things thumbs can do.

But Mac had promised he wouldn't ever ask me out again. We were at last on the same, sensible just-friends page—truly—and all I wanted to do was kiss the boy, like, now.

"No," Mac said. "I guess it's kind of like a double-date thing."

Keep it together, Kyla.

"Oh. Wow. Okay. Is it someone I know?"

"Como? No, I'd never do that to you. It's just some girl. It's a favor to Victor more than anything else. He's been trying to get with this girl's sister for, like, ever."

"Okay, well, thanks for letting me know." I had no right to be upset. Yet my traitorous eyes filled with stupid tears. "I'll get your Doc for you."

I hurried inside. What had I thought, that if I said no, he—Mackenzie Rodriguez—would just happily go on not making out with other girls? Actually, yes. That's what I'd thought. Because I believed him when he said we were different. Because not dating but still being each other's person was what we did. Because I still had his reminder in my Doc to *say yes to Mac asking me out* a month from now. And when it went off, I had fully intended to show it to him with a little smile and say "Yes, please."

I snatched his Doc off the kitchen table. Back outside, I chucked it at him from the top of our steps.

"Thanks for coming with me today. And for the record, from now on you don't have to tell me every time you go out with someone. I mean, we'll never talk about anything else."

I slammed the door before he could say good-bye. I peeked out the window. Mac stared at our house, looking like it was a place he'd never ever return.

Eyes closed tight, I leaned against the door and felt the dead air of my empty house. When I got home last night after Mr. E.'s, Mom was in her office with the door closed. This morning when I went to school, it was still shut. Apparently her "on deadline" was perpetual. I didn't have the heart to be around the same avoidance technique this evening. What I needed was a hearty dose of my best friend. I also needed to know that I still *had* a best friend. And if I left now, I'd be right on time for dinner.

When Audra answered the door fifteen minutes later, her eyes lit up with happy surprise.

"Mac's going on a double date tonight."

"Oh, ew," Audra gasped. "The Mother just told me she thought I could benefit from a nose job."

"Ack, that's terrible."

We locked in a mutual hug of relief. I hadn't realized how much I'd missed her, this snarky, acidic friend of mine. It felt like years since we'd had those few moments alone in the stairwell. This feeling wasn't helped by the fact that since I'd last seen her, she'd grown a full head of mahogany hair.

"I was starting to worry you didn't exist." I gently tugged her hair and felt it give. Not extensions, a wig. "Or are you Audra's evil twin?"

"Evil twin?" She laughed. "Audra is the evil twin."

The Parents didn't look up when I entered the dining room. Audra set out another plate.

"If I'd known one of the girls was coming for dinner, I would have ordered more food," the Mother said.

I txted Audra.

moi One of the girls. I wonder if she even knows my name.

"*Kyle* can have my dinner, seeing as I still don't eat meat."
Audra slid a plump lamb chop onto my plate. Being with my Doc again felt like having a life-sustaining IV reinserted into my arm; being back around Audra felt just as mollifying.

audy The Father knows your name. He told me last night at din that he voted with the board to suspend that "Kyla girl" I was friends with.

moi Wait, your dad is on the board?

audy Yup. Thanks for telling me about your suspension btw.

I looked across at him. He was calmly cutting a lamb chop. I had the impulse to swipe his knife and jab him in the hand.

moi Did you at least defend me? Or tell him not to do it?

audy What do you think?

Audra's eyes narrowed, but then crinkled into a smile.

audy I'm so happy to see you.

On the wall screen behind her, the news was about the oil exec and the US senator who Woofer footage caught with prostitutes in Dubai. The story had broken a week ago. It was developing into a mess of government and foreign kickbacks, falsified property rights on remaining Arab oil reserves, and so many unacceptable errors in morality and judgment that I was surprised our government functioned at all. A spokesperson for something called

Awareness for a Safe America was calling for the senator to step down. Finally.

Audra followed my eyes and said, "I'm sick of the news. Wall: Wallpaper."

Instantly, the screen behind her was a paisley print.

"Audra," the Father sighed. "I was listening to that. Wall: News."

The screen flashed back. The news cycle had moved on to a story about the skyrocketing price of bottled water.

"Wall: Wallpaper." Audra grinned.

You wouldn't know unless you were looking at her, but Audra wasn't being bratty; she was trying to get a little attention. She was also trying to cheer me up. Only the Father didn't look up.

"Audra, stop being childish."

The humor was instantly gone from my best friend's expression.

"Has it escaped your attention that I *am* a child?"

"And here I thought you were an independent eighteen-year-old. Guess we'd better take back the platinum Amex then. Wall: News."

"I haven't used your stupid credit card in months."

No. That couldn't be possible. Audra was dropping loads of money—the Elites, the expensive clothes, the museum memberships, H-double-L, my boxing lessons. Just the other day she'd come to school carrying a bag that she insisted was a knockoff, but when I Sourced it, my Doc said it sold at Barneys.com for three grand. No way could she afford that without her parents' money.

Audra pushed away from the table, her eyes bright with tears. "Enjoy the news."

She stormed out of the room.

All this time, I'd been wondering what I'd done to motivate AnyLies to make the video. I'd assumed it had something to do with competition (Jessie). Or vengeance (Ailey or Brittany). Or distanced dislike (anonymous you-tell-me). But what if it wasn't as complicated as that?

Thanks to *EToday*, my video had now been watched over eight million times. If the person who posted it made even just a penny off each view thanks to the ads, that was at least eighty grand. What if this had only ever been about money?

"Someone's having a dramatic day," the Mother sighed.

I slid away from the table without thanking the Parents for dinner. I wished I could shut off my brain. Who loved Audra better than me and the girls? We were all she had. I couldn't think these things about her. I also couldn't stop thinking them.

"Kyle," the Mother said, as I was nearly out the dining room door. Though she continued to stare at her Doc, her light complexion burned red. "If you ever have children, hope for boys."

On the landing outside her bedroom, I tried Audra's doorknob only to find it locked.

"It's only me, Audy; can I come in?"

"No," Audra wailed.

On the other side of the door, I heard her check the lock.

"Are you mad at me?"

"No, of course not."

"Then let me in, silly. I hate seeing you miserable. I found a new baby panda vid for you."

"I can't right now. I'm not decent. Kylie, all I want to do is take a long bath. I'll Face you in a few, okay?"

Out on the stoop, I had a brilliant idea that would hopefully not only cheer Audra up but remind me that the only title she held in my life was best friend. If my plan also distracted me from spending the rest of the evening thinking about Mac's date then we all equaled winners.

Group txting all the girls, I wrote that I'd discovered important info about my hater that afternoon and invited them all to an impromptu school-night sleepover at the Cheng house. As I waited for their replies, I couldn't help noticing that the recycling bin in front of the Rhodes brownstone was filled with cardboard from various tech purchases. As Sharma's and Fawn's affirmative responses came back, I looked up at Audra's window.

She would hate me for this.

Screw it.

I hurried down her steps and rifled through the boxes.

All the shipping labels were addressed to a Ms. Audra Rhodes. I was about to stop—this didn't prove anything—when something caught my eye. There, wedged down between the boxes for a new camera lens and a backup drive, was the slim cardboard packaging for a GoFetch drive.

My Doc buzzed with Audra's txt tone.

I whirled around and looked up at her window. It was dark.

audy Catch your hater-themed sleepover? Wouldn't dream of missing it.

60

"Let the Crush Kyla's Hater—subtheme Ninja Comfort—sleepover commence," Fawn cheered two hours later, hoisting a wineglass of grapefruit juice and seltzer.

On my walk home from Audra's, I'd txted my mom to get permission for the Monday night sleepover. She replied that it was fine, that she was too busy to run out and grab us snacks, and that tonight everyone in the Cheng family would be using the EatIn account to order food for themselves when they got hungry and that we were welcome to do the same. I think she was just as relieved as I was that the girls were coming over. It meant another night's distance from our fight. Tomorrow, we'd go back to being in the same room. Day after that, we'd be back to having stilted conversations, and life would return to how it had been for the last three-plus years.

Now, white takeout bags littered my floor. Fawn, Audra, and I were lying shoulder to shoulder widthwise on my bed, all of us dressed in black-on-black pairings of pj's and sweats. Audra was on her back in the middle; Fawn and I were on our bellies on either side with our ankles linked in the air. Sharma sat on the floor with her Doc on her lap. And Kyle sat in front of Fawn, looking like the time his raffle number was called at Kicks and he won a new pair of trainers. I didn't normally beg Kyle to hang out with us when the girls were over, but right then I needed my family.

My blood was boiling.

Audra owned half the tech on the market *and* a GoFetch drive. Audra had been suspiciously averse to helping me figure out who made the video, when I'd once seen the old Audra go all lioness-protecting-her-cub on Charity Knowles for pointing out that my shirt was wrinkled. "The only thing wrinkled here is your [C-word], betch." Never mind that Audra kept telling me I should be grateful for what was happening to me. Or that she suddenly had loads of money. Or that she'd taken a weird liking to Mac.

"You want the rest of my flautas, boy-Kyle?" Fawn said. "I can't finish them."

"Since when?" Audra snorted. "Or are you just hoping for a bite of boy-Kyle's burrito?"

As Audra got an elbow in the ribs from both sides, Kyle grinned ear to ear. Fawn tickled the back of his neck with the string on her hoodie. I loved watching Fawn play with other guys, but this was my little bro and she was getting intense. Audra wasn't the only one known to go into lioness mode.

Clearing my throat, and giving Fawn some seriously furrowed eyebrows, I said, "As Rory and I discussed at the café today—"

"'As *Rory* and I discussed,'" Sharma mimicked under her breath, still annoyed that it was someone other than her who had provided all this new information.

"—our goal is to find the fake profile. We've already narrowed down the orginal forty matches between our accounts to these twenty users. We've flagged these CBers because they almost never post or log in and have very few Woofer pics linked to them. If we can find the fake profile from among these twenty, then Rory can use his CB access to get us the attached e-mail account and Doc digits—more than enough info to figure out the RL person behind all this."

"How do you know any of these *are* fake?" Audra asked. "You're assuming that your hater is one of these twenty people just because you and the other girls are all connected to them on CB?"

Without looking, she reached an arm off my mattress and groped around for food. She picked up a carne enchilada torta, then tossed it back and tried again. Sharma pushed a bag of suckers beneath her hand. Audra pulled one out, unwrapped it, and stuck it in her mouth.

"Yes—" I said, as Fawn grabbed Audra's sucker and popped it in her own mouth.

"Gross," Kyle said.

"—and because there isn't any way someone could access all our Woofer footage otherwise."

"Except for the fact that he's a hacker and probably doesn't need CB to access those videos. And what about AnyLies?"

Audra reached for another sucker. Sharma snatched it away before Audra could put it in her mouth.

"What about AnyLies?" I said a little too defensively.

"We're supposed to believe that AnyLies travels around the country doing this to different people? Was he in—where'd you say one of those other girls was from?—Kansas City taking pics of her talking to her teacher?"

"Nooo, because those vids were forged too, remember?"

"Still, these feel like two different things. What if AnyLies only found the video and posted it. And the person who made the video is some armchair psychopath—"

"Don't call her that."

"—with a popularity complex. If you ask me, you've pinned too much on a coincidence. I think you're way off base here."

"And what information do you have that leads you to that conclusion?"

Audra scoffed. "Didn't I just tell you?"

My bedroom was silent.

Kyle stood up. "Yeah, uh, thanks for the food. This room is getting too female for me."

"Unacceptable descriptor," Audra and I said even as we glared at each other.

"Whatever," Kyle laughed. "I'm going to bed."

"And I have to pee," Fawn said.

"I'm not trying to be mean," Audra sighed after Fawn and my brother escaped. "But, I mean, there's got to be something else that connects you all IRL. *Think.*"

"I don't know. You tell me, Audra Rhodes."

"How should I know?" If we were in a video game, Audra's blue eyes would have turned red with rage. "Sharma, tell me I'm right."

We both stared at the back of Sharma's head as my room screen stayed motionless. After a few beats, choosing her words more carefully than she'd chosen her latest Doc case, Sharma said, "You equal sign good points, Auds, but going about it this way can't hurt. You *are* onto something, Kyle."

Taking away my suspicions and the severity of her words, all Audra meant was that we couldn't have been chosen at random. It wasn't a terrible point. *Or*—my debater brain kicked in—she was only saying that she had nothing to do with the other five girls' videos. I chose to follow the first line of reasoning. Why were we specifically chosen? I sat up.

"Oh my gosh, that's it. Auds, how many posts has the *Bra&Panties* slut done of me?"

Confused, she said, "Three?"

"What if it's her?" Audra rolled her eyes. "No, no, no, listen. It makes sense. The morning the video posts, I get those countdown-clock messages. The same day, the *B&P* slut launches *her* countdown clock. We know she lives somewhere in Brooklyn. And why did she pick up on my story so fast?"

"But what about the other girls?" Sharma asks. "What do they have to do with her?"

"Did you ever read the *B&P* slut's comments? Maybe these girls are some of her haters. She could have made the other videos solely as revenge, but then mine exploded and she saw a different opportunity. Her site even says she wants legitimization. What better way to sound lofty and get more views than create this scandal and then be the champion against it? Sharm, pull up her page, por favor."

Sharma looked between us, her fingers motionless. Impatiently, I connected to the hub with my own Doc. I was onto something. I knew it.

"Look. The views on the post she made with the girls imitating me and Mr. E. in the classroom? Two million and climbing. Meanwhile the post she did the week before only received seven hundred fifty K. Who benefited? This chick. Plus, she knows about editing. There isn't a single pic on her site that she didn't edit the asterisks out of or put an anti-Woofer filter on. I mean, Auds, what do you know about this girl? Who is she?"

"All I know is that this is a useless tangent." Audra's face flushed as she struggled into a sitting position, jostling me hard in the shoulder. "And for the last time, would you stop calling this girl a slut? Maybe she's no President Malin, but at least she has better hair and her office isn't broke."

"Audra, I'm warning you. Don't make fun of the president."

Slowly, as if savoring every word, Audra said, "Malin botched her Middle East foreign policy and she all-caps HAS NO FASHION SENSE."

"Uh-oh." Fawn was back, looking more rumpled than ever. "What'd I miss?"

"They're insulting each other's role models," Sharma said.

I turned back to the screen so Audra couldn't see my eyes well up. I knew I was being ridiculous, but New Year's Eve wasn't for four more days. I still had lots of time before my drama-free New Year's resolution took effect. On-screen the *B&P* slut and co. were in a sparsely furnished room wearing neon wigs.

"Whatever." Audra yawned. "You take everything so person-ally. Ping me when the Harriet the Spy portion of the night is over and we can go back to having fun."

I scrolled through the pics. There was something familiar about them. The post was about making new friends, and the three girls in the pics were all over one another, their bodies linked with a hand on a waist here, arms entwined there. If they'd had their clothes on, instead of bright pink and purple mixed bra sets, there'd be nothing sexy about the pics. The girls and I draped our-selves over one another like that all the time. Even now, Fawn had settled back in and was braiding Sharma's hair, while Audra rested her head on Fawn's butt as she played on her Doc.

It wasn't the *B&P* girls who were familiar. It was the room behind them—those wide wraparound windows with the shades drawn.

I'd been in that room.

I knew that space.

It was in the Cimorelli brownstone. Before they discontinued using me as a babysitter this past week, I used to show it for them when they weren't home. They rented it out as office space to help pay for their kid's nanny care.

I didn't just recognize the *Bra&Panties* slut's new space. I'd suggested it to her.

It was after midnight. It had taken me nearly an hour to pull myself together. Now, in the kitchen, I watched my petite best friend root around in my freezer, trying to think of my opening line.

Of all the girls, Audra stayed over the most. Prior to this fall, when the numbers had inexplicably, or now not so inexplicably, reduced, it hadn't been unusual for her to sleep over three or more times a week. Sometimes, like when she complained that we were having cereal for breakfast *again*, having Audra over got on my family's nerves. But never mine. Anyone whose family was so terrible they didn't even want to sleep in their own bed—my favorite place on earth—deserved a little leeway.

Tonight I had no such sympathies.

"So when were you going to tell me you're the *Bra&Panties* slut?"

Our refrigerator was a side-by-side model. Audra stooped down to look through the bottom shelves of the freezer even though she only ever wanted blueberry gelato. It was the only reason my mom bought it. Her back stiffened, but she nonchalantly grabbed the deep-blue pint container, as if I hadn't spoken. Stepping around me, she took a spoon from the drawer next to the sink, then hoisted herself up onto the counter. Her heels lightly tapped the cupboards below as she said, "I didn't think the future president of the United States would understand her kind of entrepreneurial—"

"'Her'?" I cut her off. "'Her' who? You *are* her. This is why you always keep your Doc on private. Why you never sleep over anymore and always have unelaborated 'plans.' This is where all your money comes from. You sell pictures of your boobs and tush, to what? Buy shoes?"

Audra dug out an enormous scoop of gelato and took a tiny bite.

"Please, Kyle." She licked her lips. "You're seventeen. It's time for you to say tits and ass like the big kids. And, yes, you've got me all figured out. I just couldn't stand not shopping enough."

"So then why do it?"

"Why should I tell you?" She slammed down the gelato, launched herself off the counter, and shouldered past me to grab a juice box from the fridge.

"Because I thought I was your best friend."

Audra jabbed at the juice box until the flimsy straw broke. She set them both on the counter.

Without looking at me, she said, "The New Year's Eve reveal should net me close to five hundred thousand dollars. The countdown clock alone, at fifty thousand purchases at two ninety-nine apiece, has earned me a hundred and fifty thousand. That Vogue.com thing I was telling you about? It's real. They want me to start in February. What's all this for? It's for never again letting a douche like Cobi Watkins have power over my body and image. Or anyone else's, for that matter."

I knew Boobgate had scarred my friend, but becoming the queen of nudie pics as a response? It was either the most brilliant or most misguided way of dealing with boyfriend betrayal that I'd ever heard of. Leave it to Audra, I guess. Girl never did anything small.

"And it's for never *ever* having to ask the Parents for another dime for as long as I live. I know it's hard for you to understand, coming from your perfect family, Kylie, but living the rest of my life independent and free of my parents is the only future goal I have right now. I already have a down payment on an apartment in Williamsburg. I'm moving there as soon as school's over."

AnyLiesUnmade. It was all lies. This hadn't been going on for just a few weeks. *B&P* had started almost ten months ago. That meant nearly a third of our friendship had involved Audra keeping a huge secret from me. And not unintentionally. I thought of all the times her Doc had been set to private when we were together. Feeling light-headed, I slid down and sat on the floor.

"You're moving to Williamsburg?"

I knew Audra had been more withdrawn and short-fused since the summer, but it wasn't that out of character for her; I'd thought she was just getting anxious about graduation. Whenever I asked what she was planning to do with her gap year—travel, intern, volunteer—she'd shrug and say she hadn't decided and leave it at that. Pressing her on it never seemed worth the nasty ripples it created in our day-to-day.

Never mind that she was the *B&P* chick. I txted Audra when I couldn't decide if I should buy a new blouse. Meanwhile, she'd been apartment hunting without me.

"I tried to tell you a bunch of times," Audra continued. "Life would have been a whole lot easier these last couple months if I could have. But every time I tested the waters, you, like, created a tsunami of hate toward her. And I get it. You're the leader of every club at our school. You say you're going to be president, and I believe you. You won't even date the hottest, most interesting catch at Prep because he has a history that isn't as squeaky-clean as yours—"

"That isn't the only reason why I won't date Mac," I interjected halfheartedly.

"—so you can't be mad at me for not seeing how you could ever comprehend a project like this. Sorry I checked out on you the last few days, but we've been shooting for the New Year's reveal. I've never been so stressed in my life. I just couldn't handle both our dramas at the same time."

It was like my best friend was a stranger. If her big reveal hadn't been coming up, if all this junk hadn't been going on with my hater, would I have found out about *B&P* at all? Or would I only have found out after the reveal, along with the rest of the world?

"Aren't you gonna say anything? Come on, Kylie, lay into me already." Audra slid the gelato and spoon down the counter to me. When I didn't reach up to take them, she said, "Did I mention that *B&P* earns me enough money to buy way awesome clothes? Come on, laugh. That was a joke."

"I can smell the drama from upstairs. Who burned the toast?"

Fawn's bare feet smacked lightly on the floor. She looked like another person when she was tired. Her eyes turned down at the corners; her whole face got puffy.

"Kyle knows about *B&P*," Audra said.

"Geez, it took you long enough." Fawn yawned.

In the third grade, Aubrey Torr-Jones accidentally punched me in the stomach during a PE volleyball game. I remembered all the air rushing out of me, and for a split second panicking because I couldn't bring any back in. This felt exactly like that.

Fawn eyed Audra's pint. She grabbed a spoon from the drawer and padded over to the freezer.

"I so sleepy. Need sugar. Got anything other than blueberry? Chocolate peanut butter, maybe?"

"You know too?" I whispered.

Fawn's eyes cut to Audra. "Aw, uh-oh, worried face. Yeah, but only because Audy needed help. I mean, who else do you think would be dumb enough to ride a horse in Prospect Park in her undies? I totally expected you to recognize me months ago. It's why I kept sending you so many links. I mean, I know this doesn't make up for it, but I'm buying a Peddler, one of those self-guiding bicycles, with all the money Audra paid me. Zoom, zoom."

Fawn knelt next to me and gave me a hug. When I remained unresponsive, she reluctantly got up and went back to digging around in the freezer. I was doing my best to choke back a sob as Sharma came in.

"Was messaging one of your maybe haters that also plays *Z-Wars*. Said nitrogen gun exists. Stashed in a safe in the principal's office. Comes with a hammer so you freeze the zombie's head and then..." Her words fell off when she saw my face. "What now?"

I didn't even bother to ask if Sharma knew. Of course she did. Who else would have helped Audra set everything up?

From deep inside our freezer, Fawn said, "Kyle knows about *B&P*."

Sharma went to the snack cupboard and pulled down a bag of snap-pea crisps. She popped one in her mouth and crunched loudly.

"Good. It's about time. Kyle, you okay? How bad equals your freak-out?"

My eyes filled with tears. "So I'm the friend my friends have to keep secrets from. Do you know how crazy that makes me feel?"

"We know how crazy it makes you look."

Fawn pulled her Doc from the waistband of her pj's and snapped my pic, then held it up for my perusal. I shoved the Doc away.

"Who's the third girl in the pictures?"

It wasn't Sharma, and it certainly wasn't me. Fawn and Audra exchanged glances. Audra shook her head no.

"I'm sitting right here. I can see you, Audra Bethany Rhodes. Who's the third girl?"

She shrugged, in a *have it your way* gesture.

"Fine, betch, it's Ailey. Sorry. I know how much it bothers you that she and I have become friends. Even though you've blown me off to not screw around with Mac for the last four months and I never once held that against you.

"And for the record, maybe you're hurt I didn't tell you about all this, but at least *I* never doubted your loyalty. Did I stick up for you when I found out my dad voted to have you suspended? We only fought about it for *two hours*. And how do you think it makes me feel that he still went ahead and did what he wanted? Thanks for the vote of confidence, friend."

Tears filled her eyes.

"Audra. Kylie," Fawn said. "Come on, ladies, don't fight."

Audra looked at me, waiting for me to apologize. Ailey was the third girl. Audra had trusted Ailey with this secret when she wouldn't trust me. No. Worse. She'd included Ailey in it. Ailey had been hanging around with my friends, for months, behind my back. She knew a whole world of things about my best friends that I didn't. Things she knew I didn't know.

"How much do you trust any of the girls?" she'd asked.

Right, because Audra was the *Bra&Panties* slut. Everyone knew but me, and *I* was the one who got put into the fake sex video? I thought of the posts that Audra had done to "defend" me. Li'l Miss Straight-A, she kept calling me; she wished I had more courage to stand up and set a better feminist example about the entire situation. I shook my head.

"Did you make the video, Audra?"

Audra laughed, then clapped her hands, slow and sarcastic.

"That's perfect. You have some serious trust issues, Kyle. I mean, here you are blaming everyone else, but did you ever stop to examine why this is happening to *you*?"

"Only about a thousand times!" I yelled. "And maybe I have trust issues, but at least I'm not vengeful. How is hating your best friend for nearly a year better than being honest with her and working through the aftermath? I'm not such a beast you couldn't have told me about *B&P*. This is just like your mother not changing the pescatarian setting. You'd rather feel vindicated and misunderstood than actually address the issue and feel better."

My voice was shaking with emotion. Tears streamed down Audra's cheeks. This was normally the part where one or the other of us would realize what a big scene we were making, crack a joke, and hug in a flurry of tears and apologies. Instead, Audra's nostrils flared.

"You don't know anything about my relationship with my mother." Audra jabbed a finger into my face. "At least she's awful to everyone. Your mother is amazing and she only despises you."

I smacked her hand away. We were over. We were so completely over.

"You still haven't said you didn't make the video," I said.

Audra put the lid on the gelato and tossed it back in the freezer.

"FCK you, Kyle," she said. "I'm calling a car. Anyone else want a ride home? I'll pay with my slut money."

62

Audra pinged a car and went to wait outside. Fawn and Sharma swore they weren't leaving because they were mad or were choosing sides, but, well, dot-dot-dot. After they left, I stayed downstairs and cleaned up the kitchen, trying to make sense of everything. When I finally went up to bed thirty minutes later, Mom was at the top of the stairs. It was the first time I'd seen her since our fight on Sunday.

"Everything okay?"

"Yeah." I nodded.

She frowned, an exhausted *I expected exactly that kind of answer* frown. She patted my arm and went to her room. I wanted to say that I was sorry. That I loved her. That, please, could she and I be okay now? Instead, as her hand touched the doorknob, I blurted out, "My hater cracked my Scholar app and sent off my unfinished college applications. And Audra is the *Bra&Panties* slut, which means all of my friends have been lying to me for months now. Also, I think I screwed up my relationship with Mac."

"Whoa." Her expression became pinched. "Why didn't you tell me about the Scholar app immediately?"

Naturally this was the one she would pick.

"Because every second my life gets worse and I can't keep up." A small dry sob escaped me. "What if I don't get in anywhere? Who's going to accept me?"

Mom wrapped her robe tighter and cleared her throat. Here came my lecture. Instead she let out one short laugh.

"Thank God I'm not a teenager anymore."

With a nod of her head, she herded me into my bedroom. She held the covers back as I climbed into bed. Then she sat next to me.

"First of all," she said, brushing aside my bangs, "you just finish those applications and I'll contact the admissions offices. And can I say, without you getting mad at me, that just because President Malin and I went to Ivies, it doesn't mean you need to too. If college is about anything other than robbing families of money or filling up your time between your late teens and early twenties, it's about what *you* make of it."

Terrific. At the moment, I couldn't make anything of anything.

"And if I know you, whatever school you end up at will one day have a building named after you. Second, as for Mac, honey, I saw how he looked at you at the All Brains on Deck meeting. He clearly adores you. Now, don't bite my head off for asking, but why *aren't* you dating him?"

I pulled at a loose thread on my bedspread.

"Because Mackenzie Rodriguez doesn't date. He scores, then moves on, and that's that. It's like I told him, history doesn't lie."

Mom picked up Teddy and fiddled with his nose. She started to speak, stopped. Then, very carefully, she began again.

"Let's not forget Mac is a teenage boy. Not only is he prewired to want to make out with every available face, but he's cute enough to actually get to do it. You can't blame him for that. But how long have you two been close now? Since September? Has Mac scored with anyone in that time?"

"No," I said begrudgingly.

Though who knew if that still held true. Oh gawd—my stomach constricted—the date. It had to have gone well; he hadn't txted me even once.

"Has he tried to score with you?"

"Mom." I rolled my eyes, but still said, "No. Not really. He actually asked me to be his girlfriend."

"So then what about *that* history? Isn't it possible he feels differently about you?" She put her hands on my shoulders and gently shook me. "Regardless, baby, save all this relationship anxiety for your thirties. It's not like you have to marry him. Actually, for the record, you should not marry your high school boyfriend. That's how you end up miserable in your late twenties. If you didn't like Mac that way, that'd be one thing. But I've also seen how you look at him."

I played with the hem of her robe and then finally said what I'd been worried about this whole time.

"What if he breaks my heart? I'll feel like such an idiot."

"Well." Her gray eyes crinkled at the corners. "That's all part of the experience. It's a given—an absolute fact—that at some point in life a person you love will tear your heart to shreds, but I don't think that makes *you* stupid and I don't think that person is Mackenzie Rodriguez. If anything, it will be the other way around. And then you'll move on."

Miraculously, problem by problem, Mom was making me feel better. Why had we been at each other's throats so much these last few years? I let out a long sigh.

"That's right," she said. "Deep breaths. Also, before I lose the opportunity, might I add that if Mac does try to score with you, please use a condom."

"Ew, Mom. Gross."

"I'm sorry. It needed to be said. And lastly, I know she's your best friend, but, honey, Audra's always been kind of a bitch."

Shocked, I laughed, "Mom."

"I'm sorry, but it's true. Living with that family doesn't give her much choice. Granted, before the other night I hadn't seen her for a while, but honey, Audra is clearly going through it."

"What did you two even talk about?"

"At first, business. How the Paris stores were coming along, whether or not I liked my bookkeeper and accountant. I thought she was asking me on her parents' behalf. Though, come to think of it, she did sound like she knew what she was talking about. I mean, what teenager knows about C corps? Then we mostly talked about you. How much she respected you, envied you. How she wished she could make you see and appreciate how perfect your life was. To be honest, it was a little intense. But I thought that's what you *liked* about Audra. Her intensity. I mean, are you really that shocked that Audra's this bra-and-panties girl?"

"Yes," I huffed, but then, quieter, I said, "No. But it's more than that. Instead of just telling me about *B&P*, Audra's been increasingly resentful and nasty. And all along everyone knew why but me. Fawn slips up and spills secrets all the time. It's not just Audra. I'm not sure I can be friends with any of them anymore. I mean, now I'm not even sure that I was to begin with."

"Honey, the girls have known each other since they were babies. I'm not sure you can expect to have the same kind of friendship and trust that they do, coming in as late as you did."

But then how come Ailey got let in on the secret?

"What do I know?" Mom sighed when I didn't respond. "I always thought as far as friends are concerned, you reap what you sow."

Poof. Gone went the relaxed vibe. In the dark I sensed Mom tense, like those last words accidentally got out and she wanted to bite them back in. I actually kind of felt sorry for her. Even in our times of peace, she still couldn't quite like or forgive me. Audra was a bitch, my friends all let me down, and I'd reaped what I'd sown. Did this moment count as the person I loved tearing my heart to shreds? I rolled away from her so I was facing the wall.

"That didn't come out right," she said quietly, putting a hand on my back.

"It's okay." I forced out a laugh. "It's good advice."

She cleared her throat, then brightened. "How about I tell you the story of us?"

When I was growing up, anytime life seemed bad, Mom told me the story of us. It began with how she met Dad and continued to the present day. The moral of it was that life might not be easy, but we four Chengs were scrappy, we somehow always clawed our way to the top, and most importantly, we had each other.

But we didn't anymore. And I wasn't interested in this new ending.

"Nah, I'm pretty tired."

She lingered for a few more seconds, then tucked Teddy in next to me. At my door she paused and said, "I love you."

I didn't respond. After a beat or two, I heard the soft click of my door shutting. As soon as it did, I grabbed my Doc.

> moi I think we've both hurt each other. Maybe more than we meant. I just wanted to let you know, I'm sorry for everything that's happened.

Only after I sent it did I realize I could have written the same words to half the people in my closest circle. Maybe I really did need to examine how I treated people. Not to sound like a cheesy song lyric, but why do we damage the ones we hold most precious?

Before I changed my mind, I added one more line.

> moi I'm sorry, but I'm not going to be txting you anymore.

AnyLies's reply was instant.

😈 Why. Not.

moi I need to focus on other things now. Like my friendships, my family.

😈 I AM your friend. I'm the one who told you there were other girls. I'm the one who is looking out for you. Aren't you tired? Tired of having to pretend all the time? Tired of no one understanding you? Tired of friendships that aren't everlasting? Tired of being watched, but not seen? I get it. But you still don't. Do you?

I put my Doc down. I could feel the rage radiating off it.

😈 You will regret this.

That was too much.

moi Leave the video up for all I care. I have nothing left to lose.

😈 I wouldn't be so sure. Enjoy the fall.

63

TUESDAY, DECEMBER 28

The next morning, I left for school early. I checked my Doc and looked over my shoulder the whole walk there. Every second I expected a new something awful to drop from AnyLies. It felt like the countdown all over again, but this time it was silent. *T minus three, two, one...*

I made it to Park Prep unscathed. After the security sensor checked me in, I used Ankle Breaker to hurry to the second floor, waited ten minutes until the Walk had to be over, then doubled back downstairs to Dr. Graff's office. I told her secretary that Graff was expecting me.

Dr. Graff's expression clouded when I slipped into her office. Yesterday she'd given me a very specific directive and time frame. I'd ignored both. You just didn't do that.

"Kyle."

"Good morning. Sorry to interrupt. I know you're probably busy, but I wanted to stop in before class and tell you I'm feeling fine today."

She tilted her head. "That's good."

"And I have a feeling I'll be feeling fine tomorrow and the next day as well."

She was getting it now. A haze of disapproval fogged her unblinking eyes.

"So if you'd like to go ahead with what we discussed yesterday, you may call my mom and tell her I'm suspended."

My heart was beating like it was competing in a speed-beatboxing competition, but my voice stayed steady—thank you, debate prep. I almost apologized for being too forward, but I didn't. "Never apologize for speaking your mind," President Malin said in her televised special *Elementary: Our Young, Our Future.*

No, let Dr. Graff endure *my* unwavering stare, because, in five hundred words or less?

Today?

I was someone you got the F out of the way of.

64

"Thank goodness you're here." Fawn took my hands in hers. "Wait—*are* you supposed to be here right now? What about Graff?"

"F Graff," I said.

So much for dodging the Walk. Fawn and Sharma were both waiting for me outside Graff's office. Nothing about their outfits matched. It was the first time the girls and I hadn't conspired on a theme in over three years.

This morning, I'd woken to txts from Fawn about her mom nearly calling the cops because she thought the brownstone was being broken into when she got home last night. Sharma had txted the exhausted-face emote. It was their way of assuring me they hadn't all gone to another house without me after they left. I wasn't entirely sure I cared.

"Why's your Doc off?" Sharma asked.

"Are you still mad?" Fawn asked.

"All my friends have been lying to me for ten months. That doesn't go away with a good night's sleep, Fawnie. Sorry. I have to go. I don't want to be late."

283

"What does it matter?" Sharma asked. "Sub already thinks you slept with Mr. E."

"Which is precisely why I refuse to create the impression that I'm tardy as well."

Fawn tugged at my arm and pulled me to a standstill.

"None of us knew," she said. "We had no idea *B&P* would be this huge. We thought we were just helping Audra with a goofy pet project and then it exploded this summer and at first we were just trying to help her keep up, and then we all felt like total scumbags for not telling you sooner, but were also kind of afraid of how pissed you'd be, and I totally understand if you never want to see our faces again. Only I hope that isn't the case, because you're one of my best friends and I'm so sorry I've been lying to you." Fawn's lip quivered dangerously close to the border of Sob Town. "I shouldn't have taken that pic of you last night when you were upset. I thought it would lighten the mood. I feel like this is all my fault. Audra didn't even come to school today."

"So what?" I said. "She was absent yesterday too."

"Yeah, but then she equaled busy. Now she equals upset. Are we all breaking up?"

Fawn's lower lip had fallen open as if she were emitting a silent wail. Sharma whipped her head to look at me, like, *Are you seeing this?* I let out a rush of air. Fawn and Sharma were good people and great friends. Without question they definitely belonged in the fostering-friendship category. I brushed Fawn's hair off her shoulders.

"Mommy and Daddy love each other very much, but sometimes Mommy and Daddy fight, and it's no reflection on you...."

Fawn flicked my hands away, but she was smiling now. "Doofus."

The half-minute chimes sounded over the loudspeakers. We all bolted toward the back stairwell.

"B-T-W," Sharma said as we ran upstairs. "Guess who came back from her li'l family vacay early?"

"Jessie?" I asked.

"Y-E-S," Sharma said. "Saw her online Sunday night. Asked how the trip was going. She said: Finito. Said best part was her parents let her fly back early. Christmas night, I guess."

"Which means she could have taken those pics of me at Mr. E.'s. Maybe that was her on the train. Is she in school? Sharmie, did you say I'm dying to talk to her?"

"Uh-huh. She quit the game soon as I brought it up. And no, she equals pretending she's still away."

"Lucky," Fawn said, thoroughly out of breath.

"Fawnie, why are you up here? Your class is on one."

"I know," she wailed as I powered on my Doc. "I didn't want to miss anything."

I laughed and hugged Fawn, then Sharma and I slipped into class. But not before I sent a rapid txt. Just two words.

moi   Jessie. Please.

The next four periods passed with me expecting to be called out of class at any moment. I had cold-brew jitters but with none of the perks of actually drinking a cold brew. But Dr. Graff never sent for me. And AnyLies never posted anything. So either both threats were only that, empty threats, or two different people were crafting my downfall right at that very moment. Either way, my attendance record was safe for one more day.

Then, finally, lunch. As Sharma lost herself in her online worlds, I stared at the cafeteria door. The one lucky thing about discovering yesterday that all my friends had been lying to me was that it had wiped Mac's date almost entirely out of my head. I *still* hadn't heard from him, so I thought there was no way he would visit me in lunch. But then, ten minutes into the period, he was sliding into the seat next to mine.

I'd resolved to give him the cold shoulder all day. Was it immature that I was mad he went on a date with someone else immediately after I said I wouldn't be his girlfriend *at that moment in time*?

285

Sure.

Was I okay with being immature in this instance?

You bet I was.

But now that he was there, all I felt was relief. I couldn't wait to tell him about my fight with Audra and AnyLies's new threat and how I'd stood up to Graff. He met my smile with a relieved one of his own. Sharma polished her glasses, put them firmly back on the bridge of her nose.

"Wowza, guys. Mackenzie Rodriguez, is that a hickey on your neck?"

The bite of liverwurst sandwich I'd taken fell out of my mouth onto my lap. Mac flipped up the collar of his shirt.

"Nah."

"Yes it is." An enormous un-Sharma-like smile lit up her sharp features. "Happy New Year to you two. Finally."

"Yeah, um." I crumbled up the rest of my uneaten lunch, cleared my throat. "Mac went on a date last night."

Sharma's head rocked back like she'd put on an EarRing and the volume was on high.

"Whoa." She held the next one longer. "Whoaaaaa. Yuck. Just, all-caps, YUCK."

Out the corner of my eye, I saw Mac's expression fall. Dark circles ringed his eyes. He looked like he hadn't slept at all. It was almost as if . . .

"Is that the same outfit you were wearing yesterday?" I asked. Mac shrugged.

"It must have been a really excellent date if you didn't even go home."

"What do you care?" Mac didn't shrink from my gaze. "Not everyone thinks it makes them dirty to kiss me."

I wanted to mush my sandwich in his face. I wanted to scrub that hickey—could it be more enormous?—off his neck with my keys. So much for Mom's theory that he didn't want to hook up with anyone but me. I wanted to hunt down the chick that gave it to him and throw her in a solar trash compactor. Luckily, my Doc buzzed. I jumped.

Rory—FaceAlerting me. I angrily swiped accept.

"What?" I answered.

"Have we reached an age when no one says hello anymore?" He was clearly at Headquarters. Behind him, two people were playing holobadminton with their hands. "So it's not any of the girls."

"You're sure?"

"Uh-huh. Or the nerdy guy, either. Turns out that *I* was actually friends with that guy, so I did a little profile scrolling. Dude's darkest secret is that he belongs to a live-action medieval-battles club. I stayed up all night watching vids. Peeps run around a park in crazy getups and smack each other with foam weapons. It's amazing. This one guy's foam battle-ax was literally the size of a Hydrogen Coop. The dude and I got to messaging. I might join."

"Hydrogen Coop? Why'd you choose that reference?"

"Uh, 'cause it was accurate?"

A holobirdie flew straight at Rory's head. One of the guys lunged for it. The collision rolled Rory out of the FaceAlert window. He wheeled himself back in.

"Come on, you guys. I'm on business here."

"So that leaves eleven names." Despite the fact that Sharma and I were pelting him with eye daggers, Mac swiped into CB, pulled our list from yesterday up on holo, and flicked away the girls and the medievalist. "My money's on this normal guy with the avat profile pic. I mean, mira, what dude listens to oldies like Dave Matthews and Eminem, and also Primal Rage?"

"A dude with no musical legitimacy." Rory ducked and looked over his shoulder, waiting for another birdie attack. "Bro has traveled a lot for being only twenty. I'll look into normal guy first thing after lunch."

"Already did," Sharma said. "No activity on his account for two days now."

"Who said that?" Rory asked.

Sharma shook her head and waved her hands in front of her: *no, no, no, no.* I kept my Doc trained on me and Mac.

"Big deal," Mac said. "So normal boy doesn't like to be online. I haven't checked into my accounts for at least two days."

"Technically, you have," Sharma said. "Look, CB accesses your other sites. Click here, your profile shows what you've looked at online, where you've checked in, who you've . . . ew." She stopped speaking. Her eyes shot up to me, then quickly away. "Normal boy doesn't have that, which means . . ."

"Ew"? What did that mean? And why had she looked at *me* when she'd said it?

"Could be a dummy profile," Rory finished. "Or he's purposely covering that tracking stuff up, and why do that unless you've got something to cover up?"

Behind me there was a loud crash. I squeaked in surprise—actually squeaked—and jerked around. Brittany Mulligan must have stood up too quickly and knocked her chair over.

"What?" she asked when she caught me staring. "Afraid Ellie was coming to get you?"

And although I desperately wanted to say, *No, I just saw your shirt-and-pants combination,* I shook my head. When I glanced at my Doc again, Rory was peering into the FaceAlert screen.

"Are you actually in your school's cafeteria right now? Kyle, do a wide-angle reverse view. Are you, like, surrounded by kids in space-agey uniforms? Is everyone eating adorable box lunches? Are owls delivering your homework assignments?"

He snuck a finger beneath his glasses to rub his eyes, as if to better see the private school wonders previously denied him.

"Rory, it's a cafeteria. Not an anime spaceship for wizards."

"Feed a programmer's offline experience points and reverse angle already."

I sighed. "Fine, there's someone here I want you to meet anyway. Rory, computer hacker extraordinaire, allow me to introduce Sharma, computer hacker extraordinaire."

Sharma shook her head, whispering, "Don't you dare," even as she took her hair down from the pencil it was twisted up in, so when the Doc camera landed on her, glossy black hair was swishing across her shoulders.

"Whoa," Rory said.

Sharma blushed and flapped her hand halfway between a greeting and a *go away.*

"Sharma, meet Rory. He dropped out of college. What does 'ew' mean, Mac? What did Sharma see on your CB page?"

Mac fully turned toward me so I could see just how far back on his neck that thing went. His *nah-it-isn't-a-hickey* was the size of Greenland.

"Oh my gosh. That's hideous."

"What's the big deal?" Mac asked. "I thought you liked being proven right."

Then he pushed back his chair and left. If Fawn or Audra were here, I would have been wrapped in a hug right now, but Sharma just studied me quietly.

"Sorry," she said. "Awkward."

When I turned my Doc around again, Rory was scowling. A txt from him hung over his FaceAlert screen.

rory (cb techie) Hey. That whole dropping-out-of-college
line only sounds good when I deliver it. It also means
I'm only nineteen. Please turn the Doc around again?

"Just find out what you can about normal boy, okay?" I forced a smile. "Oh, and Rory? Sharma wrote a program that makes Universal Translate recognize pig latin."

Rory clutched his chest and collapsed on his desk.

"Not fair," he murmured as I hit disconnect.

65

Rory's next FaceAlert came while I was in study hall. Before I accepted, I sent invites to Fawn and Sharma to silent conference the call. Two tiny FaceAlert windows immediately popped up on my screen. Now they could see and hear everything that I could and I wouldn't have to try and repeat any of this later. I blew them kisses, then tapped accept.

"Am I on speaker or are you plugged in?" Rory immediately asked.

"Plugged in," I murmured. "Study hall."

"Okay, gotcha. You can't talk. Is your foxy friend there?"

"Not the one you like."

I reversed my screen so he could see Fawn. She was sitting next to me, smiling at her Doc. When she noticed herself on my FaceAlert window, she angled her own Doc away so we couldn't see her screen, probably so Rory wouldn't know she was silent conferenced in.

Rory shrugged. "Not my type."

Gorgeous isn't your type? I wanted to ask, but the study hall monitor was already looking at me, so I just shook my head in exasperation.

"So, it's definitely normal boy," Rory continued. "I counted five firewalls around his profile. Or, you know, his dummy profile. Plus, get this, all the travel pics in his cache? They're all stock photos. He bought them off this site *BeenThereDoneThat.com*."

moi   Wait. You're serious. You found him?

Rory laughed. "Yeah, I told you we would. I mean, if it is a 'him.'"
Rory actually *found* him. Which meant this was all almost over. I felt the tingly rush of adrenaline of winning a debate, except this prize was so much bigger. I'd just won my life back. Fawn reached across the aisle and gripped my hand.

"And hey, be careful. Nobody puts up this many firewalls without having something major to hide or without being serious about protecting it."

Who of the half dozen people who hated me would go through this much effort to make a fake profile? Intentional or not, there had to be a clue, either in the awful movies or music they made the dummy profile like or in the uber-WASP-y clothing sites they made him shop at. The fake boy's avatar profile pic actually reminded me a little of Cobi Watkins. I couldn't help thinking that this entire account reflected the exact kind of have-it-all-prepster that Audra—or Jessie, for that matter—would hate.

moi   You're telling me this person's dangerous?

"No. I'm dangerous. This kid's a guppy who's about to get caught and doesn't even know it."

moi   Do you find these lines on some kind of B-movie
        quote site?

291

"Nope." He grinned. "One hundred percent Rory's original recipe."

Damn.

moi So what do we do?

"You let me do a little more digging and then we talk in a few and come up with a game plan. Also, wait, don't disconnect. Can you put in a good word for me with your foxy friend?"

moi Sharma?

"She's not like sixteen, is she? You're all seniors, right? No, don't tell me. But maybe tell her I'd be so good to her, it would crash her system. No, don't say that. Make something up, but make sure it sounds nerdy so I could have actually said it. But not *that* nerdy! Like suave nerdy. Just think about it. But make it clear I'd kill to meet her without sounding desperate."

moi I got it, Rory. I'll come up with something.

"Don't make me sound too desperate," he was saying as I hit disconnect.

Rory clicked off FaceAlert. Sharma and Fawn's faces became 50 percent larger on my screen. I tried not to think about how one face was noticeably missing. Luckily, watching Sharma squirm made up for this fact.

"One word," Sharma said, "and I'll freeze you out of your online memberships for life."

Maybe it was impossible to find Jessie's Doc digits, but as I already knew it was very easy to locate the address of where she and her bazillionaire family lived. So, less than three miles yet still somehow one bus transfer later, I was pressing the RingScreen of an enormous marble edifice that could have been mistaken for a museum but, apparently, was the Rosenthal residence. Through a wrought iron gate that shielded the front doors, in the thin line of regular glass that surrounded the frosted door panes, I could just see into the Rosenthals' massive foyer. An enormous chandelier that was shaped like an overturned rowboat with lightbulbs in it hung from two stories up. Beneath it, a perfectly dust- and clutter-free elegant wood table held an enormous vase of completely out-of-season hydrangeas. And beneath the table lay a pile of suitcases.

I'd had my finger on the RingScreen for two minutes now. As dark and quiet as the interior of the—let's be honest—*resort* felt, I knew Jessie was in there.

Sharma didn't do bad intel.

My wrist was just starting to tire from pressing the screen

when I heard the sound of a window sliding up. I stepped back on the portico. Jessie's house was bigger than Park Prep. It was nearly bigger than the Barclays Center. I craned my head back. Three stories up, a thin, pale face surrounded by a mound of curly hair sneered down at me. As was her way, she wore a fine black blouse with a stiff ruffled collar.

Still, when I spoke, my words contained such relief you'd think I actually liked the girl. "It's you."

"Surprise, surprise, seeing as I reside here. What do you want?"

Oh, how I wished vomiting on cue were a talent I possessed, because I would have let loose right there on her perfectly swept marble steps. How had I forgotten? Jessie spoke in a light, fake British accent.

"Are you AnyLies?" I called out.

"What's that?" She dramatically held a hand to her ear. A hand covered by a black lace glove, trimmed with more ruffles. "I can't hear you."

"Jessie, will you please just come outside so I don't have to shout?"

"Are you batty? I most certainly won't. You've been blowing up my Doc like it's Los Alamos. Anything you have to say to me you can say fine from there."

With the house, and her in all those ruffles, and the posh accent, I felt like I was in some Off-Broadway production of *Mary Poppins*. This was ridiculous. It was all I could do not to stomp my foot in frustration. After a quick glance both ways down the street, I cupped my hands around my mouth and shouted, "Why are you doing this to me?"

Jessie held a finger to her lips—playing pensive—then cupped her hands around her mouth and shouted, "Why the FCK should I tell you anything?"

Laughing merrily, she slammed the window shut. Before completely disappearing from view, she held up a fist, then four fingers. Point four. The exact number her grade-point average was below mine. This time, *I* gave her the unfriendly finger. Trilling her fingers, she disappeared from sight.

Cursing, I swung my bag onto my shoulder. I'd transferred for this?

No sooner had I turned the corner from her estate than my Doc shrieked with AnyLies's txt sound. I gasped. I'd been waiting for this moment all day, wondering when and how my hater would finally make good on her threats from last night. Now, finding out AnyLies's freshest revenge was only a swipe away. I looked back at Jessie's mansion. It equaled as impenetrable as the firewalls around *Whitehouse.gov*.

Suddenly something crashed into the back of my legs, like someone took a pipe to my calves. My knees buckled. I fell to the ground, scraping my palms. My Doc sprang from my hands.

"Oh goodness, I'm so sorry."

It was a nanny, pushing a double baby stroller. She came around to see if I was all right.

"Are you okay, honey? Five a.m. call time plus PHD plus stroller equals accident. I even made you drop your device. Here, let me get that for you."

"No, don't touch it!"

Her hand stopped an inch away from my Doc.

"I was just trying to help," she said, then abruptly crossed the street.

Last night, despite what Sharma had already said, I'd double-checked with the other five girls. None of them had received txts from AnyLies. Only me. Getting to my feet, I slowly reached over and retrieved my Doc. Honestly, what could be worse than that hickey on Mac's neck?

 Not to bother you, but thought you'd like to see who your so-called friends really are.

Three pictures followed. All of them appeared to have been snagged from Woofer.

The first pic was a Woofer of Sharma and the girls. They were in the background of a pic someone had taken of his latte. It must have been captured the day Audra and Fawn re-created the photos of me and Mr. E. for the *B&P* site, because even though their backs were turned and Fawnie was still sporting Mr. E.'s pompadour wig, I'd have recognized those outfits anywhere. Sharma *was* facing forward, and she must have swiped the Kyle wig from Audra, because she was sporting it on top of her own long black hair, and you could just tell by the way she held her head that she was mimicking me.

I knew right then that I should delete the rest without looking at them. These wouldn't be photos you were supposed to see; they happened in the background of life for a reason. They were supposed to be forgettable. But like that time Kyle searched the word "nude" and it brought up pics of people with paintbrushes stuck in their tooters, I couldn't stop looking if I wanted to.

When I scrolled to the second pic, I immediately sat down on the curb. And nobody sat on the curb-your-dog curbs of Brooklyn, even in Brooklyn Heights. But I suddenly felt like that stroller had run me over again and dragged me a few blocks besides.

It was another Woofer pic. This one had been taken at some kind of Mexican restaurant or club. I now knew what Sharma had seen when she was looking at Mac's profile. In the foreground two girls were holding up margaritas. In the background was Mac, my math genius, with his derivative all tangent to the curves of some chick.

Correction: Nothing could be worse than Mac's hickey, except for seeing a pic in which he was receiving it. Her hands were embedded in his curls. Their pelvic regions were plastered together like two sides of the same holoscreen. The time stamp was from last night. I guess I realized Mac hadn't been kissing other girls these last four months because he wanted to kiss me, and I guess I knew that couldn't continue *indefinitely*, but I hadn't figured he'd go back to his old ways so quickly. The familiar sick-to-my-stomach, get-me-out-of-Brooklyn-my-skin-my-life-ASAP feeling came over me.

There was no way I was looking at the last pic. I wouldn't give AnyLies any more power over me. My Doc screamed again.

😈 Thoughts?

I meant to only reply with a string of threats about lawyers and leaving me alone and karma one day coming back to crush her or him or whoever this was, but instead my eyes found the third photo. At first I didn't know what I was supposed to be looking at. It had to be from one of our recent snow days. It was a wide shot of a pretty, white-frosted street in Brooklyn. But there in a slice of an alley was a mess of curls that could only belong to one person. I zoomed in. Sure enough, it was Fawn leaning against a building, making out with some boy.

So what? Like this was news?

Except when I zoomed again, I realized the boy looked a lot like someone I knew.

I zoomed again and squinted at the screen. Kicking the tire of every car on that street, thereby setting off every single alarm, still wouldn't have covered up my sharp shout of surprise and rage.

Fawn, apparently, was making out with my brother.

67

Fuming. All I saw was red. Screw the bus. I ran home. The entire one point nine miles.

When I got there I slammed the front door and hurled my bag into the living room. Nobody was home, so I was stuck with myself. I paced the first floor in anger. No wonder Kyle had been in such a good mood lately. No wonder he was always so clean. But was he aware that Audra's period-predicting app told us Fawn had been creating blue dots aka *having sex* with some boy?

I stopped where I was and closed my eyes. For a moment, I was glad Audra and I weren't speaking, otherwise I'd have felt compelled to txt her what an idiot I equaled. The "some boy" Fawn was logging blue dots with *was* my brother.

I stomped upstairs to my room and threw myself on my bed.

moi Fawn. What the FCK. My brother?

Just to make sure she knew what I was talking about, I forwarded her the pic that AnyLies had sent me.

Her avatar immediately went from green to red.

It wasn't Fawn's or Kyle's fault I knew about this. It was AnyLies's. And as I seethed in my room, I reminded myself that I never had been and wouldn't start now being the sister who went through her brother's stuff. I further reminded myself that I wasn't the kind of girl who scanned Woofer looking for more pics of her not-boyfriend making out with some skank.

Except, apparently, I was. Also I now not only called girls sluts, but skanks as well, because let's face it, some of us just were. And why the H-double-L did Mac's skank have to be so pretty? And, according to her profiles, interesting. A Natty History Museum volunteer and a Summer Relief aid worker? Speaking of exceptional sluts, it was then I realized that AnyLies hadn't sent me a pic of Audra. Did that mean something or was it just that Audra's secret had already come out? And if it *was* that Audra's secret was already out, how did AnyLies know that? And did we still have any of Nãinai's tea for migraines, because so much wondering was making my head hurt.

Regardless, it took a lot to make Audra look like the angelic one. "Screw it."

I went across the hall and shoved open Kyle's door.

I knew my brother was a slob, but usually Mom closed his door against it. So I hadn't realized what an extreme state of gross he lived in. Clothes were thrown everywhere. Tech stuff was just as sloppily strewn about—game consoles, earbuds, outmoded Docs that he was too lazy to trade in. As I poked around the mess, I wondered how AnyLies lived with being such a creep. Just being in Kyle's room uninvited felt squirmingly gross and morally wrong. Still, I pulled open his top dresser drawer.

The papers stood out like a flock of flamingos in the Gowanus Canal.

There were sheets and sheets of them. They were all primarily the same. My name was written in every color and every style imaginable. Okay, not my name. Kyle's name, boy-Kyle's name. Now I knew why Fawn's face had paled the day these fell out of my bag.

She'd written them. I thought of the look she and Audra had given each other. Why hadn't I realized it before? It was a *W-T-F, how did those get there?* look. Which, B-T-W, was still a great question.

At least now I knew who'd been inside Fawn's house the day I fought Ellie. And why Kyle had snuck into the house that afternoon and then lied that he'd been upstairs the whole time, the jerk. And why they'd both snuck off so much at the sleepover.

I slumped to his floor. Why hadn't Fawn just told me? I got that she was afraid I might be upset, but come on. I wasn't the scary-temper one in the group. Audra was.

I banged my head lightly against Kyle's dresser. F it. I pulled out my Doc and txted Mac.

moi Come for dinner? I miss you so much it hurts.

But before I could hit send, my Doc buzzed. Rory—FaceAlerting. I didn't even have this much face time with my parents. I almost didn't answer. I didn't have the heart for this anymore. I just wanted my life to go back to the way it was. My Doc continued to buzz. Then again, Rory was the only person left who could help me get back to normal. Or as close to normal as I was now capable of. Because so much of what I used to take as a given in my life—the girls, my solid relationship with my bro, Mac's adoration—would never exist again.

I swiped accept.

"Got him!" Rory cried when I answered. "Or at least I got the schmuck that the fake CB account is attached to. His real name's Jonah Logan. He's got at least four other dummy accounts that I could find. Meanwhile, his actual profile is mi-ni-mal."

No, it couldn't be. My hater was Jessie. Or at the very least Audra. I'd even believe dumb Brittany or Ailey. Not some kid named Jonah. I'd never even met a Jonah, let alone interacted with one enough to make him hate me. And this whole time I'd been txting a boy? That definitely didn't feel right. What boy called someone *pookie*?

I guess Mac had nailed it. I had no idea who my hater was, so why was I giving him open access?

"Hello?" Rory tapped his screen. "Why don't you look happier?"

"Sorry. I'm just surprised. I was expecting a girl. Are you sure this is my hater? Did he view the clips used to make the sex videos?"

Rory smiled. "Yup. I checked his view history on the fake account that linked to the other girls and teachers. He viewed all of their Woofer accounts. And guess what he was looking at a week ago?"

"My Woofer account."

"Yep, hard-core stalked it looking for that footage of you in the cafeteria. Plus, you know how all you girls kinda look like each other? I'm sending you what might be the reason why. Check your mail."

"Check mail, Rory sender," I said.

A small window opened over Rory's FaceAlert screen. The photo of a girl in a glittery semiformal dress uploaded, her hair swept into a fancy updo. Like me, she was some kind of Asian-white mix. If not downright twins, we most definitely could be long-lost sisters.

"What am I looking at?"

"The dude's ex-girl. Best I can tell, they broke up six months ago. She dumped him right before their winter formal. She and her girlfriends drove to his house to pick him up, and when he stepped outside, they collected his ticket, hopped back in the car, and sped away. Didn't stop her from having a terrific night."

"How do you know all this?" I asked.

"He set up a one-post hate page about it. Along with this picture."

One new message from rory (cb techie), my Doc said. I clicked it. It was the same pic, but this one was grossly doctored, so the girl looked like she'd been beaten to an inch of her life. Her white smile was now filled with gaps and broken teeth; both her eyes were black-and-blue; a thin stream of blood dribbled down from her cracked forehead. A giant bruise bloomed on her cheek, and what looked like fingerprints—strangle marks—dotted her neck.

"Tell me you know where this waste of space lives."

I full-screened Rory. He quietly watched his screen, watching me. He nodded.

"Jonah Logan is a Philly boy."

68

"Where's Kyle?"

Two hours later there were only three plates on the counter next to the Thai food Dad brought home. This was when I should have shared what Rory had discovered, but quite honestly, I was too pissed at Kyle. And that came first.

Mom was loading up a plate to take back to her office, clearly back in the midst of the same old avoid-Kyla deadline. Dad had the living room screen cued up for the last few episodes of that anime series Kyle had turned him on to. Now he frowned.

"Kyle's at Nate's? I think."

"Yeah, right. Dad, it's important to know where your children are."

"Just as it's equally important," Mom said, juggling her plate, her Doc, and a glass of wine, "not to yell at your parents."

Everyone looked immensely relieved when the doorbell rang.

"Maybe that's Kyle now," Dad said.

"If we'd invested in a RingScreen," I said as I went to answer it, "maybe we'd know."

If we'd invested in a RingScreen, I could have strategized with my heart.

It was Mac. (What was with him not pre-txting his arrival?) Even though Mac ran hot and the evening temperature, exhausted from its ups and downs, had finally flatlined in the bland upper forties, he was graciously wearing a scarf.

"Can you come outside for a minute?" he asked.

"Let me grab my coat."

As I layered up, I thought of the thousand things I wanted to say to him. And none of them had to do with the South America-sized hickey on his neck. I knew it was only there because I'd said no. It was not too far from a petty vengeance I would have enacted myself.

(Fine. Yes, it was.)

When I went back outside, Mac was pacing.

"I just came by—" he said at the same time as I said, "So Rory found out—"

We gave each other strained smiles.

The last time Mac had come over unannounced we'd been pulled further into our "just friends" mess. This couldn't be good. If only for postponement purposes, I quickly went first. I told him about Philly and Jonah Logan and how the whole thing didn't feel right and how I planned to take a bus to Philly tomorrow to get to the bottom of it all.

"You sure about this?"

"No."

In fact, if Ellie's slap-happiness had taught me anything, it was that rapid-fire decision making did not always lend itself to the best results. So I was pretty certain it was a bad idea to face off with Jonah. But I also knew that if I told my parents, they'd call the lawyer, who was on vacation. And even supposing they could reach Rick, in a few days he would draft some kind of cease-and-desist doc. Shortly after that, he'd mail it to Jonah. Jonah would then lawyer up. And during that whole process, we'd lose all element of surprise, and I'd be past my college-application deadlines.

"But I don't have a whole lot of other choices."

I'd practically lost every single friend I had over this video. If taking a gas-guzzling, Philly-bound death trap toward an unpredictable, possibly dangerous scenario *might* salvage my future? Sign me up.

This was where Mac would normally offer to skip school and come with me. Instead he squinted up the street like some weary gunfighter in an old Western.

I swallowed hard. "Your turn."

"I can't do this anymore."

"Can't do what?"

Mac chewed on his lower lip.

"Us," he croaked. "It's like I said from the start. I can never be just your friend, Kyla."

I was suddenly aware of the weirdest things. How our breath made perfect cumulus clouds. How all this fluctuating weather meant the subways would be filled with sick people. And how utterly unsurprised I was by Mac's words. I'd been expecting this. All those times I knew Mac would dump me after he got what he wanted, it looked exactly like this.

"Say something," he said.

What was there to say? Mac was "just friends" breaking up with me. And that meant we'd never again lie side by side and say our words directly into each other's mouths. He wouldn't send fake messages to my teachers from Dr. Graff that pulled me out of class because he'd found a song that would, like, change my life. I wouldn't hear his cackle laugh anymore and I'd never see him get ubersentimental after watching that dumb underdog soccer movie. And there was definitely no possibility he'd be my first. Mac hadn't gotten what he wanted. Neither had I. What was the whole stupid point?

I struggled out of my coat. Then I whipped it at him.

"I hate you, Mackenzie Rodriguez!"

"Kyla—"

"I fell for you the second I saw you, freshman year." I flung my scarf at him. "And since then I have watched you make out with almost every female on the planet and still you've managed to be the best part of any of this, you dumb jerk. But you want to stop being my friend? Now? What, because some new skank is there waiting for you? Go ahead!"

Hat.

"End our friendship."

New faux-leather gloves.

"Ruin the entire point of this whole crummy exercise in not dating because you're impatient and you can't wait a little longer for me."

One shoe. "This is what I was trying to prevent all along..." Other shoe. "...you complete and total a-hole."

Fresh out of winter wear, I stood gasping for breath. It looked like Mac had been standing next to a snowman that melted. He pressed his fists to his forehead almost like he was going to laugh, but then he flung his head back and kind of, like, howled instead.

"So what are we supposed to do?" His voice cracked. "Because you clearly don't trust me, which means you'll never date me. And this 'look but don't touch' thing we've got going on? It makes me crazy, so we can't be just friends."

And then all of a sudden his eyes filled, his lower lip kind of trembled, and Mac, my Mac, started to cry. Clearly not pleased with this development, he gave an exasperated huff. Yet tears kept sneaking out. He brushed them away with his thumb, sniffed. More tears came. And watching Mac try to not cry while fully crying— at the thought of losing me, mind you—I mean, it was almost as upsetting as watching the Mr. E. video for the first time.

Whatever other labels he fell under, Mac was one of my best friends. We were supposed to protect each other from hurt, not cause it.

All my anger dissolved away as if I *had* melted out of my clothes. Picking up my coat, I rummaged through the pockets until I found a tissue. I handed it to him. He blew his nose. I picked a fleck of tissue off his cheek.

"Thanks."

He held his arms open. I walked into them and, in my socked feet, stood on his shoes. I messed with his curls. He pressed into my touch. We put our foreheads together. And it was then I realized I did trust him. Mac had been there for me this week. More than my mom or my dad or my brother, and, with the exception of maybe Sharma, more than any of the girls. So what did the past matter? Mom and Audra were right. The thing about history was that it was freshly created every second.

I've never understood indirectness or people who were afraid of definitive sentences. It's actually really easy to get what you want. You just say it. And what I wanted was Mackenzie Rodriguez.

"Mac—"

He kissed the side of my head and untangled himself.

"It's been real, amiga. Be safe tomorrow in Philly, okay?"

Sure, I could have stopped him. I could have completed my sentence. But if Mac so badly wanted to walk out of my life without any further discussion, then I figured it was probably best that I let him.

69

At two a.m. my Doc belched. It was the new txt sound I'd given to AnyLies. President Malin always said that we are born limitless and then proceed to chip away at that status throughout our lives. She said we create our own fears. So I figured why give AnyLies the power of a scary txt tone?

Audra could worship the *B&P* chick, or, well, herself, I guess—ew, hello, narcissism—all she wanted. Corny as it might be, I still thought President Malin was the SHT, and her Limitless speech still equaled my all-time fave. I'd first heard it after a particularly rough spell with my mom second week sophomore year. Up to that point, I'd been using my mom as my sage-advice wellspring. But since I began at Prep, all her advice had gone down the "maybe you should try being less *you*" route.

President Malin had been my go-to guru ever since.

My Doc belched again.

🐱 I know we're not txt friends anymore.
Was wondering tho how it feels?

After a lengthy pause, I replied.

moi How what feels?

😈 Coming in last. Not on top anymore, are you? Look at
what weak foundations you built. I took it all away in
a matter of days.

moi That's what you think.

My Doc spooled angrily.

😈 THAT IS WHAT I KNOW.

Grinning, I fluffed my pillows, then clicked off my light. Before
muting my Doc and hunkering deep under my covers, I shot off
one last message. I even happy-sighed as I closed my eyes. It would
be a good sleeping night.

moi Sure thing. I just hope you're ready. I am SO coming
to get you.

WEDNESDAY, DECEMBER 29

A HopSkip bus to Philadelphia took two hours and cost eighty-five dollars round-trip. Sharma and I arrived forty minutes early and still had to wait in a line at least a hundred people long. Last night, I'd group txted all the usuals about going to Philly, and then one by one I'd deleted names from the list. Mac's went first, then Audra's, then Fawn's, and last Kyle's. So it was only Sharma who'd received the Rory debriefing, along with the Woofer pic that AnyLies had sent me of her wearing the Kyla wig. Her reply had been instant.

> sharm Ha! Where'd you find that? Wore it all night.
> Me + extensions = awesome. What time we leaving for cheesesteak central?

Earlier that morning—almost exactly one week to the hour that the video dropped—Sharma and I were excused from classes before we even set foot in school. Off-grounds passes, signed by each of our dads *and* a deputy secretary of Homeland Security, were sent to each of our teachers excusing us for the entire day so that we could attend a classified meeting.

"Whoa, a little over-the-top, don't you think? How'd you forge that?" I asked when I saw the e-sig. "Graff will never—"

"Will never say anything. Only forged the parent signatures. Hubert owes me."

"Sharma, sometime I'd love to hear more about what you do in your free time."

Now, as a glacial wind blew up Thirty-Seventh Street, we huddled together for warmth. It was so cold, Sharma wasn't even on her Doc—a first. It also equaled the first time we'd hung out alone, ever.

"And then they were down to two, huh?" she said, as if she'd hacked my brain. "Man, winter is by far my least favorite season."

"Sharm," I snorted. "It's so cold, you just made a complete sentence."

"Kylie, did you know only one percent of people are thought to have an IQ higher than one hundred thirty? When they tested mine for Code to Work, they estimated it at one-sixty-eight. The test's wack, because there are infinite kinds of intelligence, but Einstein's IQ was only estimated at one-sixty. I'm pretty sure I'm able to speak in complete sentences, but no one wants to hear what fourth-wheel Sharma has to say unless it's about amping up their connection speed or, like, hacking Destiny Spark's Doc. Which is not even that interesting, B-T-W. She totally underutilizes her tech. It's okay. You don't have to make consternation face. I was a fourth wheel even when there were only three of us."

I couldn't have been more surprised than if Sharma had peeled off her face, yelled *Ha-HA*, and turned out to be an alien. I'd known Sharma for three-plus years. She'd been talking in gamer-speak this whole time because otherwise she thought no one would listen to her?

"Do I know my friends at all?"

"Better than anyone." Sharma blew warm air into her gloved

hands. "Don't look so upset. We all do it. If I didn't watch you online, I'd never know how amazing you are. The chats you have with the people in your clubs, the essays you write. Audra thinks I'm the smartest, but Kylie, I think we tie. Every morning, when I give newsreel, you already know it all except for the funny trending vids. Trying to trump you equals the most interesting part of my day. But around us, you way scale back your smarts and natural interests."

"If I didn't, you guys would think I was even more unbearable."

"Who thinks you're unbearable? Kyle being more Kyle only equals more awesome."

It was without question the sweetest thing Sharma had ever said. Possibly to anyone. Ever. With her hair hidden beneath her beanie and the magnification on her giant old-skool lenses she looked 90 percent eyes. They widened further as a puffball of winter clothing appeared and held up a gloved hand for a high five.

"Rory!" I cheered. "What are you doing here?"

"I'm tagging along on this Hunt the Hater Hacker, er, Hunt. Oh, hey, you must be Sharma. Nice to meet you IRL. Didn't know you'd be here. Figured it was too nice out to sit in the office all day. Might as well get some vitamin D sunshine and whatnot."

The only part of Rory not covered by his oversized pants, boots, winter parka, scarf, gloves, and fisherman's cap was the lower half of his face. We all looked skyward. There had never been a bleaker NYC day.

"Think you forgot what sunshine is."

Sharma spoke this in the general direction of Rory's shoulder, like she was addressing the elderly grandmother in line behind us, who didn't look all that happy that her line had gotten longer by one. Rory laughed like he was txting it—all-caps HAHAHA followed by dozens of exclamation marks. He smacked his cheek to stop.

"Well, it feels like sunshine being in present company," he bellowed.

Sharma gave him such a frosty look, it made the air feel tepid in comparison. Then I realized it wasn't Rory she was glaring at. It was the person behind him.

It was Mac.

I put my hand into his airspace, thinking he might be one of those holo-ads that plugged in people from your favorites list. My hand hit coat. It was really him. He was holding a tray of steaming hot teas.

"Oh, thank G-O-D," Rory breathed. "You made it."

"I never let down a primo."

As Mac and Rory did a one-armed bro hug, the grandma behind me swore in what my EarRing told me was Russian. As a peace offering for cutting, Mac handed her a tea. Grumbling, she snatched it, then sighed at its warmth. He passed out the other three to us.

"You came," I said.

"Well, I kinda needed to urgently tell you something. Plus, what kind of friend would I be if I didn't stick around to find out who your hater was?"

"The kind who gets slutty hickeys and then ends a cool relationship?" Sharma intoned.

She slid her glasses to the bottom of her nose and glared at Mac over them like a librarian scolding a talker.

"Oh, hey, Sharm, nice to see you, too." Mac took my elbow and resolutely turned us so our backs were to her and Rory. The Russian grandmother smacked her lips, pleased to now have a hot drink *and* entertainment. "When did Sharma start speaking in full sentences? Never mind. So I had this realization after I deserted you outside your house last night. Before you, I never got the point of holding hands. I mean, it's two bony appendages pressed together. No me importa. But as soon as you took my hand on our date—"

"I recall you taking mine, amigo."

"Agree to disagree. That day, I got why people dug it. I'd never felt so connected to someone or so ready to be immersed in all their messiness. I never felt happier and all I was doing was holding your hand."

"Aw," Rory sighed.

We glanced behind us. Startled, Rory looked skyward, like the clouds had just called his name. Sharma simply stared at us, not even trying to pretend she wasn't listening.

"Keep going," the Russian grandmother said.

Mac cleared his throat; even quieter, he continued, "I know you think I want us to go out so I can, like, run your bases, but it's not that. It's that I kinda knew from the first time we held hands that we fit—really nicely—and that it was special. And, well, yeah. That's sólo todo what I had to say. That's all I got."

Rory clomped his ski gloves together in muted applause. Sharma discreetly wiped at her cheeks, then punched Mac lightly on the arm. Mac's eyes roved over my face.

"Nah," he said. "That's not all I got."

Tea sloshed on the sidewalk as he lifted me off my feet. With our noses touching, he swung me back and forth. Just as Mac angled his lips down to kiss me, I snuck a hand up and clamped it over his mouth.

"I don't want to be your girlfriend." Before all the happy drained from his eyes, I hurried on. "I haven't just been worried that you'll break up with me; it's that I don't ever want to experience a day when either of us 'moves on.'"

Mac set me down. I kept my hand over his mouth.

Through my glove, he said, "So now we're getting married?"

"No, dummy. I'm saying 'just friends,' 'going out'... the labels don't work. They're all too limiting, because I love you, Mackenzie Rodriguez. And—fingers crossed—I'm also going away to school for four years. Which means if we date, we'll have to break up at the end of summer, because everyone knows you don't date your high school boyfriend past high school. And I can't imagine a day when I won't want you in my life."

We both got a little teary. I wiped my nose on my coat sleeve.

"Gross," he sniffed. "So this means you promise to be in my top five lost contacts when the Virus strikes?"

I nodded. "Macky, I am exhausted with not kissing you. But be warned, if anybody other than me gives you a continental-sized hickey in the next few months, I will get Sharma to delete your fantasy-fútbol team faster than you can say 'skank.' And, for the record, even though you're taking me to prom, I refuse to do it with you in the back of some car or, like, dirty motel room afterwards." I took my hand away from his mouth. "Now say something."

"Lo siento. I spaced after 'I love you, Mackenzie Rodriguez.' So we're not going out again?"

"Correct. But we are also not not going out."

Behind us, Rory said, "Uh, so what's your CB relationship connection gonna read? On-Again, Off-Again?"

"Free Spirits?" Sharma asked.

Mac danced that eyebrow up. I bit my lip, trying to hold back my smile. There was only one out of the hundreds of connection descriptions that fit us.

"You Wouldn't Understand," we said together.

And just as we leaned forward to kiss, the bus arrived. The line surged. Rory hurried forward. Sharma looked back at me with a *you'd better not stick me with this guy* glare. Russian grandma behind me ran her suitcase into my heels.

"What I understand is that the line has moved."

I took Mac's hand. He smiled at our interwoven fingers.

"Yeah, that's better," he said as we moved toward the bus. "And, hey, did you just ask me to prom?"

71

Two and a half hours later, a little before noon, we were off the bus, and the Elite Rory pinged—now that Sharma was present, look who had credits—was pulling up in front of the tan, aluminum-sided house that Jonah Logan called home. Mac let out a low whistle. The whole neighborhood didn't look more than ten years old, but I got the feeling that in those ten years newer, fresher neighborhoods had been built and all the people with lawn mowers and, like, hedge trimmers had moved there. Maybe it was the gray day, or maybe I was used to living in a building that had nearly two hundred years of character built into it, but Jonah's home equaled so dingy it was unnerving. Mac squeezed my hand. He hadn't let go of it since we got off the bus.

"Wait for us, please," Rory said.

"I got you," the car replied.

The woman who opened Jonah Logan's door was wearing a bright pink sweatshirt, mom-khakis, and running shoes. I already knew what Jonah's mom looked like. She was in one of the Goog-Satellite pics. What it failed to capture was her warm smile. When I told her we were there to see Jonah, she brightened even more.

"Ooh, friends from school?"

"Sure," I said. "Why not?"

"Come in. Come in. He didn't tell me friends were coming. I would have cleaned up."

From the small foyer, we stepped down into a living room that was not a whole lot larger than mine. I'd thought suburban homes were supposed to be huge. Granted, there was an identical space right across the hall. Like a second living room. With a whole other set of couches. The décor was a little bit country, but the tech was top-of-the-line. Each room had a home hub—*each* room—plus holo wall screens and a voice-tech system I didn't think came out until next year.

"Mira," Mac said, and ran his hand through the Christmas tree in the corner.

It was such a good holo, I'd thought it was real. And from what I could see, there were three of them, all with different light combinations. I was beginning to wonder if the furniture was even real when Mrs. Logan said, "I'll tell Jonah you're here."

All four of us traded glances. I don't think any of us had expected to get this far. It felt so not like real life.

Mrs. Logan went to the bottom of the stairs, started to holler, then slapped a hand over her mouth in an overexaggerated way and waddled back into our living room.

"He gets so mad when I don't use the gadgets. But I never remember how they work."

Next to the holoscreen in the living room, an old flat-screen HDTV blared an afternoon game show. Considering all the tech, Mrs. Logan could have watched the game show in interactive, life-sized 3-D. But hey, my dad still read paper books.

With my back toward the mom, I whispered, "This is like totally—"

"Redundant technology," Rory and Sharma murmured at the same time, and not at all what I was going to say.

As Mrs. Logan swiped through different screens on the Speak

Panel, Rory and Sharma patrolled the perimeter. I caught only snippets of what they were saying.

"...money they wasted installing three home hubs?"

"...faster and easier interface."

"I hate—" Rory began.

"Vanity tech," Sharma finished.

"The wonders of technology," Mac murmured to me. "Bringing people together."

Suddenly, a boy appeared next to the very panel that Mrs. Logan was standing in front of. When she saw him, she let out a little scream. It was my hater. In the digital flesh. He was kind of what I expected any good Internet stalker to be. Doughy and pale, medium height, with bad posture and greasy hair hanging in his eyes. He clearly hadn't washed it in weeks, though considering all his tech, until they created an app for cleanliness maybe he never would. Even in holo mode he couldn't look his mother in the eyes.

He had yet to notice us. I was holding my breath. I couldn't wait to see his expression when he did.

"If you'd watch the vid I linked you," the hologram huffed, "you'd know how to work that."

"I did watch it, JoJo. But I can never remember if it's a swipe or a tap, and when I'm supposed to say 'speech activate.'"

"Never! 'Speech activate' is only for when you install it. You swipe once, say 'Jonah,' and then talk. How less complicated can you get?"

"Oh, well, much less complicated, actually. I could have called up the stairs to you. But now that you're here, I was trying to tell you, JoJo, you have guests."

"Guests?" He flattened his hair with one hand, realized we could see him, and stopped. At first there was confusion on his face, like he was wondering who we were and why we were in his living room. Then his eyes quick regarded me and grew wide. "Oh SHT."

The image instantly evaporated. All four of us looked at each other. I wasn't the only one holding my breath. Mac clearly wanted to run upstairs, but he settled for peeking out the living room windows, as if Jonah might jump from the second floor and make a quick getaway.

I group txted:

moi What do we do?

rory (cb techie) Wait him out.

sharm And if that doesn't work?

mac Drag that little p*ta down here by that oil slick he calls hair.

"Yeah, playah," Rory said as he and Mac bumped fists.

"Drinks for anyone?" Mrs. Logan asked, worrying an LED bracelet that changed color every time she touched it. "You kids hungry?"

I shook my head, unable to speak from the anxiety of anticipating what Jonah was up to.

Mac, however, said, "Starving, and I would love a coffee. If you have any on. Please."

Mrs. Logan's face lit up. "I'll put on a fresh pot."

"Oh, and Mrs. Logan," Sharma said, "may I borrow the home hub password? My Doc won't sync to a signal. My mom's trying to txt me."

No one would ever give out this information. Knowing the password to a home hub was like knowing someone's Social Security number, bank account number, and password to said bank account all rolled into one. But Sharma asked for it like it was no big deal. Not syncing to a signal didn't even make sense.

"Sure, hon, are you ready? It's pretty complex. Jonah made it up."

319

Mrs. Logan took a piece of paper out of a sideboard, put on glasses, and read aloud, "Capital *A*, one of those underslash things..."

Meanwhile, Rory inspected the home hub like he was admiring its specs. Even though I was watching, I barely saw him insert the minuscule jump drive into one of its ports.

"Lowercase *a*," Mrs. Logan finished. "You want me to repeat that?"

"Nope," Sharma said with a bright smile. "Got it."

"Now about that coffee."

No sooner was Mrs. Logan out of the room than Sharma said, "G-A-S-P."

Hologram Jonah was back. Standing barely an inch away from me.

"You have ten clicks to tell me what you want before I fry your operating systems."

'm not sure what I was expecting. For the past week, I'd been daydreaming about how it would go down when I came face-to-face with my hater. Still under the impression AnyLies was a girl—namely Jessie—I'd imagined lots of tears and yelling. A smug hologram boy was not a scenario I would have dreamed up in a million years. It all felt...wrong.

From what the holoimage captured, Jonah's room was even more tricked out than the downstairs. It looked like he was at the helm of an alien fighter jet. All around him were holoscreens running with green code. I wondered how many girls' lives that code was destroying.

"So what do you want?"

"I think you know what we want," I said.

"What, am I a mind reader now?"

So he was going to play it like he didn't know who I was.

"I want to speak face-to-face," I said.

"And I'd like to get with Destiny Sparks." Jonah blew air out his lips. "Sorry, sweetheart. No can do. You want the parental controls removed on your Internet? Leave me your operating system ID, the main password to your Internet hookup, and a hundred bucks on the coffee table. I can get it done by tomorrow afternoon. Now get out. I don't do houseguests."

"Don't make me pull you down here by your EarRing," Mac growled.

"Don't bother," Rory said.

Sharma nodded. "We can do better."

They hadn't stopped working their Docs since Mrs. Logan gave up the hub password. Via his hologram, we watched as Jonah stopped swiping. He peered more closely at one of his screens and then expanded it.

"What the heck," he murmured. "My CB was suspended?"

Rory cracked his knuckles and grinned at Sharma, both eyebrows raised.

Sharma tsked. "Too subtle."

Suddenly the screen in front of Jonah went black. The music shut off in Jonah's room. All the lights went off as well. Other than the kitchen, where Jonah's mother could be heard opening various cabinets, the whole house fell silent and dark. Mac whistled under his breath. Rory looked ready to cut his heart out and hand it to Sharma right there. The only thing that stayed on was Jonah's hologram and, on his end, the feed of us in the living room.

"W-T-F, man?" Jonah pushed back in his roller chair and then fiddled with the connection on the hub under his desk.

"It's not your hub," I said. "It's us. Now how about you come downstairs."

It wasn't a question.

"Who the hell are you guys?" Jonah squinted at the transmitted images of us.

We all looked to Rory.

Swiveling his head to stare down the hologram, he said, "We're the people who decide what the rest of your life looks like."

73

"Wait, this is my favorite part," Jonah said. "You know how long I spent on that edit? I mean, it was fine after a half hour, but I really wanted to make it clean."

"A half hour?" I said. "Don't you mean half a day?"

Jonah snorted. "I would if I was a tool."

One minute and ten seconds ago, Sharma had cued up the Mr. E. video.

"Oh," Jonah said, "you're that one. I couldn't tell."

"Racist," Sharma said.

Jonah shrugged and then proceeded to provide an audio commentary track to the video the entire time it played. Now that we were coming to the end, I tuned him out. I'd never expected my hater to be so enthusiastic about his work. And I'd never expected my friends to be so absorbed by my hater. You'd think Sharma, Rory, and Jonah were at a hacker convention. Only Mac seemed to get how crazy this made me, patting my leg, kissing the side of my head, cracking up at the test video Jonah played where he put a lizard's face where Mr. E.'s girlfriend's should have been.

"This part is amazing," Rory said. On-screen I flicked my hair up. "The blend is perfect."

"I know, right? It's the program—EffectsMaker. It literally melds the pixels of two different vids together. It's the same software they use in special-effects studios, but way more user-friendly. It's not even available anywhere yet. It's all tied up in the courts because of security and identity concerns. Right now you need a Japanese birth certificate to even test a copy. Unless you know someone." Jonah laughed—"Hehehe." He sounded like the evil villain in an anime movie. "And in my case, I am that someone. Safe America got a deal when they booked me."

Rory and Sharma were silently, insanely jealous. Clearly, they both added EffectsMaker to their mental checklists of software that needed to be cracked.

"Am I the only person who remembers why we're here?" I asked. "What's Safe America? I've heard that name before."

"It's nothing," Jonah said, and clamped his lips shut.

"We don't have time for this." Mac stood up like he was going to beat it out of the kid.

At the same time, Jonah's mother staggered into the living room carrying a tray loaded with a crumb cake, full coffee mugs, and a veritable coffee shop array of creamers and sweeteners. A stack of paper plates was wedged beneath her arm. Mac and Rory jumped up to help her.

"Aren't you two sweet."

Mac set the tray on the coffee table.

"Oof," Mrs. Logan said as, knees cracking, she hovered over it and began doling out mugs of mocha nut. "Don't mind me, kids."

Jonah sank into the couch with a satisfied grin.

"Actually, Ma." He smiled sweetly. "Stay. Have coffee with us."

"Oh, okay," Jonah's mom said brightly, though this could have been her intention all along as there were six cups of coffee on the tray. "It's so nice to meet some of Jonah's pals."

As Mrs. Logan spooned sugar into her coffee, the wall screen behind her flickered to life. Jonah's main G-File page—his real one—was on view. His profile pic was a joker from a deck of cards. Douche. Otherwise there was scant information about him. He was tagged in a few family photos, but they looked blurry, like someone had taken a filter to the parts just over his face. Other than that, there were only a few banal memberships to various movie and comic streaming sites.

"So," he snorted.

Sharma smiled but didn't look up from her Doc. The list of memberships updated first. Every site that Jonah had joined under an alias was now attached to his G-File. There were sites for making weapons. Sites for looking at porn—whether it was girl-on-girl, guy-on-guy, teacher-on-student, the list was nearly unending.

"Those are for work," Jonah muttered.

But already other memberships were edging the porn ones off-screen. Amidst the hundreds of sites that were suddenly scrolling along, I swore the *B&P* site flew by. Audra sure had reach. Jonah spilled his coffee on the floor as he stood up and quickly sat back down.

"Whoops," his mom said, and dabbed at the carpet with a napkin as, on-screen, avatars appeared for all of Jonah's aliases, for his role-playing games, and for what I could only assume were hacker memberships.

"Jonah was just about to tell us about this new club he joined," I told his mother.

"A club," she said hopefully. "Like a school one?"

"Extracurricular," I said.

Jonah pressed his lips together. "It's nothing."

"Well, I'm sure it's not nothing." Mrs. Logan had finished with the spill and now turned her attention to the coffee cake. "Who wants cake? Sorry, kids. Jonah always gets the first piece."

Rory gazed at Sharma. "Be still my beating heart." Then, cracking his knuckles, he said, "My turn."

Now on Jonah's G-File, under the video section, small clips

filled the screen. It was all the videos he'd authored. Mine and Mr. E.'s was first, as it had the most views, but the other girls' came right after.

"Wait," Jonah said. "What are you doing?"

"Is that too big a slice, hon?" Mrs. Logan stopped cutting cake; in an aside to me, she mock-whispered, "Jonah thinks he's getting chubby."

As if his mother's humiliation of him weren't enough, on-screen there were now what appeared to be a bunch of old Batman movies that had Jonah's head superimposed over Batman's. Rory selected one. It whirled to life. It was immediately obvious, as Batman faced off against the Joker, that Jonah was playing all the parts.

"Harsh," he whispered, then louder: "Stop it."

"You don't have to eat it all."

Beneath the video, all the pics that Jonah was Woofered in began to surface. Pics you could normally only see through ConnectBook could now be viewed by anyone. Rory and Sharma had just uncoded his life and privacy faster than it took Jonah's mom to cut a slice of cake.

"No!" Jonah shouted. "You can't put all that ... dessert ... on my plate for everyone to see. This will ruin me."

Mrs. Logan blinked once, twice, then chuckled. "Jonah, it's just cake. You love cake."

But then the sheer delight on four of the five faces around her finally caught her attention.

"What's everyone looking at?"

She turned to face the wall screen.

Jonah shouted, "Safe America. It's called Awareness for a Safe America."

The wall screen flipped back to Jonah's original, bare G-File.

"Dear me," his mother said. "That sounds like quite the dope club. What does it do, JoJo?"

Jonah's face was white. With shaking hands, he took the huge slice of cake his mother offered him.

"I'll tell you about it later, Mom." Jonah set the cake on the coffee table and sat on his hands. "Do you mind if I hang with my friends now, alone?"

Now that everyone was served, Mrs. Logan had just been about to sit. She covered the hurt over her revoked invite with a bright smile and patted Jonah on the head, then left. Sharma or Rory—who could tell which at this point?—was already bringing up the Encyclo screen for Safe America.

"You won't find much written there," Jonah said, correctly.

The definition stated that Awareness for a Safe America was a privately funded Internet-safety watchdog group. And that was about it.

"They found me. Messaged me through a *Kruel Killers* board—"

"Detective game where you hunt and kill serial killers," Rory chimed in.

"—things like: 'Interested in being a Kruel detective in real life? Make money finding RL Kruels.' I thought it was spam. Except a dude I'm connected with on the game said he worked for them. That they're legit. Said the work was fun and all-caps DOLLAR SIGNS. Zipped-lips face what *kind* of work. Didn't take me long to find out. I totes hacked my friend's e-mail. ASA had him scooping up Woofer pics of congressmen with chicks who did not equal-sign their wives—I sent ASA my e-sumé stat."

Jonah couldn't make eye contact worse than anyone I'd ever seen. It was like an invisible hand was pushing his head down and to the left. And it was horrible listening to him. He practically spoke in emotes. I was tempted to have Sharma give him subtitles. Wait. *That* was where I'd heard that name before.

"Safe America brought down that shady senator, right?" I asked. "They're behind the Dubai scandal exposé."

"Couldn't say." Jonah smirked. "The focus they assigned me

was to stop-sign child molesters. It was all up to me to find the supporting vids and pics. It's not hard. You find raunchy home vids, then use Woofer software, then write a diff program that cross-references against employment info, one that cross-references against age info. Found a doctor, a guitar instructor in Jersey—"

"And then, let me guess, you stopped finding people so you started forging the videos instead? That wasn't me with my teacher."

Jonah shrugged. "Well, it could have been. In the original vid the girl's face was all blurred out, but the guy was clearly a teacher. That's clearly sex in a classroom. I just connected A to B. I mean obv the guy's got issues if he gets off on that kind of thing. Is that someone you want around impressionable sixteen-year-olds?"

"But it's fake. And he got fired. You're ruining lives."

"I posted one vid on your school's faculty message board after hours. It was taken down five minutes after it posted. Your life equaled ruined in five minutes? Please."

"No, it was ruined the next morning when you reposted it to the Student Activities board."

"I never reposted it. The only people I need to see it are the administrators. My job is done as soon as pervy gets caught."

"What about those photos you took of me and Mr. E. by his apartment? What about that video you shot of me through FaceAlert? What about AnyLiesUnmade?"

"What's that?"

"Your alias."

"No it isn't," he laughed. "Trust me. Why waste all that effort when the vid is the clincher? The last time I touched anything having to do with your case was when I posted the vid to the faculty board, like, a week ago. Look, you saw all my aliases up there. 'Any lies unmade'? That's just dumb. *All* lies unmade' is more like it and better English."

Said the guy who barely spoke the language. Yet it matched

up to what Mr. E. had said about the video first posting the night before on Prep's Faculty Activities board. Jonah's whole life was exposed before us. Why would he lie?

Jonah snorted. "Sounds like I'm not the one who ruined your life after all."

74

"So who did?"

"You figure it out." Jonah took a huge bite of coffee cake and then coughed on the powdered sugar topping. "I'm sure you have frenemies abounding."

I couldn't believe it. We were back to square one. Mac stroked my thumb with his. It felt nice, but it was more of a...you know what? I needed to focus. We were back to square one. Sharma txted me a pic of a French bulldog that looked like it was bowed down in prayer. The caption said: *Have Faith*.

"How come you picked Kyle?" Mac asked.

"Like that equals rocket science? Found the vid of your teach on some wronged women's dating site, then browsed your school's online yearbook for a current student that mirror-pic'ed the girl in the vid. Two girls fit. You belonged to more extracurrics. It meant you had more Woofer vids to choose from. You and me became connected two weeks ago. Nothing personal."

No, that couldn't be it. "Nothing personal"? *That* was why this had all happened to me? Because Jonah had randomly selected the

girl on the left instead of the girl on the right? I wondered who the other girl was, the girl whose life was almost ruined instead of mine.

"Lying," Sharma said, without looking up from her Doc.

"My guess," Rory said, "is you also picked Kyle because of her."

A G-File for a girl named Ananda Stevens came up on-screen. Jonah shifted in his seat. He coughed and bits of cake flew onto the coffee table.

"What about her?" Sharma's lips pursed.

A folder on Jonah's desktop labeled *Homework* opened to reveal another folder, which led to another and then another. Suddenly there was the photo of the girl with all the retouched bruises marring her face. The thing about high school was it all felt so personal. Every slight felt specifically, solely crafted for you. And the only thing worse than your "unique" agony was the belief that no one else had to deal with anything as bad. So you wildly inflicted slights of your own. I saw how impossible it was. No one would ever escape high school unscathed.

"You're sick," Mac said.

Jonah reached across me and grabbed Sharma's Doc. With her PHD in his hand, he looked capable of breath for the first time. Mac immediately launched himself at Jonah, like he'd only been waiting for a reason. As they tussled, Jonah swiped at Sharma's Doc, then in a loud voice said, "Home hub, reboot. Enable backup pass code. Okay, okay, here."

Mac let go. Jonah handed Sharma her Doc back. I gathered this meant Jonah had regained control of his house.

As the system rebooted, he said, "Our moms worked together. I was her first friend when she moved to Philly middle of sophomore year. She was so shy she barely spoke in school, so I built her worlds to roam. But then she 'blossomed' over the summer and made friends with some of the pretty girls and suddenly it was all about needing space. As soon as junior year came, she couldn't wait

to go off and play in more hi-def pastures. You aren't supposed to just drop people like that."

"Jonah," I said. "I'm not Ananda."

"It's pronounced with a long *A*."

"I couldn't give a swipe," I said. "I'm not her. She's not me. We're not all the same. You're not just screwing over a teacher, who at least in my case was innocent; you're hurting us. And we never did anything to hurt you. Delete it—now. All of it. My video, the other girls' videos, everything."

"Fine. All right. It doesn't matter to me. I've already been paid anyway."

Once the hub was back up, we watched as he swiped through, deleting source files.

"Your profiles might as well make you the same. Tens of thousands of friends. Vids without a care in the world. Clothes, shoes, boys." He snapped his fingers. "Now I remember why I picked you. You do that stupid air-kiss thing with your Docs. How annoying can you get?"

"So I'm annoying. What you're doing is terrorism."

"Oh, boo-hoo." Jonah selected the source file for the vid of me and Mr. E. and clicked *Trash*. "Did pretty rich girl not get a date? Did I mess with her shopping? There. It's deleted. Are you happy?"

I looked at my G-File on my Doc. The video was still the first thing attached to my name.

"No. It's still there."

"Not possible."

Using his Doc, Jonah brought up the video on the home hub.

"What does that mean?" Mac asked. "You have it stashed somewhere else?"

"No," Sharma said. "It means someone else downloaded it before Dr. Graff removed it, and then that person stuck a DRM on it."

"You have got to be kidding me!" I shouted.

From the kitchen we heard Mrs. Logan say, "Oh dear. Everything okay, JoJo?"

Her son gave his evil-villain laugh again. "Everything's great, Ma. See? I told you it wasn't me. I only posted the vid to your school's website. I never linked it to YurTube. How unlucky are you? Someone really has it out for you."

"But the money to buy all this tech in your house..."

"It came from hard-earned hacks. Safe America pays me pocket change compared to what I make off of my other fields of expertise. Actually, this equals plagiarism. Whoever reposted that vid is making dollar signs that should be coming to me. That's my content. I oughta sue. How come you haven't found out their IP address and leveled their ass?"

"They used GoFetch to reroute the IP," I said.

"So crack the GoFetch reroute."

"With what?" Rory asked.

Sharma's head was already whipping up to stare at Jonah, like *Don't even tell me...*

He withered under her gaze, but smiled and said, "Don't feel bad; the South Koreans don't even know I have this. Where'd you say it was rerouted through?"

"NY Public Library at Forty-Second Street," Sharma said.

"Uh-huh, only three GoFetch users found at that site in the week before and after the vid posted."

Jonah's fingers flicked and swiped at his Doc so ridiculously fast, it didn't seem possible he was doing anything other than pretending. But a click later, a computerized receipt for a GoFetch modem along with a name and billing address came up on-screen.

"Ta-da. This one cross-lists with your school. Ring any bells?"

Sharma, unimpressible Sharma, RL gasped. I felt numb and vindicated and like I wanted to use one of Jonah's hologram generators and send myself back to Brooklyn to immediately wreak some havoc. This was what I'd been expecting. Not some kid in

Philly—someone who knew me better than anyone else. Finally, everything made sense.

"Whoa. Oh, whoa," Mac said. "That little bruja."

"That one's for free," Jonah said. "You're welcome."

Mac's hands clenched into fists. The veins in his arms popped. Just knowing he wanted to crush something as badly as I did made me feel a hundred times better.

"There's a car waiting out front?" Mrs. Logan poked her head back in. "I wish you kids would have told me you took a cab here. I could have driven you all home."

On our way out, Rory handed Jonah a business card. "Better options out there, man."

"Corporate? No way."

Rory shrugged. "It's a stepping-stone, plus three meals a day, and you get to bring your dog to work. Besides, I'm going to keep checking back on you."

"Is that a threat?" Jonah snorted, as I txted Sharma,

moi He's offering him a job?

sharm He might have just saved the world. Hacker with
       God and Napoleon complex = cyber ow.

I snapped a pic of Jonah with my Doc.

"You blinked," I said. "Doesn't matter. You so much as post one more video of a girl, even if it's only of your cousin cuddling a kitten, and I will send your mom, your aunts and grandma, your cousins, teachers, and friends, not to mention whatever person is dumb enough to one day date you, everything you've ever done. Sharma has it all backed up on her Doc. You sneeze in the wrong online direction, and we will link and woofer you in all the worlds you're a part of until there will be so many people coming after you, you can't move online."

Sharma had the good sense not to look at me like I was crazy. Instead she adjusted her glasses and smiled malevolently. For all I knew she *had* downloaded all of Jonah's files.

"And that's a threat," Rory said, tipping an imaginary hat. "Well played, Ms. Cheng. Finally."

75

The whole ride back to New York, all I saw was that name on the screen.

"Just to be clear," Sharma told me, "you need to obliterate the source file, which means the original download she got off the Faculty Activities board. It must be on her Doc."

How ironic that we'd gone all the way to Philly to do what I could have done a few blocks from my house. On the bus ride home, as Rory and Sharma mused over all the nasty things they could do to her, including changing all the sizes on her InStitches filters so everything she ordered would always be four sizes too small or link a paparazzi drone to her Doc signal so she could feel what it was like to be stalked, I filled in all the gaps.

"Oh gosh," I said when the city came into view. "Quick, I need pen and paper."

I met with three blank stares. With only ten more minutes until we hit midtown, my seat was poked gently from behind. The woman looked seventy but was probably much older.

"Here, dear. I always carry a pen."

The note card she gave me had little frogs on it. As I wrote out *AnyLiesUnmade*, I finally, after seventeen years, saw what Mom meant about the advantages of paper. No wonder it was such a mysterious code name. How blind could I be? I txted her as the bus pulled up to our stop on East Broadway, quickly switching out her profile icon on my Doc for a much more appropriate one.

moi Hey, I feel bad about the way we left things. Where you at?

Her reply was almost instantaneous.

(x.x) About to sit down to dinner with the Parents.

When we disembarked, Rory and Sharma said they were getting Korean BBQ and asked if we wanted to come.

"Yes, but no thanks. I have to go talk to my ex–best friend. And Sharma"—I grabbed her arm and pulled her into a hug—"you were never a fourth wheel. Don't you dare condense yourself around me ever again."

"Awkward."

But she was smiling when I released her, and I was treated to a half second of Sharma's sparkling eye contact.

After that, Mac and I dodged tourists and made a beeline for the trains at Herald Square. My palms were already sweating. It was like before I stepped up to the podium at a final. Watching the other rounds proceed, my stomach was always a knot of nerves, my arguments running through my head, and it was like my twitching legs were saying, *Seriously? Fight? Flight is the best way to handle this situation.* And then they started the timer and all my preparation fell into place. What I'd forgotten amid all the nerves was that I all-caps LOVED a good argument.

And then?

I crushed you. Sorry, but it's true.

On the Q train back to Brooklyn, I clutched Mac's hand.

"Let me come with you," he said.

I shook my head. "I need to do this alone. I'll be okay."

"Yes, you will be, bonita."

After only a second's hesitation, Mac tilted my chin upwards and kissed me. And just like when he kissed me on our date, I knew I was in trouble.

"Macky?" I said, between the kissing.

"Mm-hmm."

I whispered into his ear, "Will you do that thing with your thumb to me sometime?"

His eyes clouded—*that thing with my thumb?*—then he laughed. "Turn around."

"You're going to do it here?"

"Just turn around."

I did. We were on a two-seater, so now I faced out into the aisle. An older man across the way tipped his hat. I waved. Meanwhile, Mac collected my hair and slung it over my left shoulder. After giving me a quick kiss on my neck, he ran his fingers down my back. And right at the arch of my back, he pressed his thumb into my spine. It hit just, like, every knot of tension I'd ever had. An inappropriately loud groan escaped me. Fawn was right: I absolutely melted.

"Macky, I feel like we've lost so much time."

I turned back to him.

"Nah, our time's just beginning."

Then we kissed again. Maybe more than once, because when I opened my eyes, we were at the DeKalb stop, Mac's transfer.

"I have been waiting so long to do this," he whispered.

"Let's do it again later," I whispered back. "Let's do it all the time."

He laughed, "Deal."

After one last quick smooch, he darted off the train, making it just as the doors closed. Grinning, he gave me the thumbs-up until the train pulled out of the station. Across from me a woman in a turban and ankle-length down coat winked. My cheeks flushed.

"I remember the first time I fell in love," she said. "Lucky girl."

The first time, because there would be more. And right at that moment, I didn't care. I couldn't stop smiling. *Lucky.* Debaters scoff at luck, but you know what? I did feel lucky.

Just like that, my predebate jitters were gone. When I got off at my stop, I was as serene as a lake on a windless day. When I got to her brownstone, a yellow Hydrogen Coop was parked in front. That solved that. She'd wanted her own car for as long as I could remember. Said she knew it was overindulgent, but there it was. She must have bought it with the video earnings. I took the steps two at a time. Rang the bell bouncing on my toes. I couldn't wait for this to start. As Mac would say, I was so aces right now.

It all pretty much unraveled from there.

76

Audra answered the door. She was clad in slouchy gray sweats, a tattered white tank with no bra underneath, and not a stitch of makeup. This wasn't Audra caught unawares. This was as much a look as if she were decked out in Gucci. A typical teen's casual attire didn't involve popcorn-sized diamond studs. *Popped-popcorn-sized studs, mind you—no kernels there. They were like the earrings that Mac's cousins all sported, except Audra's rocks weren't fake. This time we didn't exchange a squealing hug.

"Have a photo shoot today?" I asked.

"Yup." She elevated her chin.

"Cool. Are you still eating or can I come in?"

"We're almost done." She looked back over her shoulder, hesitated, then shrugged. "Why not?"

Locking the door behind me, she asked, "So did you confront your big hater?"

"Not yet."

I'm about to.

As we made our way through the downstairs, I pulled up the AnyLies txt thread.

I typed,

moi Gotcha

then hit send.

Up ahead in the dining room, there was an old-skool beeping alert. Audra heard it too but didn't say anything. Weird as it sounded, I was going to miss txting AnyLies.

In the dining room, judging by the level of wine in the Parents' glasses and the empty bottle on the table, they had indeed come to the final minutes of the meal. Neither Parent looked up when I entered.

"Hello, dear," the Mother said.

The Father said nothing.

"Father, we need your chair."

"No, don't get up. I can stand," I said.

"That's silly. My parents are finished anyway, aren't you?"

Clearly, Audra was trying to get them out of the room, probably afraid of what they were about to hear. Normally, I'd be cringing, waiting for the sniping to start. For once I wasn't at all concerned by their icy remoteness. Or by the wall screen blaring violent news. Or that the chicken bones on the plate indicated that the Mother had forgotten again that Audra was pescatarian. And not because I'd written Audra off, but because there, sitting in my usual seat, bearing this torture with a grateful smile, was my old best friend and current hater, Ailey.

77

"Kyle," Ailey said brightly. "So glad you stopped by."

She said this generously, as if this were her house, her friend, her life I'd just been invited into. Not as if she was stealing mine.

"It looks like we're finished eating," the Father said, but made no move to stand.

Something like surprise flickered in the Mother's eyes, that her daughter had *two* friends over. I imagined pulling up Audra's naked pics on the wall screen. Seeing if that could wrench a stronger emotion from this woman. But I didn't want to steal Audra's thunder. No doubt she'd been looking forward to that moment since she turned eighteen two weeks ago. I wished I could be there to see their reactions. But then, shockingly, the Mother pushed back in her chair and picked up her plate.

"Do not think bad manners will always be rewarded in this household, Audra Bethany. Gregory, let's let the girls chat."

While Audra cleared, I stared at Ailey. Her braids were piled high on her head, as if she'd had them shoved under a wig. She was clad in comfy yoga sweats, but her tank was more form-fitting than anything I'd ever seen her wear. I shouldn't have been surprised that Ailey had developed so much. It wasn't the first time I'd seen her cleavage recently. Only the first time I'd seen it in person.

Her eyes flicked to me, then away. Her right hand moved to twirl her braid as it did when she was nervous, but it only met air and settled for her earlobe instead. She checked if I was still staring at her. I was. A tiny nervous whicker escaped her.

"Smiley face," she said.

When the Parents left, Audra closed the dining room doors. Ailey took her Doc off her lap and placed it on the table. I wondered if she and Audra had been engaging in the same surreptitious dinnertime color commentary that Audra and I always had. I realized I didn't care.

"So?" Audra asked, hands on hips.

"Sorry to interrupt. Ailey, I was about to tell Audra that I figured out who made the sex video. It's this hacker in Philly. I was going to show you guys what we swiped from his home hub, but my Doc died on the bus ride back. We left in such a hurry to get there, I forgot my charger. Ailey, can I borrow yours real quick?"

"My charger?"

"No. Your Doc."

She clutched it to her chest, glanced at Audra, who rolled her eyes impatiently, like, *what's the big deal?* Only then did Ailey meekly nod and hand it over.

"You actually tracked down the person that made the video?" Ailey asked.

"We did." To Audra I said, "He was one of the ConnectBook guys after all. We got him to delete the source file."

"So that's it?" Audra asked, begrudgingly interested, begrudgingly impressed. "The video's gone?"

"Not quite. You were actually right too. There was something that linked us all. We all looked like his ex. And there was a reason I was chosen more than the others. Oops, Ailey you deleted me as a biometrics user. Is the friends' password prompt still the same?" Before Ailey could answer, into the Doc's microphone I said, "Flipper Fourteen."

The Doc whirled to life. By the nervous way Ailey glanced at Audra, you'd think I was about to, like, delete her movie queues or reading shelves. Maybe while I was at it . . .

"So, one of the things I learned today was how to search for hidden files. Audra, you already know this, but Ailey, you would be amazed at what Sharma can teach you over a two-hour bus ride. Apparently, there's this way to scan all Doc files solely based on gig size. Doesn't matter where you store them; the program simply looks for bulk fileage. So, say your hi-res nude selfies are all in a double-encrypted folder, this special search will bring them to the front of the list. See? Here they are."

I put the folder on fast slide show and swiveled the Doc around so the girls could both see Ailey's previously hidden pics zip past on-screen. Since they were originals from Audra's shoots, the girls' faces weren't cropped out yet. In half the photos, while the girls posed ubersexy, they were crossing their eyes or sticking their tongues out or just caught midblink. They were the antithesis of the sexy selfie face. My mouth got all bile-y. I guessed it was the taste of jealousy, because the girls also looked like they were having so much fun.

"Granted, this doesn't work if what you're looking for is stored on a separate drive, as I'm sure all your *B&P* files are, Audra. But how many people back up their data on the home hub like they're supposed to? Besides, if a gal's worried about her folks accidentally decoding it—say if her dad's some big gig over at Eden—she definitely wouldn't take a 'crypted file off her Doc and stash it on the home hub. And most especially not if it was the first official download of her old best friend—air quotes—'having sex' with her teacher."

Audra's perfect little heart-shaped lips formed an O. Ailey's pouty lips formed a flat, angry line. A few more swipes and I'd logged on as a guest to Audra's wallpaper screen. Behind Ailey, my sex video came to life.

"I told you, I didn't make the video."

"Correct. And I only blame myself for not seeing that statement for what it is: suppressed evidence, aka the lie-by-omission technique. Very crafty. So while it's true that you didn't make the video, what you omitted is that you did find it on the Faculty Activities board of Park Prep's website.

"I still don't know why you were looking at the dead-zone Faculty Activities board—have mucho time to kill, do you?—but you must have been all-caps SHOCKED to see it. You downloaded it pretty quick, huh? Because you knew that as soon as anyone else saw it, Dr. Graff would zap it from existence. Then you created your own account for it and reposted it. First on YurTube, then on the Student Activities board, which you very well know is as much a part of every Parkside Prepper's five-minute checks as ConnectBook.

"Your G-Calendar says your mom was choreographing the Rockefeller Center Christmas show the day before the video dropped. I'm guessing you were killing time at the Forty-Second Street library, waiting for her to get out, before your annual holiday-windows walk?"

I was getting good at this detective stuff. It was almost as easy as they made it look online.

Ailey gazed out the dining room windows. "I don't know what you're talking about."

"Okay. Sure, so I guess it's a total coincidence that AnyLiesUnmade is an anagram of your name. Kind of clunky, no? Did you come up with that yourself? Or did you use an app? I'm guessing app."

"Kyle," Audra said. "Stop."

"Almost done." I held a hand out to Audra, warding her off. "I see the proceeds of the video let you buy that car you always wanted—told your parents you were using your savings, right? The rest is probably already stashed away in your money-market account. You know, I never figured you for a stalker, Ailey."

"What makes you think this is even about you? And who's been stalking who? You're the one who wouldn't stop txting me."

"I didn't know it was you. I was trying to get my hater to take down the video."

"Wait," Audra snapped. "You were txting AnyLies? Why would you do that?"

"To be honest? I thought it was you, Audy."

Ailey burst out laughing. Not in a comical way, but like in a she-might-go-for-my-eyes kind of way. Audra stepped back. The outside streetlights cast a sickly pallor on Ailey's face.

"Of course," she said. "Of course you'd still never see me. All those txts we sent each other? It was just like old times. Don't you remember how we stayed up until two a.m. txting? You think Audra would ask you if your friendships were good for you? Don't you see? *I* believed you were innocent before any of them. *I* tried to help you. I dug around online and *told* you there were other girls. But did you thank me? No, instead you got famous." She laughed. "You're indestructible, Kyla Cheng. And that means you'll probably never get it."

"Get what, Ailey?"

But she just stared blankly into space. I was at a loss for words. I hadn't intentionally hurt Ailey all those years ago, but I guess I'd known she had to be hurting. But it wasn't like I'd been her only friend. She'd had those swim-team girls. And then she'd found Ellie. Was it my responsibility to make sure she made it through high school?

But Ailey was right. She'd believed me when I'd told her it wasn't me in the video. Instantly. Her AnyLies txts had filled in all the gaps that Audra's lack of txts had left in my life this past week. In her own weird way, Ailey had stepped up. And if I had done the same all those years back, even a little, we probably wouldn't be here right now.

I tried again. "Jessie and I spoke on the bus ride back from Philly."

I'd sent her a txt that said,

moi   Sorry I = psycho. But I know it's not you who's been doing this. I know who is. Mind running over some things with me? Know this isn't great for you either. Truce?

She'd called me—*voice* called me—immediately.

"Jessie said she never posted those videos. That she doesn't even own @JessieRosenthal. All her profiles are under @DarkEnchantress. I'm guessing it was you who organized that flash mob via Regrets Only? It was you who was in the locker room at the Y?"

Ailey rocked forward a little, nodded. "Catching the fight was just a lucky coincidence. I was going to surprise Ellie and walk her home. And then I heard Ellie say that Jessie was her best friend. And I knew. It was happening again."

"What was happening again, Ailes?" Audra asked.

"I was losing her. Ellie this time, I mean. Once again, I was falling out of my best friend's graces."

It felt like the entire dining room was one giant screen and we were watching Ailey's avatar. There wasn't an ounce of emotion in her voice. I never expected Ailey to put up much of a fight, but I also wasn't expecting this toneless, dronelike honesty. Audra and I were transfixed.

"Ellie clarified and said Jessie was only *one* of her best friends," I said as gently as possible.

"I guess that makes everything okay, then, does it?" Ailey tilted her head to regard me. "Do you even know what true friendship

347

is, Kyle? I don't think so. Every time I was around Fawn, she was doodling your brother's name—you're welcome for sharing those, B-T-W. Mac's out slurping it up with other girls, letting me be all handsy with him in the hall. Even Audra—sorry, *Senpai*—she knew I took those pics of you with Mr. E. We were shooting *B&P* when I saw you check in at those apartments. We even searched the building together, squealed when Mr. E.'s name was listed as a resident. It was her idea to drive all the way out there. Audra sat next to me as I snapped away."

Audra shook herself a little, surprised to be dragged into it. She cleared her throat, took a sip of water. Reluctantly her eyes left Ailey and met mine.

"I was concerned," she said. "I thought you might be in trouble."

I snorted. "You'd never drive half an hour to anywhere, especially somewhere like Brighton Beach, out of concern. Oh my gosh, Audy, you never did believe me, did you? You were trying to bust me."

"Sharma said there was no way someone could make that video." Audra sounded as exhausted as I felt. "I didn't see how it couldn't be you. Even when you 'found' the source video, next second it mysteriously disappeared? I believed someone was after you. But, no, I didn't for one second believe that wasn't you. And then when Ailey said you were at Mr. E.'s, I thought catching you in a secret might make you less high and mighty when I told you mine. Guess I was wrong."

For once she wasn't being nasty. All our fury had been burned away by Ailey's bizarre monotone speech. So I nodded, like, *Fair enough*. Audra's expression became less pinched. We almost reconciled right then. I could imagine after Ailey went home we'd go upstairs to rehash this very fight, but then something occurred to me.

"Wait. So then you knew it was Ailey. She took those Mr. E. pics Sunday night and posted them on the Student Activities board under AnyLies. That was on *Monday*. You've known for almost three days now."

Audra's lips pressed together. She fiddled with one of her ridiculous diamond studs.

"I've had real-life creeps stalking me because of all of this, Audra. Every organization I'm a part of dropped me from their contacts. All the parents I babysit for think I'm a tramp." My anger was full-on back. "Ailey submitted my college apps, Audra, and you knew."

"This isn't about her!"

Ailey pounded a fist on the table. I'd never seen her look so furious. Not when Coach DiPietro suspended her from a swim meet in the sixth grade because she was too competitive. Not when Moon Li called her hair a gutter weave in eighth grade. Both those times Ailey was angry. Now, she looked...crazed.

"Audra knew I was AnyLies because *I* told her. I told her how satisfying it was to watch you get your comeuppance. I didn't do this so I could buy a car. I did it to completely humiliate you. Guess I'm not the only one who doesn't change her passwords. Hiii, Harvard."

"You ruined my life because I too abruptly stopped being your friend *years* ago?"

Ailey gave a tiny laugh. Tears welled in her eyes. Her voice quavered, finally carrying some emotion in it. I'd never wanted to hurt someone so much in my entire life.

"I did it," Ailey snapped, "so *you* could see how it feels. Knowing that the people you thought loved you best—Mac, Fawn, Sharma, your brother, Audra—aren't at all who you think they are. Or did you all just 'grow apart' this past week?" Ailey snorted. "We 'grew apart,' Kyle? You 'too abruptly' stopped being my friend? We were best friends for nine years—nine years—and do you know after Audra came up to you in the cafeteria freshman year, you never called me, not even once, ever again?"

Audra gasped, like this was the most shocking fact of today.

"That can't be true," I said.

"Trust me," Ailey laughed tearfully, "it is. At first, I figured once the girls knew you, and once you were settled with them, you'd, I-D-K, pull me along. It wasn't so that I could become popular. I could give two swipes about being popular. It felt like my Doc crashed. We spent every click of our time together for nine years, and then you suddenly stepped away. It was like you died, but worse, because I could still see you. Or maybe it was like *I* died, because I could see you, but you didn't see me anymore.

"Who do you confide in"—Ailey was sobbing now—"when the person you told everything to won't answer your calls? You used to come over to my house two or three times *a day*. Whenever you were upset or bored or you just wanted to raid the cupboards, I was there for you. After Audra, you'd pass me in the halls and not even say hi. I knew you weren't doing it to be mean, but I wished you were. At least then I'd have known I did something to make this happen. Or that I at least mattered enough for you to despise me.

"I didn't have a few lonely months, Kyle. When you dropped me, my life dropped. They put me on antidepressants."

Ailey shook her head, fought for a smile, sobbed in her breath. Audra tentatively rubbed Ailey's arms, as if she was trying to warm her up. Audra wouldn't look at me. But Ailey couldn't stop.

"Thanks, pookie," Ailey hiccupped. "I'm okay."

I should have listened to my mom. Her experience was from Ailey's perspective. Only someone I'd irreparably damaged could have wanted to ruin me so badly. None of what Ailey was saying I'd done had been intentional, but that didn't mean I was innocent. Audra was right. I did deserve this—all of it.

"It doesn't matter," Ailey continued. "I'm better now. Because then Ellie came along the end of freshman year and saved me. Unlike you, Ellie is a good, loyal friend. She told me how sweet I was, how much fun she had with me, how indispensable I was. I mean, she slapped you for me.

"And then she and Jessie met in some troubled-teens therapy

group, and suddenly Jessie 'got' Ellie the way no one else did, and suddenly Jessie was Ellie's top contact. And Ailey wasn't good enough again. At least I can rationalize you dumping me for the girls, but Jessie is awful. I don't know why Ellie can't see it. I mean, if I don't equal better than Jessie Rosenthal . . ."

Ailey wiped her nose on one of the Parents' fancy napkins. She immediately apologized.

"So when I stumbled across that vid on the faculty wall—I was doing research for a piece I was making on Ms. Valtri, FYI—I didn't know it was fake. I just knew you needed it exposed. I was going to take it down that very afternoon. But then not only did you come to my house—to blame me—but when I invited you to dinner, you looked so disgusted by the mere thought of sitting down to a meal with us . . . and then later that night when I txted, offering help, you blocked me. And I knew you hadn't learned your lesson.

"AnyLiesUnmade was perfect. It was all a lie, your whole life. I almost posted the flash mob under AnyLies, but then I saw the two-birds-with-one-stone beauty of it all. Maybe Jessie didn't post those vids about you, but I mean, hello, who spends their time making stalky 'human projects'? With a little help from me, Ellie would have to see what a nightmare Jessie was.

"Except it didn't work. Ellie *hated* that flash mob in the hall, all right. She and Jessie had a huge fight about it. Ellie voice called me, sobbing about it. But they made up, like, one click later. And I knew all-caps-to-period FRIENDSHIP IS THE BIGGEST LIE OF ALL. No one actually cares about their friends; they just care about how their friends make *them* feel, what their friends can do *for* them. I mean, you're the perfect example, Kyle. You want to change the world, but you don't give two craps about the people trying to survive in it."

I looked to Audra for help. She was biting her thumbnail, trying not to cry.

"I don't know what to say," I said. "You're wrong, Ailes. I did care. I still *do*."

"No, *I* cared." She sniffled a laugh. "I cared enough to hate you."

This wasn't supposed to be how it turned out. I was supposed to feel victorious. This was supposed to be my win. Instead I felt dirtier than the first time I watched the Mr. E. video. I was too dumbfounded to offer any kind of rebuttal or apology. I just wanted to get out. Out from under Ailey's glare, out of this house, out of my own skin.

Without any fanfare or celebration, I held my finger down on the Mr. E. video file on Ailey's Doc. On the wallpaper screen we all watched as the file quivered for a click and then disappeared when I selected delete. I quick checked my G-File. It was still a mess of links and nasty comments, but now they led to an error message—*Content Deleted*. The video was gone. I'd deleted it from Ailey's Doc. I'd won.

I'd never in my life felt more miserable.

"Sorry. I'm just gonna go."

Giving Ailey a squeeze, Audra said, "I'll walk Kyle out."

Snuffling, Ailey nodded. I silently got up to leave. When I was at the door, Ailey called out, "Scarred or worshipped, isn't that what you always said, Kyle? Welcome to being scarred."

78

Out on Audra's stoop, it took us a few clicks to know where to begin. The lingering deadness of Ailey's voice had wafted outside with us.

Finally, I said, "Three days, Audy. You knew for three days."

"I know."

"That means even at the sleepover."

"I tried to point you in the right direction. I tried to say it had to be two different people."

"Which isn't the same thing as telling me you knew it was Ailey."

Audra shrugged like I could be mad all I wanted; *she* didn't care. But I knew she did, because right up until a few minutes ago, we'd been best friends. Fighting—knock-down-drag-out-style, maybe—but still best friends.

"I know, but it's not that simple. Ailey was lined up to do six different shoots with me between then and New Year's. The pics with multiple girls in them get twenty percent more likes than the ones with just me. She's a natural at it.

"I asked her if she made the video when those Mr. E. pics

surfaced the day after she took them. She told me she didn't make it, just reposted it. I figured whoever made the video put the DRM on it, not Ailey. I didn't know that she was the only reason it was still online. It wasn't like the video could do you more damage at that point. And after we got in that fight in your kitchen, I couldn't tell you that I knew. I just couldn't."

"A fight is a fight, Audra. It's not friendship-ending."

Unlike this. I knew Audra thought not telling me about being the *B&P* chick was as much my fault as it was hers. I knew she thought that didn't make her a bad friend. And I suppose I could see her logic. But Audra not telling me about Ailey? That was unforgivable.

"Friendship?" Audra scoffed. "Is that what we have? All I kept thinking for the last few months was that if you knew anything about me—the real me—you'd disapprove."

"So why bother giving me the chance to prove you wrong." I fought to keep my voice level. "Am I such a monster that my friends won't be honest around me? Am I that scary?"

"Scary?" Audra laughed. "It's not that we're afraid of you, silly. It's that we're afraid of disappointing you.

"You know, Kylie, I've wanted to tell you something for the longest time, but I always worried you'd take it the wrong way. All this pressure you put on yourself to do the right thing all the time? Like if you don't get a perfect grade in life it's all for nothing? That's not real. There is no one right way. I think the closest you can be to getting it perfect is enjoying yourself and being happy fifty-one percent of the time."

"Are you happy, Audra?"

"Oh, hell no," she snorted. "Clearly. But I'm working on it."

I realized then that I had felt more connected to Audra in the last three years than I had to Ailey in the entire nine I'd been best friends with her. But I thought about what AnyLies had said: Was Audra there for me no matter what? No. And about what Mac had said on Christmas: If the Virus struck, what would I be left with?

Would I have good people around to be stuck in the dark with? When it came to Audra, it was more like who *shouldn't* I be alone in the dark with? But I guess my mom nailed it after all. As far as friendships went, you *did* reap what you sowed.

Maybe I'd taken down the video, but before my life would feel "like"-worthy there was one major aspect I needed to fix. Assuming I still could.

"I'm sorry you didn't think you could talk to me," I said, as tears welled up. "I didn't mean to be a bad friend. I would have supported you as much as I could."

We hugged good-bye.

"I know, betch. But that's the problem. 'As much as you could' wouldn't have been enough."

79

There was only one place I wanted to be. I couldn't get there fast enough. I almost pinged an Elite. Instead I ran down Fifth Avenue, dodging baby carriages and post-holiday shoppers.

Ten minutes later, my heart was pounding as much from my run as from where I was standing. During the entire last week, I hadn't wished I could make time go backwards as much as I did right then. I knew now that there weren't any good or bad guys in real life. Not really. It was all just life. And *none of us* were perfect at it. As it turned out, even the worshipped were scarred. Everyone was. And never *ever* again did I want to contribute to the scarring process, which meant there were a few things I needed to make right, and one more urgently than all the others.

Swallowing my nerves, I knocked on the door.

"Come in."

Mom was at her desk with her back to me. Her closet-sized office was a mess. Spreadsheets, e-mails, and website mock-ups filled her holoscreen. Her desk was piled high with to-go coffee cups. Clearly, her "deadline" didn't need the air quotes after all.

This also solved the mystery of where all the plates in the house had gone. A dirty stack of them teetered next to her desk.

"There's the girl I've been looking for," she said, still typing. "I received an e-mail from Dr. Graff this afternoon. Something about was I aware you used an off-grounds pass this morning? Know anything about that?"

"Probably. Maybe. Yes. But can it wait till we're all together?"

Too busy to argue, she sighed. "I guess."

"Where are the guys?"

"Some kind of sport thing...hockey, basketball. I forget."

It was my cue to leave. Instead I picked the empty paper cups off her desk and tossed them in the wastebasket.

"Mmm, that's okay, honey. I'll get those later."

While she tried to regain her focus and quietly read her last few sentences out loud, I perused her shelf of old cell phones. How fast would she stop working if I told her about Audra and Ailey? I picked up one of the clunkier phones. She called them design "artifacts." She swore they'd all been top-of-the-line when she first bought them and that someday they'd be worth money, the same way old turn-of-the-century, like, electric cars were. Mom being Mom, the cord was taped to the back of it.

I sat on the floor. The phone lit up when I plugged it in. All the pics on the phone were old. Like before-I-was-born old. I snorted at one of her and Dad grinning ear to ear, decked out for Halloween as an old-skool book (Dad) and an even older-skool e-reader kind of thing (Mom). Mom glanced over, probably ready to say, *Can you do that somewhere else,* but whatever expression I was wearing stopped her. She pushed her glasses up on her forehead. Her fingers hovered over her holokeyboard. Her gray eyes softened.

"Screw it."

She saved her screen. With a groan, she lowered herself to the floor next to me.

"That's right around when Daddy and I started dating. Look at his hair! There was so much of it." We sat in companionable silence, scrolling through the old pictures. After a few minutes she bumped her shoulder against mine. "So I've been thinking, a lot—a lot a lot—about our last few conversations."

"Oh gosh." I bit my lip. "Can we please forget this whole last week?"

"No." She shook her head. "Because it finally dawned on me that you think I don't like you, and I need to rectify the matter immediately."

Instant tears, all down my cheeks. They were exactly the words I'd craved hearing my mom say for the better part of the last sixth of my life. She reached for the box of tissues on her desk and handed me one.

"I hardly think you're evil, Kyla. And to be clear, I *never* liked Ailey more than you. When I said you changed after you met the girls and it was like the stuff from your old life wasn't good enough anymore?" She took a deep breath, then quickly said, "I meant me."

I let out a short, disbelieving laugh.

"It's true. I felt like I got left behind or like I didn't fit in anymore. And yes, maybe just a little, that reminded me of being back in high school.

"I'm probably not supposed to share these feelings with my kid. I'm probably supposed to suck it up and commiserate with Daddy. But you and boy-Kyle spoiled me. All my friends whined about how hard parenting was, but you two were a breeze. So when we started having problems, I didn't know what to do. There are thousands of books out there, but when it actually comes to raising your kids, there isn't a fail-safe manual."

She put an arm around me. I rested my head against her shoulder.

"I can't stop worrying that once you go off to school we'll fall completely out of touch." Now she reached for a tissue. "Then next year Kyle's off too, and then the only person I'll have to talk to around here is Daddy."

Mimicking the inane voice that Kyle gave my avatar, the one that rose at the end of every word, I said, "And Daddy's, like, the worst."

Mom snorted and wrapped her other arm around me. She kissed me once, twice, three times on the top of my head.

"You will never understand how much I love you. I am so proud of what a smart, smart girl you are. And that is a fact. You are my favorite daughter."

I dabbed at my eyes but still executed an expert eye roll. "Mom..."

"I'm not kidding. Even if I had more, you'd still be my favorite."

"You're playing favorites with me and your imaginary daughters? That's not fair."

"You're also the funniest of my daughters."

"I'm gonna tell them you said that." Mom gave me another squeeze, then blew her nose. Before she could say she desperately needed to get back to work, I said, "Mama, will you tell me the story of us?"

"Now?" She glanced toward her desk but then started playing with my hair. "Seventeen years ago—"

I lifted my head off her shoulder. "That's not how it starts."

"Seventeen years ago," she said firmly, "I lay exhausted in a hospital bed because a tiny being with an enormous head had just come out of me. And after they cleaned her up and put that little beast on my chest, I knew right away that I would love her even if she cried through the night every night until she was two, even if she threw tantrums in restaurants. I'd love her even if she grew up to be mean.

"I shouldn't have worried. She never did become a single one of those things, but even if she had, I knew it wouldn't matter. For the first time in my life, I was experiencing fierce, unwavering love. Friends come and go. Men do too—don't tell Daddy I said that. But this little girl and I were going to be with one another my whole life.

"The next couple of years, your mommy went through a lot. And every time I felt like I couldn't live in my own skin, because there was so much anxiety festering beneath it—"

"You felt like that?"

"Yup." I felt her nod. "Almost twenty-four hours a day. And when it got really bad, you would come to me with your arms out-stretched, smiling, and I knew no matter what happened with the stores, our finances, my marriage, I was blessed. Even during the roughest patches—"

"Like the day after Christmas?" I interjected.

"Exactly," she laughed. "Even then, I loved you as fiercely as I did when you were that little girl who held her arms out to me when I felt like I was sinking."

Now we each took a tissue and blotted at our eyes. Mom reached across to her room screen and untacked a tiny piece of paper. I unfolded it. It crackled with age. In my mom's cool block printing, in faded red ink, it read:

WHAT WOULD KYLA DO?

"No matter what obstacles we face in the future, if we create them or if others do, you are my greatest strength and my greatest love. Don't tell your brother I said that." We laughed. She gave me one last squeeze. "And that is the story of us. To be continued."

ELEVEN MONTHS LATER

In January, a week after I took my video down—Wait, sorry, who took down her video? Oh, that's right. This girl!—my parents and I went to the offices of Awareness for a Safe America, located in downtown Washington, DC. Our lawyer set up the meeting. Once we were inside, two forms of ID were needed to check in at reception. Everyone's tech was remotely powered down by security. When we were deemed nonthreats, we met with the head of ASA's public relations department, a Ms. Smythe—no joke, just like in a spy movie—who explained that, contrary to what our lawyer insinuated via e-mail, ASA wasn't entrapping people.

"We're a watchdog group," she said. "A privately funded corporation that works in conjunction with Homeland Security. Since technology isn't growing in a bubble, ASA's job is to hold the criminals that grow with it accountable for the very traceable, very real, very evil—I don't think I'm overselling it by using that word—footprints they leave on the stream."

Cool. Ms. Smythe was one of those people who called the Internet the *stream*. I imagined her riding the building's soundless elevator to a pod in the basement every night, attaching a giant hose to her back, and powering down.

"While we sincerely apologize for your inconvenience, I hope you will view it as forgivable. There's no end to the benefits of monitoring men who frequent or set up child pornography sites. Or, when it's true—we're reevaluating our vetting process as we speak—of pulling teachers who slept with their students out of schools. As stellar as you are at debate, Kyla, even you can't argue against the advantages of preventing grown men from befriending children on apps that were meant for ages two to six."

Clearly, Ms. Smythe didn't know who she was dealing with. Or maybe she did. As I explained how that was heroic and all, but that there were still five other girls suffering through the mess Jonah Logan had made of their lives, she replied that she'd already signed them up for a pilot software program that erased selected materials as soon as they reemerged online—i.e., the other girls' un-DRMed sex videos.

When we left, Mom got all teary-eyed. "That was spooky and terrifying, but honey, I am in utter awe of how awesome you are."

I wasn't as impressed. When I'd asked about Mr. E., Ms. Smythe had said, "We'll look into it. But in his case, I fear the damage has already been done."

Awareness for a Safe America had done that damage. Them. But this was politics, wasn't it? And if this was where I was headed, I needed to learn the game. Maybe today there was nothing to be done, but someone worked above Ms. Smythe. There was always another channel.

Speaking of politics, while, ahem, I did take down my video, I was not the recognized valedictorian of my high school graduating class. I should have been. I had the highest grade-point average. But a few days before the ceremony, Dr. Graff called me into her office for one last visit. With her unblinking eyes, she informed me that though I was technically valedictorian, due to the circumstances in December my giving the commencement speech would be too controversial. It would open the school, and myself, up to too much scrutiny and negative publicity. So it was that Jessie Rosenthal, with her lousy 3.89 GPA, her three senior-elective art periods, and her crap British accent, won the honor of being the class speaker at graduation.

And actually?

She crushed it.

"We're all about to go off and see and do many miraculous things, but I'd like to spend a few minutes now reminding you about what we don't see...."

While she spoke, she scrolled through photos from a series she called the *Humanity Project*. It was the man in the diner, and the woman feeding the birds, but also a woman putting on makeup on the train, a man walking his bicycle, a mother with her five children staring into space as they waited to cross the street, all these lonely souls, moving through the world, crying out for a little contact and a little something good to happen.

"...In conclusion, I'd just like to remind everyone to be kind, to be mindful of those who don't have what we do, and for heaven's sake, to look *up*."

As an added bonus, I still got called up onstage for having perfect attendance.

In college app news, two days before the admissions deadlines, Mom and I contacted twelve different admissions offices and begged them to let me resubmit the essay portion of my application. It turned out to be no big deal. Apparently, Scholar screwed up constantly and students were always pleading to upload new documents.

Still, I didn't get into Harvard.

But I did get a partial ride to Yale.

I was also in that year's class of summer White House interns. Funny, but as it turned out, I think my sex video nudged me into

363

both places. In their acceptance e-mail, the head of the White House review committee told me she was "moved" and "overwhelmed" by the video addendum to my application, and that she was "excited" to have such a voracious crusader on board. In my reply, I thanked her for her kind words and said it was only too bad that my teacher, Mr. Ehrenreich, had been a casualty of the whole ordeal.

I'll get Mr. E.'s record expunged yet. After all, I'm the girl who took down her video!

Okay. That will be the last one.

Although, actually? I didn't take down the video.

Yes, I deleted it from Ailey's Doc and YurTube faster than you could blink, but not before transferring it to my Doc. A few days later, I posted it to Whattodo.org along with my story—this story. Of course, the video had a DRM on it, and Mr. E. was no longer tagged to it, but if at some point in all our lives we'll be attacked online, we need to muster every resource to fight it. And there's nothing I love better than a good fight. (Or at least a good *theoretical* one.) Besides, a friend once told me I'd be an idiot not to use the incredible platform I'd been given.

Speaking of Audra, the photos for her big New Year's Eve reveal were staged on her parents' dining room table. I didn't see them right at midnight on New Year's. I was too busy toasting my mom and dad. But I did try to flip through around one a.m. Unfortunately, a billion other people must have too. All the traffic temporarily crashed her site. When I saw the pics the next morning, I had to admit that Audra looked beautiful. The photos were tasteful, fairly showy, and yet coy. I'm not sure any of that mattered to the Parents.

As I'd hoped, Sharma said that Audra showed the Parents the photos on the dining room wallpaper screen after yet another nonpescatarian dinner. Audra's bags were already packed and waiting by the front door. Which, from Sharma's telling, was a good thing as, shortly after the Parents viewed the pics, Audra was no longer welcome in the Rhodes brownstone. Apparently, she's lived quite happily in her one-bedroom Williamsburg apartment ever since.

Dr. Graff was also not thrilled with Audra's entrepreneurship and this latest Park Prep sex scandal. I'm guessing Audra opted for a suspended-until-graduation deal, as she never sat next to me in English again. By then I highly doubt she cared. Because it just meant, by early January, her life was exactly where she wanted it to be.

After her New Year's pics posted, *Vogue* did indeed scoop her up, but she must have pissed off someone, because her column only ran for four months. Fawn said Audra was now working on a lifestyle brand and had a contract with a major national retailer— apparently she was thinking of naming it Slut Kitten. Leave it to Audra to take over the world, one repurposed word at a time.

There was a lot of leftover junk related to the video on my G-File, and right before the January 1 deadlines my parents paid a file-sweeping company to make it go away. Before they did, Audra thoughtfully untagged me from the *B&P* posts.

I immediately txted

moi you =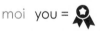

audy You know it, betch. Keep being good. And don't forget to be bad, too.

I did not come to such charitable terms with my other ex–best friend. Ailey's currently enrolled in Cornell's new NYC Tech undergraduate program. Judging by her profiles—fine, I look—she seems happy. I need to know that, because almost daily I think about her sobbing in Audra's dining room, and the same sickening shame I experienced that day washes over me. For someone who prided herself on never making a mistake, it doesn't get much worse than how I dumped Ailey. And yet she nearly ruined my life, so I can't quite forgive her, either.

I tell myself the best way to deal with the ick feeling of it all is to make sure I never treat anyone like that again. And that at least Ailey got what she wanted. I will never, ever forget her. Maybe one day I'll even get to a place where I can wish her luck.

Currently, that day seems like a million clicks away.

As predicted, Fawn and Kyle lasted for about two months. On New Year's Day, Fawn dropped by with flowers for me.

"I didn't know how to tell you," she squealed. "It just kinda happened. At first I didn't think it was anything serious. And then I did. Does it help to say I think he's loaded nachos with extra jalapeños?"

"Only if you don't ever mention his jalapeño in front of me again."

"Kylie, a penis joke? I'm so proud."

Fawn dumped him right after Valentine's Day. Kyle still insists it was the best two months of his life. And I suppose in an extremely creeped-out, please-let's-move-on-to-other-subjects way, I'm happy she was his first. Everyone should be so lucky as to love the first person they sleep with. Still, things weren't quite the same with me and Fawn after that. She's currently enrolled in the French Culinary Institute and washing dishes at this hot young chef's new restaurant in the LES. We mostly check in with each other when we need a little e-love pep talk.

Kyle continues to make overanimated facial expressions and remains one of my favorite people on earth, though it will be some time before I bring any of my single friends home.

Sharma, meanwhile, lives on an undisclosed campus in Virginia not too far from DC. I imagine she is fighting off e-ttacks or building apps that assist small businesses in developing countries or, who knows, hopefully fixing the free American universal Wi-Fi program. Aside from saying how much she loves it, she isn't really allowed to talk about it. But that doesn't matter. Since we agreed never to edit ourselves, it turned out we had lots of other things in common.

Over the summer, during my White House internship, she and I met weekly for lunch. (Weekends were reserved for her and Rory commuting to visit each other. Yup. Who didn't see that one coming?) We're closer now than we ever were at Park Prep. For the first time, when I say she's my best friend, I mean it.

The weekend after I started at Yale, I had an erasing-Kyla-Cheng-themed sleepover. My college roomie, Electra, was the only person physically present. Sharma, Kyle, and Rory were there via FaceAlert.

Sorry, I don't mean I erased myself completely. It wasn't like I was going to stop listening to music or reading e-mags or commenting on *Unicorn Wars* or shopping—truth is, I *do* like clothes—and no way was I going to freshly enter a password every time I wanted to do those things. I only mean I canceled my ConnectBook account. It was actually a relief. Rory gave me two days before I reinstated it. Sharma gave me a week.

sharm   Kyla = 💪 + 😷 + 💄

rory (cb tech god)   Nobody's 🕶️ + 💎 + 🚂 enough
to not have a CB profile.

Nerds.

But I had to be strong, because the one huge perk about canceling my CB was that it effectively prohibited me from online Woofer stalking the daily life of Mackenzie Rodriguez. And I needed all the help I could get.

For 239 days—give or take some minutes—of our senior year and summer, Mac and I existed without labels and didn't not date. And we grew cataclysmically close. But even good indefinite things must come to an end. And the morning my parents drove me to New

Haven, Mac was inconsolable. He hugged me for so long that my mom teared up and my dad had to jingle his keys and say, "Traffic."

"Promise." Mac linked his pinky with mine. "Top five contacts when the lights go out."

Initially we txted about a thousand times a day, but as our semesters geared up, those numbers fell off. With that hair and those eyes, Mac wasn't going to have a hard time finding a girl-friend at NYU.

Oops, hold on.

My weekend guest wants to insert something. . . .

Insert something? Gross, Kyla. Y en verdad, Mac wasn't going to have a hard time finding a girlfriend wherever he went. But he was certain none of them would compare with the unlabelable Ms. Cheng, the one he would always be fondest of.—M.R.

For real, Macky? Unlabelable? And you can't end a sentence on the word "of."

You just did. You're also not supposed to start them with "and."—M.R.

I can do what I want. I'm the girl who took her video down.

Remind me how long you'll be saying that for again?—M.R.

Yeah. Clearly we're still pretty close. And maybe one day I will outright "date" Mackenzie Rodriguez, or maybe I won't. But for sure I'll do my best to keep that boy in my life. If the video taught me anything, it's that you'd better do everything in your power to hold on to the good ones.

So as for me? I can't possibly wrap up myself here.

As I told Yale in my amended application essay, *who you are in five hundred words or less* is an unanswerable question, yet another constricting label. I'm not just the pretty one or the smart one or the slutty one. I'd be disappointed in myself if I could be narrowed down to so few words. Considering there is so much life, knowledge, and emotion to experience, I like to believe there's room for growth. I firmly believe that we make our own history.

So I, for one, fully intend to screw up, try new things, and, most importantly, have a little fun. Because that's another funny thing I'm figuring out. The moments in my life that have mattered the most aren't the ones that everyone "sees," but the ones that they don't.

AUTHOR'S NOTE

Often, non-English or unfamiliar words are italicized in novels. The author believes that this is an antiquated tradition that should have ended yesterday. Not only does it cast a weird sheen of "other" on perfectly normal words that millions of people speak daily, but it hinders the natural happy process of your language becoming mine and vice versa. As you might guess, it is the preference of the author that italics not be used to accentuate non-English words in *The Takedown*. Thanks to translation technology, there will soon come a day when we're all communicating easily across language barriers. Hopefully, a little of that begins here.

ACKNOWLEDGMENTS

A tremendous thank-you to my agent, Sarah Burnes, for her relentless belief in this book and her all-caps enthusiasm and insistence that we get it RIGHT. This book would not be in the world if it wasn't for you. To my editor and soul sister, Kieran Viola, who thought the most important thing was maintaining my voice. I am constantly astounded by how excellent you are at doing yours and how willing and supportive you are of letting me do mine. This book would not be any good if it wasn't for you.

To my copyediting team for making sure all my trains ran correctly, my publicity and marketing team for being so pumped to get this book out into the world, and especially to Marci Senders for creating a cover so wonderful, I can no longer imagine the book without it. Also, to Ellen Goodlett, who read more early drafts than is humane. To Rose Costello, whose enthusiasm for a middle draft provided the oomph to finish. And to Julie Schiena, who read one late draft and knew all the right fixes. This book would not have such good bones without all of you.

To my inner circle of women who have provided shoulders, ears, and sanity along this entire journey. Christine, Anne, Julie, and

Cyr, I am eternally indebted to you. Thank you to Rick Purcell for his smashing legal advice. Also a huge arigato, y'all!, to our vast Short Grain crew for making the two years it took this book to pub the most thrilling of my life. And to my broader Buffalo, Brooklyn, and Charleston contingent of support, there are too many names to list, but I hope you all know who you are, because I do and I couldn't have done this without (venting to) you. This book would not have any soul without all of you.

I can't say it often or well enough, but thank you to my mom, for her constant loving encouragement and for infusing me with her passion for the written word. (And for being muy amable about all my last minute "will you read this??" requests.) I wouldn't be me without you. Also many thanks to my dad for all those pre-orders and my stepdad for catching the overflow of stress I send Mom's way. To my sister Amanda for reading an early draft and saying "We're gonna be rich!" And to my sister Annie for being my favorite sounding board and most enthusiastic promoter. And lastly, to my husband and partner in shenanigans, Shuai. You, sir, make life fun, even when it isn't. Thank you for loving me even at my most teary and for unknowingly schooling me in how to write an adorable good-guy character. This book would not have any heart without you.